To Ruth Ann
— May this be the first
of many exchanges between
us about writing and
literature —

Caroline
May 20, 1986

Sweet Country

CAROLINE
RICHARDS

A Fireside Book
Published by Simon & Schuster, Inc.
New York

Copyright © 1979 by Caroline Richards
All rights reserved
including the right of reproduction
in whole or in part in any form
First Fireside Edition, 1986
Published by Simon & Schuster, Inc.
Simon & Schuster Building
Rockefeller Center
1230 Avenue of the Americas
New York, New York 10020
Originally published by Harcourt Brace Jovanovich, Inc. Published by
arrangement with the author.
FIRESIDE and colophon are registered trademarks of Simon & Schuster, Inc.
Manufactured in the United States of America
10 9 8 7 6 5 4 3 2 1 Pbk.
Library of Congress Cataloging-in-Publication Data
Richards, Caroline.
   Sweet country.
   "A Fireside book."
   Originally published: New York : Harcourt Brace Jovanovich, 1979.
   1. Chile—History—Coup d'état, 1973—Fiction.
I. Title.
[PS3568.I3152S94 1986]   813'.54   86-1886
ISBN 0-671-62285-4 Pbk.

The author wishes to thank the
following publishers for permission
to quote from the sources listed:
   Dell Publishing Co., Inc.,
Selected Poems by Pablo Neruda,
© 1970 by Anthony Kerrigan, W.
S. Merwin, Alistair Reid, and
Nathaniel Tarn. © 1972 by Dell
Publishing, Inc. By permission of
Delacorte Press, Seymour Lawrence.
   Ediciones Carlos Lohle, de
Buenos Aires, *Salmos* by Ernesto
Cardenal, © 1969.
   Limes Verlag, *The Poetry of
Gottfried Benn*, © 1963, as translated
by Howard Richards.
   Macmillan, Inc. and the
Macmillan Co. of London and
Basingstoke, Miss Anne Yeats, and
M. B. Yeats, *Collected Poems of
William Butler Yeats*, © 1912 by
McMillan Publishing, Inc., renewed
1940 by Bertha Georgie Yeats.
   Pantheon Books, a Division of
Random House, Inc., *The Chilean
Revolution: Conversations with
Allende*, by Regis Debray, copyright

Princeton University Press, *George
Seferis Collected Poems 1924–1955*,
translated, edited, and introduced by
Edmund Keeley and Philip Sherrard,
copyright © 1967 by Princeton
University Press. Reprinted by
permission of Princeton University
Press.

The epigram on page 3 is from an
autobiographical document by
Father Juan Alsina, a Spanish priest
whose body was found floating in the
Mapocho River shortly after the *coup
d'etat* in Chile of September 11,
1973.

The final address by President
Allende quoted in full on pages
79–81 is authentic.

The account of the torture of the
Socialist deputy Perez on page 225
appears in Klaus Mischkat, "Are You
a Jew?", *International Documenta-
tion on the Contemporary Church*,
no. 58, December, 1973.

IN MEMORIAM

Salvador Allende Gossens
and all of his
fallen comrades

And you will ask, why doesn't his poetry
Speak of dreams and leaves
And the great volcanoes of his native land?

———PABLO NERUDA

Sweet Country, Accept our oath
Which we have sworn for your sake:
That you will be either the tomb of the free
Or a refuge against oppression;
That you will be either the tomb of the free
Or a refuge against oppression.

——CHILEAN NATIONAL ANTHEM

Sweet Country

Eve's Memoirs
August 15, 1973

The word was becoming flesh—
and we couldn't stand it—it
is the scandal of the cross.
We have never been able to
stand it.
——JUAN ALSINA, "Testament"

Santiago: August 1973

For two weeks there have been no buses to catch and scarcely
any taxis. At seven o'clock in the evening, when thousands of
workers and clerks trudge home after a day's work, the streets
themselves seem stretched too tightly, nervous and wary like
the humans who crowd each other off the sidewalks. This is the
time hardest to endure, when the tepid rays of a late winter
sun disappear along the broad avenues, leaving the city in fear
and darkness. Sober-faced women stand in queues waiting for a
chicken or a kilo of flour. Hoarse-voiced newspaper vendors
scream headlines: the strike of the middle class will succeed,
the Government will fall, there will be civil war. We tense

and walk a little faster, eager to reach our homes and shutter ourselves in against these shrill alarms. Except for the lights which glow feebly behind heavy curtains, all is inky shadow, ghostly suggestion. The passing cars seem like menacing presences bent upon unspeakable errands. We hurry on, afraid to lift our eyes, astounded at the horror which threatens what was once a blessed land, a happy place: Chile, Santiago....

Dr. Carvajal

Monica had arranged for me to see Dr. Carvajal at 9 P.M. on August 15 at his home in Providencia. I didn't expect much good to come from the appointment, but I was mistaken. It was Dr. Carvajal who first suggested that I write my memoirs.

I started walking there from the Moneda at six-thirty, stopping briefly at Mother's house for a bite to eat. Arriving right on time, I was shown into a library which sometimes doubles as an office. The bookcases were stuffed to bursting and the oak sideboards stacked with papers and journals. A sputtering fire tried feebly to warm the draughty quarters.

Dr. Carvajal stood up and leaned across his desk to shake hands with me. "How are you, Eva Maria?"

He seemed so genuinely glad to see me that I felt reassured. "You are kind to save this late hour for me, don Alfonso," I replied. "I'm very grateful."

"Well, sit down in the chair there by the fire: that's comfortable, isn't it? I want to take a look at you. You are too thin, just as Monica said."

I tried to smile. "Don't take Monica too seriously. She exaggerates things."

He walked to the fireplace and stood with his back to it rubbing his hands together behind him. The low flames threw shadows on the walls: I could see the outline of his straight-nosed profile, the great crown of silver hair which stood in tall, tight waves. "These logs should catch in a minute," he said. "I'm sorry I didn't have a chance to warm it up in here before you arrived."

He peered at me again for a second or two and smiled benignly. "You have always reminded me of your father, you know," he continued. "There's something about your forehead and the shape of your mouth. He was a fine man though we didn't see each other enough. He was involved in so many things. It was a great shock when he died in July. I wanted to talk to you at the funeral, but you disappeared while I was with your mother and Monica. You know, you were the one I was especially worried about, Eva. Your father died only a week or two after the abortive coup. I suspected that you were under a terrible strain."

"We're all under a terrible strain these days, don Alfonso. But I appreciate your concern."

"Still, it must be especially hard for someone working in the Presidential Palace. I suppose that's where your office is. Or maybe a special assistant to the First Lady works at the President's private residence."

"No, you were right. I work in the Moneda."

There was a pause. I felt him encouraging me to confide in him, but I hardly knew where to begin. "Honestly, don Alfonso, I never dreamed that I would need your professional help. I never thought of you as a psychiatrist; you were always just my father's favorite chess partner."

We both smiled a little, remembering happier times, but I could feel my tears surfacing. I took a handkerchief from my purse and fingered it as I talked.

"I guess Monica told you that I can't sleep," I began. "I cry a lot. My nerves are rubbed raw from worry. It's getting to the point where my mental state interferes with my job: I'm very forgetful and I snap at people—something you can't get away with in my position. I misplace important papers. Sometimes I just stare into space and don't do anything. Meantime the work piles up. All my problems make my head ache. The country is about to explode, and so am I. How else should I feel? That's why I was annoyed with Monica for making this appointment. 'Don Alfonso can't change anything,' I said to her. 'He's a psychiatrist, not a politician. Maybe he can help neurotics, but can he save Chile? And if Chile goes, what chance is there for me?' "

He sputtered a self-deprecating chuckle. "Well, at least I can prescribe some tranquilizers for you, Eva, and I think you'll find me a good listener. It always helps to talk your problems over." He leaned to his right and picked up a pair of tongs. "Just let me turn this log. Then I'd like to hear a little more about your situation."

He continued fussing with the fire for a little while. Finally he sat down on a three-legged stool across from me. The room was beginning to warm up; I could feel myself relaxing. He laced his fingers between his knees and looked at me in a kindly way. "You're right about the country exploding. Yesterday, when I heard that General Prats had resigned as Commander-in-Chief, I thought to myself, This is it. The Fascists have finally driven him out. Now there's nothing to prevent them from taking over. It won't be a silly little affair like what we saw last June: it will be the real thing."

"Yes."

"But what about you, Eva Maria? In your job do you handle anything that is likely to get you into trouble later?"

"I don't know. I'm certainly not in a policymaking position. My job is a catchall. I was originally hired by Mrs. Allende to do the things that fell outside her regular secretaries' responsibilities. In particular I do a lot of translating and photographing. I'm now an expert on Chile's social welfare program. That's something I hadn't bargained for. Maybe you know that there is a tradition of the First Lady being Lady Bountiful: her office doors are always supposed to be open to the poor and helpless."

"I had heard something of the sort, yes."

"There had always been a trickle of unfortunates who came to ask the First Lady for help, but once the Left was voted in the trickle became a torrent. Every day they would line up outside doña Tencha's doors: cripples, terminal cases, drunks, women with sick children, unmarried pregnant girls. At first she talked to everyone, but it was too much. Doña Tencha isn't well, you know. Finally we came up with a division of labor so that she could save her strength. I became doña Tencha's official almoner, to put it in her words. Directing these poor people to the right channels became one of my main responsibilities. I do other odds and ends, as I said. Sometimes I make the arrangements for receptions and luncheons and benefits. I do a lot of writing and editing."

"Maybe you're working too hard, Eva. It sounds like a heavy load."

"Well, how could I stop even if I wanted to? Doña Tencha loves me like a daughter: I don't want to let her down. Think what a hard time she's having now."

I began to cry. Don Alfonso put his elbows on his knees and rested his head on his hands. When I had calmed down a little he asked softly, "Eva, have you ever thought of leaving?"

"Chile?"

"Yes."

"Did Monica mention it to you?"

"No, but I remember your father saying something about a young man in Germany. He seemed to think you might join him, or so I remember it."

I dabbed at my eyes with my handkerchief and paused to blow my nose. "His name is Helmut," I said. "I met him last summer when he was in Chile as a tourist. When his ninety-day visa expired, he had to go back. He wanted me to go too, but my job was very demanding just then, and there was no one to take my place. But I expected to join him sooner or later, long before now. Something always prevents me." I hesitated a second or two but then decided to say it: "My witch insists that I shall never go, and I'm inclined to believe her, I'm afraid. I feel paralyzed, as if everything were already decided: I'm to stay here and suffer whatever Fate has in mind for Chile; there's no fighting it."

Don Alfonso frowned. "A fortune-teller: I'm surprised, Eva Maria. I must admit I had assumed you were too sophisticated for such nonsense."

"Both Monica and I consult our favorite witches, don Alfonso. Father always said he didn't know how he could have produced such superstitious daughters."

"Well, witches apart, I hope you're willing to consider the options objectively. About whether you should leave, I mean, and about the young man in Germany."

"I consider them endlessly. As I said, I almost left three or four times. But it is not a choice I can live with easily. For one thing, Sergio has never agreed to annul our marriage. I'm still officially his wife. Until he does I can't marry. Helmut's family is fairly conservative about these things."

"You mean they disapprove of his relationship with you?"

"That's what I suspect."

"Do you think you could live with that?"

"I don't know. Helmut has been very understanding: it makes me miss him more than ever. The last time I prepared to go I really felt sure of myself. I had reservations for the first of July. But the coup attempt of June 29 spoiled everything: I could hardly leave doña Tencha during a crisis, even supposing I could leave my country."

"Doña Tencha is fortunate to have such a loyal young friend. I wouldn't expect less from you, Eva. But if she knew that you wanted to go, I bet she would encourage you. She's a mother with three grown daughters. She is sure to be sympathetic in matters of the heart."

"But ever since, things have been getting worse. Father's sudden death on July 9: I think I'll never get over it. And I'm still grieving for Miguel Medina. I saw him in his office at Navy headquarters just the day before the Fascists assassinated him. Monica and I loved him like a brother. I can't get used to the violence, don Alfonso. The country seems to be racing towards chaos. The truckers are on strike, the buses aren't running, schools aren't in session, food is scarce. You know how it is. How can I abandon ship, I ask you? How could I face myself afterwards?"

"Well, I admire your spirit, Eva, but at the same time I'd like to suggest that you have an obligation to save your own life."

"True, but I don't know for sure that I'm in danger. Even if the *milicos* take over, they may leave me alone. That's one of the things that's driving me crazy, the uncertainty of everything."

"What does Monica think? And your mother?"

"Monica pushes me to join Helmut. Mother thinks she'd like me to leave, but in truth I wonder how she'd manage without me. She's been depressed since Father's death. I think she needs me." I attempted to laugh. "You see, that's one of my little vanities: I think everybody needs me: Mother, Monica, doña Tencha, just to name a few. I feel as if I owe something to them, as if I owe Chile something."

"Well, Eva, are you telling me then that you've decided? You're going to stay?"

I should have been able to answer that question without hesitation after having thought about it for so many weeks. Yet I paused. I wanted to be sure. Dr. Carvajal waited patiently. In my confusion I felt wretched and absurd. "No, I'm still wavering," I finally said. "I can't make up my mind." I started to cry again into my wet handkerchief. He offered me a fresh one and tried to soothe me.

"My dear, I know how desolate you must feel. You've been over and over the same ground, and the solution never appears. Maybe the time for thinking is past; what you need is not an argument but an insight. Monica and I and the others, we propose various arguments: the insight must come from within yourself."

He rose slowly from his stool and reached for my hand. I stood, clasping in my other hand my handkerchief and purse. "Maybe it will come to you now," he continued. "I think it will. Try to stop worrying. You've done all you can: you've described your situation every which way; you've named your fears. That's very good. You're delivering yourself of them, as if they were creatures struggling to be born, only temporarily housed with you."

We walked to the front door. "I almost forgot the prescription for tranquilizers," he said, reaching into his pocket for a tablet and pen. "But let me tell you something, Eva Maria. I have less confidence in pills than I have in the powers of the mind." He scribbled a few words and handed me the paper. "I don't know if you've heard about the mental health program I've been helping with at the prison. We've got all our patients writing poetry and stories and keeping journals. It's been very exciting to watch. That's what I'd like to recommend, Eve. Try writing something down." He leaned down to kiss me on the cheek. "I think you'll feel better right away."

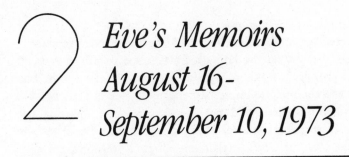

2 Eve's Memoirs August 16– September 10, 1973

Through all the lying days of my youth
I swayed my leaves and flowers in the sun;
Now may I wither into the truth.

——WILLIAM BUTLER YEATS

Father

He was an enormous man, both physically and emotionally. He died unexpectedly in July. For a long time I was distressed that I couldn't recall his face, but once last week I saw him clearly in my dreams; he was like Balzac.

He would have loved his funeral, for scores of friends and relatives attended, and the Allende family sent flowers.

When Sergio and I separated, Father said to me, "Latins can't tolerate a clever woman; you must never forgive them for that." To Monica he used to say, "You are tall and blond in a nation of short, dark people: assert yourself!"

Grandmother Thibault

My French grandmother: she could be quite severe. I remember her as she was on the holy days, when she would have us all kneel as she led the rosary on her heavy black beads. She gave me the lifelong impression that God speaks French.

Sometimes she would pet Monica and me, admiring our curls, instructing us in our knitting, enjoying us. But often she would push us away, exclaiming: "Family of females! ¡Qúe vergüenza! May God grant me grandsons to carry my coffin. Who will carry my coffin at my funeral? There is only Max. Lord, give me grandsons!"

Last night, when I was going through my desk, I came across her old, heavy missal with the onionskin pages which used to rustle so pleasantly when she read the long liturgy on Good Friday. Twice I opened it at random, taking the first verse I saw as providential: "*Courons avec persévérance dans la carriere qui nous est ouverte*" (Heb. 12:1) and "*Retenez ce qui est bon*" (1 Thess. 5:21).

Monica

She is golden and sparkling like the noon sun on the high sea. She is like a hardy receptacle through which currents of life rush, as breath through the Indian flutes of the North, the *quenas*, rumored to have been made originally from human bone. She is like a white-barked eucalyptus tree which towers over all the little trees, whereas I am like a tortoise, lodged within a mental carapace, as if consulting with some secret power. She is simple, like tinkling bells, or like spring water. Compared to her I feel opaque, impenetrable.

Mother

She is more beautiful than Monica or I, and rather high-strung. Since Father's death I have noted in her little nervous quirks, like hiding bills in teapots and cannisters, as if saving money were a possibility in this inflationary economy.

Last Sunday we dined with her and, because of a sudden

rain shower, delayed our departure. When it was time to go, we stood together at the door which faces the Parque Forestal. Little puddles of rain were shining under the streetlights, and in front of the Bellas Artes, half a block to our left, we heard cars passing. Even in the darkness we could see the snow-capped *cordillera* glistening brilliantly.

"Chile is such a pretty country," Mother remarked. "It is blessed in everything except its people. We're quarrelsome and vindictive and lazy and thieving. May God have mercy on us. Why can't we be peaceful and productive and export wines and fruit? Why can't we be a nice, progressive little country like, say, Norway or Sweden?"

Helmut

Peru: sausages, cutlets, and entrails roasting on spits at street corners, a whisper of seaweed along the quay, ancient foot-paths worn into rock from plain to dizzy heights. The relics of eons of effort in an inimical world: always the wind in the sierras, the thin air, the barren rock.

Once, after Helmut and I had visited some ruins outside of Lima, we walked along the beach where the surf had turned up curious bits of wood and shells. Helmut came upon a perfectly dried starfish lying upon the sand. He delighted in such simple sensual pleasure. In the Mapocho Station in Santiago, where on another occasion we were purchasing tickets, he clutched my arm: "Listen!" I heard only the comings and goings of hundreds of people and the monotony of the arrival and departure announcements. He repeated the voice of the microphone: "Yungay, Quilicura, Batuco, Colina, Polpaico, Tiltil, Montenegro, Llay-Llay, Ochoa, La Calera, Illapel, Coquimbo, Ovalle, La Serena. Chile: even its names I love."

Marriage: RIP

When people told me that Sergio was seeing Julia again I decided to move out. That was a year ago last May.

"You shouldn't, I really wish you wouldn't," he kept saying as I packed up. "It's not as if I don't love you, Eve." His eyes were large and sad and beautiful, like a hound's. He always made me think of ox-eyed Hera.

"And Julia?" I snapped. "You want her too? Are we supposed to share you?"

Yes. He needed both of us. Julia, his first wife, the one who had loved him longest, who had borne him two children, was indispensable to his happiness. He had never forgiven himself for having walked out on her a few years before meeting me.

That was something I was a long time finding out.

"Julia and I no longer quarrel, you see." He said it as if he expected me to congratulate him. "It's clear that we have precisely the same faults and virtues. There's no point in accusing the other of one's own shortcomings. We couldn't tolerate each other before, but now that we can.... She isn't always competing with me, Eve; maybe you can realize what that means.... The children are so glad to see me.... Our relationship is one of the few long, strong threads in my life." He shrugged his shoulders and waved his hands about helplessly. "I can't give her up, Eve. I'm sorry."

"What about me?" I was pouting and storming, falling into the role (which I detested) of spoiled child.

He embraced me with his soulful look. It reminded me of our early days together, when he would kiss me from head to toe. Then he couldn't get enough of me. "You're springtime, Eve," he said coaxingly. "You're health and freshness. You're a prize to a middle-aged, sickly man like me. I don't know how I'd manage without you."

I started to cry. He held me close. Then we both cried, and we argued on and on between kisses.

We repeated this sequence of scenes for several days. Finally Julia called and broke it up: she had been waiting, distraught, for Sergio.

He left. I finished packing my things and moved in with Monica.

doña Tencha

Tower of Ivory, Morning Star, Comforter of the Afflicted, Mystical Rose.... When I think of her the words of the great litany come to mind, those wondrous globes, perfect tributes to femininity and motherhood.

Chile

Where daily life is a slog, interrupted only by bus rides, boiling and eating beans, and sleep; where, for those of us who must work for a living, life is an eternal battle against spontaneity: we are often bored and crave an explosion into blood lust, the experience of fear, the exhilaration of inspiring fear.

Helmut's Departure

Searching the apartment for a trace of him, only the matchbook.

Mother

When Monica and I were little, we had to memorize the names of all the geological epochs since creation and the flora and fauna of each. When relatives came to visit, they would ask us to sing or to recite a poem, like other children, but Mother would say, "No, no; that's not for my girls." And we would instead name and describe the principal dinosaurs or trace the evolutionary tree from lemurs to *Pithecanthropus erectus* to modern man. Occasionally we would get a prize for performing especially well: a book about Schliemann's excavations at Troy, for instance, or Bingham's discovery of Machu Picchu. Since I was four years younger than Monica, I made numerous mistakes which she corrected in what I took to be a condescending manner. There were many quarrels: Mother had to intervene.

One of my earliest memories is a trip to the National Museum to see a traveling exhibition of Father Le Paige's finds from the Atacama Desert. Mother was ecstatic. "When you grow up, girls, you can be like Father Le Paige. You don't have to imitate the women who knit themselves into old age and die in their rocking chairs. You can explore the wide reaches of the world and finally put your heads down on your spades for an eternal sleep. You can disappear into the caves of the Atacama or the jungles of the Yucatán. . . ."

That sort of thing doesn't appeal to everybody.

"You'll have to do it yourself, Mother—that Yucatán number," we said when we grew up. At first she greeted our challenge with a stony silence. But then, two years ago, she surprised us. "All right, I will," she said.

When she enrolled in the university, Father at first sulked over the inconvenience she was causing him. He soon came around. "Mrs. Archaeologist," he would call her, or sometimes "Mrs. Fossil." When she went on a dig in the northern desert the summer after her first year, Father was so lonesome that he drove all the way to her camp, near Arica, so that he could see her every day.

After a year and a half of schooling, she was fourth in her class. Then Father died. She was so broken up she couldn't continue. Now the universities are disrupted with strikes and quarrels; she couldn't go on if she wanted to.

"Remember, Mother, you always said you want to be buried with your spade," we tell her. She doesn't say yes; she doesn't say no. For her name day we bought her a book on archaeological finds in China since the revolution. The old light came into her eyes. It's just a matter of time.

Leaving

As a child I knew scores of people who conceived of life as a contest in which the winners were rewarded with permanent residence in Europe or the United States. That was a prize I never wanted.

Uncle Max

He is short and paunchy with a hairy chest and a deep voice.
For twenty years he has worked as sales manager for a drug
company. No one would call him attractive, good-natured, or
nice to children. His habitual expression is fierce and inter-
rogative. When I was a child, I was dazzled by his presence. As
Grandmother used to say, *il est formidable*.

He and Aunt Sara used to have fights periodically which
disrupted not only their lives but the whole family's. They
argued only about remote issues: Is Hitler really dead? Did
Beethoven ruin the last movement of the Ninth by including
the chorus? Did the Polynesians reach America? Will there
be another Ice Age? On a more mundane level they were perfectly matched. They were tidy, prudent with money, indifferent to food. They read late into the night and seldom went
out.

Even though he is over forty now he will always be Mother's
baby brother. When he and Aunt Sara separated last May, he
called Mother immediately. "Sara calls me an old *momio*, and
I call her a leftist fanatic. Soon it will be a civil war. I'm
getting out."

Mother started clucking over Uncle Max in her habitual
way, finding him an attic apartment in the house next door
to hers. At first Monica and I feared that looking after him
would be too hard for her while she was going to school, but
after Father died, we were glad to have Uncle Max around.
No one could comfort her as he could. It was the only situation
Monica and I had ever seen that brought out the best in him.

One night not long after the funeral, when Monica and I
were spending the weekend with her, Mother couldn't sleep.
We stayed up to keep her company. Finally about 1 A.M. she
called Uncle Max. "I can't sleep," she cried; "you must do
something."

"Just hang on—I'll be right over," he replied.

In a minute he walked into the living room, dressed only
in his underwear and a robe, carrying his viola case under his
arm. By this time Mother was talking to another night owl on

the phone; she motioned to Uncle Max to sit down. He ignored her. He opened his case and lovingly removed the beautiful instrument. He put a cloth on the neckpiece and then fixed the viola in place and began to play a movement from one of Mozart's sonatas.

Uncle Max plays very well, and he was in especially fine form. But he looked so ridiculous standing there in his bare feet—his paunch visible under his thin robe—that Monica and I began to laugh. Mother attempted to continue her phone conversation, but she grew distracted; soon she was giggling into the phone, and finally she hung up. We laughed and laughed.

Uncle Max, eyes closed, didn't deign to notice. When he was finished, he carefully returned the viola to its case and prepared to go. "When Saul couldn't sleep, he called on David and his lyre; you, dear sister, may always call on your humble servant." He bowed a few times when we clapped and went out as he had come.

Youth

"Do you renounce Satan and all his works and all his pomps?"

In his splendid robes and stoles, the familiar parish priest who challenged us with this portentous question was hardly recognizable.

We, in our turn, dressed in long white dresses and veils, looked less like eight-year-old schoolgirls than like miniature nuns.

"Yes, we do," we piped in unison. "We renounce Satan and all his works and all his pomps."

There were other pledges, but compared to that one they must have been lackluster affairs. Only that solemn, irrevocable oath, witnessed in heaven, reverberating with its suggestions of lurid and depraved deeds, has remained with me all these years.

Work

I love my office, its tiny proportions and its brightness. I sit here staring at the large photograph above my desk, a sunny street scene I once snapped in Valparaíso, confident for the moment that the world is tidy and manageable. Through the single large window to my left I can hear the cheerful tinkle of water falling into a tiled pool and the chattering of birds. I should get back to work—I really should. There is the foreign mail to go through, the clippings to take from foreign newspapers. Doña Tencha is hurrying me to make a selection of photographs for enlargement and press release. I have an article to write on the Allende family's efforts in education. But the day is full of springtime, and finally I feel serene. Perhaps it's because I've had a few nights' sleep. I'm inclined to think, however, that Dr. Carvajal was right: giving birth to these little verbal children is so comforting that now and then I can relax completely, forgetting the melancholy circumstances which led to their conception.

Assassination of President Allende's Naval Attaché, July 31

When Enrique brought me the news about Miguel, I at first thought that this was the tragedy to which the witch had referred, as I had thought in the case of my father, who had died three weeks previously. She had foreseen the death of a father figure, which would have catastrophic consequences.

Miguel was a young bachelor—thirty or thirty-five—but with his bony ridges and protuberances and immense size, he had the aspect of an ancient armoured dinosaur. His visits to Monica's apartment during 1972 and 1973—always with Enrique—were unexpected and jolly affairs. Usually Miguel would bring a *charango*, a musical instrument of the North resembling a tiny guitar, and frequently a bottle of *chicha*, of which he considered himself a connoisseur. Speculating happily about, say, the comparative merits of apple *chicha* from Chillán and peach *chicha* from La Serena, he would suddenly deliver an expert rendering of Victor Jara's classic about political fence sitters (who were, I must confess, by that time virtually nonexistent):

You are nothing
Neither *chicha* nor lemonade

He was the only Chilean I have met who was completely free from an exaggerated, morbid fear of making a fool of himself. (What do all little children learn in first grade? "I don't want to appear ridiculous!") I remember one afternoon when he astonished us by his energetic encounter with flies, slapping them between his palms, leaping on chairs, crawling on his hands and knees, explaining, as he did so, the nature of the Chilean fly. "Only in Chile," he said, "are flies so indolent that they can be swatted with your hand. Their sluggishness is attributable to a process of Natural Selection: they have had no enemies swatting at them. Those of us who aren't too apathetic to bother with the pests are too proud to give combat to insects."

When Enrique brought me the news I took him to bed where we comforted each other the night through. Kissing soulfully and crying, we were each of us calling up the memory of our dead friend, celebrating in our wordless way the tender friendship that had united all of us. And, as with my father's death, I had to face the self-doubt which a loved one's death seems to produce: have I been a good friend? Did Miguel die not knowing, perhaps, what a difference he made in our lives? But in the case of Miguel there was the additional horror that violent death produces: which group of Fascist terrorists had slain him, and what did such a seemingly gratuitous murder mean?

When I saw Monica in the morning (I was living in her apartment then), she looked slightly annoyed. "You'll sleep with anyone," she said. "For you, sex is like a Band-Aid: good for any pain." I could not think of an appropriate reply to such crudeness. She frowned. "Appearances to the contrary," she continued, "I'm more traditional—a true frigid, Latin woman, for whom sex is an instrument with which to beat a husband, or perhaps a lover, into submission. It can't be helped."

The Harriet Beecher Stowe School

This great monument to the egalitarian spirit of nineteenth-century America is still alive and well, but the present establishment is as conservative and elitist as the original one was radical.

Mother and Father pulled a lot of strings to get us into the Harriet B. School. They wanted us to be bilingual, and they were pleased to think that their daughters went to the best there was.

On the faculty today there is one well-meaning American director, twenty *momias*, eight *momios*, five wavering Christian Democrats, and Monica.

The custodial and grounds staff consists of nineteen leftists and one rightist. The rightist is the doorman and gets to wear a uniform. He's the only one who's thinking about which side his bread is buttered on.

Sergio

I talked to Sergio today about annulling our marriage. He said that he would agree to it if there's a coup.

I felt impatient. "But why wait?" I asked. "If there's a coup I won't want any legal hang-ups. I may need to get out of Chile fast."

He was flippant and playful. "Because I still love you. I'll give you up only to save your life. Besides, there's no need to hurry. Getting an annulment is the only thing in Chile that goes quickly and efficiently. You merely hire a lawyer and claim to have perjured yourself in filling out the original marriage contract. It's a matter of a few hours. We'll say we lied about our legal address. That's the going excuse these days, I understand."

He looked youthful and healthy when I met him, although

I didn't say so, since he has always cultivated the demeanor of a sick old man, slightly stooped, fumbling in his pockets for bottles and pills. When he coughs he examines his handkerchief carefully as if eager to see blood. That I was ever attracted to him may seem astonishing since my robust family views illness in the pagan way—as shameful. But initially I was fascinated by his neurasthenic good looks, by the impression he conveyed of experiencing delicate feelings which the rest of us could scarcely imagine.

I am grateful to him for helping me to grow up. He was a well-known conductor and composer of thirty-eight when we met, and I a nineteen-year-old university student. He was speaking at a forum on indigenous elements in Latin American film scores. Although I had stayed up studying for exams the night before, I attended the talk, determined to get to know this impressive person who had lectured to my class several times on film. But how could I capture his attention? Finally I scribbled him a note which an usher delivered to the chairman of the conference who passed it on to Sergio. I was breathless with embarrassment and anxiety, but he nodded pleasantly and wrote a brief reply.

After the forum he took me to his apartment where, having served me a good American whiskey, he introduced me to his amazing collection of recordings and ancient Indian instruments. It was my introduction to Santiago's avant-garde, which seemed glamorous then. It exercised an influence out of proportion to the income of its leaders, since, being leftist, it was patronized by many political figures, and, further, being talented, it was cultivated by the aristocratic jet set, whose raison d'être was its good taste.

As we became acquainted, I realized that my French was as good as his and my English a good deal better—a fact I was too naive to conceal. But the unfamiliar whiskey coupled with my exhaustion made me feel ill. I stayed in the bathroom such a long time that Sergio became disconcerted. Finally he knocked softly several times and called my name, but there was no answer. When he opened the door anyway, he found me sitting on the toilet, my head dropped low, soundly sleeping. I was humiliated when he awakened me and fearful that my inexperience, so inexpertly hid, had made a bad impression; but, as he remarked later, I had given him repeatedly that evening the supreme human pleasure, which he hadn't experienced for years—that of being taken totally by surprise.

The Hoarder

She had begun long ago, before there were shortages, in an effort to save in an inflationary economy. Some of her treasures dated back to President Frei's term, when they cost a hundred times less than today's official prices. First she had filled the kitchen cabinets, then the broom closet, and finally she had spilled over to less likely areas, like the coat closets and the guest room.

She took comfort in the rare and valuable commodities no longer to be found in the shops: pyramids of toilet paper, shelves stacked high, library fashion, with toothpaste, razor blades, sugar, detergent, cocoa, oatmeal; bottles of cooking oil, jars of honey. On a good day, when it was announced that detergent, say, was available, two boxes to a customer, she would stand in line with her mother and four children, in that manner coming away with twelve; and if it were early enough in the day, the six of them would hurry on to queue at the other markets in the vicinity. It was time-consuming, but it paid off; she now had enough salt, beans, noodles, jams, flour, and canned goods to last for several years.

Then there were the bonuses. The Co-op, to which she belonged, in an effort to distribute fairly among its members during the hard times, made monthly deliveries of staples. Her husband was in the school teachers' labor union which provided commodities regularly. When the Popular Unity government finally set up the neighborhood food co-ops (the "JAPs") in an effort to get around the middleman and provide food at low prices, she found it easy to resist taking advantage of them, preferring the pleasure of moral indignation at this leftist political maneuver to the comfort of adding even further to her stash. We like being indignant; getting angry is a pleasure.

Helmut

In A *Sentimental Education* Flaubert describes a love affair which totally changed the lovers' manner of perceiving life; the loved one was for him "a general manner of feeling, a new way of existing."

Departure

Heads, I stay; tails, I leave. Heads, tails....

My City

City of tinny old cars on endless avenues, low buildings, earthquake scarred, and instant high-rise apartment houses. City of overworked buses, the odor of wine and garlic commingling with cigarette smoke. Hungry, scabby children hawking newspapers with their puny voices.

Acrid smelling manholes eternally open; padlocked refrigerators; starving dogs running in packs at night through treeless slums. Swarms of street vendors with lottery tickets, combs, clothes hangers, spices, gelatin, mirrors, gum, toys, wicker furniture.

Ancient odor of mildewed walls, smell of cologne, urine, sweat. People everywhere, elbowing one another in streets too narrow for their number; queuing up in interminable lines to process official papers; racing, arms outstretched, towards crowded buses which don't stop.

A Sunday Dinner, May 1973
(shortly before Father's death)

UNCLE MAX: You know what you can do with your Chilean Road to Socialism....

MOTHER (nervously): Now, Max....

UNCLE MAX: Your UP Government is nothing but fat cats who run the banks. The banks lend to the nationalized industries. The industries use the funds to pay themselves higher wages. The workers, the ungrateful bastards, sneak goods out of the factories and sell them on the black market.

AUNT SARA (slamming fists on table): If they do, they're just imitating the *momios* who cheat on their taxes and stash dollars away in foreign banks. They learned from the example of their so-called betters!

MONICA (hands over ears): Just once, can't we just once—

UNCLE MAX (more loudly): The *momios* at least know the facts of life. Your fatuous comrade heroes couldn't wait to take on the U.S., but as soon as Uncle Sam retaliated by ruining the economy, they screamed in indignation.

AUNT SARA: If only you'd let us govern! We can't do a thing! You block all our legislation. You even vote against the things your party is supposed to be in favor of just to ruin us!

UNCLE MAX (roaring): What do you expect us to do, you ugly *rota*, lie down and surrender?

COUSIN MARGARITA (standing up with Gonzalito): Look, now you've made the baby cry!

UNCLE MAX (pointing his fork at Aunt Sara): The Christian Democrats are the largest party in Chile, don't forget that. We have a right to drive you out! We'll fry you! We'll watch you sizzle!

AUNT SOLEDAD: I'm not going to stand by and watch you abuse your own wife, you brute!

MOTHER: Mercy! My stars! Mother of God!

UNCLE MAX: You are all soft in the head. When the Armed Forces step in they'll have to lock up the feebleminded people, including you!

FATHER (fiercely): All right, Max, that's enough. We don't like that kind of talk in our house!

UNCLE MAX: Don't pull any of your pious legal flimflam on me, you Commie toad!

FATHER: Shut up or get out! I don't care if you are my brother-in-law! I'll knock you cold!

MOTHER: Quiet, everybody, quiet! I'll have a nervous break-down!

UNCLE MAX: Oh, go hang! You're chickens, all of you. Brain-less cowards! Peep! Peep! That's what's wrong with this country: the people! You! (Throws napkin down and marches out.)

MOTHER (to Aunt Sara): He'll be back. Don't cry, Sara. You'll see. He always comes back.

MONICA: Yes, she knows. Why do you suppose she's crying? *¡Por Dios!* why does he have to be in *this* family?

MOTHER: Now, Monica....

Helmut, July 1972

Like most *santiaguinos* whose marriages have just failed, I sought peace of mind in June of 1972 by getting away, this time escaping into an ancient and mysterious past, the world of the Incas. ("You have left him?" Monica had said. "Good. Then you must make a pilgrimage with me to the tethering place of the sun, Machu Picchu.")

By now my memories of Peru are inextricably mingled with those of Helmut, the lanky German tourist with an awkward walk, whom I grew to love with an unseemly haste.

To change lovers is to change worlds.

Monica was accompanying some students from the Harriet B. School on a two-week excursion to Peru. I went along. After we had settled down in our hotel in Lima, we made trips to nearby archaeological sites. It was on our way back from Chan Chan that I met Helmut.

Monica, the girls, and I were sitting on a public bus crowded with mute Indian women, live chickens in burlap sacks, scream-ing children, a dog or two in the aisles. The odor of sweat and dirty underwear was stifling; I ate peppermint candy to calm my stomach, trying to offer some to a small boy who was too shy to accept. Finally I took his scabby hand, opened it, and deposited five lozenges in his palm. He did not smile, he did not move, he did not eat the candy; yet his joy manifested itself in some mysterious way, charging the air around him with a palpable emotion.

Monica and her thirteen charges had been singing. Suddenly she was surprised by a foreign-looking fellow who had made his way down the corridor of the bus to her side.

"Excuse me," he said in a thickly accented Spanish. "My friends and I have been listening to your group singing and talking. Although you speak Spanish, we have a feeling that you are tourists here. We have made a wager about your nationality, and I have been sent back to inquire."

We were pleased at the interest we had inadvertently generated.

"May we know a little more about the wager?" asked Monica.

The foreigner struggled with his words. "We have been in many Latin American countries, but not yet in Chile. We have not met any women who enjoy themselves so much in public. One of my friends thinks you must be Cuban refugees living in the United States; two of us guess you to be Chileans."

We laughed and applauded when he finished, and he held up two fingers as a victory signal to his companions. It was obvious that everyone wanted to be friendly. Before Helmut returned to his seat, he had the address of our hotel.

When Monica, the girls, and I came in the next evening, we headed for the bar for an evening treat. Helmut and his friends, Wolfgang and George, were there, evidently waiting for us and eager to go out. But Monica, who had ordered breakfast for seven in the morning, thought that the girls should stay in, which meant she had to stay in too. As Helmut turned to me to inquire about my decision, it seemed to me he caught his breath a little. I flushed.

"Well, Eva?" he asked. "And you?"

"We were told there is an interesting *boîte* just two blocks from here. Maybe we could peek in and be back by one."

Everyone said good night, leaving Helmut and me at the front door of the hotel. As we began our walk, I took note of his stature; he was the only man I could remember standing by who was taller than my father. Though about twenty-eight or thirty, he gave an impression of adolescence, almost of teenage gawkiness; he appeared thin, yet one could see from the size of his feet and hands that he was big boned. With his heavy blond hair hanging straight to the nape of his neck and eyes like the winter sea, he made me think of a Viking.

He was the first man I had been out with since leaving Sergio, and I felt shy. My uncertainty somehow communicated itself to Helmut; by the time we reached the *boîte* we were almost looking for an excuse to end our evening together before it had begun. It occurred to me that, dressed informally in pants and ponchos, we might not be admitted to the night spot, giving us an opportunity to say good night and go our separate ways. But the *boîte* turned out to be a psychedelic wonderhouse, low-ceilinged, plastered with stalactites in rainbow hues, the walls punctured with caves where tables with candles were set. Once we had entered by sliding down a fireman's pole, we discovered that no one took any interest in the patrons' dress.

How can I describe the way I felt as we joined the crowd of dancers? The band was playing American rock, and colored lights were casting vivid beams of green and red and yellow and purple over everything. I was excited and giddy, yet somehow frightened because, in that barrage of sensations, with a stranger who barely spoke my language, I could only with difficulty keep my sense of individuality, of oneness. It seemed as if I might decompose into a flash of blue and green, a wail upon a horn.

But as Helmut took my hand and led me in the dance, I had an experience I can describe only as religious. His sense of rhythm was expert, and his footwork deft and quick. Our shyness was dissipated in a sure communion of movement with melody, a faultless communication older than civilizations, truer than speech.

We danced to rock, then to Latin American music. I do not remember thinking anything, but once, inexplicably, I had an image of myself dancing with Sergio, how he used to push me around the floor like an asthmatic custodian leaning on a broom. But the scene seemed definitely over, archaic, so distant from my present situation that it might have been someone else, that woman who had been used like a household utensil. My sense of liberation was enormous, and I burst into tears. Helmut, without asking, without even wondering, merely cupped my cheek in his palm for a second or two; I knew that he would be an important person in my life.

In that extraordinary atmosphere couples came and went, and the band played on and on, as if the exigencies of time were superfluous. Finally, when even the horns sounded tired, the place was left to Helmut and me and perhaps three other couples. By then the songs were old-fashioned favorites from the forties, and we were dancing cheek to cheek, except that my face didn't reach that high. I was happy with Helmut, intoxicated by his warmth and touch, and soon yielded to an impulse to shower kisses on his chest through his shirt. He immediately responded to me, taking my face in his hands and tasting my lips. Then we were leaning against one of those improbable stalactites which reached from ceiling to floor, tightly locked together while, when we weren't kissing, Helmut whispered to me in three languages words which I scarcely understood but somehow intuitively knew; words no man had ever said to me before.

I felt almost sick with desire for him but there was no place for us to go, for I was rooming with Monica, and Helmut with Wolfgang and George.

We left the *boîte* and stumbled down the street, Helmut half-carrying me as we kissed and embraced. Riding in the elevator, he fumbled clumsily for my body under my poncho. Before the door to my room he held my head between his palms, covering my eyes so that all I could hear was my own blood rushing through my head; and with so many kisses I could hardly breathe.

He finally held me at arm's length and whispered one word in perfect Spanish: *mañana*. When I somehow fell into my room it seemed as if I had just returned from another world, from an opium dream, perhaps, or from a long swim under a warm sea among wondrous coral reefs, except that my nerves felt played out for such silent realms. How difficult it is to explain these things.

I was astonished to find Monica still awake and smoking with the light on. I made my way to the dresser where I began brushing my hair. As my breath returned to normal, I peeked in the mirror at Monica who, propped up by several pillows, was inhaling deeply and staring at my back.

"You seem upset; did something happen?" I asked.

"Did something happen!" she gasped. "You come in at five-thirty in the morning and ask me that! Whore! It is I who should do the asking: *what happened?*"

Then I felt annoyed. "But Monica, I'm not one of your charges, remember. Besides, you know I was with Helmut."

"I knew nothing. You could be whoring around with anyone. And what do I know of Helmut? Not even his last name. Maybe he goes in for unspeakable perversities; he could have abducted you and sold you into white slavery. Don't laugh—it happens here! Or he might have left you in an unsafe neighborhood among criminals. *¡Por Dios!* Eve, I have a dozen young ladies to watch over. I must ask myself, 'Are they sneaking out at night? Do they take the pill? Do they have IUDs?' But it turns out that all my fretting is misdirected: *you* are the one who can't be trusted!"

As she talked, I finished brushing my hair and got undressed. I had been standing before the mirror, and it occurred to me, eyeing myself nude, that I did not look much older than Monica's charges; perhaps my appearance partially accounted for her unreasonable reaction. What little makeup I had worn had been vigorously rubbed off in the wrestling with Helmut, and my hair, hanging straight at shoulder length, made my face look small and round.

Then, still looking in the mirror, I happened to glance at Monica's image. Behind the rings of smoke she sat cross-legged under a sheet that was pulled to her waist. Her breasts plunged abundantly against the silk and lace which stretched tightly against them, revealing her large nipples. She hadn't succeeded in washing off all of her eye shadow, and in her excitement, her cheeks had flushed slightly. Her magnificent masses of blond hair fell in every direction down her back and over her face. And as she spoke in her throaty way, her slight overbite was noticeable. She reminded me of a buxom Melina Mercouri playing a naughty role.

When I giggled, she stopped talking and stared at me in wonderment. I carried over to her a silver-backed hand mirror which we had bought in an Indian market earlier that day and held it before her face. "Now tell me: which one of us would pass for the virgin, and which for the whore?" Finally, she smiled broadly and pushed the mirror away; she gave me a little slap as I moved to turn out the light.

"Why do you always get the last laugh?" she asked.

Peru

For several days Helmut and I continued to live with the tide of desire for each other that had begun to roll in the *boîte*. It was a splendid, almost insupportable yearning. I was amazed that the force of it didn't jolt other people out of their normal paths, causing them to point and stare at the commotion of currents that was disturbing the atmosphere. Yet the world seemed unaware of the new thing in its midst, this ocean of sense and imagination whose waves we simultaneously wanted to stay and to quicken

Finally the girls, Monica, and I flew from Lima to Cuzco in one of the famed old Fawcett planes, unpressurized, which provide oxygen in a tube to be held under the passenger's nose for comfort at high altitudes. Breathing deeply of pure oxygen, I dreamed of Helmut who had left his friends in Lima and was waiting for me in a hotel in the old Incan capital.

The first night I left Monica's room for his, I was wearing a coat thrown over a satin gown and high-heeled sandals. What followed I have relived a thousand times in my dreams, just as a person plays over and over again a beloved record.

He met me at the door of his room which, though unlit, was strangely illuminated by a magnificent moon that shone through the French doors leading to a balcony. In the thin air at 14,000 feet, the moon glows as it never does at lower altitudes. He removed my coat, and I stepped out of my sandals. He buried his face in my hair for a few seconds. I was trembling. Then he picked me up and carried me to his great rug of llama fur which he had spread on the floor before the French windows. From the bed, he grabbed some pillows for our heads. I was dazzled by the light of the moon, full and wine red: it cast its glow on everything in the room.

Later we were to love and lust in Chile, and I suppose that we could love and lust in Europe. But neither of us expects ever again to break the confines of ordinary human emotions as we did for those few weeks in Peru. Chile, more than the other Latin American countries, is made to human proportions, like the Mediterranean lands it so closely resembles, and that is perhaps why her people seem civilized, why they seem to know how to live well. No one would say the same of Peru: there people's impact on the wild environment seems as tenuous and uncertain as a child's footprint in sand. The stark, snow-covered Andes, penetrated by depthless volcanic lakes scarcely known by humans, with furious rivers spanned only by the twisted Incan rope bridges, lord it over a primeval, inhuman world. Among the bold condors, with their seven-foot wing span, who dive in troops on goats or mountain lions; or the huge flowers with leaves so thick that the Indians float upon them as rafts: in such a world the monsignors in their stiff brocaded robes, who for centuries have permitted the Indians their soporific *coca*, their religious flagellation, seem like hieratic figures from an ancient temple relief.

Before Helmut my lovemaking had been vaguely disappointing, an uncontrollable rush from anticipation to anticlimax, in less than a twinkling of an eye, like an adolescent boy. So much fuss, it seemed, about some graceless fumbling in the dark. Now for the first time every gesture and smile became part of an endless sexual act in which stimulation and peace followed each other in an ever-renewed cycle.

Helmut said that only in ancient Greek is there an expression to describe such passion: Ἰουλίαντοθῶ "Oh, I desire too much."

The Moon

I have read that the origin of sexuality probably lay with the tides when, in response to the moon's movement, myriads of microscopic creatures, not yet differentiated into plant and animal, were washed ashore and stranded until the sea rescued them again. In those terrible ventures onto the perilous land, made every twenty-eight days, those that were to survive learned to mingle and reproduce.

How is it that this great celebration, which occurred monthly for eons on the ocean's barren beaches, came to manifest itself in the female cycle? What other primordial secrets are locked away in the structure of our being? Some profound truth about our universe and ourselves seems to lie here, more mysterious than art, deeper even than Greek tragedy or Neruda's poetry.

Allende

"The Right is our enemy—the PDC is our opponent."

There was a time when I thought Allende made such facile, benign remarks for reasons of state, but now I wonder if he doesn't believe them. He was elated at his good luck—this three-time loser who had had so few hopes of winning in '70 that, on election night, he had no place ready to give his acceptance speech. He had dedicated his life to a long chance and felt morally vindicated, as if his election were a revelation of History's intentions.

He dined at the Cardinal's house last night. Jorge Cisneros, second in command of the PDC, was also invited. It was the sort of occasion Allende loved: a gift for the cardinal, a *bon mot* here and there worthy of a tangy wine, a solid dinner. Allende once said that Cuban socialism tastes of cigars and rum while Chilean socialism is meat pies and red wine. His observation suggests his preferences; always the gentleman, always the comforts of a practiced taste and of an old and amiable culture.

I have never noted in him a sense of irony. What was he thinking as he exchanged stories with the Cardinal's other guest, whose political party is in collusion with the military for the overthrow of Allende's Government? It's hard to believe that he doesn't know. Does he find it impossible to believe that History will let him down so badly?

doña Tencha

Your chauffeur drives the limousine as close to the main entrance as he can, and you thank him as you gather your things. A soldier opens the door. You lean on his arm as you climb out, smiling, moving your right hip carefully to minimize the pain at the base of your vertebrae. V. and B. are standing in the patio. They join you at the wrought-iron gate and relieve you of your parcels. Together you walk down the corridor to the office door, high heels tapping on polished tiles. The sound of water splashing gently in the fountain, birds chirping, feminine voices laughing softly: you feel happy and mildly excited, forgetting for a minute to move slowly and cautiously. A shooting pain down the right side: you hesitate briefly, eyes clouding. V. and B. watch anxiously. No, it's nothing, it's all over, you say, but you glance at the clock by the stairway: at 11:00 you may take a Percodan, not one second before. It is now 10:30.

X. and I, clipboards in hand, meet you at the door of your reception room and escort you into your office. Three appointments today, not bad, X. says; a luncheon at 1:00 with Señora L., wife of the Venezuelan ambassador. Is a little gift ready for her, you ask—is it wrapped prettily? And the flowers, you remember: they must be red, yellow, and blue—those are the colors of the Venezuelan flag.... Yes, it's all arranged: don't worry, I assure you. You are sitting on the sofa of Persian silk across from X. and me. You glance at the clock: 10:45.

The trip to Mexico this weekend; everything is almost ready,

I say. I read the itinerary: breakfast and a briefing with the Chilean ambassador to Mexico at 8:30 on Friday morning. At 10:30 a private tour of the National Museum.... You try to focus on my words, but the pain is there again. You shift position and grind your teeth; finally you stand, pressing your hip with your hand.

12:00. The Percodan has taken effect; for an hour you have been free to forget your body, losing yourself in the pleasant details of an eventful and useful life. You throw yourself into last-minute arrangements for the trip to Mexico, a country you know and love. You are concentrating fully, hardly aware of your surroundings, so that you are startled when M. touches you on the elbow: "Señora, the President," she murmurs. "Ah, the President, the President...." You hear our whispers as X. and I silently gather up our papers and look expectantly towards the reception room.

He approaches, smiling, his arms outstretched slightly. Your hand starts towards your hair, but you stop it. A swift kiss on each cheek, sweet smell of shaving lotion and hair lacquer. He turns to greet X. and me as we tiptoe back to the reception room. A little joke: a wave of laughter. He sits down at your side, peering over your shoulder at the travel itinerary. "You won't forget to see P., will you, darling? And remember not to mention.... How I envy you the.... It will be wonderful to...."

Of course, of course. You feel excited, your eyes are bright. "If only you were coming too, Salvador...." "Yes, I know...." "Everything is more fun when you...." "The last time...."

He becomes sober, referring to the political situation. You try to follow him, but you are distracted by all the little imperatives staring at you from the agenda on your lap and by the general sense of well-being that comes whenever you are free from pain and your husband is sitting beside you.

He rises to go. "So soon?" you object. "Yes, yes, so many duties, so many people making demands...." "But dinner tonight?" You try not to sound plaintive. "My last night before the trip, Salvador." "Sorry, so sorry," he murmurs. "Up all night last night, dinner tonight with the Minister of Defense. These are the crucial days, everything depends on...." He kisses your cheek and squeezes your arm. "But for Isabel's birthday I'll drop everything," he promises. "We'll have a whole day...." "Yes, yes, wonderful," you agree; you grasp his hand.

He walks swiftly to the door, pausing there to blow you a kiss. From the reception room a ripple of laughter as he chats a minute with X., M., and me. The click of the door.

You put your reading glasses on again. Suddenly it is too quiet. You look up quickly at X. and me as we enter with our notebooks. You attempt to banish the suspicion that we have been exchanging glances. Your hand strays to your hair. For a second you allow yourself to think of the other, the doe-eyed one, the favored one, on whom clothes seem like an impertinence. A surge of pain again, this time down your left side. A muscle in your face twitches, your pupils dilate. X. and I gaze at you with concern and love. You look away. You know that we know.

don Nestor

By the time Helmut arrived in Chile a little over a year ago, there was a good deal of speculation about a compromise between the UP and the centrist PDC since the latter was effectively blocking the passage of Government-sponsored legislation in Congress. Some thought a compromise would save the Government, others expected a sell-out, and still others, including many Christian Democrats themselves, preferred that the UP fail.

Helmut, fascinated by the incredible degree of politization among the population, engaged everyone he met in conversation as soon as his Spanish would allow it. Before long he had his favorite haunts where he went for gossip and debate and eavesdropping: the bar of the Sheraton-Hilton, the Café Haiti, the Goethe Institute, where his fellow Germans gathered. His favorite, however, was his tailor's shop where, among heavy rolls of yardage, long tables for cutting and basting, and numerous catalogs of men's clothes, don Nestor Salas would serve *pisco* to his clients and friends in the afternoons.

Don Nestor, who had been apprenticed to his craft at the age of fourteen, had inherited when twenty-five a few acres from his father, whom he had never seen. He sold the property, bought a plane ticket to Miami, and in twenty years built up the most fashionable tailoring establishment outside of New York City, making smart hand-tailored suits at $500 apiece which were prized by leading financial and political figures. His luck threatened to change when, in 1969, his wife divorced him and saddled him with enormous alimony payments ("I was a Latin lover married to an Anglo-Saxon," he would explain); but by selling everything and returning to Chile, he managed to save his fortune and to continue the style of life to which he had become accustomed.

In a country where tailors are without pretensions, don Nestor—his prices much sobered by the move South—became an instant success. The *Don Nestor*, done in thick carpets and chandeliers in the former French cultural institute, employed sixteen subordinates who discreetly stitched under the master's supervision, though they were not permitted to do the fitting or cutting. "Any experienced tailor can sew," he would say, "but cutting: that is the test which separates mere competence from genius."

He loved his role. At fifty he was still a handsome man with a shock of thick curly hair and large blue eyes. He would smoke incessantly, filtering his cigarettes with an ivory and onyx holder, and speak to Helmut in a heavily accented English. "Americans," he would say, "they make the best husbands in the world; they stay home and change the baby's diapers while their wives go out drinking with their lovers. But American women!" He would roll his eyes in despair.

It was at don Nestor's that Helmut heard the most about what was going on in Chile. The tailor seemed to know everyone of consequence, and in the late afternoons, when the shop was comparatively quiet, he would obligingly share his impressions with his close friends.

"Chile is a microcosm of the continent," he liked to say. "It's even more, it's a *laboratorio* for the *conflictos sociales* that will continue to wrack the world as long as capitalism prevails." Then he would frown. "That's why it's important that the Government doesn't botch everything. But it looks bad—what a bunch of incompetents are running things. The inflation, it starts spiraling again, there are shortages of foodstuffs; the black market, it is flourishing—the Christian Democrats are loving it up with the right."

He would cast a glance towards the back of the huge shop where his assistants worked and lower his voice to a whisper. "You observe I speak the English so the wrong people don't hear.

"There is an office in Providencia: on the wall is a huge map of Santiago—it is stuck with flagged pins, red, yellow, green; they show how the city will be organized for a massive strike of truckers, *profesionales*, and businessmen to be staged in October. There are files too with reports on the movements of all the key Government people.

"October 1972 to October 1973: within that year the subversive groups intend to bring down the Government. They have Brazilian and American money. And they know how; they are advised by the Brazilians, by the same capitalists who toppled Goulart in 1964, the ones who work for the multinational corporations. And some of the top boys from the CIA have been sent here to set everything up.

"The recipe for a coup d'état: the creation of economic and political chaos, the fomenting of discontent between bosses and workers, the blockade of Government-sponsored legislation, the organization of demonstrations, terrorist acts."

He would extinguish his cigarette as he spoke and immediately open his slim, gold case for another, making a little ceremony of offering his guests a smoke, filling his holder, and lighting up.

"These Brazilians, they are so proud of themselves, they talk too much. One said to me, 'We teach intelligence work, we import into Chile machine guns in boxes marked "coffee" which are addressed to Señor Rodriguez, your estimable senator who, when he isn't working with us, runs his instant-coffee company and his supermarkets. It's all well done. But most of all we have taught the Chileans to use their women against the Marxists. In Brazil we created a successful campaign of women demonstrators, and Chile copies us. You remember the march of the empty pots.'"

He would pause to yawn and stretch his legs, waiting for his words to sink in. "A pity, Helmut, you were not here for the famous march. The rich, fat women of Santiago, they squeeze themselves into their tight pants and waddle down the Avenida Bernardo O'Higgins to complain they go hungry. So much corpulence gathered in one place: you could find the like only in a Turkish whorehouse."

After sharing such a confidence, don Nestor, like an actor who has just played a hard scene, would pour himself a *pisco* and stretch out on his Victorian fainting couch. Helmut, who could never sit still for long, would pace up and down before the wide windows at the front of the shop, mulling over what he had heard.

"What you've told me, about the arms, does the Government know about this?"

"Of course. Some dockworkers reported in June that the Brazilian coffee boxes they've been unloading are filled with arms. Government *inteligencia* has infiltrated some terrorist groups like Patria y Libertad." Don Nestor paused to sip at his drink. "P and L leaders meet frequently in the American Ambassador's office; they're getting technical assistance on arms from the Americans besides the arms themselves, which are channeled from the United States through CIA front export-import companies and the U.S. Army."

"Why doesn't the Government do something?"

"You have heard of the Arms Control Law? It is a bill presently before Congress. It will be passed almost unanimously so that the authorities can raid stashes of arms laid away by terrorist groups. Allende expects to give the orders: you must go after Patria y Libertad; instead, the Fuerzas Armadas will raid the leftist terrorists, the MIR."

"It is rumored that Fidel Castro makes illegal arms shipments to Allende in boxes labeled 'art objects,' " Helmut added.

"It's possible. Allende's a fool if he's counting on illegal arms to help him in case of a coup. It will be the *Fuerzas Armadas*, not the extremist groups, who will determine the fate of this country. Once the terrorist groups have helped bring on the crisis their work is done."

At 6:45 or 7:00 don Nestor would begin to eye the gilt clock that hung above the mantel, and at 7:15 he would lift himself from his prone position and pour his final *pisco*. "Young man, you are keeping me," he might say. "I have a date with a *señorita exquisita* in just an hour, and first I must go to the jeweler's for a little trinket I had made for her. Women appreciate such things."

"One last question," Helmut would say. "You have depressed me with your sad talk. Now tell me: what hope is there that the UP can reach an agreement with the Christian Democrats and thereby prevent its own bloody downfall?"

Don Nestor would close his eyes and frown. Rubbing his forehead he might ask: "Do you know anything about the Chinese Revolution during its early period, the twenties?"

"Only what I've read in Malraux's novels."

"There is much to be learned. What do we have: on the one hand, workers and peasants and some fanatics who want a revolution but who lack power; and temporarily allied with them the bourgeoisie who because they want national liberation will fight *los imperialistas* but who fear *el pueblo* more than *los imperialistas* and join the struggle in order to take it over. At first the bourgeoisie and the workers are successful against the British; then the crisis comes. Chiang Kai-shek says to the Communists who have fought for him: 'Now you must surrender your arms.' The Communists either do or they don't: it makes no difference; in either case Chiang has the power and forces them to submit: In Shanghai and elsewhere, he butchers thousands."

Helmut, always bewildered by don Nestor's elaborate analogies, would interrupt: "I'm not following you. What has your little story got to do with modern Chile?"

"My friend, as I always say, Chile is a microcosm, and China, she also is a microcosm. Let's compare: The Christian Democrats are on the side of social change because they want to control it. If they talk about a 'revolution in liberty,' or whatever, it is in order to divide and conquer the working class, which they fear. What can the Government do in the face of their demands? To compromise means to give up the UP program; the Christian Democrats will not permit the Government even a token, even a face-saving portion of it. To refuse to yield means to risk the collusion of the PDC with the Fascists, who are already plotting a coup. We yield, we don't yield"—here he shrugged his shoulders, his palms extended upward—"either way we are done for."

Helmut would wait while don Nestor prepared to close shop for the evening. There were conversations with his chief assistant about tomorrow's appointments and a necessary purchase or two. The custodians were given directions about the evening's cleanup. It was apparent that don Nestor involved himself in every aspect of the business, sometimes even personally sorting scraps to be saved or sharpening scissors.

To Helmut, the tailor was a curious figure, the mixture of clichés and insights in his conversation compounded in an unexpected way. Yet, Helmut asked himself, as he eyed the beloved scene—the Chilean Baroque of three-legged tables topped with doilies and china figurines, heavy mirrors and skylights, girlie calendars with saints' days, massive buffets lined with rows of glasses and bottles (with one touch from the American experience: an ice bucket)—would don Nestor's ready talk of women and arms shipments and international plots seem as thrilling anywhere else?

Once, shortly after Helmut had returned to Germany, when his absence was still an agony for me, I visited the shop with Monica. I suppose I expected to be enlivened and entertained as I had been on former occasions with Helmut. But I soon grew unaccountably annoyed at don Nestor's conversation, which seemed excessively frivolous, like his clothes. Suddenly it seemed as if his wit, which had never failed to delight Helmut, depended on his faulty English to act as a medium for his typically Latin expressions and attitudes; in Spanish, he—like most of us—seemed to be a balloon of inflated hyperboles. Certainly he was nothing like what I had led Monica to expect, a fact for which I absurdly felt he was to blame. Piqued, I attacked him, challenging his sincerity, asking him how he could claim to be a socialist when he was such a high-liver.

For a second or two, he looked as if he might become annoyed, but finally he smiled and took my hand. He spoke in a slow and courtly Spanish: "My dear, you must have me confused with someone else—with a Christian, for instance. The socialists have always had a healthy respect for material things: so much protein a day for every person, so many pairs of pants, so many years in school. These very tangible things we fight for.

"It is the Christians who preach voluntary poverty, though I must confess I do not see them practice it. 'Consider the lilies of the field'—you remember the words? But the Christians have always preferred to be gilded lilies. It was the Christian nations which invented that ingenious arrangement through which some toil and others collect interest on their investments.

"Socialists, indeed, are not obliged to practice charity, since alleviating people's suffering to the smallest possible extent to prevent revolts is a splendid method of social control among the capitalists. I must confess, however, that I am not a purist in matters of the human heart; I give my *centavos* to those in need. But I never fool myself that charity absolves us from the necessity of being just.

"It is true that I do not abandon my business and go with my numerous dependents to starve in the streets. I'm not for misery, or for magnificent gestures which make one feel less guilty but do not change the social order. I am for an economy which aims only to serve people's needs, where everyone works, where everyone is owner of the national wealth. I do not expect to see it in my lifetime; but I assure you, my dear, that without that dream—which I have dreamt since I was twelve years old—I would not care to live. My good luck has provided me with the means to keep myself in my old age and assure a dignified burial. What of the others? There is no dignity in misery. Dignity: for this I am a socialist; I cannot bear the constant humiliation of those who work that others may be rich. For this I shall live and die a leftist."

Memoirs

When I began to fill the pages of this notebook, I wrote hurriedly, expecting to bare in haste what normally lies hidden under the courtesies and constraints which make human beings bearable to live with: I mean the unique conjunction of feeling and event which, I presumed, forms the matrix of our histories like the memory knots on an Incan *quipu*. Somehow I expected to peel off the mask of my everyday self, revealing half-forgotten mysteries and surprising meanings.

False: stripped of my actions, I'm as bare as night spaces.

I had thought of striving for some principles to keep me whole in a country of terror and uncertainty (*my* country). But what is emerging is far different: memories like rain on the sea; a series of perspectives which I sometimes take comfort in, sometimes reject.

3 *Monica*
September 11, 1973

Dreams are not private; they don't belong to us. They are
the nocturnal part of an individual's experience; like all experience,
dreams are the result of biological and cultural determinants
which affect everyone. Since human action shapes both the physical
environment and the spiritual environment, we are each one responsible
for the dreams of the others.

————A. YAROSLAV JURASEK

1

Monica awoke to a sound of distant rumbling which might
have been a small earthquake if the air had been quickened, or
the roll of trucks on the Alameda except that they were on
strike. Another armed uprising, she whispered to herself. She
observed with approval that—except for the ache now almost
permanent in the back of her neck where her nerves, reacting
to possible danger, seemed to stand alert—she was calm. "So
it's to be this week, just as Eve warned, and I find myself ready

to confront whatever comes." But she reflected sardonically that it was easier to be brave when it is another who is endangered: *Eva!*

Someone on the sidewalk below was raising the squeaky iron door of his newspaper stand. "Here Felix! Here Felix!" His command was followed by the sudden silence of the *san agustines* who lived in the trees across the street, and the splatter of a dog's feet in a puddle.

Monica propped herself on one elbow and listened to the silence. The gravelly sound as of artillery moving on big avenues had died away; or perhaps, she thought, she had been mistaken.

She had to decide whether to arouse Eva. Wrapping herself in a quilted robe cold to the touch, she walked towards the golden bar of light which warmed a large square of the tiled floor. She could see a few magenta-colored tulips which had blossomed during the night, bowing to each other in the breeze by the entrance to the market across the narrow street. With the paralysis in transportation since the strike had started, the air had been as pure as she remembered it from her youth, with a faint country smell. "Even this ugly old city can be lovable sometimes," she thought. To her east stretched the *barrio alto*, the homes of the elite: solid, shuttered houses, each protected by a German Shepherd watchdog and a high wall topped with glass. The European architectural styles combined with unmistakable signs of luxury reminded her vaguely of an Old World city though it would have been hard to say which. Monica looked towards the Andes which dominated the horizon, imagining the drive through the foothills which eventually brought one to the orchards and gardens of La Reina and El Arrayán. From there, taking tea on a terrace or walking through the woods, one could view, when absence of smog permitted, Santiago in all its enormity, houses and buildings crowded together in the bowl which the mountains made for them. Only from that altitude, mused Monica, did the city suggest grace and mystery, though on a spring morning after a rain it seemed to lift its grim spirit.

Suddenly the quiet was broken by the roar of distant gunfire. Peering out, she strained to listen to the disturbance, but the sounds of muffled explosions, of sirens, and of widely circling helicopters coming from every direction only confused her. "Violence is noisy, but it is mute," she thought. She continued to listen. Finally there was a moment of silence except for the faint drone of a neighbor's radio playing military marches. She banged the window shut.

She turned towards the room. The dawn, which had now fully illuminated the Santiago streets, cast a comforting haze, softening sharp contours and disguising a disorder of books and clothes and breadcrusts. Tangerines left from a midnight snack gave off a pleasant odor. Absently she corked a bottle of brandy, remembering as she did so Eve's small face as it had appeared last night, dominated by the great circles under her eyes. "Why can't conservatism die a natural death in Chile?" Eve had thought aloud. "Instead, seeing that in the natural course of things it's bound to expire, the *momios* will try to impose it by force." Later, too tired to worry, she had said jokingly, "If anything happens to me, or to Chile, try solving this dilemma: was the failure of this government—our government—inevitable, or did we bring it on ourselves?"

"Failure?" Monica had replied, but from Eve there was no response.

2

Bate, bate chocolate
Con harina, con tomate
Monica heard the children's voices chanting in rhythm as she walked the block to Felipe's office to use the phone. Even at this early hour they were out, as certain a sign of spring as the hedges of lilacs which were in bloom everywhere. She stopped

to watch the little girls who jumped adeptly to the swing of the heavy rope, their hair shining in the brilliant morning sun. "Whoever heard of a catastrophe such as what I fear, which hasn't already been anticipated by all animate things, and the elements themselves?" she thought. Yet how peaceful the world seemed now. She remembered from her youth the earthquakes which measured the passing of years more surely for Chileans than any almanac. "The cathedral fell in 1906," someone would say, "and Maria Paz was born during the summer tremors of 1967, and two thousand houses collapsed during Allende's first year."

But always an unusual tension in the air preceded a major upheaval, a weird, ominous premonition which one learned to interpret like shadows on the moon. A cock would unaccountably crow at midday, birds would fly crazily without alighting. And finally currents of magnetism would seem to pull the air itself asunder. But nothing suggested the sense of doom which Monica felt unless perhaps the course the children's play had taken. Abandoning the jump rope, they had begun bickering over who should ride the bicycle first, each one insisting loudly on her rights.

The booming of guns in the distance recalled Monica to her errand. She crossed the Alameda, suddenly aware of the people hurrying about with shopping baskets as if they had a deadline to meet. Up one flight of stairs, in the office building on the corner of Miguel Claro and Providencia, she reached her destination. "Food and Agricultural Organization (FAO), Providencia Office," she read on the door. Letting herself in with a heavy set of keys, she took in with a glance the dust-covered single desk and chair and bookcase that furnished the small room. By the telephone lay a nearly full pack of American cigarettes which she pocketed though they seemed dry and old.

Monica had often suspected Felipe of having rented this office, so seldom used, for her own convenience, so that she could use the phone. It was the sort of generous solicitude she had come to expect from him. "It's so that I can spy on you: see how nice your apartment looks from the vantage of my desk." There was a time when she had disapproved of him for his glibness, his self-indulgence, his way of getting on no matter which party was in power, but after reading his book, she had admitted to herself that she hadn't understood him. On their first weekend together she had made a clumsy effort to apologize, but he had cut her off with a shake of the head. "You have decided, revering the creature, that the creator cannot be a 'dirty old man.' "

"There is a Japanese saying, 'A man's character is apparent in every one of his brushstrokes.' "

He had laughed. "Monica, you are a good deal wiser than when I first met you, but being a woman and a leftist, you imagine man's whole duty to be an eternal battle against despair."

She pondered. "And you?" she asked finally.

"My dear, being noncombative by nature, I am free of those onerous obligations which you earnest people would lay on everyone. For me there is only this moment and a delightful walk in the sun with a beautiful woman like you."

The phones were functioning: a comforting suggestion that the country wasn't yet at civil war. "Hello." The high-pitched, trembling voice was that of an older woman. "Is that you, Monica?"

"What's happening, Maria Inez? Can you see the Presidential Palace from your window?"

"Dear, there are tanks and machine guns everywhere. There are even snipers on the roof of our apartment building, which means that those below will be firing at us." She started to cry in tidy little gasps like the sneezes of a cat. "I haven't taken my eyes off the Moneda. Sometimes one of the Presidential Guards appears helmeted and fires a machine gun. Once I even imagined I saw the President himself."

"And the loyal regiments?" Monica felt herself panicking. "What are the Commanders-in-Chief doing?"

"But Monica," Maria Inez replied in ashonishment. "Haven't you been listening to the radio? It's the Commanders who are betraying us. And the Navy took over Valparaíso this morning.

We're finished!" Emphasizing the words, she sounded oddly triumphant as if, working overtime, she had completed an improbable task.

Monica knew that she would neither cry nor faint, but she could not control the trembling in her knees.

"Doña Tencha," she asked finally. "Where is she?"

"You should know better than I," replied Maria Inez. "Doesn't she send the car to your place to fetch Eva most mornings? But Monica"—her voice became soft and confidential—"*El Compañero Presidente* will see to doña Tencha, no need to fret about that. He'll see about his wife. You shouldn't be worrying about her but rather about us."

"About you?"

"When the Fascists break into the Moneda, they'll search through doña Tencha's papers and find Eva's name and mine among others, and then they'll be after us. We weren't, after all"—she spoke slowly and distinctly—"without considerable importance in the smooth functioning of the Popular Unity Government."

In spite of Maria Inez' chilling use of the past tense, Monica couldn't suppress a giggle. She had never known a person who took such childlike pride in her office. As a reward for years of friendship, she had been appointed at the age of sixty to the First Lady's staff. She had respected herself more ever since. She was like a piece of pewter which, having been ignored for many years, was finally displayed in a prominent place.

"I don't think you need to worry," Monica replied. She started to add, "You are just a secretary, and Eve's just a girl Friday," but checking her tactlessness she concluded, "and in any case there's no escape."

"Monica, dear," Maria Inez was almost whispering now. "You and Eva have been like daughters to me. I'd do anything for you." She hesitated. "I want you to know that I have some friends in high places who might be useful." The old lady was enjoying her role of potential benefactor. "Just give me a call if you need me."

"If the telephones are working." Monica hung up and quickly turned towards home.

3

The apartment smelled of chocolate and toast. "Eve," she started to call as she closed the door, but Maria Paz, her finger on her lips, silenced her. "Shh, mama; the President is speaking on the radio."

The familiar and beloved voice; it comforted her like a favorite old wine. Suddenly she felt wild with hope; how often had Allende turned apparent disaster to advantage! She went to stand by Eve, who was sitting in front of the radio, her face buried in her hands. "Listen," she whispered to Monica.

I say goodbye to you, in these minutes the airplanes are flying overhead; it is possible that they will fire, but....

The sound of aircraft momentarily drowned out the words. The President continued:

Workers of my country: I have faith in Chile and in her destiny. Other men will overcome this gray and bitter moment where treason tries to impose itself. May you continue to know that much sooner than later the great avenues through which free men will pass to build a better society will open. Long live Chile! Long live the People! Long live the Workers! These are my last words....

An announcer continued: "The President of the Republic has addressed the country; the Constitutional President has just declared that the people should be at alert and in their places, ready to defend what years of struggle...."

"With what?" thought Monica desperately. "With sticks and Molotov cocktails?"

Again the voice faded, died out, and together the sisters cried in exasperation. Monica began to bang her fists against the old radio, supplicating it with tears and oaths. But suddenly the interference disappeared, and they sat stone still as if at a death bed. "...cowardice and treason," concluded Allende.

There was a few seconds' pause. Then, like an offertory hymn, the national anthem began to sound. Monica wanted to swear and to weep, but she was checked by Eve who motioned towards the child. Maria Paz had clutched her great masses of dark hair and, her eyes tightly closed, had begun to moan slightly as she rocked to and fro. Monica was reminded of pictures she had seen of ancient, careworn Jews, in sackcloth and ashes, at the Wailing Wall: she was struck with the resemblance between the very young and the very old, their instinctive distrust of human efforts to thwart death and suffering. "She is wiser than we," Monica thought as she listened to Eve's attempts to soothe the child. Maria Paz shook her head ambiguously as if despising the weakness of adults who must dissemble in their profoundest moments, or perhaps she was exerting herself to be calm in an effort to please: for she suddenly became still, her great eyes turning from her mother to her aunt, mutely replying to their unarticulated questions.

"*Tía*," she finally said. "Tell me about June 29, when the *milicos* tried to overthrow the Government."

Eve looked astounded. "But Maria Paz, you know that story. I've told you so many times. . . . "

"I like to hear," she said supplicating. "We need to hear." She shrugged like an adult, her palms extended upwards, as if to suggest that her meaning, though unexplained, was obvious.

"*Tía* isn't in the mood for stories," said Monica; "let me tell; you help." And she began to unwind the familiar tale, her deep voice, from birth unaccountably suggestive of whiskey and cigarettes, charged with unshed tears.

"It was a chilly winter morning, June 29th of this year: your *tía* was walking to the Presidential Palace rather early, about nine o'clock. It was during the third year of President Allende's term of office—"

"Doña Tencha didn't send the car for her," the child interrupted.

"No, she was ill that day. She is often ill. It is a sad thing to see someone suffering so, though she bears it bravely." She spoke the words mechanically like the refrain of a ballad.

Maria Paz nodded solemnly, allowing a few seconds for

respectful silence, but obviously pushing onwards, like a chess player eager to see all of the well-worn pieces on the board. But she saw the world less as a series of moves and checkmates than as a suit of playing cards, each splendidly colored king or queen or fool playing eternally his or her predestined part.

"And what was she wearing?"

Monica smiled at her daughter's love of spectacle. "A coat of suede with a mink collar; and a blond wig." She paused and turned towards Eve. "You know how we *upelientos* are: we expect our leftist leaders to dress as smartly as the opposition. This is an astute observation I'm making, Eve, worth a shelf of books on the 'meaning' of the Chilean road to socialism."

Eve managed to laugh. "Or the Chilean road to nonsocialism."

"Mama, *Tía*," interrupted Maria Paz, "you're forgetting the story."

"Not at all, how could we forget?" replied Eve. "But your mother must relinquish the telling to me; she will spoil it with her endless editorials. Be quiet, Monica, let me tell it: when I got off the bus at the Alameda and Morandé, there was a most extraordinary sight, stranger even than a pride of lions tracking prey through the Plaza de la Constitución."

"A big tank regiment," Maria Paz almost whispered the words.

"And how many people have been faced with moving tanks, grinding the pavement under their enormous weight, turning their guns from side to side like the suckers of prehistoric sea monsters? They surrounded the Moneda and the Ministry of Defense, firing in every direction, terrifying the pedestrians who, like me, tried to seek shelter somewhere. Many were hurrying towards the bank on Teatinos, planning to walk through it to safety on the other side. But I was too far. So I crawled under the nearest car. I was cramped; my stockings were ruined. There was an inhuman smell of grease and cold that made me want to weep."

"The little old lady," urged Maria Paz.

"Ah, the little old lady. She approached with a lapdog on a leash, and she was decked out with gloves and hat, like someone from a former era. For some reason she spotted me, and, surprised, exclaimed, '*Mijita linda*, whatever are you doing under there?'

"I couldn't resist teasing this silly creature, so oblivious to the danger around her. 'Waiting for a bus,' I replied. A look of bewilderment crossed her face, but as she paused to consider, there was another round of fire. 'Get down,' I urged. She swooped her dog into her arms, and in a second was lying beside me. How long were we there, I wonder?

"Finally it became apparent to me that this attempt at coup d'état was stillborn although, of course, I had no way of knowing that it was farcical. How the professionals from the CIA, who were no doubt planning something for later, must have laughed at the rebel colonel and his boys, driving their fine tanks up the Alameda and stopping at the first gas station with a peremptory 'Fill 'em up!' 'And to whom do I present the bill?' asked the dubious owner. 'To the Government.' And naturally our poor, law-and-order-minded Government later had to pay, furious as they were. But I digress. There we were under a car when General Prats appeared unarmed, urging the regiment to surrender peacefully to him as their Commander-in-Chief, talking personally to the tankers one by one. He was heroic. One of the rebels refused to surrender and pointed his gun threateningly, but it was a futile gesture since Prats' assistant succeeded in disarming the soldier.

"Things quieted down. It seemed like a good time to escape. 'Don't run, someone might shoot,' I said to my companion as we emerged from our hiding places. We were so frightened that it took all of our self-control to walk at a normal speed. Yet just in front of us, also heading towards the bank on Teatinos, a man broke into a run; he was killed before our eyes."

"I saw that on television," interrupted Monica. "I was in Llay-Llay that day, remember? What could be more peculiar than watching an attempted coup d'état on TV, in a small

provincial town, not knowing for certain what the outcome would
be? I wasn't afraid for our country, Eve—you know that.
Allende had been broadcasting all morning from his house on
Tomas Moro, urging people to go about their business while
the Armed Forces took care of the rebels. But I didn't know
where you were! I thought you might be in the Moneda!"

Monica felt her throat tighten. She paused and swallowed
hard. "That night when I was returning to Santiago I saw the
campesinos getting ready to attend the Government's demonstration to commemorate the rout of the traitors. They were
riding into town on tractors or in trucks—thousands of them.
There would be thousands of workers there, too, unmistakable
in their hard hats. I could hear singing in the streets when I
reached the city.

The people united,
will never be defeated!
The people united,
will never be defeated!

And paradoxically I fell into a fit of depression. Yes, I thought,
we've earned ourselves a respite; yet what stands between us
and the next attempt of the right to take the government?
These workers, so quickly and efficiently mobilized for enormous demonstrations: what will they do, unarmed, when the
Armed Forces start firing at them?"

Eve did not reply, and Maria Paz seemed restless. Finally
she turned towards her aunt. "*Tía*, you haven't finished. What
did Allende say to you on the twenty-ninth?"

Eve shrugged helplessly. "I've told you, I don't know—I'll
never know for certain. After escaping from the Plaza de la
Constitución, I hurried to the president's house on Tomas
Moro to see what I could do for doña Tencha. She was with
the President, so I made my way down the hall and into his
office, through throngs of reporters and officials, trying to reach
her. But I was closer to Allende than to her, and as I passed,
he surprised me by reaching for my hand and squeezing it
between his palms."

"What did he say?" repeated Maria Paz.

"There was so much noise in the room that I couldn't quite make it out, I've told you. But it seemed to me that he made a remark uncharacteristic of him and unsuited to the circumstances, which were turning to our advantage. I had just mumbled something humorous about the scare I had had at the Moneda, and he grew very sober. He suddenly looked old. 'Some things are more important than life,' he said."

Maria Paz started to cry. Monica rose and walked to the window. She was smitten with a sudden loneliness, like a person whose welfare is dependent on fickle or malevolent powers. Outside the traffic had almost ceased, and there was silence except for the laughter of a group of teenagers who were drinking champagne on the balcony across from her. In the distance she could see the window of Felipe's office which looked even emptier than usual. Then, unaccountably, she lost interest in her own situation; with the energetic surge of pity which she sometimes felt for the old and spent, she remembered Allende under fire in the Moneda. He would die, it seemed certain. It was his duty to die; if he couldn't win, he must give his life, as he himself had said. Yet she feared that even now he might weaken in his resolve; the traitors would be offering him amnesty, a flight to Argentina for himself and family. Perhaps he would be tempted. He had always bargained, maneuvered, trusted his luck; what was needed now, an indifference to life born of despair, was alien to his temperament. She found herself grinding her teeth. "Don't fail us at the last," she said. "There's no way back. See, you have consecrated your life to realizing our dreams, which you helped create, which for a few moments in history charged us with magnificence. Now you must die a death worthy of such dreams and such people."

Eve, who had been listening to the radio, joined Monica at the window. "In a half hour the traitors will bomb the Presidential Palace," she said.

4 *Ben*
September 11, 1973

... and let it be known among men of commerce and
gentry who wish to come to settle, that they should
come, because there is no better land in all the
world for living and founding a line. Say it
because it is flat, very healthy, agreeable, it has
only four months of winter, and in those months, if
there is no quarter moon, it rains only a day or two.
All the other days are so sunny that there is no need
to light a fire. The summer is so mild, and the
winds that circulate so delicious, that all day long
a man can remain in the sun without endangering his
health. It is the most abundant land for pasture
and gardens, and for every kind of cattle and plants
that one can imagine; much beautiful wood for making
houses, and an infinity more of firewood for the
service of the houses, and the mines very rich in
gold, and all the land, and wherever you wish to get
it, there you will find it; all you need for sowing and
for building, and water, firewood, and grass for your
cattle. It seems that God made the land deliberately
as a place where everything needful is at hand.

———FROM A LETTER TO THE EMPEROR CHARLES V
FROM PEDRO DE VALDIVIA (1497–1553),
LA SERENA, CHILE, SEPTEMBER 4, 1545

In the country Ben always arose before dawn, awakened by the crowing cocks or by the squealing pigs who waited impatiently to be driven to forage at the river's edge. Santiago confused him. He squinted in amazement at the luminous dial on the clock on the floor near the cot: 8:00. Through the forlorn-looking curtains he caught a glimpse of bright sky and nacreous clouds; it would be a good day for walking to work.

He dressed quickly, shivering in the morning freshness, and searched his pockets for a match with which to light the water heater in the minuscule maid's bathroom to his left. Then he began his morning routine: urinating, teeth brushing, gargling, hair combing, and finally—overcoming a fleeting temptation to ignore his black shadow—shaving with soap and razor. He was rinsing the sink of murky water peppered with his black whiskers when inadvertently he caught a glimpse of himself in the mirror. He started in surprise: it was not his own reflection that he saw, but that of his mother, as she was, at least, when Ben was a boy. "It's the eyes," he thought, "their violet color and their long lashes." Then he suddenly remembered something she used to repeat to him when, as a teenager, he had been unable to participate in sports due to a slight limp which a bout with polio had bequeathed to him: "Resist the notion that your ungainly size and your limp are impediments; without them you would seem too pretty for a boy." He had been neither offended nor pleased by her remark; unable, as a child, to decipher the meaning of her compliments, always tinged with contempt, he had ended up ignoring them.

He returned to the bedroom where he folded the blankets on the cot and neatly piled his clothes in little heaps on the floor. Then he went through his backpack, feeling the various compartments like a policeman frisking a suspect. Everything was still there. Since the beginning of the strike he had had to walk from the Mapocho Station—thank God the trains were running!—to Jaime's apartment, almost five miles away. He had early on tired of carrying bundles and suitcases and had switched to a backpack, in spite of Carmen's disapproval: "If you can't see to the back of you, how are you going to prevent people from stealing your things?" Sometimes, remembering her words, he tried to catch a glimpse of his zippered pockets, turning round and round like a dog chasing his tail. But his main strategy—if his childlike plotting deserved such a designation—was simply to raise himself to his full broad-shouldered stature and to walk too rapidly for his would-be despoilers.

He carried the pack with him from the "maid's" room, where only he ever seemed to sleep, to the kitchen, where he quickly removed an oblong bundle wrapped in newspaper and a small tin of "English Breakfast" tea which Anna had included for Jaime. ("People who don't have anyone to keep their backs warm at night deserve a little pampering," she had explained.) But Ben wondered if Jaime would appreciate the largesse; Anna had hoarded the tea since her return from the United States over a year ago, never finding an occasion grand enough to break the seal for.

He lit a match to a ring on the stove and put the kettle on to boil. Then he unwrapped the bundle and smiled: biscuits. He wouldn't have been more pleased with cake or pastry. He felt proud of Anna for remembering biscuits when the bread lines at the bakeries had grown intolerably long the past few days. She had even given the recipe to the neighbors, who, although they munched dejectedly on the odd *gringo* dish, agreed that it would do in an emergency.

Ben took from the cupboard the only cups which weren't chipped, and two knives and spoons which were lying with their mates on a cloth napkin. For plates there were two silver-plated trays, both rather scratched and worn; on the back of one there was an inscription: "To Father Jaime Venegas J., S.J., on the occasion of his ordination, from the choir at St. Ignatius, 1955." Jaime usually set the table with the green soup bowls made of tin, but Ben—although he wasn't normally a fussy man—refused to eat from tableware he deemed appropriate for hospitals or army camps. ("Sometimes I suspect you are imperfectly acquainted with the circumstances of your adopted country," Jaime would say to him. "It *is* a hospital full of critical cases who, if they don't succumb to germs, die from despair or delirium tremens as their would-be physicians squabble over the proper treatment.")

It was only after Ben had found some jam in an old yogurt carton that he felt the time had come to awaken Jaime. Yet, as he listened for a moment to see if his friend were awake, he suddenly realized that the streets were rumbling with the sound of tanks. Indeed, it dawned on him that he had shut out from his mind since arising the unmistakable racket of moving artillery. "One quickly becomes inured to infernal conditions," he thought. He remembered the faint traces of tear gas, left over from who-knows-what street fight, which had irritated his nose and eyes as he walked to Jaime's the night before.

A pair of narrow French windows led from the kitchen to a balcony, just large enough for one deck chair and three flower pots, which overlooked the apartment's gardens and narrow Eugenia Street four stories below. Ben had just decided to step out in an effort to get a glimpse of the busy streets which Eugenia Street intercepted when Jaime appeared. "I wouldn't do that if I were you," Jaime said. "There are snipers on the surrounding buildings."

Ben blinked in confusion. He felt alarmed and disoriented. "You're dressed in a Roman collar," he said irrelevantly. He was amazed that his mind continued to work in the usual way, registering ordinary sights and sounds, and that his voice sounded perfectly normal, in spite of his acute anxiety.

"You are impressed by my resemblance to the giraffe," Jaime stated; "don't deny it."

Ben grinned. With his big teeth, his enormously long eyelashes which his thick lenses magnified, and his fantastic neck, Jaime did indeed look like a giraffe.

"I'm very fond of giraffes," Ben said, "and in any case I don't come here for the sights. I come for—"

"For spectacles, I hope," interrupted Jaime. "That is what you'll be getting. Think of it, my friend, you've a ringside seat at a coup d'état. We're not more than a mile from the Moneda. Now if we can avoid attracting attention to ourselves, we may live to tell stories to your grandchildren." He sounded fearless and self-confident, if a little overexcited. He tugged at his collar. "I dressed in my harness this morning because I was to have lunch with the papal nuncio at one. You see how we presume, making plans as if the world will continue to conform to our expectations. The papal nuncio is no doubt just this minute countermanding yesterday's instructions to the cook."

Ben moved to peer through the panes of the French windows. Although he couldn't see much to either side, he knew that there was a row of identical balconies for every story of the large building. Directly across the narrow street there was a similar apartment house, and on the roof were perched several helmeted men with rifles. He was about to make a comment about them when a boom of distant artillery, followed in a few seconds by a shell burst, stopped his thought. His mouth was dry and he felt a lump in his throat; he was surprised at the sense of infinite sadness which smote him; this coup d'état, after all, was not a shock—he had expected it for weeks.

Jaime joined him at the window for a few seconds and then moved to turn on the radio above the refrigerator. Every station was playing military marches. Ben and Jaime gazed at each other in silence for a few moments, in perfect communication, and then sat down at the table. As Ben poured the boiling water into the teapot, he reflected that his deep friendship with Jaime depended less on their conversation—although he valued it highly—than on the mood and atmosphere they managed to create together. More than anyone he had ever known, Jaime intuited the longings of the heart.

Jaime took a few sips of the tea but seemed lost in mournful abstraction. In the painful silence which the marches on the radio seemed paradoxically to amplify, Ben became suddenly conscious of the lack of comfort to which he had grown accustomed in Santiago. The kitchen table at which they sat was hardly big enough for the breakfast dishes, and when two men sat at it, one found himself scraping the sink, and the other the door. From the cement floor emanated a cold sometimes intense enough to produce chilblains. From the ceiling a sixty-watt bulb hung suspended on a short wire. It was the same in the rest of the apartment, one of the hundred or so in this modern high-rise building into which Jaime had moved when he and his fellow priests had decided to live among the community they served instead of in the traditional, attractive Jesuit houses which dotted the city. ("What I find peculiar about Chileans," Anna had said, "is their indifference to their physical aspect. How odd it is to see people dressed in sensational, tailor-made clothes, adorned with real jewels, partying regally in grimy-walled rooms with peeling plaster or wormy woodwork. They don't seem to notice.")

Jaime's apartment was not yet decaying; it had, however, lost whatever trace of dignity it might have had under all the impertinences committed against it: unwashed cupboards, unswept floors, stained rugs, and amorphous piles of clothes and papers. In an effort to save his most important documents from the ever-rising tide, Jaime had taken to taping them to the walls. Among them were to be found some of his little jokes. Above the kitchen table, for instance, he had posted a quotation from Diego Portales, Chile's leading nineteenth-century statesman: "I don't believe in God, but I believe in priests." Under it Jaime had drawn a particularly gruesome skull and crossbones. And then, as if engaged in a private dialogue, he had penciled: "Marx's insight that the domination of man by God mirrors the domination of man by capital is true, but it is insufficiently comprehensive."

"The tea is exquisite," Jaime suddenly said; "I'm sorry you couldn't find a crust or two to go with it." But as he talked, he looked expectantly at the bundle wrapped in newspaper which Ben had unceremoniously deposited between the cream and sugar.

Ben began to unwrap it. "Biscuits!" he said emphatically

in English, enjoying the little explosions the hard consonants made. "American biscuits!"

"Scones!" exclaimed Jaime, rubbing his hands together. "Scottish scones!"

Ben quickly prepared to defend his claim. They were both aware of the sounds of mysterious movements outside which made the tea cups tremble in their saucers. "In a way we're both right," he said. "A fascinating example of cultural diffusion." And he tore a biscuit in half as if to demonstrate a truth about it.

Jaime held up a finger as if suddenly inspired. "The Americans adopted the recipe from the Scotch-Irish who settled in Pennsylvania," he declared.

"Not at all," replied Ben. He paused to take a bite of biscuit with jam. "Indeed, it was the other way around. A commonly overlooked fact is that at the time of the American Revolution one-third of the colonists were Tories. Many of them fled, ending up in Canada, or even returning to the Old World. When a number of Scotch-Irish who had lived in western Pennsylvania returned to their place of origin in Ulster or in western Scotland, they took this typical frontier recipe with them. These *panes* have been known as 'Scotch scones' ever since, except in the United States, where their true origin is appreciated."

Ben talked as if engrossed in the conversation, but his hearing was acutely attuned to the street noises. He felt fully alert, like an animal scenting danger. "Why are we carrying on this way," he asked himself. "Is this how you confront a coup d'état on your doorstep, with aimless conversation?"

Jaime narrowed his eyes. He chewed thoughtfully for a few minutes, methodically spreading jam upon three or four biscuits which he lined up in front of him. He drained his cup, quickly finished eating, and then sat back in his chair, sighing deeply. "Willing, you've done it again. When you're not here, I don't know what I eat; you can imagine the state of my cupboards. But just when my stomach starts to flap against my backbone, my international chef shows up again."

He rubbed an imaginary swelling in his bony middle. "I may even grow a paunch."

Ben smiled at the thought of it and at the absurd myth which Jaime was creating about his culinary abilities. It hardly seemed possible that it had begun only a few months ago, when Ben had asked around the office for a place to stay in Santiago three or four nights a week. A number of people had thought of Jaime: "He was supposed to set up housekeeping with Father Duran, but Father Duran got a grant to study in Belgium. Jaime could use some company and a hand around the kitchen."

Ben's reverie was interrupted.

"Do you remember the Mexican muffins?" Jaime looked at Ben in an ambiguous way. It wasn't clear if the priest was making fun of him.

"Do I remember the Mexican muffins? How can you ask?"

"And the Old Believers' Holy Saturday bean pie. I've always hoped you'd make that again."

"It's just a question of finding the ingredients. It isn't easy, you know, when I arrive on Tuesday morning and find only soda crackers, maybe, or a plate of stew."

"But you work miracles, Willing. In the last month we've had Norwegian pancakes and Bengalese peanut curry and Polynesian raisin-pumpkin pudding. I wonder what you would come up with if the country were functioning normally and commodities were readily available."

("You should be ashamed of yourself, teasing a priest like that!" Carmen had objected when she had heard of Ben's culinary frauds. But Anna enjoyed the joke; sometimes she helped Ben with his stories.)

Jaime excused himself and walked towards the living room, returning briefly for the transistor radio on the refrigerator. "I'll relieve you of these damned marches," he said. He looked hard at Ben for a few seconds, then averted his eyes. "If there's any news, I'll call you."

Ben began to clear the table, reviewing in his mind how Jaime had paid him back a week ago in priestly style. It had happened Monday evening, when Ben had arrived at Jaime's about 10 p.m. "Have a piece of cake," Jaime had said, offering him a slice on a paper plate. "Today's my saint's day. My sister surprised me with a little party this afternoon."

"Tastes good," Ben had replied, "plain, maybe, but good. Happy Saint's Day. Whose recipe is this?"

Jaime had nibbled at a few crumbs from the cake plate, conspicuously moving his Adam's apple. "God's."

"Well. And what else is new?"

"Surprised, are you? Why shouldn't God have a favorite recipe? It's harmless enough."

"I just never associated God with honey cake, that's all. Where did you get your information?"

"In Genesis, of course." Jaime had laughed deeply. "You can check it yourself!"

As Ben remembered the incident, he mumbled to himself and finished the dishes. Jaime's joke had only momentarily deflated him. The priest wasn't as gullible as he had at first seemed; Ben would either have to transform his little fancies into art or abandon them altogether. He wasn't ready to give up.

He was about to take a stand at the French windows when Jaime, his face ashen, motioned to him from the living room. "There's news," he said.

With a few steps Ben crossed the kitchen and stood before the radio. The announcer's voice, deep and sonorous, seemed to be intoning rather than speaking. There was a bit of static; then Ben heard distinctly:

In view of the extremely serious social and moral crisis through which the country is passing, the inefficiency of the government in controlling chaos, and the steady increase of paramilitary groups trained by the parties of the Popular Unity coalition which would inevitably bring the people of Chile to a civil war, the Armed Forces and the Police have resolved:

First: the President of the Republic must immediately release all his powers to the Armed Forces and Police of Chile.

Second: the Armed Forces and Police are united in their

efforts to initiate the historical and responsible mission to fight for the freedom of the country and prevent it from falling under the Marxist yoke and to insure the restoration of order.

Third: the workers of Chile can rest assured that the economic and social achievements which have been reached to date will not undergo any fundamental change.

Fourth: the press, radio stations, and television channels serving the Popular Unity coalition must suspend their functions as news media forthwith. Otherwise they shall be attacked.

Fifth: the people of Santiago must remain in their homes in order to avoid becoming victims.

Signed by: Augusto Pinochet Ugarte, Commander-in-Chief of the Army; José Toribio Merino, Commander-in-Chief of the Navy; Gustavo Leigh, Commander-in-Chief of the Air Force; César Mendoza Duran, Director General of Carabineros.

The two men continued to stare at the radio as the talking ceased and the marches resumed. When Jaime finally began to stir, Ben observed that his friend's face was drawn and pinched, suffused with flashes of pink and lilac like a famished llama's. Suddenly, in addition to his other sensations, Ben felt an alarming sense of his own intrusiveness, as if, after forcing himself on an almost total stranger three months ago, moving into his home and, as it were, demanding that the priest expand his emotional sweep to include a complex and perhaps even eccentric *gringo*, he was now about to witness what he had no right to see: the relaxation of Jaime's control over his own nervous intelligence. Ben wanted to leave the room, but he felt severed from his body, which slumped lifelessly in a chair. Then he heard himself enunciating, "Pinochet and Leigh, it's what I expected, but who are Merino and Mendoza?"

Jaime swiveled his head on his long neck, registered his friend's question, and seemed to recover his composure as he spoke. "Well, you see, in the case of the Navy and the Police, the top dogs wouldn't go along with the plot, the conspirators had to go several places down the seniority lists to find officers who would cooperate. Mendoza: I believe he was in sixth place."

He got up and began to pace the room, pausing always at

the windows to peek from behind the curtains at the street below.

"You know what that means. The military people have already been fighting among themselves. Last night there must have been mutinies among some regiments, and enlisted men murdering officers loyal to the UP, and agonies of indecision among junior officers with divided loyalties. In one night the toll of widows in this country augmented by the hundreds, I'll wager. And this is just the beginning, Willing."

He turned suddenly to face his friend, his eyes glittering. "I never wanted this, you know. I was against the UP, yes, against their stupidity and shortsightedness. But a day didn't go by that I didn't pray that Chile be spared a military take-over."

"I don't think the Church has anything to be ashamed of in this particular national failure," replied Ben. He was thinking of the Cardinal's long efforts to set up a dialogue between the Christian Democrats and the UP.

Jaime suddenly sat down, his elbows on his knees and his hands hanging loosely between his legs. "My dear friend, like most converts, you are a menace to that institution you most cherish. How can we enliven it when you refuse to face the truth about it?"

It was another thrust in their months-long duel; Ben allowed himself to stretch psychologically into a form of consciousness which fitted him comfortably, his wits on edge, ready for intellectual sparring.

"How can you justify the way we Christians allowed the political scene to bring out the worst in us?" Jaime continued. "We weren't interested in sanctity: we wanted ecstatic feelings. We egged one another on, not taking into account our duty to prevent the very cataclysm which excited us so. What a disjunction between intellect and gut! Those of us who are critical of the left, we watched the death throes of the UP with a smug sense of self-justification, we were cynical about their intentions, and we were amused, and—let's face it— even exhilarated by the brilliance of the catastrophe which threatened us. Every morning we ran to the papers to read about the latest development, vaguely disappointed if there were no assassination or street fight or disastrous political maneuver to intoxicate us."

"You exaggerate."

"But what I wonder is: where was our love of God during all those extraordinary days? I mean: when the last drop of blood has been shed after this ordeal is over, the last orphan placed in a home, how can we possibly rest assured that we didn't do our bit to create this hell?"

Ben felt moved. "There is no way to answer such scruples."

The sound of bullets flying, sporadically—a subdued accompaniment to their conversation—was suddenly amplified; now it was joined by a cadenza of machine-gun fire, apparently from the roof of the building across the street. Jaime, whose back had been to the windows, moved quickly to the sofa, and Ben, seated in an armchair, stood up abruptly as if to leave. "I'm not a brave man," he said to himself, trying out the idea. He felt comforted by his cowardice: surely heroism was an unworkable ideal nowadays. He noted with interest, however, that Jaime was putting up a courageous exterior. Perhaps, Ben reflected, that was a good way for a priest to control his emotions; or perhaps with years of spiritual discipline one becomes indifferent to the hour of one's death.

Jaime finally seated himself on the floor near the front door. Ben paced about the living room. "Do you ever listen to Angel Parra's songs?" Jaime asked.

For a second or two Ben couldn't focus on the question. He stopped pacing and stared at his friend. "I guess you're proposing to carry on normally in spite of . . . this." He motioned towards the window.

"But Willing, this calamity has hardly begun. It could go on for days. You and I, we may be forced to share the pleasure of each other's company indefinitely. Don't you think we might as well make the best of it?" His tone was friendly and cheerful, but as he talked he ran his fingers through his hair, and his eyes seemed abnormally bright.

"As I was saying," Jaime continued, "I'm a great fan of

Angel Parra's. He says everything that I mean but much better. Sometimes he says things I don't mean, too, but I forgive him because of the good songs."

Ben sat down on a pile of sofa pillows opposite Jaime. "I've probably heard him, but I get the folksingers mixed up. I'm not very musical."

"One of his songs never fails to make me feel ashamed and saddened. Let me see if I remember the words:

Does God care for the poor?
Maybe yes, maybe no.
What I know for certain is that at lunchtime
He sits at the boss's table
What I know for certain is that at lunchtime
He sits at the boss's table.

If there's anything on earth
More important than God
It's that nobody spit blood
For somebody else's benefit.

Jaime banged his fist on the door behind him. He made a few inaudible sounds but apparently changed his mind about what he was going to say. There were a few seconds of silence except for an echo of voice and movement on distant streets.

Ben watched the play of light on a dirty window and on the lush Wandering Jew which covered the sill. It was nearly springtime, he thought idly. All the juice gathering behind living membranes, crazy to rush through limbs and stalks, made itself manifest even in the city air, even inexplicably on weatherbeaten windowpanes. He found himself thinking in images of colored eggs and rabbits and Easter lilies, remembering with a jolt that in the Southern Hemisphere everything is upside down; it was spring but soon it would be Christmas.

"You don't have to look at things that way," he finally said. "One can sympathize with the poor man, but, at the same time, one knows he's made an error. He doesn't know that he himself is God. He thinks God is dining with the rich—it seems reasonable. But God isn't there; Christ isn't there. Christ is the poor man."

Jaime smiled. "Are you playing Jesuitical tricks on me, mixing up the One, the Omnipotent, with a poor old *roto?*"

"It's hardly a new idea, the unrecognized God. Do you remember the verses from Isaiah?

there was in him no stately bearing
to make us look at him,
no appearance that would
attract us to him.
He was rejected and avoided by men,
a man of suffering, accustomed to infirmity,
one of those from whom
men turn away,
and we held him in no esteem.

"That's the Chilean lower classes, as far as I'm concerned," Ben concluded. "And my job as an expert in nutrition is to help them to nourish themselves adequately, to teach God what to eat, so to speak. And now if you don't mind I'm going to make another pot of tea and set to work. It's kind of quiet out there now. As you said, we've got to carry on somehow." He rose and stretched and started for the kitchen.

"Willing, I'm astonished at your ability to quote Scripture," Jaime called after him.

"It's because I was brought up Baptist," Ben shouted back from the kitchen. "The Protestants ground their children in the Bible." From the living room he heard what he had expected, a small "Damn!" He smiled: one of Jaime's peculiar quirks, an envy of what he considered to be the model piety and virtue of the Protestant churches, was reaching sinful proportions. Ben started humming "Rock of Ages" as he got out his slide collection and paste and colored pencils to begin work.

2

At ten-thirty and again at eleven that morning they heard over the radio the ultimatum signed by the chiefs-of-staff: Allende must surrender immediately or the Moneda will be bombed. There were a few conflicting reports; once it was announced that Allende had agreed, and the time limit was extended. Two or three groups of UP supporters left the Moneda, hands over their heads. The continual firing of heavy artillery and of machine guns provided an accompaniment to the announcer's voice.

Sometime between eleven-thirty and twelve the planes came, two of them, Hawker Hunters, flying from the direction of Los Cerrillos. At this point Jaime and Ben began to watch through the French windows in the kitchen. They saw the planes, like dancers, fly in perfect unison towards the middle of the city. Suddenly they dipped, making a large and graceful curve along the San Cristobal hill. Then with a terrifying noise they picked up speed, racing low over rooftops as they neared the Mapocho River. It was there that they let loose the rockets which dived straight towards the Moneda. One rocket, two, three: as they struck, the explosions reverberated in a city as silent as death. Ben and Jaime felt the building rock on its foundations. Then the planes climbed upwards as they approached the target, which was by then in flames. They circled briefly before flying away as gracefully and serenely as they had come. Over the Moneda a screen of smoke was rising. By radio a voice called intermittently for firemen to extinguish the blaze.

3

For the next few hours Ben sat at the kitchen table, his work spread before him, unable to do anything. Anna and Damaris would be worried about him, he thought. They had probably gone to the Ortegas' earlier in the day to use the phone; they had called him at work, but there had been no answer. By now they would be locked in the house with Carmen. Anna would be crying: tears were a great comfort to her. Damaris would be afraid of this unaccustomed display of adult sorrow. "Anna, Anna," he called silently. "Can you forgive me for this, for everything?" And again, "Please, don't let this get you down." Then he stopped, surprised at his own apology, troubled by his obscure sense of culpability. "Anna, you know I love you," he implored. But he could not conjure up her presence. He felt alone and afraid.

Sometimes Jaime, as he paced the length of the apartment, overcome by curiosity and boredom, would approach the French windows. Ben would forcefully tug him away. They both knew it was dangerous to expose themselves to snipers; earlier in the day they had heard a splintering of glass, and a snap and whiz of bullets as they penetrated some apartments in the building opposite.

Since the bombing of the Moneda, the street-fighting had increased. The armed men on the roof shot intermittently at the *carabineros* below who kept firing and shouting, "Surrender! Surrender!" At one point the building (fortunately built to withstand earthquakes) had been struck by a bazooka.

It was about two-thirty or three in the afternoon when they heard a peremptory, impatient knock at the door. Taken entirely by surprise, the two men stared incredulously in the direction of the noise, unable to believe the evidence of their own senses. At first Ben felt frozen with fear. Jaime, apparently paralyzed into inaction, finally took told of himself and turned to answer the angry-sounding summons. As Jaime moved towards the door, the quaking of Ben's heart could not be stilled. He wanted to cry out "No!" but he could not make a sound. In any case, Jaime proceeded cautiously, at first opening the door only a crack. He stared hard for a few seconds and then broke into nervous laughter. "Ah, my Canadian friends," he exclaimed. "What a fright you gave us! But don't stand out in the draughty hall—come in, come in!"

Ben stared in amazement at the young people who crept in silently like cats. The woman, who came first, about twenty-five years old, was large and angular, with deep-set eyes and a wealth of freckles across her nose and cheeks. Her hair was a flaming red. The young man, apparently her husband, was dark-skinned and clean shaven. He would have appeared quite youthful had it not been for his baldness, which circled out from his crown, giving him a monkish appearance. Both were dressed in American blue jeans and their heavy woolen socks with Indian moccasins seemed exotic in the Chilean environment.

Everyone sat down. Jaime seemed to be enjoying the situation. He spoke in nearly flawless English, and the couple, after a few attempts to reply in Spanish, gave up. "Let me introduce my houseguest," Jaime said to the newcomers. "This is Benjamin Willing who works with me at the Catholic University's adult education center; you know—UCADULTOS. And this young Canadian couple—"

"Not Canadian, 'Québecois,' " interrupted the young man somberly.

"Ah, you must excuse me," said Jaime, coloring slightly. "This is Paul and Evelyn Pouillon. They've been in Chile only two or three weeks. They both spent the past few years at Berkeley, and now they're planning to study economics or sociology—"

"Planned," interrupted Paul again.

"Let me assure you, my friend," Jaime continued, turning to Ben, "—and I can tell from your mystified expression that you are wondering—that Paul and Evelyn didn't come here in a taxi. They live in our building, you see; they took an apartment on the top floor just last week."

"What an introduction to Chile!" said Ben. "I wish you

could have arrived at a happier time. Is there anything we can do for you? Do you have everything you need?"

"You can talk to us," replied Evelyn in a frightened voice, "and advise us. You can't imagine what a scene it's been."

Together the couple began to describe their experiences, starting with the morning, when Paul had gone out to buy bread about seven. He hadn't really expected to find any; yesterday there had been none in this quarter of the city. When he reached the bakery, there were already about sixty people waiting ahead of him. He had stood in line for an hour, listening to the talk of trouble, which fluttered everywhere. And he had taken it seriously, for he himself had seen a tank driving down the street as he had left the apartment house.

"Only one tank moving in the direction of the Moneda? It might have been Allende," Jaime suggested.

"That's what we think," replied Paul.

He had run home to awaken Evelyn and to listen to the radio. Upon learning that Valparaíso had been taken early in the morning, he had gone out to buy food, but evidently everyone else had heard too, for there wasn't a scrap to be seen, and the shops were closing up. Then the machine guns had begun to fire; at first he had started to run, but, realizing how dangerous it was to appear to be involved in the disorder, he had forced himself to walk at normal speed. Two policemen with automatic rifles passed him on motorcycles; farther down the street he could see a barricade.

When he reached home, he found Evelyn busy with preparations for a long ordeal. She had put a large pot of beans on to boil and had filled the bathtub and numerous pans with water. "I learned my lesson the first or second day we arrived," she explained. "That was when a terrorist group dynamited the power stations in half of Chile as the President started to make a speech by radio and TV. We were without lights and water for a day."

"Then we proceeded to get on each other's nerves," continued Evelyn, giggling. "There wasn't much to occupy us except listening to the snipers' fire and to the stupefying marches they played over and over again on the radio. We did

get Allende's speech, though. Paul even thought to record it."
As she spoke she took a small recorder from her pocket.

"Allende's speech? What speech?" asked Jaime.

"You missed it? Allende spoke to the nation over Radio Magallanes before it was finally silenced. The station has a mobile unit, you see, and although the Armed Forces systematically silenced all the other government stations last night, that one remained."

"It's a magnificent speech," added Paul. "You'll want to hear it. We've already made arrangements to sneak it out of the country via a Canadian airlines plane. By tomorrow it will probably be heard all over the world."

Ben was impressed with the competence and self-possession of the young people. He wondered vaguely if they had acquired political experience in the liberation movement in Quebec. He started to formulate a question, but Evelyn interrupted his thought, continuing with her story.

"I don't know how bad it has been down here, but we're on the top floor, you know. I was furious with Paul for inventing a little fantasy which freaked us out: what if one of the snipers above us were to be wounded and were to fall onto our balcony? We have one just like yours, Jaime, although ours is off the living room rather than the kitchen."

"You can see the dilemmas such a scenario would present us with," interjected Paul. "We couldn't be so inhuman as to leave the man outside to die, yet if we were to help him, we'd surely be punished for it. The *carabineros* might even storm in and kill us."

Ben looked at the young man curiously. He gave the impression of thriving on thorny terrain.

"We talked it over for a long time," Paul continued, "and although we never made a firm commitment, I think we were both fairly confident we'd do the right thing. And then, wouldn't you know it, life imitated art. The situation we'd invented—well, it happened!"

"But, how extraordinary!" exclaimed Jaime. "Did a wounded body actually land on your balcony?"

"No, but there was a pounding at the front door. Not a

polite little knock, you understand, but banging and kicking. I still don't know which of us went to open up, or what we thought about it. I half-expected to be done to death."

"Well, and who was it?" asked Jaime.

"Jacques Durand," said Evelyn.

"Jacques Durand? The name means nothing to me."

"He's a reporter from a Quebec newspaper whom we met when we first arrived in Chile," she explained. "Some friends of ours had given us his address. We had had some good sessions with him; he'd shown us around. And this morning he looked utterly fagged out. He sort of collapsed at our doorstep, holding his lungs, as if he'd never catch his breath again. So we helped him in and laid him down on the sofa. And finally he said, 'Do you think you could hide me for a couple of days?' "

Ben suddenly felt struck with a fearful premonition of deep trouble. "Well? And what's the problem?"

Evelyn hesitated and spoke softly, as if afraid of her own voice. "He's into politics. A lot of the foreigners found themselves becoming involved—you know that. Jacques had been covering the scene for a long time, and he lived in a working-class area. When the transportation strike began, and the food shortages here in Santiago were becoming serious, he helped to organize some trips to the countryside to purchase food which could be distributed in poor areas in the city. He and his friends would highjack some trucks. It was a dangerous business. Sometimes they got shot at by terrorist groups. But it was good; they were really exhilarated by it."

"Does he expect to be picked up by the military forces?"

"Yes. He says they had infiltrated everywhere. His name is sure to be on their lists of unwanted foreigners."

"I have an idea," said Jaime. "Why don't you hand him over to me?" His face brightened as his plan took shape. "I could dress him in a Roman collar and drop him off at a nearby Jesuit house once the curfew is lifted. The police are likely to respect the Church's right of sanctuary."

Paul looked thoughtful. "What about his friends?"

"Which friends?"

"Jacques' *compañeros*. He isn't the only foreigner in danger, of course. We agreed to let a number of Canadians and others hide out for a week or so in our apartment."

Ben put his palms to his forehead and pushed hard as he frequently did when faced with a problem. "No," he said as he waited for his thoughts to surface. "No, no." He was appalled at the recklessness of the young couple at the same time that he admired their nerve.

"I know what you're going to say," Paul interrupted. "Forget it. Listen: this morning before Jacques showed up at our place, he went to the apartment of some friends of his who live—lived —near here; some Brazilian refugees, some of those fourteen thousand political exiles that Allende admitted into Chile. Jacques knew that the military would go after the foreign leftists first, and he wanted to help hide them. But he was too late. The front door to their place was ajar; everything inside was a mess. He walked through, absentmindedly looking for clues as to their whereabouts; he assumed they'd fled, you see. And then he found the couple murdered in their bed."

A weight of silence descended on them, as plaintive as a funeral chant. They looked at one another as if waiting for something. Finally Jaime said, "Maybe it wasn't the Chilean military who did it. Maybe the Chileans are giving the Brazilian intelligence service a free hand."

"That's what Jacques thinks," said Evelyn. "But in any case, a lot of people are up against it now. And our apartment is a good place to hide out. We're new in Chile; we're not known...."

"But you could be imprisoned for years for harboring fugitives," said Ben.

"Who says we will be there? We're going to seek refuge in the Canadian Embassy."

Jaime slowly smiled. "Can you do that? Will you be admitted?"

"We've read the rules on it," said Paul. "The Embassy is obliged to admit Canadian citizens whose lives are in danger.

Jacques is afraid to go over there; he might get picked up on the way. He's staying at our place. But we're going. There's our child to think of. Evelyn is pregnant," he added hastily. "She has already had three miscarriages. Her health requires perfect calm and serenity."

Ben allowed his mind to wander as the couple filled in the details of their proposal. They occasionally tried, not always successfully, to speak Spanish. Evelyn's accent was quite nasal, as if she thought Spanish should sound like French. Ben felt certain that she was not a true *Québecoise*: her big-boned, ruddy beauty as well as her mannerisms seemed either English or American.

Jaime went to the kitchen for a bottle of sherry and some glasses. Everyone seemed comforted by the little ceremony of making prayerful toasts. Jaime suddenly remembered the remains of the American biscuits which he served on one of his silver trays.

"I guess we're fiddling while Rome burns," he said. "I honestly can't think what else to do."

Ben was about to ask Paul about his reasons for having come to Chile when the young man suddenly anticipated him.

"I think Jaime mentioned you to us before. You're the guy who lives in Villa Inez de Suarez and commutes into Santiago?"

"That's right."

"Why not save yourself the trouble? You could live here."

Ben smiled. "If you could see Villa Inez, I think perhaps you'd understand." He hesitated, entertaining and then rejecting a temptation to describe the ancient village set at the foot of the coastal range, which, along with the *cordillera* farther inland, forms the length of the stony ladder which shapes Chile. "And I hope you will visit us soon. It's a lonely life for my wife, Anna, although she prefers it to coping with this infernal city. I should warn you, though, about our accommodations. We have a tiny house, about six hundred square feet, I'd say, which sleeps my wife and myself, our daughter, Damaris, and Carmen. Carmen is..." He hesitated, searching for explanations he couldn't formulate. "She's the one who keeps things going."

"Ben is a *campesino,* you see," added Jaime. "He has two hectares of good fruitland. It's a charming place. And best of all, there's a cement reservoir for irrigation water which they've converted into a pool."

"Villa Inez, that's a funny name for a town," said Evelyn.

"It's named for Pedro de Valdivia's mistress," replied Ben. "She was Chile's first heroine and probably the only female conquistador. Valdivia rewarded her with a huge land grant and she built a mansion on the Suarez River near our house. But her place disappeared long ago. Only the name is left."

"Well, we'll come out to your place sometime," said Paul. "And maybe we'll ask for some professional advice. Jaime told us that you're an M.D."

"It's been a long time since I practiced. I had to give it up when I decided to stay in Chile permanently, since my license isn't valid here. But of course my present work in health education for adults is similar to what I've always done."

They exchanged pleasantries as Paul and Evelyn got ready to leave. Paul was just opening the door when Evelyn suddenly exclaimed, "The recording! We forgot to listen to the recording."

They returned to their chairs. As the tape rewound, Ben felt tension in the room. "This speech is going to be hard on us," he thought. "We want to hear it, yet we don't want to." There was a bit of static and then the familiar sound of Allende's voice, as calm and dignified as if he were giving a state of the union message.

4
_____

Surely this will be the last opportunity I will have to address myself to you. The air force has bombed the towers of Radio Portales and Radio Corporación. My words do not come out of bitterness, but rather deception, that they may be the moral punishment for those who betrayed the oath they took as soldiers of Chile, titular commanders-in-chief.... Admiral Merino, who has self-designated himself commander of the armada.... Mr. Mendoza, the callous general who only yesterday declared his loyalty to the Government, has been named director-general of the carabineros.

In the face of these facts, the only thing left for me to say to the workers: I will not resign! Placed in a historical transition, I will pay with my life for the loyalty of the People. I say to you that I have the assurance that the seed that we plant in the dignified consciousnesses of thousands and thousands of Chileans cannot be forever blinded.

They have the power, they can smash us, but the social processes are not detained, neither with crimes, nor with power. History is ours, and the People will make it. Workers of my country: I want to thank you for the loyalty which you always have shown, the trust which you placed in a man who was only the interpreter of the great desires of justice, who gave his word that he would respect the Constitution and the law, and that I did.

In this definitive moment, the last thing which I can say to you is that I hope you will learn this lesson: foreign capital, imperialism united with reaction, created the climate for the Armed Forces to break with their tradition, that of General Schneider, and which Commander Araya reaffirmed, a victim of the same social sector which today finds them in their houses, waiting to retake power, by strange hands, to continue defending their huge estates and privileges.

I address myself above all to the modest woman of our land, to the peasant woman who believed in us, to the working woman who worked more, to the mother who knew of our concern for her children. I address myself to the professionals of our land, to the patriotic professionals, to those who were working against the auspicious sedition carried out by the professional schools, schools of class which also defend the advantages which capitalist society gives them.

I address myself to the youth, to those who sang, who gave their joy and spirit to the struggle. I address myself to the Chilean man: to the worker, and peasant, the intellectual, to those who will be persecuted because fascism has already been present in our country for many hours: those terrorist actions which blew up bridges, cutting railway lines, destroying oil and gas pipelines, in the face of the silence of those who had the obligation of pronouncing themselves. History will judge them.

Probably Radio Magallanes will be silenced, and the calm mettle of my voice will not reach you: it does not matter. You will continue to hear me, I will always be beside you or at least my memory will be that of a dignified man, that of a man who was loyal.

Workers of my country: I have faith in Chile and in her destiny. Other men will overcome this gray and bitter moment where treason tries to impose itself. May you continue to know that much sooner than later the great avenues through which free men will pass to build a better society will open.

Long live Chile! Long live the People! Long live the Workers! These are my last words. I am sure that my sacrifice will not be in vain; I am sure that it will at least be a moral lesson which will punish felony, cowardice, and treason.

5

The national anthem started to play ("the most beautiful national hymn in the world," Anna always said). Both Paul and Evelyn were weeping silently, and Jaime's skin was once again diffused with curious pavonine shades. Ben began to pace the living room, pressing his palms against his forehead. He had been moved, yes, but he also felt irritated, as if he were being compelled to share in a nexus of feeling which slightly distorted his own shape of grief.

"Allende: I never really liked him," he finally said. His own words surprised him; he hadn't expected to be so hard.

The flecks of gold in Paul's eyes once again spread and then suddenly contracted. He looked at Ben enigmatically, as if he were measuring him against a standard too private to be found out by others. "Was it his, well, his style you found offensive? The way he had of living and dressing like a bourgeois though he was a socialist president?"

The question had been put to Ben, but Jaime answered. "You know, I've heard that criticism only from North Americans and from Chilean *momios*, who, of course live well themselves. It's a curious thing: the Chilean working class, so far as I can see, never begrudged him his food or his women or his imported liquor. I remember when Fidel Castro was in Chile— in 1971, I believe. Fidel was seen a great deal in public and in the newspapers, and everyone made a big fuss over him. I happened to be in Puerto Montt when Fidel and Allende were about to make a boat trip through the southern fiords. The weather was dreadful, as it usually is in the South, but I went down to the docks to see them off. Puerto Montt is just a small town, a stroll to the docks is such a small effort. Well, there were many people standing about, and I was next to an old, toothless man who kept elbowing me and pointing to the ship in port, 'It's *el Compañero Presidente*, it's *el Compañero Presidente*.' And suddenly Allende and Fidel appeared on deck, Fidel, as usual, dressed in army greens, but this time sporting an enormous Chilean poncho and some kind of sheep-herder's cap. Allende was his usual elegant self in a heavy suede coat trimmed in fur and with a Russian astrakhan hat. Just to joke a little with the old man at my elbow, I said, 'Yes, I recognize *el Compañero Presidente*, but who is the giant standing beside him?' 'Oh him,' he snorted with contempt: 'that's Castro, *rotoso pero no roto*.' It's a Chileanism hard to translate, but in essence it means looking like an outcast while not really being one. I must admit I was taken aback by the old man's scorn, but I think I learned something from it. I learned for one thing that Allende had correctly gauged the temperament of his supporters. It will be a long time before they'll accept a president who lives as they do."

"I have a favorite story about Allende," Evelyn said. "It's about the March elections, six months ago—the congressional elections in which the opposition hoped to sweep everything before them, enabling them to impeach Allende. It was their last chance to get rid of him by legal means." Her voice trembled slightly. "I wasn't here then, but I understand that conditions were bad, the UP was pretty pessimistic about their chances. Jacques says the left thought they'd be lucky to poll 25 percent of the vote; they came through with 44 percent. This is the story: it seems that when Allende heard the news, he went into the office with his secretary, Olivares, closed the door, and danced the *cueca* all by himself, waving about his handkerchief." She giggled. "That's pretty neat, a president who can express joy like that."

"How well informed you people are," said Jaime. "I'm surprised you know what a *cueca* is."

Paul turned towards Ben. "But you still haven't told us why you have never liked Allende."

"Never mind. It doesn't seem appropriate now. I'm sorry I brought it up."

"Nothing seems appropriate, does it? We sit around eating and telling little stories while the country goes to hell. A few more days of being cooped up together like this, we'll be murdering each other."

"Have you noticed how quiet it's become around here?" said Evelyn. "Maybe it's all over—do you think?"

"The fighting will probably continue in the working-class areas," replied Jaime. "But the snipers who were here before seem to have moved on."

Once again the Canadians made their way to the door. Ben realized as he watched them tiptoe down the hall that he felt close to them, as if he had lived through something important with them.

"Aren't they a nice young couple?" said Jaime. "I must admit I'd quite forgotten them—a terrible oversight."

"But how did you get to know them?"

"Divine Providence, my friend. You know how I'm always writing my pieces and sending them off to various religious publications; I like to think I'm contributing to the sum of good in the world, but quite frankly, years go by when, so far as I can see, only my close friends—six or eight of them scattered over the earth's surface—avail themselves of my wit and wisdom." His face brightened. "It's the ordinary sort of 'you scratch my back and I'll scratch yours' arrangement: we read one another's works religiously—if you'll permit me a bad pun—and sometimes, I must admit, we're afraid we're destined to write only for one another. Then like a thunderclap a new voice rends our little circle: it just happened that in 1970 it was Paul Pouillon. He came across a Jesuit publication in a train station in Montreal, if you can believe it, in which I had a few things to say about the Chilean elections, a topic of world-wide interest then." Jaime slowed down and pronounced the next sentence with a nonchalant air. "He was sufficiently persuaded of the truth of my argument that he sent me a little note of thanks. We exchanged a few words over the years."

"That's fascinating," said Ben. "What did you say in your article?"

"The whole of it can be ascertained from its conclusion." Jaime arched his eyebrows as he slowly quoted: " *'May God forgive the revolutionaries. If in order to do one's share in the overcoming of human misery it is necessary to die in mortal sin, then it is a duty to burn in hell forever.'* "

He shut his eyes and leaned on the chair in front of him; he looked tired and depressed. Ben was swept with a wave of compassion for him. "Why is it," he thought, "that we are so simpleminded about religious people? They seem transparent to us, smooth, guiltless, wise. As for priests, when we don't envy them for their serenity and faith—which we regard as pure gifts of Grace—we despise them for their intellectual surrender to dubious and untestable affirmations. That's the greatness of Jaime's writings: he makes it impossible to doubt the anguish of others, including his own. Anyone can see that his life is no smooth gyring around some sort of conversion experience of his youth, but an infinite series of agonizing choices made from minute to minute, by a man who is perfectly sincere—that is, a man with no interests to protect."

Jaime had roused himself from his reflections and was again shuffling through the mess on his desk. "Willing, you really are a Godsend," he said. "Not only are you a first-rate cook, you're also a perfect captive audience. Now you've inspired me to read to you from my latest composition, if I can find it." His face grew anxious. "Well. I'm afraid we'll have to forgo the pleasure until I get a chance to clean the place up a bit." He glanced from the desk to the shelves and rocking chair which were also overflowing with papers and books.

"Well, you must give me at least a clue as to what you're working on."

"I started it in August when the transportation strike was beginning to strangle us *santiaguinos*. It's called, 'On Coming to an Understanding of the Alternatives to Civil War and Military Takeover Which Are Still Left Us, or: Does Making Sense Make Sense?' "

"It's already out of date, Jaime. That's the trouble with writing on the latest in an infinite series of crises."

"Tell me, Ben, now that we're alone. Why were you so hard on Allende when the young couple was here? You surprised me."

"I don't know. In truth I've nothing against him personally. I'd imagine he's a mixture of strengths and weaknesses like the rest of us, but he has the unfortunate characteristic of not sufficiently resisting weaknesses."

"Such as?"

"Such as resorting to *machismo* to win support and intimidate his opponents. That's a subject worthy of you, Jaime, the *machismo* of the left.

"But Willing, every Chilean politician has to be a *macho* whatever side he's on. Why single out Allende?"

"Because his responsibility is greater than that of the others. In his more rational moments he knows it doesn't serve any purpose—indeed, it is dangerous. No conscientious leader is going to encourage the masses to believe that they can resist a modern army solely by virtue of their greater bravery, the righteousness of their cause, their solidarity. Yet sometimes he appears to. We will see the results: thousands of his followers will be mown down today, and the rest will be helpless against the severe repression which is coming."

"Well, to the extent that Allende has done it, I think he has tried to appease that part of the UP coalition that wants him to stand up to the reactionaries."

"It wasn't just that. I think he allowed himself to be swayed by the rhetoric of the romantic left, and they were an unreliable bunch, that fact has to be faced. It irks me to think that the wildest of them are probably already safely refuged in foreign embassies while the poor fellows who believed in them are being marched off to prison camps."

Jaime removed his glasses and rubbed the lenses with his handkerchief. "Allende was trying to straddle a fence: on the one side, he had to be tough enough for the members of his own party; on the other, he had to work out a compromise with the Christian Democrats—unless, of course, he was to use force to keep himself in power."

"Which was unrealistic. Had he attempted a coup, he would have lost. I think that in the privacy of his heart he knew that."

"That's an issue that's going to be debated till the end of time, Willing. I've always maintained your argument, but I've never won over anybody committed to the other view. I remember just a few months ago talking with a fairly highly placed socialist. I said, 'OK, so the working classes of some urban areas are organized to defend themselves. How are they going to do it? How will they stand up to a well-equipped army when the contest comes?' He replied, 'The soldiers will go along with us.' I replied, 'Come on! If the twentieth century teaches us anything, it's that soldiers obey their superior officers (most of whom, in the case of Chile, have been trained in the United States).' You know what he said? 'A soldier is nothing but a proletarian in uniform!' He seemed to think his nicely turned phrase was a mortal blow to all of us skeptics. He kept repeating it, 'A soldier is nothing but a proletarian in uniform.' "

"That's typical of what I've observed. Too much sloganeering, too much nose thumbing in place of sober thinking. And although Allende engaged in it, he more than the others was a victim of it, since he had to govern."

"Listen, Willing, I'm going to share a confidence with you. In my capacity as priest I have had occasion to talk with some of the junior officers of the Navy who are on trial for planning a leftist coup to save the UP government. That was back in June and July. One of them told me that he was motivated by his knowledge of the seditious plotting among his superior officers. He wanted an official OK to head them off; he actually talked to Allende and to some of the left-socialist leaders including Montero and Montt. Allende said that, although he appreciated the danger his government was in, he couldn't approve a coup. 'It would be political suicide,' he said. As to Montero and Montt, they couldn't quite bring themselves to sponsor it, or at least before they pronounced on it, the younger officers' plot had been discovered. You know the rest. I think all this shows something about Allende's character; he had a sense of what was feasible and what wasn't, and in spite of provocation from both right and left, he couldn't be moved to challenge the bourgeois system which he had agreed to respect and which in some ways he admired."

"He backed himself into a corner but refused to admit it," replied Ben. "He couldn't bring socialism about either by force or by compromise with the Christian Democrats. Now the left will have to pay for that. Compromise would have been the sensible solution, but after all the rough talk, he couldn't do it without appearing cowardly—the only sin that makes the superleftists tremble. And, of course, the rougher he talked the more unreasonable the Christian Democrats became; they loved to see him squirm."

Jaime was staring absently past Ben at a shelf of dictionaries. "We're already speaking of him in the past tense."

Ben paused. He felt uncomfortable. "You're right. This is like a postmortem."

"Well, I'm sorry it turned out as it did." Jaime sighed. "But I expect that Allende will be a better martyr than he was a president. Dying for your beliefs is easier than institutionalizing them, if you're a Chilean."

"I suppose we'll eventually be lighting candles to him; that's the way we humans are: we hound a man to death and then we canonize him."

"I'll light a candle, gladly. He gave his life, he deserves it. And now, Willing"—Jaime's eyes suddenly lit up—"I have an idea for a new piece: it will be entitled, 'Allende and Baptism by Fire and by Desire.' "

5

Eve's Memoirs September 20-30, 1973

For God's sake, let us sit upon the ground
And tell sad stories of the deaths of kings!
———SHAKESPEARE, *Richard II*

A revolution, more than any other enterprise,
has to be carried through to the end.
———LEON TROTSKY

Arrest

On September 11 there were radio announcements throughout the afternoon of people who should turn themselves in immediately to the police. The summons, theatrical in tone, seemed to punctuate with exclamation points the various names, always beginning with "Abarca" and "Arguedas" and proceeding in alphabetical order through a list of UP notables.

It wasn't until the following morning that I heard my own name called.

Monica and I were lingering over breakfast. "Eva Maria Soledad Thibault!" the euphonious radio voice intoned. We looked at each other and tried to control a nervous impulse to giggle, as if parties to a good joke.

"You see how preposterous it is, my being included among such dazzling VIPs," I said. "They've even got my *name* wrong. Can you imagine them confusing the maternal and paternal *apellidos* of anybody else on that list?"

"It's a good sign," Monica said, and she lit a cigarette. Since yesterday afternoon she had been smoking steadily although normally she didn't enjoy it. "I bet you'll be forgotten in the initial excitement of arresting an entire government. They probably added your name as an afterthought in order to make an impressive number."

At Monica's urging, I decided to follow up on Maria Inez' offer to bring influence to bear on my behalf. It was about 9 A.M. when I left the apartment. The streets were very crowded, for the curfew had been lifted only for the morning hours, and housewives were eager to do the day's shopping and gossip with their neighbors about the new order of things. I walked quickly and climbed the stairs of the office building and let myself into Felipe's office with Monica's key. In the close and dusty quarters, the telephone seemed friendly and reassuring.

Maria Inez had always felt motherly towards me, and today she sounded even warmer and more solicitous than usual. It cost me an effort not to cry. "I thought about you all day yesterday, darling," she began. "Tell me about it. How did you get along? What did you do?"

"Well, we drank a lot of brandy, Monica and I."

"Did it help?"

"No, not in the least."

"What else?"

"I went through my papers. I tried to destroy anything that might get me into trouble."

"Good, that's very good. That's what I was about to suggest."

"Then I baked some bread."

"You're kidding me."

"Not at all. I baked a ton of it, a week's supply at least. Monica had been hoarding oil and flour, you know. There was no longer any reason to save it. Haven't you ever kneaded dough to take out your frustrations? It's great therapy. You pound it as hard as you can, you strangle it, you pinch it, you can throw it against the wall if you want to—"

"OK, OK, what else?"

"What do you expect, Maria Inez? We listened to the radio; we cried."

I felt myself choking up again. There was a pause.

"I'm sorry, so very sorry," Maria Inez finally said. "After I talked to Monica on the phone yesterday, I started to pull strings for you, Eva, but I didn't have much luck. I called a certain general's wife, an old school friend. At first she thought there would be a chance for you. I also asked about Ximena and Marisol. Later, however, when she called back, I discovered that even she couldn't do anything. Ximena and Marisol had already taken refuge in the Mexican Embassy; that made a difference." Her voice trailed off.

I swallowed hard. "What do you mean?"

"Well, there's just no way that all of Señora Allende's staff can escape questioning. I'm excused; Ximena and Marisol are gone; Viviana will probably get into the Swedish Embassy; that leaves you."

I found it hard to realize that I was truly in danger. My sense of unworthiness for the role I had been summoned to perform made it difficult for me to take my situation seriously.

"Maria Inez, I have spent most of the last three years writing bread-and-butter letters for doña Tencha; why would the Armed Forces bother themselves about me?"

"Eva," she replied almost reproachfully, "you forget that whatever your duties were, you enjoyed the personal confidence of President Allende. We all did. There aren't a great number who can say the same, and many of those have sought refuge in the foreign embassies. Soon they'll be safely out of the country. If you ask my advice, that's what you'll do too, before

you're arrested; but I warn you, it's difficult to get in now.
You'll have to start working on it right away."

After I hurried back to Monica's apartment, I busied myself
with a final survey of our books and records and correspondence,
hiding and burning whatever might implicate us. We had begun the day before, when the radio had revealed that police
were raiding bookstores and libraries and private homes, "cleaning up the Marxist filth," as they put it. At first the necessity
of parting with my beloved possessions—my life—was agonizing. Each memento reminded me of something in my past that
I held dear. I had grown up in a happy time—an exciting time.
"Thank you, Lord, for making a world that is full of surprises,"
I had said on my twenty-third birthday, in 1971, when I was
about to blow out the candles on my cake. My mother had been
amused. "That is the sort of prayer one expects from the
young," she said.

But by Tuesday morning I had grown accustomed to a
regal destruction of prized objects. Every piece of paper I
burned was a step towards freedom. I was just giving my
room a final straightening up when I heard the pounding on
the front door. I knew who it was; and, perversely, I felt,
mingled with my fear, a relief that I wouldn't have to make
a decision about seeking foreign asylum.

Nine men from army intelligence rapidly filled the living
room. (Later the same number would appear from first the
Navy and then from the Police, each time to turn the apartment upside down with their searching. During the first
weeks after the coup, the branches of the Armed Forces
hadn't learned to coordinate their activities.) How incongru-
ous it seemed, such a large number of helmeted men carrying
machine guns, searching a tiny apartment occupied by three
females!

Perhaps it was my unmitigated sadness that made me
master over my emotions; my imagination was rendered
poverty-stricken so that I couldn't think beyond the reality
of that moment. Only once did I start to crack. Monica, Maria
Paz, and I were forced to stand against a wall as we were

searched. I was anxious for the child when I saw her ashen face, her somber eyes; and when, after running his hands over her body, the officer pushed his fingers between her legs, I wanted to scream. But it was over in a few seconds.

I was told to accompany a corporal into the room I shared with Maria Paz. There he searched quite casually but chanced upon a photo I had overlooked because it was in such an obvious place, wedged into a corner of a large, framed picture of "The Old Lady who Lived in a Shoe," which hung above Maria Paz' bed. He looked at it with interest, and I tensed: it showed Allende in the middle, an arm around doña Tencha to his left, and me to his right. It had been taken at the house on Tomas Moro in September of 1971, the day that the English novelist Graham Greene had been the guest of honor at dinner.

The colonel's mouth curled up to one side, and he looked at me indirectly out of the corner of his eyes. "You'd better do something with this," he hissed; then he quickly inserted it between the pages of one of Maria Paz' books. It wasn't the last time I was to meet with unexpected kindness from a military man.

When the officer in charge said that I was to come away with him, Monica fussed over me, dressing me in sweaters and stuffing my pockets with chocolate bars and bread. As an afterthought, she added the package of American cigarettes which she had picked up in Felipe's office the day before.

I have always found it difficult to express emotion in the presence of strangers. Monica kissed me on each cheek and embraced me. "I hate to leave you with such a mess to clean up," I said weakly. I glanced at the books which had been thrown to the floor, the drawers empty of contents, gaping from chests, and the clothes and linen lying everywhere. Monica rolled her eyes in mock disbelief at my simplicity and swatted my behind as I turned to leave.

Maria Paz looked as if she might bleat like a lost sheep. I touched her face lightly and suddenly remembered the set of magic tricks I had bought for her birthday next month and stored away. "Lovely one," I whispered, "there is a surprise for you on the highest shelf of the kitchen cupboard. When I come home, I'll want to see what you can do with it." She didn't smile; on the contrary, she closed her eyes and began to moan in the heartbreaking monotone I had heard from her the day before. Monica gently pulled her away from me, and the soldiers escorted me out of the apartment, slamming the door fast.

It was a chilly day with a partly overcast sky, but to the south one could see the snowcapped *cordillera*. As I waited to climb into the van, I noted almost with surprise the cherry trees in bloom, the smell of wet grass and burnt refuse, the shoppers who looked curiously at the group of soldiers taking a prisoner. With the intense self-centeredness of the novice in disaster, I had forgotten how well the world could get along without me. On other occasions I might well have been one of the indifferent crowd untouched by the calamity befalling a passerby on the street.

Once in the van, I struggled with the reality of the other victims who were to be detained with me. We were perhaps twenty—men and women of various ages, all apparently middle class. We greeted one another with our eyes, silently, communing with our fears. I was fairly certain that none of the others had been summoned on the radio; some of them, in fact—like the woman with groceries—looked as if they had been picked up by chance. There was a current of anxiety in the close air, and the smell of cold metal. It struck me suddenly that probably all of these people considered themselves victims of a monstrous mistake; they hoped to awaken from this bad dream, a cruel burden on lives already heavy laden, and laugh at their night fears. I had read about such situations, but although I tried to recall what I had learned from Dostoevsky, say, or Anne Frank or Solzhenitsyn, I was left with only a vague impression of whining sirens and sinister, thick-walled buildings. I had not read, I realized ruefully, as if these authors were writing for me.

Somehow expecting to be taken to a police station or to

Investigaciónes, I was puzzled by the length of our ride, and the direction. Someone finally whispered "Chile Stadium." I remembered the playing court where I had occasionally gone with my father and Sergio, who shared a fondness for basketball.

The van stopped and we were led to the front entrance of the stadium. There, for the first time, I faced the seriousness of my situation. Lines of army and police buses were unloading prisoners who stood gaping at the reception which awaited them: inside the fence, in front of the building, hundreds of soldiers and policemen, all heavily armed and helmeted, herded people into two groups. The group to the left was forced to carry on gymnastic exercises, and some individuals appeared ready to collapse. Various people were doing sit-ups and push-ups, but the majority were running in place. As I entered the gate, I heard one fellow, a red-faced man of middle age, say to a soldier, "I have a heart condition; if I don't stop now, I'll have an attack and die." "Well, die!" shouted the soldier, and when the man, despairing, ceased moving, the soldier knocked him unconscious with a blow on the head.

Some of the people I came with were sent to the "gymnastics group," but I was sent to the other one, which was to the right of the entrance. We were apparently waiting to get in, but, as if to break our resistance even before our internment, the soldiers kicked and beat us while we stood in single file. I was terrified and, in an effort to pass by unnoticed, looked only at the ground; everyone seemed to be screaming or moaning; and in the din I was uncertain whether I too was crying out. Suddenly, from behind, I felt a heavy blow at my kidneys, which made me double over, then a crack on the back of my head by a gun butt. After an enormous crescendo of pain, I experienced a diminishing of anxiety. How limited, I discovered, is our capacity for sensation; how monotonous is physical suffering. The ache seemed to spread over my body like a ripple from a pebble cast into a pond: soon it could not be localized.

I could no longer see clearly. I was pushed along through

the arcade of blows and kicks, which the soldiers had formed, into the stadium. There, to an obbligato of machine-gun fire, apparently from the principal playing court, the people in my group were directed towards dressing rooms, offices, and store-rooms, which were now used for interrogation and torture, or to the basement, where many met their death, or—in the case of the vast majority—they were taken to the galleries and sports center, where hundreds were massed together. Compared to them, my internment was to be cheerful and cozy: most of them, having been arrested at work or in their homes without receiving permission to clothe themselves warmly, suffered intensely from the cold, since they were obliged to sit and lie on bare cement; it was almost impossible to sleep in such crowded conditions, even for those few who weren't in constant pain from beatings. During the five days that most were there, they were given no food except small cups of coffee. Unaccountably, the percussion of gunfire and the interminable moaning and chattering of teeth, which I fancied I could hear even from the entryway to the playing court, reminded me of a poem of Lorca's: "The city, free of fear, was multiplying its doors." Here was the inverse, a city of death, where the doors swung shut.

But for some reason I was directed not into the court but into a large hall, apparently used for exercise and rubdowns, where conditions were somewhat different. There the din of groans and cries from the rest of the stadium was diffused like ink in water. From the prisoners confined within, the sounds were subdued, rather like the mumble of prayers or the supplicating monotones of plainchant. Indeed, with its elevated ceiling and numerous circular windows placed high in the walls, the hall had a churchlike quality. Even the greenish light which fell in uncertain bars across the huge white walls seemed unearthly, like the backgrounds in El Greco's paintings.

A man in uniform directed me to a wall where I was to assume the posture of the other prisoners, knees on the floor, back straight and hands on the wall. We were not to look to either side, but with such a crowd of prisoners, many of them coming and going, the rule was hard to enforce. In an hour's time I had come to know Akiko Hombo, a Brazilian refugee, to my left, and to my right N., a Communist senator whom I had met once or twice. He was the only prisoner whose arms were at his sides, and he leaned back on his heels. He seemed deep in reverie, like an Oriental monk, and once he surprised me by whispering to me, "Peace, patience, hope." I realized then that I had been crying, and I was touched by his effort to comfort me. Later I learned that his shoulders had been pulled out of their sockets when the *milicos* had hanged him by his hands, which had been joined behind him. "I am not alone," he said to me. "Do you see that priest on the chair behind me? Look at his feet, they are like cantaloupes; he was hung by them for a long time while all his blood ran to his head."

On the next day, when I shared the food in my pockets with my new friends but declined to take some myself (when I am very tense I can't swallow), he gently reprimanded me. "You must make up your mind: do you want to live? Do you want to survive this? Then you must force yourself to continue the life-giving activities—eating, defecating, sleeping. Think: with every mouthful of food, you are defying your oppressors."

By the end of my first day there I felt linked by indissoluble ties with all the others in the room. As we whispered encouragement to one another, as we shared stories, it occurred to me that the *milicos* had made an error with their mass arrests: in solitary confinement a person would rapidly lose his sense of identity and his confidence in his ideals. But thousands of political prisoners confined together experience to the highest degree the sense of solidarity which formerly was more of a longing for them than a reality. Those of us who were tortured were initiated by trial into an exclusive society whose mark we shall bear until our dying days. (That is why the Fascists must continue frantically to arrest and kill, torture and kill: it is as if they realize that the "Marxist cancer," of which they speak so contemptuously and fearfully, can never be "extirpated" now that the blood of so many has been shed in its name; they rain down death, and we thrive on it, a cycle as unfailing and relentless as the turning of the planets.)

By the end of Wednesday afternoon I had almost lost track of time and no longer fretted about what would happen next. In an effort to avoid dwelling on the weight of my own arms and the throbbing pain in my back, I attempted to think about Helmut. I had memorized bits and snatches of his letters from having read them so often; they were running through my mind like an old refrain. But I was worried about Mother and Monica and Maria Paz, who were surely beside themselves about my situation. If ever Monica had been about to crack, it would have been then, when my life and perhaps Carlos' too were in jeopardy. I had tried to probe her feelings the day before about Carlos, but she had resisted: "He is my husband only in name," she had replied dryly. "He chose his way like someone infatuated with death." I was certain she still loved him, would always love him, even though she depended on Felipe, who was so much better for her. That is a fact which Felipe accepts without comment or complaint: he must share Monica's heart with the *Mirista* husband of her youth, the guerrilla *comandante* who has become almost legendary among the Indians and peasants of the South. Where was Carlos, I wondered? Would I ever see him again, my enigmatic brother-in-law whom I had come to understand so slowly?

Occasionally, when my reveries were beginning to turn to dreams and sleep, a *milico* on patrol would pass by and strike at my kidneys with a bag of sand. "Up straight!" he would bark, and pass on to torment others. Finally, when I thought I would prefer risking death to maintaining the same posture any longer, I was called for questioning. Walking through the halls, I could see clearly the principle of inertia at work in all the "quiet" torments: some prisoners were forced to squat for hours, others to lie on their stomachs, heads down; and still others sat blindfolded for hours or days.

During my first interrogation I sat on a straight chair under blinding lights. (The next time I would be hooded.) I could sense the dimensions of the small, high-ceilinged room, and from the damp, rank odor, I surmised that it was near a lavatory. Three or four men were on the other side of a table. Before I was addressed by the interlocutor, I attempted to calm myself, for the trauma of the day's experiences seemed to have left me lightheaded and hysterical. I had to control an urge to chatter endlessly, as people do when they are high on pills. When I was finally obliged to speak, however, I felt tense and wary, like a sea urchin extending its spines.

POLICE: Your name.

EVA: Eva Maria Soledad Araya y Thibault.

POLICE: It says here that your paternal *apellido* is Thibault.

EVA: That is a mistake. My name is right on my identity card.

POLICE: Whom should we notify in case of your sudden death?

EVA: My mother, Señora Maria Teresa Thibault y Beaufort.

POLICE: Your age and address.

EVA: I am twenty-five. I live with my sister, Señora Monica Araya, at Miguel Claro 67.

POLICE: Marital status.

EVA: I am separated from my husband.

POLICE: His name.

(I had already resolved to tell the truth insofar as it was possible and to avoid involving family and loved ones. How hard it all was!)

EVA: Señor Sergio Sotomayor; his address is Avenida Apoquindo 3781.

POLICE: You mean the Marxist composer?

(I was surprised. Nothing about the interlocutor's voice—he spoke like a *nortino*—suggested an interest in serious music.)

EVA: He is a composer and conductor, but I doubt that he is a Marxist. He isn't interested in politics; he's never read any of the Marxist classics.

POLICE: What difference does that make? Most Christians haven't read the Bible either. I've heard some of your husband's music. It's nothing but filth.

(He paused as if waiting for a response. I said nothing.)

POLICE: Your political affiliation.

EVA: I have never been a member of a political party.

There was a contemptuous snort from one of the men. Under the hot lights, sweating profusely, I felt grimy and ugly. Suddenly an intense pain shot through my left hand; someone was burning me with a cigarette. I wailed. The voice continued as before.

POLICE: No lies. You cannot expect us to believe you got your job without being a Marxist.

EVA: That's another question. I'm not a party member, but maybe I'm a Marxist. I really don't know. I've never read much Marxist literature. I just have my convictions about what's just and unjust.

POLICE: We're not interested in your opinions. Tell us how you got your job.

EVA: I was hired because I know four languages, and I'm a good photographer.

POLICE: How can you account for so many skills at your age? (He sounded suspicious, as if my education were part of "the International Communist conspiracy.")

EVA: My grandmother, who was French, lived with us until she died when I was twelve; she spoke only French to us. I learned English at the Harriet Beecher Stowe School; as for the German, I'm not very fluent; I studied nights for several years at the Goethe Institute. You probably want to know how Mrs. Allende learned of me. It's very simple although long to explain. I took my degree in filmmaking at the University of Chile in 1969. There were no jobs in my field, so I settled for a secretarial position at *Camelia* magazine. *Camelia* is part of the Randolph family empire which, while partially dismantled under Allende, will no doubt resurface and. . . .

POLICE: Enough of your insolence. Just answer the questions. (Someone slapped me hard on the mouth; I could taste blood on my tongue. I chided myself for senselessly bringing pain upon myself with my sarcasm.)

EVA: I did not like my job. I didn't like translating articles on fashions and beauty from foreign magazines. In September of 1973 I announced my resignation to my boss, and the word spread around the office. One of the writers who came in from time to time was Catalina Allende.

POLICE: You mean Allende's niece?

EVA: I believe she is a cousin. One day during my last week at *Camelia* she invited me to lunch. I was surprised since I didn't know her well. It was at the Cafe Paris that she asked me if I would be interested in working for Señora Allende.

POLICE: You mean to say you were to be selected over active leftists who were clamouring for jobs?

EVA: That's more or less what I asked her, but Catalina explained, "What my aunt needs is somebody who can handle correspondence in English, French, and German." I remember replying, "But there must be many UP party members with language skills. Why me?" And she replied, "Not so many as you might think. It's the exclusive private schools that turn out linguists, and they are almost always *momios.*"

POLICE: Whom did you vote for in 1970?

EVA: Allende.

POLICE: Was that common knowledge around the *Camelia* office?

EVA: Yes.

(Indeed, it had been the source of much amusement until the day after the election.)

Suddenly the line of questioning abruptly changed.

POLICE: Explain your acquaintance with the former naval attaché to President Allende, Captain Miguel Montero, who was assassinated in July.

(I was amazed. As I paused to collect my thoughts, someone thrust into my hand a photo of Miguel which was inscribed "For my lovely *lolitas*, Monica and Eva." It had evidently been uncovered in the search of our apartment. I was preoccupied by the implications of the question, yet I drew courage from Miguel's image, the warmth of his eyes and the bony plates of his face, like those in a Cubist painting.)

EVA: My sister Monica met him years ago, about 1964, when she was a student at the University of Maryland for a year after her graduation from high school. Captain Montero was in Baltimore for some sort of joint American-Chilean naval program. When she read his name in the newspapers, she called him, and they became friends.

POLICE: Did Montero ever discuss with you some plans in the Armed Forces for a leftist coup to support the Government?

EVA: Never.

POLICE: Did Montero ever discuss the illegal stockpiling of arms by leftist groups?

EVA: Never.

POLICE: When did you two become lovers?

(I was dumbfounded and afraid of the consequences of denying the interogator's assertion. Suddenly I felt cigarettes burning into my flesh on both arms. I screamed and pushed myself to the abyss of consciousness, longing for release from pain. It must have been a few seconds, yet a vast procession of images crossed my mind, repetitious, like the gongs of a bell. There was my father's face, almost palpable in its vividness, and a number of figures like the Incan gods I had seen in the great codexes in Lima. When finally I was left in peace, I remember repeating earnestly to myself, as if afraid of forgetting, "I must review the reasons for staying alive.")

The line of questioning again changed. "Did you have access to Mrs. Allende's accounts?"

EVA: No.

The interlocutor continued as if I had given an affirmative response. "How much would you say she spent in a month?"

EVA: I really have no idea. You could find out easily enough, I imagine, by going through her files in the Moneda.

POLICE: Where have you been? Don't you know the Air Force bombed the Moneda? All of her papers were destroyed. I suppose you know she has been offered refuge in Mexico? That's how cowardly the UP gangsters really were. Allende did himself in rather than face the judgment of the people. He shot himself with a submachine gun which had been given to him by Fidel Castro.

(The speaker seemed to warm to his topic; as he added details he grew ever more excited.)

His face was a mess; he had propped the barrel of the gun under his chin and then fired. His body was carried out of the Moneda wrapped in a poncho. Today he was buried in Viña del Mar.

As he revealed this news, I had the curious sensation of no longer being present in the room. More precisely, it seemed as if the real "I" was perched above the door, perhaps, or even above the building, watching with only lukewarm interest the shell of a woman mistakenly regarded as a whole human being. The real "I" made note of the unceasing pain in the unfortunate woman's burned arms, and in her back. At the same time she could imagine the Allende's family tomb in Viña, where some miserable women, clad in black, surrounded by *milicos*, buried their lifetime companion without flowers or hymns. Then "I" thought, "How fortunate, those who live and die obscurely, eased into the world and then out of it with tender hands and holy water!" But "I" shed no tears, instead recalling for some reason the celebration of Allende's first three years in office, on September 4, less than two weeks ago, when workers in hard hats, peasants on tractors, and many others—at least 400,000 of them—converged on the Moneda, streaming past the President for six hours. He had waved at them, but he didn't speak. He looked old and sick. In retrospect he seemed almost like an old chieftain who, seeing his end approaching, called on his fighting companions to file by for a final salute.

From this point on my interrogation had a dreamlike quality. Sometimes I reminded myself to speak carefully, to avoid foolish mistakes, but I couldn't arouse myself from the lethargy into which I had fallen. I denied that Mrs. Allende had taken lovers, that she had been paid in dollars for her public appearances, that she loathed her husband. The questions somehow seemed laughable, hardly worth taking seriously; but just as I started to sink into total indifference, declining to frame answers, I would be struck again, or burned.

Finally the interlocutor started back at the beginning, repeating every question he had asked me. I was exhausted, and if offered a chance for a two-hour nap on a canvas cot, would have signed my confession; but I wasn't asked to. And finally the meaninglessness of my predicament became apparent: *I was an unimportant prisoner giving answers which the interrogators themselves were indifferent to.* That is why there would be no signed confession, just as there would be no formal charges against me. I and countless others were to be traumatized solely as a preliminary in the setting up of a reign of terror.

2

Later, when I was again with the other prisoners, a young man stationed next to me began to speak confidentially when the guards weren't looking. With his thick glasses, which greatly magnified his hazel eyes, and his pointed nose, he gave a bookish appearance. When he spoke, his jaw seemed to move in an exaggerated way which made me think of snapdragons. Yet he had a pleasant appearance; it was as though his physical characteristics, unattractive when taken one by one, were subtly transformed in the special setting which his facial movement provided.

"All day I have had a peculiar sensation," he said, "as if I weren't really here, as if I were at home hallucinating. No, that's not quite right. It's as if the 'me' who used to be known as 'Raul' is no more than a bar of wax, a template on which other people imprint their nightmares. You look amazed; I don't blame you. It must be an advanced form of madness, thinking one exists only in other people's consciousness."

"Perhaps it is. I'm not amazed at your conception, but at

how it resembles my own. In my self-centeredness I had guessed my experience was unique."

"Do you know," he continued after a pause, "for years I studied at the University of Concepción. I could explain all of Chilean history in terms of Marxist dialectic; I interpreted everyone's behavior in terms of the economic and social forces which govern our class structure. Now my whole perception has changed. I don't mean that I was wrong before; it's rather that the sweep of human history is of less moment to me now than the smell of charred flesh here in this room, right now. And the human dynamics at work seem, surprisingly, to swirl around a moral fact: some people are ethically on a higher level than others."

"Yes."

"I wouldn't attempt the hopeless task of convincing someone who isn't a *compañero*, but I'll admit it to you: I think the left is motivated by the highest moral incentives the world has yet known."

"Yes."

"Do you think that the left could ever sink to the level of bestiality the Fascists have displayed in the last forty-eight hours? No, you don't. Because we've both seen how the common loyalty and striving together against impossible odds elevated the poor and the working class in this country. I'm not referring to the last three years only, but to the whole history of class struggle. In fact, in some respects the UP period is a disappointment: the Government, in spite of its rhetoric, didn't stand by the people. There will be a lot of tears about Allende's death and the imprisonment of his cabinet, but in truth they are the ones that let the house come crashing down on us: they are responsible for the torture and killing the rest of us have to endure now. If you know someone's out to get you, you don't just stand by passively waiting: you prepare your defenses. Yet Allende wouldn't budge. His martyrdom can't make up for his refusal to arm the workers against the Fascists."

It was a variation on an argument I had heard countless

times, and I was too sad to take it up. Instead, we both listened for a while to the staccato of machine-gun fire from the patio and basement and to the quiver of window glass above us which inevitably followed. Next to us was a woman breathing noisily and with great difficulty, a horrible sound.

"The problem with the Fascists," the student finally said, "is that inhumanity is built into their world view as solidarity is into ours. And not just the Fascists: the traditional Chilean system recognizes degrees of worth in people of different social classes. Those at the top assume that the stunted, apathetic beings who do hard physical work are creatures of blunted feelings; they must be, or they wouldn't live as they do. Death at a premature age is such a commonplace that it is supposed hardly to matter to them, any more than it matters to cattle."

He paused. "The sad thing is that these ideas have governed us for so long that even the victims can't help absorbing them."

"How true. I have a sister who is blond and fair. Children in the street reach out to touch this apparition whom they're prepared to worship."

"The left had hardly begun to cure this national sickness. And now it will be as rampant and as deadly as ever."

"Not quite. I agree with what you said before; the people will never forget what they achieved at such cost to themselves. That's part of their identity now—no one can take it from them."

There were a number of such conversations during the night hours. At first the guards tried to break them up, but as the hours passed, they seemed to become bored with the effort. With their aches and worries, people couldn't sleep, and they turned eagerly to one another for courage and comfort. Sometimes I thought we all sounded hysterical with our high-strung opinings, our sudden swings from despair to the exaltations that martyrs must feel, and then back again; but now I marvel at our endless talk during those days, its poetry and its hardness.

A few hours before dawn there was a great deal of movement among the prisoners. The hall I was in became increasingly crowded, and finally a large number of us were informed that we would be transferred to a gallery on the other side of the playing court. I was at the end of the file of prisoners, and as I moved towards the door, I heard a voice counting, "fifty-seven, fifty-eight, fifty-nine, sixty." Then he stopped: "No more than sixty." An officer indicated that five of us were to wait. Finally he said, "You go to the basement instead."

Since it was common knowledge that executions had taken place in the basement, I was terrified. I remember nothing about the long walk down the stairs except the rapid beating of my heart. Yet my fears were unfounded: my transfer turned out to be a piece of good luck.

I was stationed in a small dressing room adjacent to a large hall. There were lockers along three walls, and near them several benches. Although I was instructed to kneel, the only guard on duty had to make a long walk from my little room to the other end of the hall and back again. When he left me alone (there were no prisoners with me), I allowed myself to relax, sitting on a bench. Perhaps I dropped off to sleep, for I suddenly started, aware that he was standing over me. But as I hastened to move, he waved in a negative gesture. "Never mind," he said. "Take a rest."

I put my hands in my pockets as I attempted to interpret this new state of affairs. There I discovered the American cigarettes Monica had given me. "Would you like a cigarette?" I asked the soldier. "They were good American cigarettes once, but now I fear they are old and dry."

He hesitated for a minute, then accepted. He lit one for me, too, which I took, although I rarely smoke and never on an empty stomach.

He was perhaps nineteen years old, of slight stature and extremely angular. His shoulder bones stood out from his back almost like wings. His prominent cheekbones, which narrowed his small, widely spaced eyes, protruded over the chasms to either side of his narrow mouth. He fell naturally into a relaxed position, his weight resting on his right hip. I felt wary of a certain strangeness about him, but at the same time I sensed that he wanted to be friendly.

"I'm grateful for a chance to rest," I said. "All that kneeling has been bad for my back."

"Your back is bad?" he asked. "Did you injure it?"

"I fell down the stairs of my high school when I was about fifteen. You know how highly polished the floors of schools are. All that wax makes walking a dangerous sport." I giggled nervously.

"Yes, that's the way nuns are, always waxing," he added irrelevantly, perhaps recalling his own school experience. "Have you ever thought of a masseur?"

"A masseur?"

"For your back, I mean."

"No, I've been to several doctors though. Once I was put in traction."

His eyes flashed. "That doesn't surprise me a bit. They are all the same, these M.D.s with their fancy titles; they always want to put people in traction."

"Oh, well, I guess it helps sometimes," I replied. I was having a hard time capturing the drift of the conversation.

"Listen, you ought to try a masseur," he said. "They can do wonders for you, fast and inexpensive, too. I know from experience. I have a sister who had four children in three years. One morning soon after the fourth had been born, she couldn't get out of bed. She could hardly move. So her husband arranged for her to go to the emergency ward of the Clinica San Carlos. The doctor there told her she would have to be in traction for two weeks."

"That must be hard for a mother of little children," I commented.

"It was impossible. She returned home and limped around. The doctor had given her some painkillers. A neighbor lady came in to help her. Her name was Carmen Gloria. One day she said to my sister, 'Perla, I have a cousin who is married to a masseur. I think you should see him. He knows all about bad backs.' And then she arranged a visit and went with Perla to the office."

"What do masseurs do? Rub the sore places?"

"Ha! That was nothing. When my sister walked into his office he just glanced at her and said, 'One of your legs is shorter than the other, that's your problem.' "

"You don't say. But was it true? Hadn't anyone ever noticed it before?"

"Yes, it was true, but you couldn't tell by looking. Her left leg is about an eighth of an inch short. The masseur gave her a little wedge to put in her shoe, and she hasn't had a twitch of pain since. She walked out of his office a new woman. No fooling."

After the young soldier had shared his confidence with me, I felt I should reciprocate. "Well, I think I'll take your advice, although my family will laugh at me. The only people we consult other than doctors are witches."

"Fortune-tellers?" He threw his head back and laughed. "Don't tell me. Which ones, the Gypsies in the park?"

"No, no, they'll just rob you if they get a chance. My sister and I rely on two witches with fixed studios, one lives in Vitacura and the other in La Reina. Maybe they are part Gypsy—I don't know. In any case they're fabulous."

"What sorts of things do they tell you?"

"Well, for instance, they advised each of us not to marry our husbands, but we insisted, much to our sorrow."

"I bet they told you that you would travel to foreign lands. That's what the Gypsies say to everyone."

"Well, yes, but in my case the witch was right." Then I laughed at myself. "And she told me I would meet a handsome foreigner, which I did."

He smiled, and we smoked in silence for a while. Then he put out his cigarette and resumed his patrol. I could hear the echo of his hard boots as he walked up and down. When he finally returned, he seemed to be preoccupied. "Your witch," he said, "did she ever foresee anything like this?" He gestured vaguely towards the walls and ceilings with his submachine gun. I knew what he meant.

"It's funny that you should ask. Just a while ago I was trying to recall what she said last March or April, some remarks about death. I later thought she must have been referring to my father; he had a stroke in early July. And then on July 31 an old friend of mine was killed. I don't know...."

"But you?" Stammering, he resorted to ambiguous gestures to complete his question.

I paused, trying to recollect that autumn afternoon when my witch had frightened me with her gloomy pronouncements. The sky had been a sickly white, like the whites of tired eyes, and in the crystal I had seen the same unhealthful color. Absently I had noted the witch's fine hands as she took mine; they were youthful, well-cared for, with fingers like tendrils. But her face was always old and cragged; she smelled of cloves and balsam and sweat.

"She always began by mouthing what sounded like nonsense syllables, and then she broke into a monotonous chanting rhythm sung on two or three notes. It's hard to explain. I think she said, 'When death stalks, you cannot go on with life as usual, you must tread carefully.' Whatever this puzzling remark meant, I didn't think she was predicting *my* death. I asked, 'Who...?' But she shook her head hard. 'I see children shouldering caskets.'"

We were both silent for a long time; then the soldier paced up and down the small room a few times. When he turned to me, he licked his dry lips.

"Look, I'd like to help you out a little, make you more comfortable; is there anything I can do?"

I wavered a moment, then smiled a little. "You know, I haven't been to the bathroom in over twenty-four hours. Nothing, not even a drink of water, would please me as much as going to the toilet."

"I'm so sorry," he said. "I've strict orders." He glanced around helplessly. Then his attention fixed on a mop propped in a corner of the room, where two lockers met. He looked at me. I grasped his meaning.

"It will do fine," I said. He brought me the mop and then chivalrously resumed his patrol.

3

About the remainder of my imprisonment my memories are vague and uncertain. Perhaps it's because, with the novelty of my situation wearing off, I became less observant. There was also a great deal of *ennui*; for every minute that I was interrogated or struck, I spent hours kneeling or lying on the floor. I tended to lose track of time, especially when I was alone in the basement.

Sometimes I thought I was going crazy. I couldn't figure out how I had got into that appalling situation or how I would get out of it. I began to lose confidence that I was a unique individual with an autonomous will. I seemed to be nothing but a string of synapses. I became indifferent towards my future and doubtful that there were people in the world who cared about me. Helmut: perhaps he had been a figment of my imagination. Father, Mother, Monica: I could no longer exert myself to find their reassuring presence in my heart.

I am fairly certain that it was on Friday, September 14—the third day of my internment—that I was interrogated for the second time.

I had dreaded another confrontation with the interrogators because my arms still smarted from the burns I had received the other time. I was trembling when I took my place and waited for the process to begin. If my stomach hadn't been empty, I would have vomited.

The questions were almost identical to the ones I'd answered before. I was accused of having access, as doña Tencha's assistant, to expensive luxuries (the American cigarettes in my pocket were cited as evidence!); I was quizzed about doña Tencha's reputed bank accounts in Europe; and my relationship with Miguel was dragged up again. After an hour or two I was allowed to rest while the interrogators drew up a report which was then read to me. It was not a confession, and I wasn't asked to sign it. Nor was it a set of formal charges, for (a fact I didn't know then) I was going to be released.

Afterwards I was led by an armed guard to a gallery on the main floor from which one could hear not shouts but howls. I was told to undress. Then I had to sit on a bench outside the door. There were many curses and shouts from within, and finally I was escorted inside. There I saw the table to which I was about to be tied, and the powerful lights above. The torturers put cables on my body, dampened my skin, and began to apply the current to my breasts and vagina. I have no idea how many times they did it, or how long each shower of current lasted, but each time I thought that I would die. In my agony I hardly heard the insults rained down on me, nor did I respond to any questions. I'm not sure any were asked. My biggest fear was that they would kill me by accident, that they would inadvertently apply more current than they meant to. Once I even whispered hoarsely, earnestly, "It doesn't take as much to kill a small person."

Eventually there was a break for a few minutes while the torturers consulted with someone who had entered the room. I remember thinking, "If I die, there will be no poems about me, no great novels or works of art." It seemed like an important consideration; I wanted desperately to decide if I was resigned to such ignominy and obscurity. There seemed no satisfactory way of approaching the question. Yet once the current was applied again, and I heard myself screaming, I was suddenly struck with the resemblance of my cries to those of other prisoners I had heard, both men and women, and to animals. At its extremest pitch, pain reduces us all to a wordless roar, like the voice of the sea. "I wouldn't want to be singled out," I thought. "I'd rather take my stand with the great, anonymous swell of those whose lives were tiny

affirmations and echoes, hardly audible and quickly forgotten."
There were ocean waves transforming themselves into strings
of hills, and back again. Sea gulls exploded like fireworks into
a rain of colors, which, striking the land, undulated into
flames shaped like women. These women sang melodies which
assumed square and elliptical shapes as they floated upwards,
ultimately converging in an enormous eye which, as it swam
towards infinity, shed colored tears on landscapes and on
seasons. I was transfixed by my extraordinary vision. When I
finally awoke from it, I was once again in the hall where I
had first been stationed, my clothes stacked at my side, some
other prisoners crying over me.

4

I believe it was on Saturday, my fourth day, that "gymnastics
classes" were initiated for the female prisoners. I was led,
along with perhaps twenty others, into a small basketball
court evidently used for practice. There an officer with a
whip, something like those that animal trainers use, told us
to undress. As we hastened to obey, he smirked at the four
or five *milicos* who were lounging about. The guards who had
accompanied us occasionally struck us to make us hurry.

I have sometimes wondered if the scene which followed
was an amateur orchestration of a military man's primitive
fantasies or a sophisticated psychological torment designed by
experts from the CIA. Perhaps that is a meaningless distinction. In any case, our ordeal was an exquisite exercise in
shame. Even as we disrobed, we sensed our own degradation:
our clothes, in which some had finally urinated and defecated,
reeked; so did our bodies, sticky with blood and sweat.

"Well now, you are all grown-up, married ladies," the
officer began. "I want you to have a little fun. You must be

pretty lonesome for your husbands by now, so I want you to pretend you're with them. That's right, get down on your knees, spread them out. Now: pretend you're humping away, let's hear you sigh. I want to hear you come—all of you."

None of the women moved. Some began to cry. "What's the matter with you?" the officer shouted. "Are you all frigid Marxist bitches? Start humping. I want to hear some terrific orgasms."

About this time some of the guards began to circulate among the women, threatening to strike them if they didn't obey. That many did is scarcely surprising or blameworthy, yet when I heard them I was smitten with the most profound despair I had felt since my captivity began. One guard was moving in my direction, and I shuddered.

"Come, you asshole!" he shouted at the girl next to me, who was perhaps twenty years old and pitifully thin.

"Come yourself!" she hissed at him, and as he struck her with the butt of his gun, I could hear the cracking of her bones.

About this time one of the other officers felt inspired to join in tormenting us. "I know what the problem is," he said. "Some of you haven't had a good shit in days, have you? Well, that's not right, I'm sad just thinking about it. Everybody says you Commie women are the best shitters in the world. You've missed it, huh? So spread your legs again, ladies, and this time don't come, just shit!"

Once again there was the heartbreaking sound of inconsolable sobbing. At first no one would obey. But as the guards circulated among the group, getting down on their hands and knees and showing the women how they were to grunt, there were those who obeyed. Many defecated in spite of themselves, and I wondered sadly what human beings really are, whose bodies blindly obey impulses at odds with the soul's deepest longings.

My turn wasn't long in coming. One of the soldiers shouted at me, "What's the matter, girlie? Think you're too good to shit?"

I wanted to insult him, spit at him, but my mouth worked soundlessly, like a deaf-mute's. For a few seconds I knew what it was to be literally a blathering idiot. I neither saw nor feared the blow that mercifully relieved me of consciousness.

In a more nearly perfect world such a dehumanizing experience would purge us, washing out our secret fears and envies and resentments. Perhaps it happens sometimes. More frequently, I think, it is the veneer of civilization, and good manners, that get rubbed away, leaving us with our primitive emotions exposed.

I remember that afterwards we women were sitting together in quiet torment. I was near the skinny woman who had defied the *milico*. Attempting to comfort her, I apparently uttered some sentiments which annoyed her, for she turned on me furiously. "Whore!" she hissed. "*Momia!* Don't call me *compañera!* You're not a *compañera* to me, with your elegant ways! I suppose you think you deserve some sort of decoration, now that you've been tortured. I'm going to tell you something. Torture isn't new to us; the police have tortured us always. I know about you, how you hobnobbed with Allende and his bourgeois pals at Tomas Moro. You thought you were all pure and holy, didn't you—mouthing revolutionary sentiments, stuffing yourselves with rich food and fine wine while the rest of us starved! You and your kind have had your fun, and now we're all paying for it. But next time it will be different: next time we'll have a *real* revolution!"

5

Early Sunday morning there was an announcement over the public address system of people who would be freed that day. I was one of them. In my amazement and relief I sensed what chicks must feel who have desperately chipped away at their shells in pathetic efforts to be delivered into the world. But I also felt demeaned, unwholesome: I realized that there was no release from my chamber of horrors; the evil I had known there would accompany me, spreading from my soul in concentric circles of fear and anxiety, contaminating the universe. I was even a little anxious about my reunion with Mother and Monica. They would be hurt if I failed to relate to them every unspeakable detail of my detention, mistakenly believing themselves eager to know what they could scarcely imagine.

Later we were informed that a Mass would be said during the morning, and those about to be released were urged to attend. Although I am not inclined towards religion, I have occasionally taken an interest in it. I am impressed at what a good priest can do with the Scriptures. On the rare occasions when I read the Bible, I am invariably struck with how odious God is, how quickly He is disposed to destroy His own creation just as children rub out their drawings; and how petty He is, too, with His ravings about His temple and His ceremonies, and people's diets. Yet a priest can sometimes make the most unlikely story live. I remember in particular a sermon on "The Cain in All of Us" which, in some inexplicable way, changed my perception of human nature.

There were thirty or forty of us gathered in the gallery where the Mass was said. The priest was a military chaplain dressed in his uniform. From the beginning, he made it clear that he was there to urge us to repent of "following after false gods"—the idols of Marxism and materialism. He read several pronouncements on the subject from papal encyclicals and then proceeded to show how it was God's will that the UP fail. After depicting some "Communist outrages" in great detail, he went on to the parable of the Prodigal Son, and to Mary Magdalene, to illustrate how God will forgive everyone, even leftists.

It was an unlikely sermon under the circumstances; many of the sinners addressed could barely stand. Yet everyone remained, perhaps out of an obscure sense of respect, which few of us completely outgrow, for priestly paraphernalia. More likely, we were intimidated by the guards who were stationed here and there.

I had begun to lose interest in the proceedings when the priest said, "We pause now for our private intentions." We bowed our heads for a few seconds, and he started to resume, when a voice from the back of the group surprised the silence. At first it was wavering and uncertain, but quickly it gained in force, as if fortified by our strained attention. I think that I correctly remember the words:

"Lord, even You, when You were utterly destroyed, cried out in despair, feeling yourself forsaken by our Father. Look with compassion on us who also feel forsaken in this calamity.

"Lord, help us to remember that we are but a mote in the sunbeam of history. May our descendants in some future hour find it possible to live fully and abundantly because we suffer and die now.

"O Lord, remember our fatherless children, our widows, our parents bereft in their old age.

"Lord, who promised that You would never test us beyond our endurance, brood over us in Your loving kindness."

And he concluded with some verses from the Psalms:

The days of man are like grass;
he blossoms as a flower in the fields
If a wind goes by, he is gone;
he never more will be known
in that place
But the love of God towards
those who fear him is for ever
and ever....

In my astonishment I had turned to peek surreptitiously at the speaker. He was the priest with the swollen legs whom I had seen on my first day of captivity. He still had to be supported when he stood.

A great tremor of excitement quickened the crowd while he spoke. I sensed, rather than saw, the guards glancing uncertainly towards one another and towards the priest at the altar whose face had flushed and darkened furiously. Yet, before he could resolve to stop the insolent speaker, the prayer was over; it's possible that the military chaplain felt inhibited about censoring a fellow servant of God. In any case, the prayer was concluded, and the Mass resumed. All of us who assisted there felt an odd sense of triumph and happiness, as if we had indeed been blessed in some mysterious way.

When we turned to leave, I heard someone whisper to the priest with the swollen legs, "That other, he is the puppet of the Junta; you are our priest."

6

We were released at 1:30 P.M. on Sunday, and I started to walk to my mother's house. Soon, however, one of the *milicos* I had seen at the stadium gave me a lift. As we drove towards Providencia, we said nothing, yet I felt our sentiments challenging each other like melody and countermelody. When we arrived, he braked abruptly and reached across me to open the car door. "Well, that's the way it is," he said. "You may as well get used to it." I muttered a thank you and slammed the door.

My family, including aunts and cousins, was gathered at Mother's for Sunday luncheon, as I knew they would be. I saw faces peering from the parlor window as I got out of the car, and then Maria Paz ran to open the gate. Of my progress into the house I have no recollection except for the sound of women's voices, like the whoopings of great birds, and doors swung wide, and arms outstretched.

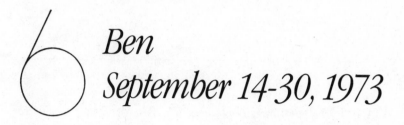

Ben
September 14-30, 1973

Pure, Chile, is your blue sky,
Pure breezes cross you too.
And your countryside, embroidered with flowers,
Is the happy copy of Eden.
Majestic is the white mountain
That the Lord gave you as bulwark,
And that long sea which bathes you
Promises you future splendor. . . .
> ——FROM THE CHILEAN NATIONAL ANTHEM

The physical information you have given us of a country [sic]
hitherto so shamefully unknown, has come exactly in time to
guide our understandings in the great political revolution now
bringing it into prominence on the stage of the world. The
issue of its struggles, as they respect Spain, is no longer
matter of doubt. As it respects their own liberty, peace and
happiness, we cannot be quite so certain. Whether the blinds of
bigotry, the shackles of the priesthood, and the fascinating
glare of rank and wealth, give fair play to the common sense of
the mass of their people, so far as to qualify them for
self-government, is what we do not know. Perhaps our wishes
may be stronger than our hopes. The first principle of
republicanism is, that the *lex majoris partis* is the fundamental
law of every society of individuals of equal rights; to consider
the will of the society enounced by the majority of a single
vote, as sacred as if unanimous, is the first of all lessons in
importance, yet the last which is thoroughly learnt. This law
once disregarded, no other remains but that of force, which
ends necessarily in military despotism.
> ——THOMAS JEFFERSON,
> LETTER TO BARON ALEXANDER VON HUMBOLDT
> MONTICELLO, JUNE 13, 1817

On Friday morning, September 14, Ben decided to walk to
the Mapocho Station in Santiago to find out when the trains
would run again. It was the first time he had been out since
the coup on Tuesday, and he enjoyed the smell of spring
grass and damp soil as he walked near the Mapocho River.
As he approached the railway station, he eyed the fruits and
vegetables for sale at the open stands, buying a kilo of Ecua-
dorian bananas, which were cheaper than Chilean fruit. As
usual, with almost a proprietary interest, he noted the prices
of produce from Villa Inez.

In the station Ben was amazed to learn that the trains
were running on regular schedule. Although he hadn't come
with his backpack, he had his briefcase, and he decided to
take the *expreso* which left in an hour. He assumed a place
in the line at the ticket window; as he waited, he read compulsively the large poster which confronted him: "In every
soldier there is a Chilean, and in every Chilean there is a
soldier." He had already seen the slogan several times that
morning. He wondered absently if the posters had been
printed before the coup.

"One way to Villa Inez de Suarez," he said when his turn
came.

The ticket vendor looked at him with fury, a deep shade
of red rapidly flushing over his face. Ben, astonished, expecting the man to shout at him, tugged nervously at his shirt
collar. But instead the man suddenly reached for a sign which
was propped against the counter where he was working and
banged it down so that Ben could see the words that had been
printed there in an enormous scrawl: "FIRST CLASS OR SECOND
CLASS?"

The people in line behind Ben began to titter. He felt
annoyed at the man's self-righteous display of temper. ("Give

a Chilean a place in a bureaucracy, and he will immediately set himself up as a petty tyrant," Anna had said.) And although he resisted such generalizations, it was hard to overlook the typical moroseness and stubborn humorlessness of clerks and public employees.

"Second class," he finally replied, embarrassed.

The vendor slammed a ticket down on the counter. As Ben reached for it, a tiny woman began to jab angrily at his back with her umbrella. "Why don't you stand up to him, *gringo?* Who does he think he is, Mr. High-and-Mighty...."

As Ben walked out of the station towards the coffee shop of the Tabor Hotel, he felt overwhelmed by the lack of tenderness in the world. Or maybe it wasn't the world; maybe it was Chile, as Anna claimed. Taking his usual seat at a table facing a window, he looked across the wide street at the ugly station, squat and gray, that lacked the comforts even of rest rooms and chairs. ("But my dear friend," Jaime had exclaimed, "how could we put chairs in a train station? People would come and sit on them!")

Ben paused to remove his poncho and jacket; the morning was growing warm. He always dressed in layers so that he could adjust to the rapid changes in temperature, and into his briefcase or suitcase went the suddenly superfluous cardigan or poncho or jacket, and sometimes the thermal underwear, too. Then he sat down again, attempting to compose himself, feeling his mind slide into a track of despondency. His life seemed dismal. The coffee shop, for instance: he had been there twice a week for a year or two, for there was no better place to await his train. Yet the broad-bottomed waitress, eyeing him as if she had never seen him before, would make him wait while she finished her picture story in *Movie Love.* Then she would approach to take his order, her calloused feet slapping against her slippers.

"We don't serve meals at this hour," she would begin. "It's between breakfast and lunch."

"A soft drink is all I want. Bring me a Fanta."

"Room temperature or cold?"

"Cold."

"We don't have cold soft drinks in the winter."

"It isn't winter, it's spring."

"We don't have them in the spring, either."

"Room temperature, then."

He would drink from the bottle, suspicious of the grimy-looking glass, and shoo the flies which collected on the sugar. Sometimes he would attempt to read the newspaper by the shy glances of light which found their way through the windows.

But this morning he had no paper to read, and in any case he had been saving something to think about since early that morning when Paul Pouillon, newspaper under his arm, had made a visit to Jaime's apartment.

"I wanted to catch you before you went out," he had begun. "Evelyn and I are going to the Embassy today. We probably won't see you for a week or ten days."

"How is Evelyn?" asked Jaime. "And how is the reporter? Is he still at your place?"

"Yes, Jacques is settling in. He and Evelyn are fine. In fact one of the reasons I'm here is to repeat something Jacques told me." He sat down and opened the newspaper, speaking as he searched through the pages. "Here it is." He folded the paper in quarters and handed it to Ben. "You can read there a statement by one of Allende's former ministers who spent the evening with the President the night of the tenth. He says Allende was writing a speech offering to call a plebiscite on his resignation. I'm sure it's true: Jacques was at a press conference given by Hortensia Allende at the Moneda the afternoon of the tenth; it was about her recent trip to Mexico. A Government press adviser there told Jacques and some other reporters that the following day Allende would make a nation-wide speech proposing a plebiscite on whether he should continue in office."

"Well, what do you think it means?" Ben asked. "Do you think the military forces would have canceled their plans if they'd known they might get rid of Allende legally?"

"Absolutely not. I think they'd been planning the coup for a long time and counted on getting total power. Allende's proposal would have been an embarrassment to them. In any case, they knew about it. They knew about everything."

The conversation had been cut short by Paul's haste. They had shaken hands, and then, as Paul had opened the door, he had suddenly turned back, saying: "Under its anemic, slippery appearance, this is a spooky country. It's enough to freak anybody out."

Ben, after walking over to the waitress and ordering another Fanta, stood at the windows for a few minutes. Somehow the morning's conversation with Jaime and Paul had changed his perception of Chile. There it was: the same slant of luminous sunlight on the iron girders of the station, the same scattering of taxis, the same peasants' carts laden with produce for the immense outdoor market nearby, the same kiosks, the same shoeshiners. Yet it had all subtly changed for him. He grasped what Anna meant when she talked about the false distinction between thoughts and events. "Thoughts *are* events," she was fond of repeating, "and a new thought can take its place in a person's life with the unforgettableness and irrevocability of a slap on the face or the birth of a child."

He supposed that he had been a dupe of his own dreams. Having decided to make his home in Chile, even proposing to change his citizenship, it had been important to justify his choice to himself. He had learned to look on the bright side of everything. The military, for instance: he would never have believed that the military would prefer a coup to a plebiscite in which people could depose of Allende legally if they wished. Perhaps he should have known: the congressional elections in March had been a kind of plebiscite, and when the right had failed to get the majority they needed, they had despaired of legality. "So," concluded Ben, "Chile turns out to be like the other Latin American countries: those with power respect the constitution and legal procedures only so long as their interests are served by them."

Suddenly he was reminded of a party he had attended shortly after Allende's election, before the popular choice had actually been ratified by the Congress, as Chilean law required. He and Anna had been in San Francisco, California, and some of the local Chilean residents had invited them to a celebration on September 18, Chile's national holiday. There had been an outdoor barbeque, an *asado*, as the Chileans called it. Towards midnight, after many of the guests had departed, about eight or ten people decided to make some predictions about the outcome of the recent elections. It was a tense period in Chile, with financial panic causing a spectacular plunge in bank deposits and a steep decline in the volume of trade. Many of the rich had left the country, and terrorist incidents, to provoke a coup, were increasing. Ben could no longer recall if General Schneider, Commander-in-Chief of the Army, had been assassinated before or after the night of the party.

He remembered the predictions clearly. A right-wing Christian Democratic professor of chemistry had begun, hoping that the Congress would have the courage to bypass Allende, who in any case had won with only 36 percent of the vote. "Congress should choose Alessandri instead," he had said. "He was the runner-up. Then Alessandri would resign immediately: he's already agreed to it. New elections would have to be called, and President Frei would run. He'd win of course." It was a clever stratagem; Chilean law provided that a president cannot succeed himself, so Frei had not been a candidate. But many took the view that, in a new contest between Frei and Allende, the Christian Democrat could not be beaten.

Around the circle they had gone. Most people, lazy and relaxed after a huge dinner, taking a sanguine view of events, refused to see anything worse than "certain economic difficulties" that the United States would make for the UP, causing Allende to lose the election of 1976. Anna had surprised everyone by comparing Allende to F.D.R.: "He will be too pragmatic; he will tinker with the UP program, taking first one line of advice and then another, the result being that the contradictory policies will cancel each other out. The bureaucracy will swell with boobs, the results will be indecisive, but like F.D.R., Allende will be well-loved, and the left will be in power for twenty years."

Ben had eagerly awaited Señor Pablo Urrutia's turn. Señor Urrutia, a senior official in the Randolph family empire, had flown immediately after the elections to Argentina, to Brazil, and to Washington. A handsome, athletic looking man, he had insinuated earlier on in the evening that he was on a mission of "international consequence." Indeed, he had quoted an Argentine banker who had advised him: "You Chilean businessmen must not sit idly by while the Marxists take over. You must talk to the Brazilians: they are experts on overthrowing a government; and you must cooperate with the Americans." Urrutia had implied that in Washington he had talked to the Secretary of State, but Ben suspected that he was exaggerating his own importance. When Urrutia's turn to speak had come, however, he had been cautious and impersonal. Yet, Ben reflected now, he had revealed a great deal.

"A government which, like the one that Dr. Allende proposes to head, is committed to profound structural changes," Señor Urrutia had begun, "must expect to be frustrated by opposition both internally and internationally." He had put his tapered fingertips together in an attitude of prayer. "While the United States will, of course, refrain from interfering in Chile's affairs, it is nevertheless undeniable that a revolutionary government is a credit risk: if for no other reason, international agencies will be obliged to refuse the government the aid it asks for."

He had raised his eyes to the ceiling, as if his text were stamped there. "Under those conditions the Popular Unity government, assuming it takes power, will have the following options: it might abandon its favorite reforms, slowing up the redistribution of income, so that the well-to-do retain their confidence. Or it might go ahead with reforms and face an extremely high level of unemployment. Or it might run down reserves and live off those parts of the country's accumulated capital which the government controls—while they last."

He had smiled broadly, as if delighted with his spectrum of choices. "There is one other option: increased inflation. That is what the UP will opt for; they will print tons of paper money, and in a year or two inflation will be so bad that Chile will have lost any semblance of monetary stability. Under such conditions the military will not have to ask for power: the middle class, never very enthusiastic about the Popular Unity's efforts to ally them with the working class, will beg their commander-in-chief to intervene to put an end to economic and social chaos."

Wrapped in his memories, Ben at first did not hear the waitress, who repeated, "Hey, you, aren't you taking the 10:15 *expreso?* You'd better hustle." He turned to her, amazed at her sudden recognition of his identity. He thanked her briefly and left the shop. Clutching his briefcase, he broke into a run as he stepped into the wide street. He knew that when he ran, he cut a ridiculous figure; and here in Chile, where he towered above the populace like a whitened minaret, he got even more laughs than he did in the States. He didn't mind; it was a way of providing people with a bit of diversion at no cost to himself. But when he approached the station doors, the soldiers on guard eyed him suspiciously. After frisking him and searching his briefcase, they allowed him to enter the building where without further problems he boarded the train.

2
_____

Ben had dozed off, but even with his eyes closed he knew that the train had reached Llay-Llay. In a few seconds he would see a windmill slowly turning, "Made in Chicago" clearly visible on one of its blades. He liked to see it; he regarded it as a genial reproof for his incorrigible tendency to romanticize the Chilean countryside, speaking of it as a refuge at the world's end where the modern alienation between man and his environment had not yet reached notable proportions. He knew better, of course, but he allowed himself, on his off hours, to take pleasure from his rural fantasies.

It seemed as if he had always known he would find his home here in the Aconcagua Valley, yet in truth, when Anna had first come into a small inheritance, they had pondered a long time before making up their minds where to settle. The southern tip of Chile, of course, was out: quite apart from the geographical isolation of the place was its physical and cultural desolation, the freezing winds which left people witless, except for those grim settlers, mostly Yugoslavs, who had grown rich with their herds of sheep. Indeed, although he and Anna had been charmed by other less remote southern areas— Chiloé, like a barren and rocky Greek island, but sunless; the city of Valdivia, built on rivers and canals, with boats for public transportation; and above all the magnificent lake country where, in water as limpid as sheets of glass, one could see reflections of snowcapped volcanoes, some of them still active —they had never for a minute considered establishing themselves there. It was lovely in summer, and like most visitors they had taken pleasure in the vast forests of Araucarian conifers, so different from their North American relatives, and in the neat German villages with their gabled A-frame houses and tidy gardens. But this was an area which suffered under ninety inches of rainfall a year, a cold and heartless torrent which took its toll of deaths from tuberculosis and pneumonia among the poor and, among all classes, from despair.

The northern desert was another matter. Ben had grown up in southern California, living for awhile in the Mojave Desert, in Ludlow and in Barstow. He and his brother Hugh had loved the immense stillness of sand and sky, the total immersion of hardy arid growths in alternate baths of sizzling daytime heat and nighttime chill. When Ben and Anna had traveled from Africa to Antofagasta and down the northern coast of Chile, he had felt again the excitement of penetrating an inhospitable environment. But Anna was frightened by the same naked indifference of nature to human needs that enthralled Ben. And as they continued south, nearing the central valley, one of the five or six Mediterranean climates in the world, both Anna and Ben were confirmed in the conviction they had started with—and which virtually all Chileans share—that the middle latitudes are meant for humans.

One last temptation remained to be overcome: La Serena, the first city of the "Norte Chico," the long, semiarid valley which lies between the great northern desert and the lush central zone. Occasionally even now Ben thought of it with wonder and longing, remembering walks on endless beaches, evening swims in warm ocean water, ample buildings with patios of flagstone, intricately carved balconies, and lacy iron grills. He and Anna had explored every corner of the city, and after a few days' stay knew just which hills to climb for a good view of the bay, where more than once the ships of Francis Drake had anchored as the English plundered the town, then a key fortress astride the route to Peru.

All of this he had written to Hugh, and once settled in Villa Inez, he had showered upon his brother his impressions of the Aconcagua Valley, glorifying everything, excusing imperfections, and whitewashing everybody, big growers and merchants and peasants alike. Hugh had not been convinced. He had responded with pamphlets and studies describing the rural misery which other students of Chile had been struck with and finally, on the back of a picture postcard of Rockefeller Plaza, he had scrawled his final verdict: "About rural Chile: you've got to be crazy."

Ben was disappointed that neither Hugh nor Anna could share his passion for the Chilean countryside, but at the same time he was amused at himself, at the emotional attachment he felt for his own systematic distortion of reality. As he confessed to Anna, he considered his romance to be constructive; it was in keeping with the social ideals he wished to promote. He conceived of it less as an apology for rural misery than as a tribute to the small farmers, who take their pleasure from sowing and gleaning. In that respect it was a counter to the traditional Chilean folklore which—so it seemed to him—unaccountably glorified the *roto*, who lived for drink. That was perhaps the only social fiction that Chileans of every class and political persuasion agreed on: that the *roto* is a life-loving, clever fellow who paradoxically does the country credit.

The train's whistle reminded Ben that soon he would be disembarking. As he reached up to the luggage rack, he found himself humming some verses of Nicanor Parra's famous drinking song, which seemed to keep perfect time with the movement of the wheels:

I'm not from Coihueco
I'm from Niblinto
Where the cowboys chew
Red wine

I was born in Portezuelo
I was brought up in Nanco
Where the cops swim
In white wine

I'll die in the markets
of San Vicente
Where the friars float
In *aguardiente*. . . .

3

Not for a long time—since before the strike—had Ben seen the buses and taxis running along the broad avenue, tented with enormous acacia trees, which formed the principal thoroughfare of the "new town," as this section of Villa Inez was called. But he decided to walk; the footpath was almost as fast. He carefully arranged his poncho and jacket under his arm, for it was uncomfortably warm. He had reached the nuns' school when he heard the familiar whistle of the milkman.

"Hey, *patron!* Jump aboard, I'll give you a ride."

Ben looked dubiously at the tiny wagon. In addition to José's weight, it held several milk cans full of the watereddown liquid which he ladled into his customers' pitchers.

"Are you through with your round? Are you going to the old town?"

"I can take you to where Amunátegui Street ends," replied José.

Ben climbed into the wagon. He had never ridden with José before, and he found the odor of warm milk, suggestive of infants, rather nauseating. But he enjoyed the clip-clop of the horse's feet on the pavement. They passed through the new town in silence. Ben had intended to ask the milkman if he had talked to Anna during the past week, but he changed his mind: José was wrapped in winey reverie. The houses thinned as the wagon approached the Suarez River, and for a while, in the sandy-bottomed canyon, the two men almost seemed to be in open country. But once on the other side of the river, the outskirts of the "old town" rapidly became visible.

It was about half-past one, and the streets were empty except for some merchants strolling to the Lebanese Social Club, where they lunched every day, and a few school children who were waiting for a bus. Ben noted with surprise the neat and prosperous air of the town under the noonday sun. Usually he arrived on the afternoon train, on winter days just before the sun went down. Then the old town wore a different aspect: he would walk along Amunátegui Street peering into the tiny shoe repair shops (how could one village support so many of them!) where the shoemakers sat at their doors trying to catch the last light. In every shop one bare lightbulb would be suspended from the ceiling on a long wire, hanging three or four feet above a low table spread with tools and shoes. Always a son or wife seemed to be there and sometimes a gathering of friends, munching on bread and drinking tea from tin cups. At the bicycle repair shops and the food shops the scene was similar, and as he passed Ben noted which radio station the shop owners were tuned into, a sure sign of their political allegiance. ("Everything is so politicized in Chile," the Irish priest at the local parish had once complained to Ben, "that if you say 'Nice day, isn't it?' you are assumed to be for the UP; and if you fail to serve a sweet at tea, you are supposed to be criticizing the government for food shortages!")

They were nearing the end of Amunátegui Street, and Ben prepared his bundles for the half-mile walk he would have to make to his home, which was situated just beyond the city limits, on a road that was no longer a major thoroughfare. He started to get down when José suddenly put his hand on Ben's sleeve and inquired drunkenly, "*Gringo*, did you come from Santiago?"

"Yes," replied Ben, alerted to the conspiratorial tone the milkman had adopted.

"Tell me," José almost crooned in a mournful tone. "Why are they killing so many people?"

A shiver of fear passed down Ben's spine. "You'd better not talk that way, friend. It could get you into trouble." And he patted the man in an awkward, fraternal way.

It hit Ben with a staggering impact that not once since the beginning of the coup on Tuesday had he heard a reliable report about what was going on in Villa Inez. Scanning the newspapers had been pointless; they had been filled with military bombast and reports of events in the major cities. He had tried to pick up something about Chile from foreign radio broadcasts, but Jaime's shortwave radio had never seemed to function right when Ben tuned in. He had supposed that Anna was safe: she lived, after all, on the edge of a dusty village, busying herself with house and family. Nobody was likely to make trouble for her.

Yet, he reflected, she was not the kind of woman who could cope with every situation. A coup d'état? He didn't know. She had been perhaps the only person in Chile who hadn't expected it. He had tried to talk with her about it, had suggested making some simple preparations, but she had regarded even such tentative gestures as a betrayal of the UP Government, which she steadfastly supported without bothering herself too much with either its successes or its problems. He had found her position baffling, yet he had declined to challenge her. She had enough problems, it seemed, without forcing her to confront an unpleasant possibility which both angered and frightened her.

And perhaps her attitude had been the right one. The coup she could neither have prevented nor influenced. All her efforts had to be devoted to surviving in the country. It wasn't easy for her. Both Ben and Anna realized that if Carmen were not there, everything would fall to pieces. Carmen was like a guide who interpreted the signals from a varied and mysterious civilization to a blind visitor. It wasn't that Anna was stupid; it was rather that she lacked the skills which a rural environment demanded. She could resolve to put the tools in the shed, only to be confounded by a tricky lock. She would dutifully feed the hens in the morning, but she would let them fly the coop; they would run wildly about while the new pup, still unaware of his duties, would pursue them, intoxicated with their frantic clucking and fluttering feathers. She never heard in time the varied cacophony on which the distribution of products depended at the village's edge, where housewives had to scurry to their gates at the beckoning of human and mechanical summons: the shrill tin whistle of the milkman, the gasman banging on an empty drum, the finger whistle of the mailman, the holler *"Tengo pe'ca'o!"* of the fishmonger, the tinkly mouthharp of the knife sharpener. (When they had lived in Santiago, there had been even more: the insistent honking horn of the rubbish collectors, for instance, or the call of the vegetable peddler, who would intone again and again the produce available that day, always descending a minor third for his final syllable.)

There had been a time when he had believed Anna when

she had described her efforts to improve, but he had long since resigned himself to his well-founded suspicion that her failures resulted from internal sabotage: it was her way of rebelling against living in Villa Inez de Suarez. She had never admitted it, and they no longer talked about it. Yet Ben couldn't help sensing in her a divided will. On the one hand, she loved him, and, to some extent, she loved Chile too. On the other hand, she could not forgive him for having persuaded her to share a life with him in a remote Chilean *pueblo* far from San Francisco, from Idaho—the places she continued to consider home.

Making his way down the graveled road, he stopped to rest under the shade of a giant avocado tree whose branches extended far over the brick fence which bounded the Ortegas' property. A problem seemed to be nettling him just under the surface of his thoughts; he wanted to get at it. The truth of the matter was that he no longer understood Anna. He had never before stated the situation to himself so bluntly, and he stretched himself out more comfortably against the brick wall to ponder his discovery. He felt perturbed by it; his heart began to flutter like the wings of a wounded bird. "It's the times we're living through," he said to himself. "Everybody in this country is being tried beyond endurance." But his case and Anna's, he reasoned, if not worse than other people's, was at least doubly trying. Chile was not their native land; he had persuaded Anna to live there on the grounds of the country's beauty and culture and peace and promise. They had resolved to give themselves utterly to it. The place had let them down.

But perhaps that wasn't it; maybe he was snatching at excuses which let him off the hook. His failure could be wholly personal. He tried to think back to the beginning of their relationship, when he had persuaded her to marry him after his breakup with Helen. "Why do you want me?" Anna had asked. "Because you are so simple." (She had seemed so then.) "What do you have against complexity?" she had responded, and although he couldn't think of an answer, he remembered now that he had associated simplicity with an open approach to the experiences which throw most people into a muddle.

"You assume that I am the opposite of Helen," she had stated. He had agreed that it was likely. And suddenly, even after ten years of marriage to Anna, he vividly recalled Helen's face, her sensational figure as she stood before a big bathroom mirror, making up for a "date" with another man. He had no right to complain: they had agreed to a free marriage, they had planned their lovers as part of their future. The problem was that, whereas she had enjoyed hers, he had been bored and discouraged by his; in particular, he had become fed up with begging and cajoling women who acted reluctant although they fully expected to end up in bed with him. And in any case, he didn't want another woman; he wanted Helen, who was never there. When she had begun to spend whole weekends away, he had protested. And when she had refused to break a "date" the evening that his brother Hugh was operated on after a nearly fatal accident, he had resolved to seek a divorce. Indeed, he had concluded that fidelity brought more comfort than infidelity brought pleasure.

Ben felt thirsty. He resumed his journey, his briefcase at his side, his jacket and poncho over his shoulder. He was tired; he felt himself limping more than usual. As he walked, he recalled the placid days before his second marriage, when even his brother's criticisms of Anna could not disturb his serene confidence in his choice. "She's got the world memorized but not understood," Hugh had claimed, capturing the way she had of immersing herself in books and lectures on every conceivable topic: a puzzled expression would furrow her brow, yet she had no discernible purpose or sense of direction. It was as if she lacked the internal machinery for organizing and collating the waves of impressions and opinions and solid data which she inexplicably loved to bathe in. Ben was willing to grant the point, but it was not the kind of thing that bothered him; indeed, there was a sort of egolessness in Anna's pursuit of knowledge which pleased him. Hugh's other objection, however humorously stated, seemed more serious: "She's the kind of woman who will use the excuse of a finger temporarily misplaced in the nose to move in on a guy's whole personality." It was true that she was captious, but he attributed her harshness less to an uncharitable soul than to a certain lack of poise and tact which he had frequently observed in plain women.

He was nearing home. From the chimney he could see a whisper of smoke ascending, a sure token of well-being; and behind the house a lineful of half-dry clothes was swaying in the breeze, the whites bleached even whiter by the relentless sun, and the colored items, after a few turns on the line, etiolated, pastel shadows of their former brightness. He felt immediately cheered. A long walk in the heat is depressing, he reasoned; it would be a mistake to confuse fatigue with problems. In regard to Anna, he was probably being overly sensitive. Secretive, melancholy, resentful: these were loaded words which, used too often, could subtly intrude themselves into his thesaurus of a woman whom, however she might be described, he valued and loved.

4

"Don't slam the door, the cake will fall," Anna said, glancing at Ben obliquely as she stirred something at the stove. She was barefoot, a scarf tied about her hair, and dressed in blue jeans. Ben noted that in the past week her normally tawny skin had almost darkened to the deep tan she would show all summer.

Then swiftly she put her spoon down and walked towards him, throwing an arm about his neck. He held her close. He could feel her chest heaving as she sobbed soundlessly. When she swallowed hard and attempted to smile, he fought the tears in his own eyes. "Who would have thought the trains were running? If I'd known, I would have got ready, I would have put my shoes on or something." She made a chuckling noise.

"You're baking a cake—that's a treat I haven't had in a long time. Where's Damaris? And Carmen?"

"Damaris is playing with the little *momios* next door. At first I wouldn't let her go over there. I was afraid that she would say something about our political views. The radio and TV networks are urging people to denounce their neighbors. I wouldn't put it past the Ortegas to turn us in. I've always suspected the Ortega boys of being in the Patria y Libertad. But Damaris kept begging me, and I relented. I warned her, though. I said, 'Damaris, if you breathe one word about what your parents think about the new *Junta Militar* or Allende or the *Unidad Popular*, the police will come and get us and we'll disappear.' Perhaps I overdid it, but I do think she understands. I know it's crazy, since she's only six, but I trust her to keep quiet."

Her voice had taken on the hard edge that served her as a defense against tears. "As for Carmen, she's out buying some of the beautiful things which are suddenly available, little packages of nuts and raisins, old wine, honey, all the wonderful treasures people overthrow governments for. That's the reason for the cake; suddenly sugar is available again. And how was it in Santiago? Were you at Jaime's?"

"I was. I hope you didn't worry about me."

"Of course I did. I felt exasperated with you for not getting a message to me somehow. I knew the phone service between cities was off, but I half-expected some heroic effort on your part to get home or to let me know you were all right. I knew I was being unfair. Then I started to have morbid fantasies; I don't want to repeat them." For a second or two her eyes filled with tears. "But tell me how it was; what happened?"

Ben delivered himself of his mixed bag of impressions, of his own sense of tragedy and of tediousness, but he was eager to return to a discussion of the state of affairs in Villa Inez.

Anna did not seem as calm as he had expected. As she sat cross-legged on the sofa cracking walnuts, he observed the exaggerated boniness of her knees through the faded jeans, and the prominence of cheekbones. ("I look like a famished old rabbi who barely survived the last Polish pogrom," she had described herself when Ben had first known her; and although she had filled out a bit after Damaris' birth, she still had a gaunt, undernourished look.)

"We ran out of gas for the kitchen stove on the morning of the eleventh," she was saying. "The Ortegas offered to lend us an extra drum, but it didn't fit our valve. But we got along all right; we turned our electric heater on its side and used it as a hotplate. All day we listened to the damned marches. About four o'clock on the eleventh it was announced that Allende and his family were OK, that they were already on their way to Mexico. I didn't believe it.

"I saw quite a bit of the neighbors, and it was pretty awkward," she continued. "All I could think about was how barbarism was triumphing once again, but I couldn't say it to anyone. I was always crying; for two days I couldn't control myself. 'It's only because I'm worried about Ben,' I repeated ad nauseam. I couldn't tell if they believed me. The Ortegas and the Valenzuelas had big fiestas after the Moneda was bombed, and their teenage children drank champagne in the streets. The Valenzuelas invited me in Wednesday afternoon. What could I do? I sat there weeping in my glass. They kept assuring me that you would be all right. They told me proudly about their kids. They were in the rightist youth brigades which busied themselves with whitewashing all the political slogans off the walls. They went around in the Ortegas' pick-up with lots of pails and ladders and brushes. This was their contribution to 'Let's clean up the Marxist filth' campaign. In the meantime the Torres family was attempting to grin and bear it, but their stoic reserve didn't help them when Luis was arrested on Wednesday. He's their middle boy, the one who worked for the agrarian reform program."

"Do you know if there have been many arrests or killings?" asked Ben.

"The stories are rife. On the eleventh the workers at the cement factory put up a show of resistance—more heroic than sensible, I should say. I suppose they anticipated the worst, since they had seized the factory extralegally two or three years ago. You remember that the government appointed that nice young schoolteacher to serve as supervisor there until the difficulties could be worked out. Now most of the workers are at the naval station at Belloto, where they are being tortured, some to death. The body of the supervisor was literally dumped at his wife's feet yesterday. He died from multiple wounds and from pneumonia: the prisoners were left outside all night in holes filled with water up to their necks."

For a moment Anna couldn't speak. She handed the nut-cracker to Ben, as if to indicate that he should relieve her. "Do you know what Señora Ortega had to say about it? She claimed that the young man had died without revealing the where-abouts of the local stash of arms. According to her, the leftists were trained in underground guerrilla schools to endure torture without confessing." Her voice assumed a hard edge again. "That's how it is: at the same time the *momios* despise their opponents they also assume that the leftists are mys-teriously blessed with extraordinary, superhuman powers."

Anna's nervousness was communicating itself to Ben. He felt like pacing about, but in the confined quarters of the house there was no room. He looked through the front windows which received the afternoon sun. In the distance the coastal range seemed to rest as serenely as ever, La Reina brooding over the worn, old peaks below her like an ancient monarch over her court favorites.

"Well, and what else—what about the jam factory?" Ben asked.

"That was more dramatic, the way the *milicos* took it over," Anna replied. "The sandman happened to be going by that morning with his cart full of gravel. He stood by the swimming pool and watched the helicopters, swooping down dropping—I don't know—grenades, I suppose, or bazookas. There were streams of smoke everywhere, and the racket of heavy machinery. Some of the sandman's friends worked in the factory. I felt sorry for him. Later I was told that it was all a show, that the workers had surrendered without resistance. Now they are at Belloto too."

"So the worst is over," Ben sighed deeply.

"I doubt it, I doubt it very much," Anna replied. The pitch of her voice rose a few notes, and she spoke slowly, a discipline she tried to impose upon herself when she was upset. "Now we must learn to live under the threat of constant violence. Every day helicopters have flown over the riverbed and the hills beyond like flocks of predatory birds. Sometimes they fire; everyone thinks that there are leftists hiding out in the thickets. Within Villa Inez they are searching every house for arms. Even here on this quiet road there are shots fired every night though I never know by whom or towards whom. I'm not out after the ten o'clock curfew, I can tell you. When I'm not housekeeping during the day, I gossip with the neighbors to find out what's going on, and at night I plan how to go about packing up."

It took a few seconds for her remark to register. "Packing up?" Ben finally asked. "What for?"

"For getting out of here," she replied, as if it were obvious. And then a look of stunned bewilderment crossed her face. "Surely you're not still persuaded that this country is Home Sweet Home!" She paused. "Since all the circumstances which led you to elect Chile have changed, I just assumed that you'd have to make some new plans. . . . "

"Such a thought never crossed my mind," Ben replied.

Even before he glanced up from the basin of walnuts in his lap, he knew that Anna's edginess and dismay was transforming itself into a sense of outrage. There was going to be a scene. He wasn't up to it; even more than usual he felt defenseless against the downpours of emotion that other people seem to unleash as effortlessly as dogs rid themselves of excess moisture with a few vigorous shakes of their backs. He recalled the judgment his mother had once made: "Ben, you are a person with no passions of your own; you're bound to be ruled by other people's."

Anna had risen and walked quickly away as if suddenly recalled to an important errand, but she abruptly stopped and wheeled about, her lips white, the corners of her mouth pulled downwards as if by invisible wires. Ben was frightened, but he was also sorry for her, for the grief which transformed her plain features into ugly ones.

"You never let the facts get in the way, do you?" she articulated between closed teeth. "Years ago you uprooted us from friends and family and insisted on moving to the end of the earth because it's pleasant here, and the Northern Hemisphere is going to blow itself up. And now that we're here, now that our lives are threatened much more by civil strife than they ever were by an atom bomb, you're content to stay. I don't understand it: for you Chile isn't a home; it's an obsession!"

Ben felt himself flush. He barely recognized himself in Anna's caricature, yet he was worrying about the element of truth in it. As he deliberated whether to answer, he tipped the basin of walnuts onto the floor. Neither moved to retrieve them. "Well," he said softly, "it's not just that Chile is pleasant and that we've established ourselves here, there's also my work—"

"Your work!" she said contemptuously. "And do you intend to carry on your nutrition education project for the Junta? Even assuming that they will let you?"

"Anna, it wouldn't be for the Junta; it's a project that's survived two governments. One can't abandon worthwhile efforts every time things go bad; there are still a lot of people to be helped."

"That's just what all those Nazi collaborators said, all those people who went about their business as usual as millions were put to death in their midst!" She covered her face and wailed.

Unaccountably, Ben remembered the cake in the oven. Somehow it smelled done to him, and he mechanically walked to the corner of the house that served as a kitchen. He took the cake from the oven and put it on the table. "The cake . . ." he started to say to Anna.

"Yes," she replied, her face still covered.

"You don't have to look at things that way," he continued. "My work. . . . "

Once more she gritted her teeth in fury.

"Your work! I spit on it. You have abandoned a useful career as an M.D., which you were good at, to become an educator, which you've no talent for. Even the level of your salary shows the contempt of your employers for you. Look at us"—she waved her hands wildly about—"we live without hot water, without a refrigerator, without dressers or blankets. And now you tell me that we must continue to sacrifice though anyone but you can see that the reason for sacrificing has disappeared!"

Ben sat down heavily on the floor. He was silent. It was the first time Anna had voiced such contempt for his accomplishments in a new career, and he felt stung. It is difficult, he thought, to live with a person who despises your efforts and achievements, even if that person is less perceptive than Anna.

He noted that her sobs were less frequent now, and she was drying her face with a sofa pillow. Perhaps she was a bit remorseful, perhaps she would begin to modify her accusations, to apologize. . . . Ben thought he couldn't bear it. He stood up. "I'm going for a walk," he said. He paused, hoping he would be inspired to say the right thing. "I'll pick up the walnuts when I get back," he concluded feebly.

He walked along the path that crossed the irrigation ditch in front of their house, past the swimming pool, and down the incline that led to the second and third terraces of the *parcela*. When he got to the animal pens he stopped, entertained even in his sadness by the way the little ducks swam like a squadron in their pool. Sometimes a few rebellious ones would venture out on their own, but soon they would lose courage and scurry back into formation.

At the dog's house he paused to unchain Pup, who was

confined during the periods when the sharecropper planted, since in his freedom the dog dug up the young shoots. In his jubilation at escaping his unhappy sentence, Pup raced up and down beside the pens as if berserk, frightening the hens who squawked in indigation. "Come, Pup," called Ben, as he walked to the gate which led from the *parcela* to the road.

In five minutes he had come to the end of the road, which intersected with a loop of the Suarez River. Here he always had to face a difficult choice; he could either cross the footbridge—a shabby, ladderlike affair just barely elevated above the swift-moving water, or he could turn to his right, following the path that paralleled the meandering stream. Each path was lovely, and each had its disadvantages: as to the second, it was a dead end, and retracing one's steps seemed aesthetically unpleasing to Ben; he preferred a circular walk. As to the first path, its beauty was marred by its proximity to the municipal dump, which the city fathers had established in the most scenic spot in the Inez Valley, where in good weather the poor came to swim in spite of the refuse and the flies.

He decided to follow the riverbank, and the pup bounded ahead, scaring the robins and *san agustines* from the trees. Some of the blackberry bushes had almost overgrown the path, and he had to walk carefully to avoid the thorny branches. When he arrived at his destination, a wide oval of California poppies stretching from the stream's edge to a stand of eucalyptus trees bordering the bank, Ben sat down on a smooth stone and attempted to reason with the pup, who wanted to proceed farther. "It's nice here, Pup—look, you can swim in the stream and cool off." He began to throw sticks of wood into the water, which the dog enthusiastically bounded after.

It was warm sitting in the sun, and after the tension of his talk with Anna, Ben felt fatigued. He closed his eyes and allowed himself to doze, starting now and then when he heard the flutter of a gull's wing or a lark's call. He never failed to wonder at the abundance of wildlife so close to the city limits. It reminded him of scenes from his boyhood, when he and Hugh used to camp out in fields of poppies, identical to those at his feet, or explore the edges of the Pacific where the gulls and herons resembled those he saw now, which somehow made their way inland as far as the Suarez River.

When he finally returned home, he no longer felt anxious, but he didn't know what he would say to Anna. She was sitting serenely in the middle of a jumble of records, apparently trying to stack them according to a system. Only in her eyes could he see any emotional distress. She smiled rather shyly.

"I didn't say I wouldn't go," he began; "it's just that I'd never thought of it before. But it will be all right; we'll leave if it's really important to you." He was surprised at his own words, yet he was comfortable with them. It occurred to him suddenly that, in truth, he no longer felt a special concern for his locus in time and space.

Anna expressed neither surprise nor joy. "I suppose it would be foolish to abandon your job before finding another one," she mused. "It will probably be a year or so before we're on our way."

"I suppose so."

"Anyway, we can get our way paid if we wish."

"What do you mean?"

"Your mother called about noon yesterday. I was speechless when she offered to send us the air fare. I suppose her crusty heart is cracking a little in her old age. She has Hugh there, of course, but it's not the same; she depends on you. Then about two my parents phoned."

"Well, I'm surprised at your parents too. They've never called before, have they?"

"No, but Dad's so hard of hearing, you know. Actually, they didn't place the call themselves; Ingrid did it for them. She's home for a few days. You know what she said? She said, 'Don't worry about being bored back in the States. I've got loads of exciting projects in mind. How would you like to open a health food store with me in San Francisco?' "

Ben looked at Anna closely. She seemed happy and excited, as if she had forgotten their recent quarrel. "What did you reply?"

"I said, 'Your problem, Ingrid, is that you think work is liberating. Actually, it's a drag. It swallows up all the precious hours you could be devoting to the really important things. Pursuing wisdom, for instance.' "

"Do you really believe that?"

"I don't know. Anyway, she contended that it was unfair to start an argument long-distance when the other party was paying. We both promised to write."

Anna paused. "It would be different if there were something really constructive that we could do here, like joining the resistance; but with the total control that the military is exerting, down to the neighborhood level, I think it's impossible."

"You're probably right. It's hard to imagine risking your life day after day."

"It would require a heroic spirit. And I'm not prepared for torture, Ben." She furrowed her brow. "Yet now that we've agreed on leaving, I suddenly feel a little confused. I know it's stupid, but some sort of doubt is creeping into the back of my mind."

"It's understandable. Big changes are always upsetting. We've had so many changes already. The best thing is not to hurry, that's what I think. We need some time to get used to our decision."

She reached out her hand to him; he pulled her up. "You're very good—you know that, Ben?" She embraced him tightly. "Now that you're here and we've had a talk, I feel as if the world isn't quite a hopeless place yet—not quite."

5

In the late afternoon Ben saw Carmen. After running her errands, she had gone to fetch her pigs who were foraging in the municipal dump. It was illegal to turn animals loose to browse at the dump, and once every five or six months the police would issue a warning that all animals found there would be confiscated. For a week or two Carmen and some of the neighbors along the river—Leonardo Olivares and the sandman and the other guilty parties—would leave their pigs in their pens, feeding them whatever they could find. But soon the pigs were allowed to return to their old haunts.

"Well, and how do you like your government now, Carmen?" Ben asked, half-teasing. She had been highly critical of the UP, especially after some squatters, encouraged by the MIR, had taken over some building sites in Santiago close to where her brother, Segundo Carmelo, after years of penny pinching, had finally purchased a small shack. The two of them had spent several weeks there, armed with a pistol to keep out intruders. They had posted a sign, "Trespassers will be shot."

Evidently she wasn't very jubilant. "The *milicos* are worse than the *politicos*," she replied. "They don't know how to run a country." She frowned. "But I can tell you one thing: now that they have taken over Radio Portales, there are new announcers who don't talk so fast—you can finally understand what they're saying."

Ben smiled broadly. The verbal virtuosity of the Chilean left was legendary.

She continued: "But you know, they go slow, but they don't tell the truth. You can't fool us about what's been going on in Villa Inez—we live here. At night I've taken to listening to the shortwave with Leonardo Olivares and his family. It makes you mad, all the things you hear. Last night, for instance, there was a newscast from Argentina about Victor Jara. He was my favorite singer, and his records are still in the blackberry bushes where I hid them on the eleventh. They said that he was taken to the National Stadium along with thousands of others on the day of the coup. One of the *comandantes* recognized him and ordered him to stand before the crowd of prisoners seated in the stadium. Then Victor had to hold out his hands, and they chopped off his fingers. 'Let's hear you play and sing now, Jara,' the *milicos* said. So he managed to stay on his feet a little while and began to sing, and he got all the prisoners to sing too. They shot him then, and as he fell he seemed to bow, as if saluting his comrades.

"I'm not for killing." She emphasized every word, as if she had been saving them for public delivery. "I thought the Junta would make Frei the president again, and instead they've killed some people I know, and they've killed Victor Jara. Some things I won't forgive. Why is it that in Chile there's never any rest; things always seem to get worse and worse!"

When Damaris returned home shortly before tea, she took Ben's hand and led him to the garden, where she had planted zucchini and chard, snapdragons and petunias. Then they sat at the empty pool, dangling their legs over the edge, while she described to him the week's events. Behind her wire-frame glasses her eyes looked sober and thoughtful. He wanted to hold her but feared disturbing her sense of dignity. When she finished her account, she turned to face him as if confiding a great secret. "Papa, I have a feeling that all of this has happened before," she said. "Isn't that strange?"

"What do you mean?"

"I think God has created the world over and over again, and each time it's been destroyed. In each world the same things happen."

Ben was intrigued. "And you and I, did we live in former worlds just like this one?"

"Yes," she replied. "We used to sit at the edge of this very pool and swing our legs." She laughed as if it were a delightful possibility, and Ben wondered at this child he had fathered, who seemed to have the sense of humor of a wise old lady.

7

Since work at UCADULTOS had been suspended temporarily due to the coup, Ben was free to spend a week at home. Every morning he arose early, working in the garden until the arrival of the sharecropper, who usually came accompanied by his horse, Jennie, and by his sons with their queer nicknames, El Negro, Oso, and El Guatón. (" 'The Black One' and 'Bear' are names I can imagine answering to," Anna said, "but can you imagine being called 'the Big Belly?' ")

Sometime about eight-thirty or nine Anna would bring Ben a glass of water and read to him from the papers. The news was always upsetting: only the smell of the damp soil and the warmth of the sun on his back could assuage the sense of desolation he felt as Anna read on and on about the systematic destruction of a world he had loved. Frequently the news was full of replies to articles in the foreign press, which no one in the country had any access to, about Chilean atrocities. "Reading the newspapers in Chile," said Anna, "is like hearing one end of a phone conversation in which the speaker is answering charges which you cannot hear."

"It's happened just as I predicted," she declared one morning as she approached with a paper rolled under her arm. "The Junta has invented another and a better reason for the coup. They claim to have discovered a nefarious leftist plot called 'Plan Zeta' to stage a coup and take over the government by force. It was to have occurred about September 18, and many military officers were to have been murdered. You remember what I said yesterday: it would be absurd for the new Government to continue to claim that they had seized power to preserve the constitution and Chile's traditional freedoms when they are obviously dismantling them. They would have to invent a more convincing reason, one that plays on peoples' deepest fears."

"They didn't have to use much imagination to invent it," replied Ben, "since there were junior officers in the Navy, at least, and perhaps elsewhere, who were in fact trying to come up with such a plan."

"That doesn't mean the UP Government was behind it," replied Anna impatiently. "Obviously they weren't mobilized for a pro-Allende coup, or they wouldn't have fallen so easily last week."

"That may be," persisted Ben, "but there were those among the romantic left who talked as if the UP could seize total power whenever they wanted to; or at least that they could initiate a civil war and ultimately win it. It was a self-glorifying assumption that the left could prevail with big talk and personal bravery against the people with the money and the weapons."

"In any case," replied Anna thoughtfully, "a coup by a legitimate government to sustain itself in office is on a different moral plane from a seizure of power by some ambitious *milicos*. Put in the worst possible light, a 'Plan Zeta,' had it existed, would have indicated the left's intention to do what the right did."

"Your problem is that you want to reduce everything to a question of logic," said Ben. Anna gave him a little push in protest and turned back towards the path. "Look, there's a VW bus parked by the house," she said. "Someone has come to see us."

A woman emerged from the car and gazed about uncertainly. Anna hastened towards her. When Ben heard the exchange of greetings, he recognized the voice of Dorothy Hemming, though he had not seen her in over a year. He smiled to himself, happy with the unexpected diversion of her visit.

He allowed the women time to talk together for a half-hour before he returned to the house, suddenly conscious of his sweaty odor and of the holes in the seat of his blue jeans. Dorothy Hemming, however, was not the type to mind. Indeed, one of the things he liked about her was her almost contemptuous indifference to appearance, including her own. It was a characteristic she shared with Anna, but the younger, smaller woman suggested a sure self-confidence that was somehow startling. It was her voice, Ben suddenly decided, the well-resined suppleness of it combined with volume out of keeping with her small size. That was quite apart from the steely quality of her mind, the way she had of chewing up people's arguments and spitting out the pieces before they had even been offered to her. Only in her love of shocking people, Ben decided, did she display the childishness that her diminutive size and rounded figure suggested.

"I have just talked your wife into becoming a spy," said Dorothy as she gave Ben a kiss. "She was trying to think of how to break it to you tactfully, but I said nonsense: cowards like Ben just love all the little deaths they must endure when their loved ones flap their wings occasionally." Her eyes suddenly glassed over and she hugged him again. "How are you, *gringo?*"

"I'm amazed at what a capitalist you've become. The last time I saw you we were both proud to be squeezed into the back of the bus with all the comrades."

"The VW bus belongs to the Methodist Church, you cynic. Alan and I use it only on church business."

"And what is the church business that brings you to us?"

"I was half-serious when I referred to spying, Ben. Do you remember that many of the wives of Protestant missionaries put together a series of newsletters on Chile during the past few years? You must have seen some. It was an attempt to get some accurate reports out to counteract the influence of the rightest press. Well, we're still in operation. Except that our work is now more dangerous. In particular, we're trying to gather and systematize stories of torture, political murder, and other infringements of human rights. We want to send them out of the country to people who take an interest in such matters; we especially want to pressure the U.S. Congress to cut off foreign aid to this government."

"But why are you expanding your network to include Anna?" asked Ben. "She doesn't seem like a likely spy to me." But even as he spoke he was weighing the advantages of Dorothy's proposal. Only that morning as he had weeded the lettuce he had wished that Anna could channel her hostile and bitter feelings in a useful direction. He was worried about her listless brooding, the lethargy that seemed to paralyze her. She would spend hours in bed, apparently in deep sleep, but upon awakening she would complain of frightening dreams. "It's a sign I'm going crazy," she said. "My dreams used to be reasonable little affairs in which I couldn't achieve an objective because I'd lost a key, say, or I had two appointments at the same hour. But the problems were perfectly comprehensible, and the world operated according to rational laws. Now my dream world is peopled only with bizarre characters and horrible events."

"Don't underestimate Anna," Dorothy was saying. "She'd do very well at this line of work. She's the kind of woman people feel drawn to confide in, and that's what we need. She can collect eyewitness accounts of the torture chambers and concentration camps around here. One of our problems," she added, "is that our group is centered in Santiago; we need contacts in the provinces. That's why I thought of Anna."

"Maybe we can think of some others who would help," said Anna. "Ben has told me about a Canadian couple who generally make themselves useful. And he could ask his colleague, Jaime Venegas. He has lots of contacts."

Anna and Dorothy continued to talk while Ben washed up. He noted with surprise their wit and their good humor. It was the first time in several weeks that Ben had heard Anna laugh deeply. "What a strange creature a human is," he mused; "what an untidy theorem, what an uneven scrawl of leaps and plunges! We breakfast on suicidal thoughts, but by lunchtime we're ready for anything. Who can understand it?"

Dorothy had risen to go, and Ben and Anna walked her to her car. "By the way," she said as she searched her purse for her keys, "I almost forgot to ask you, do you know a young woman named Eva Maria Araya?"

"I think she's Monica's sister, right? Monica is a good friend of mine but I've only seen Maria once or twice. Why do you ask?"

"Someone told me that she might be having difficulties; she was an assistant to Mrs. Allende, you know. If you have her sister's number, you might give her a call."

She put on her dark glasses and waved and drove away imperiously, as if the enormous machine were an extension of her will. Ben put his arm around Anna, and together they walked back to the house, where *Oso* and *El Guatón* were waiting with a basket of greens that they had picked for lunch.

8

Before retiring for the night, Ben always took a stroll around the *parcela*, breathing in the night air and checking the animals and locking the gates. Anna often accompanied him, but tonight she had gone to bed early. It was raining. He had felt a little melancholy as he had made his rounds alone. Upon returning to the house, seeing her lying there in a deep sleep, he had had to fight an oppressive sense of solitude. When she was sad, Anna sometimes rejected him.

The lights were off, the doors closed. He slipped out of his clothes, tiptoeing across the cold tiles and sliding between the coarse, chilly sheets. Then Anna surprised him. Her face still turned to the wall, she extended a hand backwards, searching for his fingers. They lay there quietly for a minute or two, their clasped palms a tentative question. Then she turned towards him, stretching herself out fully beside him, resting her toes on his feet.

Ben soaked in the salty warmth of her body as he listened to the light spring rain on the roof. Anna's presence was an enormous consolation to him. The crests and hollows of their bodies, barely touching, seemed as complimentary as their moods, their dispositions, their ways of looking at things.

"You know I love you," he whispered.

She shook her head slightly and pressed herself closer against him, her breasts flattening out against his chest. He turned her on her back and as he looked down into her eyes he felt tears in his own.

"So you think everything is going to be all right?" she asked.

"I do."

She sighed deeply and shivered. "Everything's fine when I can feel you loving me." She put her hand on the back of his neck and pulled his head towards hers. "Don't forget how much I need you," she whispered as he kissed her. "That's the one thing that will never change: I need you."

7 *Eve's Memoirs October 15-20, 1973*

that night you did not choose,
you did not choose, that night
——CARLOS FUENTES,
   La Muerte de Artemio Cruz

1

Allende's House

Of all the mistakes I have made since the *golpe*, moving into Allende's house seems most stupid. I have become reluctant to admit it even to people who are sympathetic with me, for they invariably look astonished and exclaim something like, "Whatever possessed you to be so reckless? You should have planned to flee the circle of your leftist acquaintances rather than to move into its symbolic center." And they look closely at me, searching for signs of a formerly suppressed martyr complex.

But we were slow to give up thinking in the old way, Monica, Mother, and I; and although I had just recently been released from my five days of internment, I rather expected to be left alone. No charges had been made against me. I had, of course, lost my job, but no one in the new government appeared especially interested in persecuting me.

Then too I seemed amply protected. It was Señor Rafael Gossens, a relative of the Allende family, who had taken charge of the former President's affairs, and in addition to being rich and respectable, he was a solid rightist. That he should agree to managing the Allende estate attests to the solidity of family ties, the one dependable resource in every national disaster.

When he talked to Monica by phone at the Harriet B. School, he was undisturbed by the fact that I had been arrested. Indeed, my joblessness and the fact that I was living in Monica's apartment had made him think that I was the appropriate person to oversee the Allende house until it could be disposed of.

"You must be referring to Dr. Allende's former residence, the house on Valencia Street," Monica had said.

"Of course. The government is seeing to the house on Tomas Moro. If Eve would do us the kindness of sleeping in the old home and generally keeping it in good order, we would be very grateful." He hesitated. "It is our impression—uh—that some items have been taken without permission. The Junta is as eager as we are to prevent lawless plundering of the premises."

On September 20 I began to move in, taking with me the minimum in personal necessities, for I saw myself less as an overseer than as a sort of self-effacing priestess. Caring for the Allende house—small and modest with its simple two-story structure, like my parents'—was a way of paying my last respects, an act of piety. I had not known Allende intimately, but I had passed this house on my way to school as a girl; I had had the comfortable feeling that a *compañero* lived here, the man my father always supported for president. Later I had frequently been a guest at dinner at the house on Tomas Moro, and Allende and I had had a few good talks. He dropped by doña Tencha's office every day. As for doña Tencha, she and I were like mother and daughter. Now he was dead, and she had taken refuge in Mexico; it seemed appropriate that someone they had known and trusted should keep watch for them in their absence.

Yet from the beginning I was miserable. I had expected the quiet and immobility of death, perhaps, but the house had not yet yielded. Isabel Allende and her family had been living here on the eleventh; everywhere there were signs of a hasty flight, drawers hanging out of dressers, face powder spilled on the rug, spoiled milk on the kitchen counter. On the desk in the study there was a picture of the family: Allende standing behind doña Tencha, seated, and on the floor the three girls, still teenagers—Maria Carmen, Beatriz, and Isabel. Other photos were lying in a scramble on the floor: scenes of birthday parties, baptisms, Masonic ceremonies, the daughters' wedding. On the mantel there was a gift-wrapped box with a card, "A Isabel: ¡Cumpleaños Feliz!"

Trying to straighten out the relics of other people's lives, I felt less like a pious well-wisher than an intruder. I seemed like a tasteless person who had called too early in the day, finding the wife with her hair still in curlers, the husband with his false teeth in a glass on the bedside table. Even though I conscientiously avoided examining whatever I found—trying, as it were, to work without seeing—I felt paradoxically blameworthy, like a snoop.

Yet I might have stayed had it not been for the extraordinary events of Tuesday, September 25. I had left the house about nine in the morning to run errands, returning with Mother, after our lunch together, about three. Though I had left the front door locked, it was ajar; and entering, it was apparent that the place had been ransacked, for books and art objects and records were in a jumble on the living room floor, the pre-Columbian figurines and pots were missing from the shelves in the study, and upstairs, where a radio set had been installed, various tapes were lying about in great confusion. No food or liquor was missing, which suggested that the scavengers were not poor.

We were shocked at the audacity of the thieves who had dared to plunder during daylight hours, having jimmied open a basement window; they had apparently left by the front door. Since we feared that the police themselves were responsible (everyone had heard the stories of their hauls), we feared to call them. Trying to come to grips with the problem, I had a notion I was later to regret.

"Mother, you remember how this house is joined to the Brodys' by a covered walk? Maybe we should check to see if the thieves pillaged over there, too. It has been empty since the coup."

She opened and closed her hands uncertainly a few times. We were both suffering from the "intruder's fever" which I had described to Mother over lunch. Entering the Brodys' without permission seemed especially improper since the former Señora Brody, now separated from her husband, was "the doe," Allende's secretary and mistress of fourteen and more years. It was easy to imagine the easygoing neighborliness of the two families in the old days, when the children ran back and forth under the arcade. No doubt a time had come when the intimacy between Allende and Señor Brody's wife had helped to break up her marriage, but I had the impression that Señor Brody was not an embittered ex-husband. He had continued to support the left over the years.

My suspicion proved to be correct; the back door to the Brody house was open, and the disarray inside suggested that the premises had been ransacked even more thoroughly than the Allende household. In the kitchen there was a fetid odor as of a kitty box that hadn't been emptied for days. In the sink there were stacked unwashed dishes stained with dried egg and sticky marmalade. Flies were everywhere. We proceeded down the hall which ran through the center of the house, rooms opening to each side. In the dining room a feisty cat jumped from the table, snarling at us as we entered. We observed the broken liquor bottles on the buffet and floor but could not judge with certainty if many items had been stolen.

As we moved on towards the living room, we were speculating on the wisdom of removing some of the more valuable things, like the electrical goods, for safekeeping. I remember the scene distinctly: Mother was walking ahead of me, gazing absently about and gesturing vaguely as she talked. I had stopped at the umbrella stand in the hall, surprised to see there a number of burlap sacks which perhaps the pillagers had left behind. As I turned towards Mother, I realized—even before I saw her—that she was mute and perfectly immobile, like a statue. With one arm extended and her lips slightly parted, she reminded me of pictures I had seen of the Romans of Pompeii who had been surprised by the torrents of lava from Mt. Vesuvius—baked eternally into their grotesque effigies of the living.

Even before I reached her, I knew that she was looking at a dead man. He was slouched on the sofa, as if he had fallen from a sitting position, a trickle of blood dried upon his chin. In less than ten seconds I ascertained all that I was ever to know about him.

Without a word or signal we both turned and left the way we had come. Mother was determined that I shouldn't sleep at Allende's house any longer, and we walked to the nearest public phone to advise Señor Gossens of the grave news. The phone in the Allende residence had been disconnected.

It was about four by then, and children were on their way home from school, carrying heavy book bags and clutching their jackets to keep out a chill spring wind. Near the phone was a bakery where some girls stopped to buy fresh buns which they ate there, without butter, as they watched the owner's TV set, which was tuned in to a popular Mexican soap opera. As I waited for my connection, I kept rereading compulsively the sign above the bakery counter: "Don't get discouraged! The disintegration of many years isn't repaired in months."

Señor Gossens was disturbed by what I told him of the plundered houses. (I didn't mention the dead man since all the phones were tapped.) He implied by his tone and abruptness that he held me somehow to blame for the jimmied window, and although I resented it, perhaps in some inexplicable way I thought so, too, for I agreed to spend one more night in the house, giving Señor Gossens a chance to make other arrangements.

Since I was afraid of further trouble, Monica spent the night with me, sending Maria Paz to Mother's. We secured the house as well as we could before retiring to our beds where we lay awake for hours.

And who could describe the night terrors of Santiago during September, when helicopters with their endless droning swooped systematically down to this house and that, in every section of the city, as if about to land on a roof? In the slums it was worse: a knock at the door after curfew meant that the *milicos* were conducting a search. Everyone had to get up then, while the house was torn apart and personal belongings stolen; men were either shot on the spot or led off to jail, frequently never to be seen again, although some bodies were recovered floating down the Mapocho River or abandoned in gutters. Even in our section of the city there were occasional shots, the screech of brakes, and the staccato of running feet on pavement.

We determined to move out the next day when Monica had finished teaching, about four, but she was delayed. It was almost six when she arrived, and since she had no babysitter, she had locked Maria Paz in her apartment.

"Aren't you afraid to leave her alone like that?" I asked.

"There's really no alternative," Monica replied. "I left strict orders that she is neither to go out nor to open the door to strangers. You know how obedient she is."

We made a quick survey of the house, seeing that everything was in order, and debated about how far our responsibility extended towards the dead man at the Brody residence. Our concern turned out to be gratuitous, for when we returned to where the corpse had lain, only a few spots of blood testified to the violence which had occurred there. I was as frightened by this mysterious circumstance as I had been the day before by our discovery of the victim.

In order to meet the eight o'clock curfew, we had to hurry. By seven-thirty the car was loaded up, except for one of my suitcases, which we were about to fetch. It was then I noticed that a police car, which had slowly passed the house, had turned around and was headed back towards us. Inside were two *carabineros*, the ones who were to make our lives a hell.

We stood near the curb watching them as they moved towards us; they were carrying machine guns. The taller of the two had a heavy, flat-footed walk and stiff way of moving, which suggested rheumatism or arthritis or some other scourge of old age, but his face was extraordinarily young looking and characterless, as if since babyhood he had been preserved in mothballs. When he removed his cap, his full head of gray hair was visible, and his little pointed ears, like an elf's. His eyes, which puckered when he smiled, reminded me somehow of the dates stuffed with fondant that my mother makes at Christmas time, for the bottom and top lids moved towards each other, leaving beween them an opening of an indeterminable color. His nose was short and straight, his lips full, and his teeth yellow and widely spaced. This was Señor Juan Andini.

The younger of the two, Mario Veras, was very dark; indeed, with his swarthy skin and his stocky, short-legged body, he seemed more Mexican than Chilean. One of his cheeks was stippled with brown spots, like an over-ripe banana, and when he spoke, one could see that he was missing a front tooth. Although his eyes were quite large and round, his sleepy lids, which fell over them like awnings, gave them an elongated appearance.

The younger man seemed to be in charge. He looked from one of us to the other, uncertain whom to address. Finally he said to the space between us, "Hey, dolly, what's your name?"

Perhaps if Monica had not been there I could have pulled myself together and made a suitable reply. But in the face of the policeman's insulting tone, and in view of the time—it was now 7:45—all I could do was fret about our situation and look to Monica to get us home by eight.

By mid-September everyone in Chile had learned that people on the street after curfew are shot on sight.

She squared her shoulders and raised her chin slightly. "You are perhaps referring to my sister, Señora Eva Maria Soledad Araya y Thibault. I who address you am Señora Monica Maria Consuelo Araya y Thibault."

When Monica assumes her superior tone, she can intimidate anyone. With her blend of pale good looks and a booming, well-accented voice, she seems too fearless and well-born to be treated without deference. The two policemen seemed abashed, as if suddenly conscious of their origins. Yet they were suspicious of us, and, as if to encourage themselves, they lifted their machine guns slightly.

"You will have to explain what you are doing at Allende's old home," said the younger man.

"My sister has been overseeing it at the request of Señor Gossens, who has been appointed by the honorable *Junta Militar* to handle the Allende estate."

He paused. "Do you have written orders from the military authorities?"

Monica glanced at me. "No," I said, "but here in my purse I have a letter from Señor Gossens which will clarify the situation. Here, I'll find it for you."

"It will not be sufficient," Señor Veras replied. "We'll have to take you in for questioning."

I felt as a prisoner must feel when he is about to face a firing squad. I knew that once we were in custody and my former arrest was known, we would be held indefinitely. In the meantime Maria Paz was locked in Monica's apartment, without a phone, with strict orders neither to leave nor to open the door. In my panic I felt an irrational urge to run away or to scream. Yet as I started to protest, it seemed as though I would vomit.

Monica was cajoling the dark one, addressing him as "Señor

Veras," when I stepped back slightly, my hand over my mouth. The older man appeared to be concerned. "Is there something wrong?" he asked.

"I'm suddenly sick to my stomach," I replied, "and now I have the hiccoughs." They were deep, painful hiccoughs that took my breath away. I wasn't sure whether they were spontaneous or I had induced them.

"What's wrong with that girl?" asked Señor Veras when he observed that Señor Andini had begun to pound my back. "Hiccoughs? I know a perfect cure." And assuming a warmth towards me now that I was indisposed, he instructed me to sit on the curb with my head below my knees. "There, you see now," he beamed. "Juan, you old fool, hasn't anybody taught you how to cure a case of hiccoughs? You were pounding that girl as if she were a fattened pig." He laughed loudly, immensely pleased with himself.

In that humiliating posture I then listened to Monica giving one of the outstanding performances of a lifetime. As she flattered, begged, and fluttered about in feminine fashion, I could almost feel the currents of attraction which she was extending in Veras' direction. Her voice was rich with emotions of gratitude toward this clever fellow who had cured my hiccoughs and whom, she implied, she would like to know better. By the time she had discreetly dropped a few names (the fathers of some of her favorite students at the Harriet B. School were the only civilians in the government), the two *carabineros* were prepared to put off the unpleasant business until another day and to escort us home, since it was past eight.

We quickly put Maria Paz to bed and wondered how long it would be until they were back. Monica bet on one hour and I on two, but it wasn't until eleven-thirty that we heard a knock on the door.

"*Ce commence*," I said. "How much will we have to pay for the favor they've done us?"

They brought their machine guns in with them and laid them by their feet. We watched curiously their reactions to our apartment, for we had carefully prepared for them, trying to create an environment in which sexual assault would be unthinkable. "We must make them uncomfortable," Monica had said, "as if they were in an unfamiliar and therefore threatening place." We had taken from the shelves our heaviest and most tedious books, leaving them on the coffee table: one was photographs of the Elgin marbles and the other an enormous historical atlas. On the table where we dine we had set up Monica's typewriter, hastily inserting a page from an old report she had once written on "Benjamin Franklin and the Spirit of American Pragmatism." Near the typewriter was stacked a Spanish version of *Poor Richard's Almanack* and the American Declaration of Independence. For music, we picked the driest, most unyielding compositions we could think of, though nothing too modern, some of Bach's partitas for unaccompanied violin. Although we had to offer our guests something to drink, we claimed to have only the sweet, sticky liqueurs which are hard to take in quantity. All suggestions of softness and comfort like sofa pillows and footstools we had removed. We expected our best defense, however, to be the child sleeping in the next room. We left Maria Paz' door slightly ajar and planted dolls and other toys here and there as a reminder of her presence.

That first night Juan and Mario were almost appealing in their efforts to strike the right tone in a situation which was in some ways as trying for them as for us. We were fairly certain they were supposed to be patrolling somewhere; they seemed to glance nervously at their watches and then at their guns, simultaneously fretting about and ignoring whatever instructions they had received. There were pauses in the conversation when they couldn't think of what to say. We encouraged them to show us photos of their wives and children.

But they managed to overcome their feelings of insecurity as the night wore on, making it clear to us that they intended to insist on the rights they saw themselves as having over us. After a few drinks they changed the record, putting on dance music. Juan ("the Italian" as Monica and I called him privately) took me for his partner and Mario ("the Mexican") took Monica.

They left at 5 A.M., establishing a pattern which was to last almost a week. Monica would arise at seven to get herself and Maria Paz off to school by eight. I spent my days like Scheherazade in the saga of the Arabian Nights, thinking up ways to avoid, night by night, an unwanted destiny.

Each time that they appeared at our door about 11 or 12 P.M., we were a little more rude than the time before; but gesturing meaningfully with their machine guns, they made their way in. They brought their own liquor now, all of which had been seized in houseraids. As they became drunker, they became more amorous, but we were saved by one circumstance: since Maria Paz was asleep in the room I shared with her, only one bedroom remained. Although each of them would eye it frequently, neither of them was willing to suggest taking turns in it. Monica and I felt almost amused and grateful that, even in the case of sexual blackmail, some amenities seemed to prevail—some romance is necessary.

Everyone understood the situation perfectly; the next step would be for one of the policemen to come alone. When the bell rang early on a Tuesday night, about nine, I somehow knew it was for me. I shuddered and clenched my teeth.

"The Italian's" eyes were bloodshot, and his walk even heavier than usual; perhaps he had had to fortify himself for his adventure. He said nothing; after depositing the machine gun in its normal place, he grabbed me tightly and kissed me hard. I noted mechanically that his mouth still tasted of his dinner, charcoal-roasted pork marinated in chili sauce and garlic. He reeked of wine.

"Let me close the door to the bedroom; Maria Paz is sleeping," I said. When I returned, he was sitting on the sofa, evidently expecting me to join him there.

I didn't, however. As if I were alone in the room, I began to undress, removing first my shoes and stockings, then my blouse. I felt neither fear nor remorse; I merely wanted to be free of this onerous obligation, free to sleep soundly and innocently like an old woman long widowed. But as I began to unhook my bra, Juan suddenly looked amazed, as if I were shocking him with a lewd performance.

"Hey, what are you doing?" he demanded roughly.

"Let's not play any more games," I replied. "My body: that's what you're here for, isn't it? That's what these night visits with machine guns are about? Well, you're in luck tonight; I'm tired of resisting you, let's get it over with."

He narrowed his eyes at me and his face reddened. "Whore!" he snarled, and he slapped me hard across the face. I staggered slightly from the blow and clapped my mouth to keep from crying out. Juan threw my blouse at me, as if to indicate that I was to put it on.

And then began the part of the evening that seemed ludicrous and obscene, when Juan, his voice shaking, his eyes brimming with tears of self-pity, foisted upon me an intimacy which I hadn't asked for, which repelled me. He had had the ordinary human measure of disappointments and resentments, but whereas I normally feel touched when people confide in me their pitiful histories, in Juan's case I felt embarrassed, as if in its nakedness his emotional life was misshapen and unsightly. As he talked, he clutched my hand in his sweaty palm, as if to wring from my physical warmth a reassuring response. I would have preferred that he rape me and then leave me alone rather than burden me with a knowledge of himself that I feared I could never forget.

Yet even in my rage at the role he had placed me in (and surely after his confession he would either loathe me or adore me?), with part of my mind I listened to him, registering impersonally like a ticker tape those utterances which seemed to have some bearing on my own situation. I had inadvertently treated him "like a *milico*," as he put it. In the spate of days since the coup, his self-image had been severely shaken by the contempt and fear he read in the eyes of everyone he met, even his dear ones. His wife had been hoarding food for some neighbors who are in hiding; when he quite by accident stumbled upon her stash, she screamed, as if she expected him to murder her.

He turned his face away from me and continued. "Maybe I haven't told you about how I play soccer. Been playing for years. Every Sunday afternoon the boys from the *barrio* play in a field that we fixed up over by the dump. I don't mind saying that I'm passable. Only my brother Jorge is better. He took after my mother's family: all the Tapias are good runners." He addressed the window as he spoke, as if I were suddenly an intruder in his private conversation with his ideal image of himself.

"We've had some good games over the years," he continued. "And when we have a chance we go to the professional tournaments. I've seen Caszely, I've seen Elias Figueroa play. I was there when Colo-Colo beat Argentina last May. You might say I grew up around ballparks; that's where I get my fun in life. When I'm too old to play myself, I've always said, just let me sit in the National Stadium and watch the big leaguers." Then he frowned, remembering as I did the new uses to which the *milicos* had put the famous playing field.

Then, almost breaking down, he said, "But now I can't play with the boys anymore. They don't come right out and say it, but I can tell they don't trust me. Last Sunday when I walked over to the playing field with them, I saw a slogan scrawled across the fence as big as life, 'Down with the murderous Junta!' Nobody would refer to it, everybody kept his eyes down, as if even mentioning it to me might mean big trouble.

"I went to a pro game at the University Stadium. I had to wear my uniform; it's the rule. Just as I got to my seat, there was a call over the microphone for Señor Andini. I thought they might mean me, though there are a lot of other Andinis in Santiago. And as I walked across the gravel towards the office, I could hear hissing from every direction, whispers: 'Death to the Fascist military men! Death to the military pigs!' "

He sobbed. "I could fire on them for that, you know. Insulting the Armed Forces and Police is punishable by death. But I tell you, there were hundreds of them, I couldn't spot any of them for sure. And anyway, these are the people I grew up with—my kind of people, you understand? Later when some children had to be chased off the field by some *cara-bineros* who were on duty, there were shouts from every direction. 'Eat shit, you murderers! Eat shit, you murderers!' It made the captain on duty furious; he called some reinforcements and they surrounded the place. But it didn't do any good. No one would tell who in the crowd had done the shouting. You can't arrest ten thousand people. Everyone was snickering and laughing up their sleeve."

There were endless stories of a similar type, none of which I remember except one, the last he told—the one that touched me profoundly. I have since dreamed about it sometimes on the rare occasions when I sleep.

"The main thing we had to do right after the coup," he began, "was to search the slums for arms. It was always the same. We would drive up in military vehicles and big trucks, maybe a hundred or two of us, sirens screaming and searchlights circling everywhere. We would go from door to door, arresting almost all the men right away (we knew who the leaders were though; later we would let the 'sheep' go, after we'd given them a good scare). We'd tell the women and children to line up in parallel lines in front of their houses and then to lie down on their stomachs. If there were any funny business, if, say, they lifted their heads, they'd be shot. And as they lay there, we searched from door to door."

He paused, as if moved by what he was about to say.

"One morning we rounded up most of the people in the *callampa* 'Mao Tse-tung' (the one that's been renamed 'Adam Smith'). The men had been taken away and the women were lying down with their kids. It had rained the night before, and although we tried to find a dry spot for them to settle down on, I could tell they were resentful because it was wet and cold. The searching had already begun when I saw about a block down the way a *carabinero* arguing with a woman who was still standing. I couldn't think why he'd argue; he could hit her or kill her, if it came to that. I went to investigate.

"She was a big, burly country woman. As I approached her from the back, I could see the veins in her bare legs; they looked all purple and sore, those legs. They made me think of my mother; she couldn't get around when she was old. But this woman was still young, I could tell by the smoothness of the skin on her forehead and by her teeth; she still had almost all of them. She was holding a baby in her arms, and from the look of her stomach she might have been expecting another one.

" 'What's the problem here?' I said loudly as I approached. And I raised my gun a little to show who's in charge. 'Why aren't you lying down with the others?'

"The woman turned towards me the fiercest face I've ever seen on a human body. With her strands of black hair flying every which way in the wind and her clenched teeth, I'll swear she seemed to be foaming at the mouth—she was more like a hyena than a woman. 'Get down,' I commanded 'or I'll shoot!'

"She didn't move. She replied without a bit of fear or hesitation, 'I will not lie down! You see this sleeping babe in my arms? You can murder me if you like, and you can bash the child's skull in with the butt of your gun, you can rip the unborn infant from my womb, but I will *never* lie down at the orders of you murderous traitors!' And then she spit on the ground."

I thought it was a heartbreaking story. I could barely stand to listen. When he concluded, I felt half-crazy from all the evil that has been let loose in our land.

"Well," I finally asked. "What then? Did you shoot her?"

I feared he was going to strike me again, but the object of his resentment quickly changed its target. He buried his face in his hands and cried a drunken cry.

He seemed oblivious of my presence. "When you go," I said, "please lock the front door."

Then I went to bed, leaving him alone on the sofa, his toes resting on his machine gun.

2
_____

We had no night visits for the rest of the week. By Friday we had almost relaxed, thinking that Juan's miserable experience with me on Tuesday had discouraged both of our admirers. We were mistaken. When Monica answered the door on Saturday afternoon about two, she saw Juan standing alone, this time without his machine gun.

"Well, you just missed Eva," she said. "I don't know when she'll be back. What a pity."

"Never mind," he replied somewhat sheepishly. "I just thought I'd drop by for a few minutes. Maybe we could share a glassful of the *chicha* Mario and I left here the last time."

Monica led him into the living room as if he were an old friend. She correctly surmised that he had something to tell her.

"I guess you've noticed that Mario and I haven't been around," he began. "Our area's been changed. We're working out in San Bernardo now."

"Ah, they've caught on about your wicked little parties on the job," Monica teased him. "You see, you talk too much to your friends: now they are so jealous of your good times that they denounce you."

He blushed. "No, no. It's a general policy. It's not good to keep policemen on the same beat for too long. Sometimes they get friendly with the neighborhood." He blushed again. Monica laughed.

"Well, I hope you don't find the change too unpleasant," she said. And as she filled his glass, it occurred to her that he was seeking to make amends for having forced himself on us. He seemed innocent then, his youthful face spread with smiles as she flattered and amused him. She wondered if he would be willing to perform a small favor as a way of expiating for his bad behavior.

"You know, Juan," she said, "we do have one little problem that you could help us with."

He beamed.

"The day that you—ah—stopped us as we left the Allende residence, we were moving out Eva's belongings. We hadn't quite finished when you drove up. So one suitcase of hers is still there. Maybe you can understand our reluctance to return for it—we wouldn't like any more misunderstandings. But perhaps you could go with me now...."

"Well, why not?" he asked. "But do you still have a key?"

"I do. Señor Gossens said he would send someone for it, but we are still waiting."

When they arrived, the place seemed subtly changed, as if someone might be there. But when they rang the bell, there was no response, so Monica opened the door and walked directly up the stairs to the bedroom where I had left the suitcase. When she came down, Juan was at the entry to the kitchen, about to descend the stairs leading to the basement.

"Did you know there's a light on down there?" he said. "You girls are running up somebody's electricity bill."

Inexplicably Monica's heart began to pound. The bare lightbulb from the basement cast an inhuman greenish haze as far as the top of the stairs, where she was standing, and she felt afraid.

"Never mind, Juan," she called to him. "The switch is here; I can get it myself. No need to trouble yourself."

But he was already pacing about below. She heard him walk from one corner to another, and suddenly stop.

"Juan, what's the matter?" she called, but for an answer there was only the sound of a heavy box being dragged across the cement. She decided to descend.

Juan had torn off the lid of a wooden crate and was now sitting back examining the contents. Monica could see nothing, but there was a strange odor, almost like a high school chemistry lab. Lichen was growing at the base of the walls, and as Monica bent towards Juan and the box, she felt a chill.

"Bullets," he said as he fingered some heavy objects in his

hand. He looked at Monica in a suspicious way, as if making an accusation.

Her voice cracked. "Bullets? But that's incredible! When Eva and I were down here before, we didn't see any boxes that might be filled with bullets. . . . "

"I'll have to report it," he said. "This is quite a find, just what the authorities are looking for. And in Allende's house too; it will be written up in the newspapers."

He looked at her cruelly, straight in the eyes, as if to assure her that he was aware of the implications.

"Juan, you mustn't," she almost whispered. "Eva was the last one to live here. If she's reported for illegal possession of arms, she'll be tortured, or worse." She felt herself trembling.

His smile was almost a grimace. "A soldier's got his duty. There would be plenty of trouble for me if I didn't report it."

Monica implored him. "Juan, it's Eva we're talking about. How could anyone suspect her of hiding arms? Who could be more tender, more fragile. . . . "

Suddenly a dark look flashed in his eyes, a crasis of lust and anger which, though new to Monica, she instinctively recognized. He wiped his mouth with the back of his hand. "She treated me like a *milico*."

Monica gazed straight at him, as if trying to hypnotize him; or perhaps she was conjuring up all the dark powers she could feel in the dank basement to come to her aid.

Then, with the artful innuendo of a practiced procuress, she said, "I'm sure that you and Eva could work something out."

There was a long pause as the two of them, kneeling on their heels over the box of ammunition, staring intently at each other, listened to the ominous silence and to each other's breathing.

"You tell her to be waiting for me at nine—alone," he finally said.

3

As I waited for him in the darkened apartment, I stared through the windowpanes at the fountains in the patio below. The spatter of rain into their depths was clearly visible in the streetlight, as were the oleander bushes, and the wisteria climbing the covered walk.

When he arrived, neither of us spoke. I led him to the bedroom which had been prepared with clean sheets and incense and a candle burning. I had dressed myself in my best robe, like a sacrificial victim.

He undressed unceremoniously, hanging his clothes over the back of a chair, and as I waited, I experienced—as I had during my interrogation—the curious sense of having become disembodied—as if my soul were perched upon the dresser or windowsill watching disinterestedly the girl upon the bed with the heavy-limbed man. Towards the male stranger, I felt neither antipathy nor affection: he seemed almost void of personality, like the countless men and women and children I had passed on the streets that afternoon, neither better nor worse. It was as if, at the last, I was to be deprived of the catharsis of despising this colony of differentiated cells, this sack of sperm and marrow and sputum that was about to satisfy himself on me.

He climbed into the bed and quickly threw himself on me. He kissed me hard, biting my lips with his teeth. He ran his hands down my body a few times and then, without further ceremony, he penetrated me, pushing and shoving as if it were a hard job. I was evidently sobbing, for the stranger suddenly turned his head towards me and barked, "Whore! Turn off those goddamned tears!" Rubbing my palms across my wet cheeks and nose, I took note for the first time of the reality of This Other, the one who, even as he finally slaked his lust, was taking little pleasure in it. And I suddenly realized how it was with him, what contempt he had felt for himself before he had had what he wanted from me, and how he foresaw the way it would be afterwards, the sad memory of it, the way it would assail him unexpectedly even during his happiest moments.

I exerted myself not to cry. I thought of how it is with all of us; we sprinkle hopes about us in our youth, like seeds whose fruits we anticipate gathering in the future, never imagining how, even if they ripen, they will disappoint us. From the vantage of this bitter moment I looked back to the young girl I had been once, even four months ago. First my father's death, then Miguel's assassination, then the eruptions of violence which reduced my civilization to memory and rubble. How could one account for such a calamity? There had been, only a few songs ago, a conviction I had assumed lightly—not even earnestly, yet joyfully—that at last Justice would come, that exploiters would be persuaded by the march of History and by our own show of solidarity to surrender their monopoly over our means of livelihood, to which they permit us access on their own terms; that they would rejoin us, not as exploiters but as fellow humans who must toil for their bread. I had put my faith in the cause which, in our time, was most abundant with human warmth and gentleness and life.

How mysterious the road from that to this! Oh, the contemptible good fortune of those who, in their youth, look only to their own self-interest!

I heard the stranger's weight as he stepped upon the floor: he was done with me. With immense relief I clenched my eyes shut, breathed deeply, and tried to relax. And inexplicably there appeared to me the image I had so often sought these last weeks but almost always failed to find: my father's face. But he looked much younger than in his last days, and brimming with a vigor I had barely remembered in him. "Papa, papa," Monica and I cajoled him, "please, you must allow us to wade in the waves. See how lovely the foam is!"

"My dears," his voice boomed, "people do not wade in the winter. How outrageous you are!" But even as he said it, we were splashing his face with ocean water, and he was laughingly removing our shoes and socks and rolling our pant legs to our knees. As we ran along the shore, daring the surf to approach us, we looked back towards him and he moved towards us, hands extended and bare-legged, ready to join us in our adventure.

There was a click as the stranger let himself out through the front door.

Monica
November 1973

Men make their own history, but they do not
make it just as they please; they do not make
it under circumstances chosen by themselves,
but under circumstances directly encountered,
given, and transmitted from the past.
——KARL MARX, *The Eighteenth Brumaire
of Louis Bonaparte*

Monica was administering a test on the Spanish conquest of
Chile to the tenth graders when her attention was diverted by
the "ping" of Señora Muñoz' ring as she tapped at the glass
on the door. "You are wanted on the phone," she said. She
looked at Monica accusingly, as if this untimely call were
further evidence in a case against her, a case whose precise
details were known only to Señora Muñoz.

"I can take the call later," said Monica. "There's no need
to interrupt my class for it."

"Never mind; it's too late now. I'll supervise your test for you until you get back."

As Monica walked to the principal's office and picked up the phone, she attempted to breathe deeply and compose herself; she regarded the telephone less as a friendly lifeline to the outside world than as a potential threat to her precarious inner peace.

"Hello," she said, "this is Monica Araya speaking."

"Hello."

There was a pause, as if the caller were unreasonably expecting her to begin the conversation, and it took a few seconds for Monica to take in that peculiar circumstance as well as the odd twangy quality of the voice, almost like a foreigner's. Then she smiled in pleasant surprise. "Benjamin Willing!" she exclaimed.

He seemed to stutter and stammer in the odd, bashful way he had sometimes, and Monica felt overwhelmed with protective feelings towards him. "You're a wretch not to have called me in over a year, but I'm glad you decided to mend your ways."

"You're a hard person to catch, Monica. You don't have a phone at home, and it doesn't do any good to write, of course, since intercity letters never arrive. I hesitated to bother you at work, but since I'm calling not just for myself but also for another friend, I feel less guilty than usual."

"Which other friend?"

"Hector Verdugo."

There was a momentary pause. Monica felt uneasy, but she could not verbalize her fears since the phones might be tapped. Ben also seemed to be choosing his words carefully. "I can imagine your surprise," he said. "Hector got back just a few days after the military pronouncement. He had been in Spain. He's been asked to assume the directorship of the Chilean Historical and Geographical Institute."

"How splendid for him!" Monica in some inexplicable way did feel pleased for Hector at the same time that she despised him as an opportunist. Evidently, she thought, he is coming out as a *momio*. Under Frei he had passed himself off as a Christian Democrat in order to put himself in a position to pocket some of the American dollars that were flowing into Chile for educational reform.

"His father is having a dinner party in Hector's honor, and both you and I are invited. When Hector told me he couldn't contact you, I said I'd try. I hope you'll come, Monica. Anna isn't able to, and I would be pleased to escort the most beautiful and charming guest."

"Of course, I'd love to," Monica said; and at the same time she was thinking, "That was handsome of Ben; he's willing to ally himself with me in a circle of *momios*." She had always felt confidence in their relationship, but this was a degree of loyalty she hadn't counted on.

He arranged to meet her in a few days for the event. As they were about to hang up she obeyed a sudden impulse to reassure herself. "You know, Benjamin, I can't help being surprised that Hector invited me." She stopped, confident that Ben understood her.

"Don't be silly, Monica. Hector holds your friendship in high esteem. I think he was as close to you and me as he was to anybody back in '67 and '68, back when we were all working in adult education. You remember how absurdly pleased with ourselves we were when we wrote our program on rural poverty and malnutrition. Then when it was rejected, we had the additional pleasure of cheering one another up."

"Yes, I suppose you're right," said Monica.

"And, well, now I remember! Hector was best man for your wedding, wasn't he? He seemed to regard himself as a nervous marriage broker to you and Carlos. When you broke up, he wrote me. I was in San Francisco then. I've never forgotten what he said. He said, 'People had assumed that their marriage, like other Chileans', would be a union of boom and echo, but it was instead the impossible mating of two roars.'"

Monica gave herself up to a deep and unrestrained laughter. "Did he really say that? What a character he is! Thanks for telling me. I feel better already."

"It's great to hear you laugh, Monica. It's infectious."

"Well, if I don't get back to my class soon, I won't have anything to laugh about. I'm already on everybody's blacklist."

"Not on mine."

"You're the same as ever, thank goodness. I'm glad you called."

2

At one Monica walked to Aunt Sara's for lunch, where Eve was hiding out for a few days. They had agreed not to talk about Eve's troubles around their relatives, but most of them seemed to know the grim details. "That unspeakable policeman called," her mother had said to Monica the day before. "He's waiting for Eva. I don't know what's going to happen." Her mother's eyes had welled with tears. "Eva, why must it be Eva? The child seems as vulnerable as spring."

Yet in some ways both Monica and her mother were surprised at the inner resources Eve had to draw on. She had always been the baby, the fragile flower; yet now she managed to sustain herself on a portion of sorrow bitter even for seemingly hardier souls.

Eve looked thin and wiry as she sank into the springy depths of Uncle Max's favorite old chair. With her dark, Semitic-looking eyes, now deeply lined with blue, and the headscarf and big earrings which she preferred in good weather, she reminded Monica of a young Gypsy who might swoop from lethargy into an ecstasy born of despair and back again, much to the spectators' wonder and, possibly, envy. In her glances, the slight downward turn of her mouth, she suggested the *menosprecio de la vida*, the classic contempt for life, of those who have passed through hope and landed on the other side. "Eve!" the silent cry caught in Monica's throat.

There was a vase of white and purple lilacs on the luncheon table, and Monica and Eve found themselves lingering there over coffee and fruit long after Aunt Sara had departed. Monica glanced at her watch; in an hour she would have to be back at the Harriet B. School for a meeting. She decided to tell Eve about Benjamin Willing's call.

"You will never guess who has invited me to a party," she began. "Hector Verdugo."

"Hector! I thought he left Chile the week Allende was elected."

"He did, but he's back, and he's going to be a VIP with the new military government. His father is using the excuse of his return to throw a party."

"It will be one of those affairs with nine glasses for each guest and the smell of French perfume everywhere," said Eva.

They were both remembering the style of life those Chileans had enjoyed who had been on an American payroll. They had lived big even as they had spoken piously about the urgent reforms they were effecting. She had despised them, Monica remembered, with the uncompromising hardness of youth. She had berated Hector to his face for his enthusiastic aping of everything foreign, from the iced drinks to the big cars. Even the institution of the cocktail party, followed by a long dinner, had struck her as an unfortunate American innovation. The traditional Chilean way, she was fond of saying, was intimate and familiar, with the voices of children and nurses and senile old people, and unexpected company dropping in. It was, ironically, the one thing that she and Hector's father, Julio César Verdugo, agreed on, for Julio César had made his reputation as an intensely nationalistic historian, and he disapproved of his son's alliance with the Americans. They had never broken over it, of course; Hector was a master at straddling contradictions.

"Aren't you surprised he's invited you?" asked Eva. "Why would he want to parade his acquaintance with you in front of his *momio* friends?"

"I wonder. Maybe he is proud of his magnanimity. He

wants to assert a certain independence of action even as he joins the Fascists. He's probably anticipating the gasps of surprise that will escape his guests as he introduces me. I'm to be the red cape before the bull."

"Why did you agree to go?"

"I don't know. I suspect it's because Benjamin Willing urged me to. He's such a good friend; I feel safe with him. It's hard to imagine being threatened if he is at my elbow."

"Benjamin Willing: I remember him. I met him once at the Moneda. He attended an official reception for Chilean educators when everyone was debating the government's educational reform bill. He was standing by the table with the hors d'oeuvres when I was introduced to him. All I remember about him is that when a waiter asked him what he wanted to drink, he replied 'tomato juice.' The waiter seemed to think this request one cross too many to bear. He rolled his eyes upwards and mumbled 'Damned *gringos!*' under his breath. I think he had to send out for the tomato juice."

"That sounds like Benjamin. He hardly drinks at all. He says his only sin is pride. You know, I've really missed him. Once I quit working at UCADULTOS, I never ran into him. He used to urge me to visit his place in Villa Inez de Suarez, but I don't care much for his wife."

"What's she like?"

"She's all bone and gristle, with a permanently pleated forehead, though she is not much over thirty-seven or thirty-eight."

Pushing her coffee cup away and resting her elbows on the table, Eve gave Monica a penetrating look. "Is he interested in you, Monica?"

"How can you ask? What a dumb question."

"Well, most men are, you know. Why should he be different?"

"To tell the truth, he's kind of strange. He's, well, spiritual. Religious. He has a weird way of mixing up talk about beauty and truth and beatitude with protein intake and neighborhood tribunals. I like it. So I excuse him for his popery. He's crazy. but he's so gentle—not like other people. And now, after what I've seen since September 11...."

"Maybe you're interested in him?"

Monica felt exasperated. "You don't seem to understand at all. We're talking about a very special friendship. Ben is the kind of person you can rely on no matter what. In fact, I'm getting an idea: why didn't I think of it before? Ben could prove to be your Guardian Angel, Eve. He's the one who could get you out of Chile. He's got contacts; he can visit the embassies. I'm going to give him a call tomorrow."

3

When Monica returned to her apartment in the late afternoon, she found a telegram pushed under her door. "Juan José is the proud father of twins," she read. "I'll see you in ten days." It bore Felipe's signature.

The message was what she had been expecting. Even before she gave careful thought to the code, she was certain it said that Carlos had gone to Argentina. Then she mentally reviewed the list of code words which she and Felipe, having agreed upon, never committed to writing. It consisted mainly of twenty-five proper names, all of which referred to Carlos. "Juan" meant "Carlos has asked for money"; "José" translated as "Carlos has escaped across the border to Argentina."

She removed her shoes and set the kettle on to boil. She loved the coziness of the kitchen and the view from the window of palms and cherry trees five stories below. It was impossible not to take comfort from that peaceful and benign setting.

It was curious, she reflected, that since the coup she had not felt anxious about Carlos' safety. And as so often happened with her, a suspicion that she felt vindicated by her husband's difficulties hovered over her. She fretted about it, but by the time she sat down to her tea, she felt free of its dark shadow. She knew that these occasional clouds of self-doubt were as close as she would get to a sustained probing of her psyche. That sort of spiritual enterprise she was unsympathetic with; it seemed egocentric and futile. People should be judged, she claimed, less by what they think and feel (so difficult to discern) than by what they do.

By anyone's standards it seemed to her that Felipe came out very well. Not only did he fill her life and Maria Paz' with loving kindness; he also never faltered in his strange friendship with Carlos who, since he refused to grant Monica an annulment, prevented Felipe and her from marrying. It was Felipe whom Carlos had kept in contact with since he had gone underground with the MIR. Carlos would make his way as far as Concepción three or four times a year, bearing gifts for Maria Paz and vague suggestions as to his whereabouts and activities. Occasionally he asked for money or left messages to be forwarded to his comrades in Santiago. It was a dangerous business for Felipe, but he never complained; and although he seemed to regard Carlos' revolutionary activity with disdain, they shared some sort of trust that went deeper even than shared convictions.

Sometimes Monica was reminded by a casual remark from a friend, perhaps, or simply by observing the lives of others, that hers was an exceptional situation. And if she had grown accustomed to it, had learned even to cherish her solitude, her financial independence, the essential femaleness of her universe of Mother, daughter, sister, and school, such contentment had been won at a cost too terrible to be thought about. She glanced at her wedding portrait which still rested on the bookshelf. How young she had been then, and how infatuated with the handsome young man at her side, tall and slightly negroid looking, with his kinky hair and tawny skin. He had been a member of Chile's Olympic swimming team in those days, and she had gone with him sometimes to practices, immensely pleased with his kinetic perfection, the dreamy and limpid movement of his powerful body, which, in the water, took on the greenish patina of old bronze. His mind had displayed the same fluidity. How could she have failed to love him?

Yet within six months she knew that she had lost him, and shortly after Maria Paz' birth he had left her for good. She remembered vividly being summoned in the middle of the night to the Military Hospital, where he had been taken, with six or eight other *Miristas*, after he had been wounded while robbing, in Robin Hood fashion, a supermarket. She couldn't understand; she was full of contempt. She had sputtered at him, "You have the ruthlessness and the single-mindedness of a missionary priest, but not the selflessness. If you are going to abandon Maria Paz and me to be a guerrilla, you should at least give me an annulment!" It was the only time that he had broken down. "Can't you understand," he rasped, "that now that I am leaving you I need the assurance of our marriage more than ever?"

And in that conviction, she thought ruefully, as well as in the others, he had never wavered, not even when he had taken another woman as his *compañera* and fathered two children by her. Monica had seen her once, at a distance, in a parked automobile, nursing a baby and staring sullenly in Monica's direction. She had suffered neither jealousy nor curiosity, yet Carlos apparently felt a need to justify himself. "You refused to join me," he said, "and a man can't live alone even when he's an outlaw."

There had been a time when she had hoped (and perhaps feared, for she was just becoming accustomed to her love for Felipe) that Carlos would abandon his guerrilla activity and support the UP in its victory. In one of her brief and infrequent meetings with him in 1971 she had declared that it was criminal for the MIR to withhold total support for the first leftist government ever to come to power in Chile. He had responded with the official MIR view already familiar to her: "The ruling classes will never surrender voluntarily," he said; "the UP could never pave an easy way to socialism even if they should try harder than they are apparently willing to. What the traditional leftist parties choose to overlook is that the conditions for revolution do not yet exist; they must be created. Armed confrontation is inevitable, and our job is to be ready for it: when you know that someone is about to strike you, you don't stand by passively and wait, do you?" And then, like the crack of a whip: "The duty of revolutionaries is to make revolution."

He had predicted again and again a long and irregular struggle for which the progressive forces should prepare with the accumulation of arms, with demonstrations, with riots, with seizures of land by peasants, with seizures of factories by workers. "That means unending violence and bloodshed," Monica had protested. Carlos had responded sadly, "It's a painful fact that for mankind to move forwards a centimeter, an enormous price must be paid." And he had added as an afterthought, "That doesn't mean that I am in favor of violence and bloodshed, of course. But there are many ways to kill people. The present social and economic structure murders half the population through malnutrition, disease, mental stagnation, despair, exposure to the elements. And it's impossible for the capitalists to improve conditions without eliminating themselves as a class."

She had felt confounded by him, but she no longer grieved. He had become to her less an absent husband than a mysterious and exasperating acquaintance out of her past. Besides, Felipe was there, if not every day, at least frequently enough to relieve her from the monotony of her round of work and obligations. "I don't think your affair with Felipe will last," Eve had predicted. "You are snobbish enough to be flattered by the attention paid you by a scion of the Medina Larraín family, even if he must work for a living, but he is too old for you, and, to be perfectly frank, his pockmarked face and his slowly graying hair aren't apt to charm you forever. Besides, his reactions to things seem too studied, too cunningly contrived." But Monica had come to appreciate his irony and wit, so different from Carlos' intense moralism; sure of himself and free from envy, Felipe was able to give of himself totally, a true aristocrat of the spirit.

Monica picked up the telegram from Felipe, reread the message, and tossed it into a wastebasket. Then she walked to the living-room windows, from which she could spot Felipe's office, almost always vacant, in the building on the corner across Providencia Avenue. In ten days he would come, he had said; but frequently his trips from Concepción were delayed by last-minute complications in his work. Her adult life, Monica mused, had been in large part a long waiting for someone who was seldom there. Yet she didn't feel sorry. She had been loved by two remarkable men. And if she had never been able to believe in the destiny for which Carlos had deserted her, she willingly conceded that he had seemingly read his stars correctly. For in two or three years of organizing peasants in the country, this "spoiled upper-class darling," as the opposition labeled the MIR's leadership, had achieved spectacular success. It was "Comandante Carlos" who had sent a shiver of fear down the backs of southern farmers, who had organized their own defense system to prevent land seizures by their peasants. It was "Comandante Carlos" whom foreign correspondents laboriously tracked down in the endless rainy forests under the MIR's control. He and his fellows, it was said, had taken more than a half million hectares, a solid area stretching along the mountainous belt, close to the Argentine border, from Cautín in the North down to Osorno. It was not an accomplishment in which she had ever wished to share, but now that the MIR along with the rest of the Chilean left was about to be hunted down and humiliated, her heart went out to her husband. She turned and studied again his face in the wedding picture, trying and failing to find in his visage the presence of the splendid young swimming star with whom she had once expected to live her life.

4
_____

Monica glanced around the ample dimensions of the Marie Antoinette to see if she could spot any informers. The teahouse was crowded, but she and Ben had chosen a table in a quiet corner. Over Ben's head Monica could see in a mirror a reflection of the waiters, dressed in black and white, rolling carts with pastries and beverages to the patrons, mostly women, who had apparently stopped by after a matinee. "I'm really glad you could make it, Benjamin," she began. "I have a favor to ask. It's about Eve."

He poured some sugar into his cup, then tea and hot water. Monica absently sipped at her coffee.

"Your sister, Eva Maria? Why do you call her Eve?"

"When you've breathed the Harriet B. School atmosphere for ten or fifteen years, your name is apt to be anglicized. 'Eve' and 'Alice' and 'Margaret' are more stylish than their Spanish cognates. It's a hard prejudice to overcome. After all this time I still prefer 'Eve' to 'Eva.' Anyway, we need your help."

"I thought that she was all right. Someone told me she had been detained but then released without charges."

"The second part is true, but she has a problem."

"Yes?"

"She needs to get out of Chile. Someone is blackmailing her sexually. Our only hope is to get her into an embassy. Once she's on foreign soil, so to speak, she can't be arrested."

Ben lifted his eyebrows, creating a row of creases across his broad forehead. "Maybe you'd better start at the beginning."

Monica suddenly felt irritated with Ben. It was absurd, she told herself, to be rude to someone from whom you were seeking a favor, but Ben's large frame, as he listened in a languid attitude, filling with apparent ease an abundance of space, seemed like an envelope for a serene and expansive psyche: no one, she thought, has the right to be so much at peace with himself under the present circumstances. She gripped the edge of the table and attempted to control herself.

"A *carabinero* has claimed her as his concubine. If she resists him he will denounce her for illegal possession of arms. It's a fantastic charge, but unfortunately there's circumstantial evidence against her."

Ben began to push his forehead with the palms of his hands, as if troubled by a buzz inside. "What did he do, move in with her?"

"It's not that bad yet. He had what he wanted from her one time, then he disappeared for a few days. We thought maybe he had lost interest. Just to be on the safe side, though, Eve was hiding out. It's a good thing she was. He came by my apartment looking for her once, and then he started calling Mother. Mother and I agreed on a story: we say Eve's in Osorno with a sick aunt. But he's suspicious. He alternates between cajoling us and threatening us. Sometimes he says he wouldn't dream of hurting Eva, his little treasure; but other times he's ready to denounce her. You get the picture. We hope to keep him in the dark about Eve's location until we can arrange for her to leave the country. My mother has been trying to make an appointment at some of the embassies, but it's impossible. You have to go there in person, and the police stop all the Chileans. Only foreigners are free to come and go. What we need is a genuine *gringo* who can thumb his nose at the guards stationed at the gates. Naturally I thought of you."

Ben put his chin on his hands and suddenly grinned. "Do you mind if I pass this one on to my wife?"

"Anna? Isn't she in Villa Inez?"

"Yes, but once or twice a week she comes into Santiago to meet with a group of Americans and Canadians. They take on cases like Eve's. They're getting so much experience now they'll soon be experts. They've got contacts. I'm sure they'd do a better job than I could."

Monica blinked and swallowed hard. "It never occurred to me that you people might be bothering yourselves about us."

"Anna is a good friend to have in an emergency."

"Will you have her call me?"

"I'll do better than that. We can meet in my office the next time Anna is in town. I'll call you at your mother's."

Ben stretched out a long arm to signal to the waiter. "The bill, please," he mouthed to a figure across the room.

"I feel apologetic. I think that I was never very nice to Anna."

"That's all right. If she succeeds in helping you, you'll be humbled. A little contrition is good for anyone."

Monica laughed a hoarse little laugh. Her eyes clouded. "Oh, Benjamin, how you always talk!" she said.

5

Monica had left her car at her mother's and walked for almost two hours, arriving at the office building across from the Hotel Carrera shortly before 7 P.M. She took the elevator to the third floor where she scanned the doors until she found the one she wanted: "Irma Freiworth, Photographer." When she let herself in some chimes tinkled pleasantly.

"I'm here for Señora Salas' order," she said to the pleasant-faced woman with blue hair who stood before the counter.

"Ah, excuse me, Señora," the lady replied with the peculiar drawl that expression assumes when enunciated by upper-class women. "I haven't had an opportunity this afternoon to make out the receipt. If you will take a seat I'll be with you in a minute."

The blue-haired woman finished with a customer and walked him to the door where they chatted briefly. She closed the door and locked it, pulled down the shade, and whispered to Monica, "Follow me."

They walked behind the sales desk and into a studio which adjoined it where various wheeled spotlights and a large camera centered on a chair situated on a dais. Then they crossed a workshop area where photos hung by clothespins from lines which spanned the room's width. Monica was vaguely aware of the photographer's paraphernalia: an enlarger, a dryer, various tubs filled with water, and everywhere the sour smell of chemicals. Finally they reached their destination, a large darkroom, lighted only by red and blue bulbs, where Monica could see three or four people sitting.

She recognized all but one. Heidi, Sister Matilde, and Pablo she had been acquainted with for years, and the last two Satur-

days she had met them at a children's matinee, where over the
candy stand and the drinking fountain, speaking in innuendos,
they had managed to make some preliminary plans for alleviating the sufferings of leftists who were being persecuted by
the military authorities. "Why are you asking me to help?"
Monica had asked, for she had never been a member of a
political party and felt unsure of herself as an activist. "Because
you've a clean record, you're not suspect," Heidi had replied.
"The rest of us have to move so cautiously that our effective-
ness is hampered."

They had agreed to keep their goals very modest, but already
Monica had found herself involved in efforts which taxed her
courage. One afternoon she had devoted to providing a disguise for a *compañera* in hiding: she had dyed the woman's
hair, darkened her skin with stains, and transported her, with
a false identity card, to a new address, where the unfortunate
lady was to set up housekeeping with her "husband," another
"clean" leftist who had agreed to the "marriage" in order to
better the disguise. Monica, who had been present when the
couple was introduced, was astonished by the cheerfulness of
the parties to this extraordinary arrangement; they never
seemed to ask themselves if the sacrifice was too great. When
she found herself fearing that she might be called upon to give
as fully, she felt diminished by her own selfishness.

The blue-haired woman, who had seated herself next to
Monica, turned to whisper to her, "The woman who is speaking was formerly an employee of the national railroads; she
was detained for two weeks."

Monica began to listen to an account which was similar to
Eve's, for the speaker had also been held in the Chile Stadium
for five days. Later she was transferred to a private house where
conditions were even worse than those Eve had described. "The
interrogators were convinced that some of my superiors were
involved in a plot to stage a coup on behalf of the U.P.,"
she was saying. "When I wouldn't give them names, I was
subjected to a gang rape. Then they inserted mice into my
vagina."

Sister Matilde interrupted. "This isn't an isolated case; we now have the name and address of the torturer who is responsible."

"We should publicize it in the outside world," one of the women said.

"Not yet; he must first be neutralized."

The nun spoke without emotion; a wordless protest made itself palpable in the peculiar mauve atmosphere of the room. Monica started to object: by using morally neutral verbs like "neutralize" to stand for murder, she argued, they were reducing themselves to the level of their oppressors.

"What do you propose? Perhaps we should report our complaint to the police?" the nun asked ironically.

There was a silence. The blue-haired woman turned to the speaker. "Well, tell us the rest. Why did they let you go?"

"They wanted names, so that's what I gave them. I picked the two fiercest *momios* in the office and denounced them as extremists and infiltrators. Now they are being tortured just as I was."

Monica shuddered and looked closely at the speaker, a blonde of apparently Germanic origin, who had the elongated dimensions of a Gothic statue. She sat rigidly, her feet pointed straight ahead, her hands folded in her lap, an inscrutable smile upon her lips. It crossed Monica's mind: "*Her thoughts at this moment are identical with mine. She's saying to herself, 'I don't belong here, I want out! It never occurred to me in my former existence that I could live such a scene as this. My icy calm belies my horror at the intolerable dilemmas I have been unfairly burdened with—for no human being deserves to be forced to choose between one moral outrage and another.'*"

Pablo spoke for the first time. "To some of us it is not given to realize the happiness of a blameless life."

They moved on to other, easier topics: the setting up of a dry-cleaning business to be run by workers who had been fired from their jobs; headquarters for experts in forging official papers; lines of communication within the country; the need for money to finance their activities. At nine-thirty the blue-haired woman interrupted the proceedings. "We have a half hour until curfew begins. Most of you cannot reach your homes in time. I assume you are prepared to spend the night out, as I warned you. Sister Matilde will come to my apartment, which is two blocks away. Monica, you go with Heidi to Pablo's house. You people should leave now, one by one; use the stairs and go out the west entrance."

Pablo lived in the second story of a building which housed a family business. As Monica walked past the shop windows on her way to the stairs at the back, she noted the woolens from Chiloé and the black Quinchamalí pottery from Chillán which were attractively displayed. CHILEAN ARTS AND CRAFTS, HOURS 10 TO 17 was written on the door.

Monica felt exhausted. She looked forward to sleeping in the alcove off the kitchen, apparently a maid's room. But she agreed to the finger of brandy which Pablo offered her, drinking it as she stood in the doorway between the kitchen and living room. "You might as well sit down and be comfortable," Heidi said. "I can't," Monica replied, "I'm too nervous."

She turned to go but suddenly hesitated, her mind and body pulling in opposite directions. "Pablo, I've been meaning to ask you about Sister Matilde."

He closed his hirsute hands over his brandy glass and curled his lip as he started to smile. With his short, barrel-chested body and his jutting brow, he looked decidedly simian, but his eyes were large and luminous and his voice surprisingly rich and velvety, like the sound of a cello. "You associate her with the Christians for Socialism movement, don't you? Well, so do we all; however, she wasn't one of the famous eighty who actually signed the original statement, and when the coup came she was apparently overlooked by the *milicos*. We should be thankful; she's a very capable woman."

"I think she's perhaps more committed than I am," said Monica. "I suppose I should be accustomed by now to Marxist priests and nuns, but they still throw me off balance. I don't see how they fit in with the official church hierarchy."

"Not very well, I should say. The official church is uncomfortable about these black sheep among their flock. The Vatican is still dominated by those who think that capitalism describes a set of economic relationships which are built into the structure of the universe, like the laws of physics." He chuckled. "But Sister Matilde has put it better than I can. She once said to me, 'The Church's spokesmen have always condemned Marxism in principle and capitalism in its excesses, but they are one hundred and eighty degrees off. It is capitalism which should be condemned in principle because it is essentially exploitative whereas Marxism is a liberating force, exploitative only when misapplied.' "

Monica hesitated, struggling with her confused impressions. "I guess I'm surprised that anyone takes seriously what the Vatican praises or condemns. What if by some miracle the illustrious canonical doctors were to reverse themselves tomorrow? What difference would it make? The capitalists certainly wouldn't sell their stocks and bonds and head for the confessional—you know that. They will go along with the Church only as long as the Church supports them."

"Ah, Monica," said Pablo, "you are a Chilean and like most Chileans an atheist at heart, although, of course, we have our superstitions. And you assume that other peoples are like us. But Sister Matilde, you see, is European, like a good half of the Christians for Socialism who were active here. In other parts of the world religion is still taken seriously."

It was obvious that Pablo wanted to talk, but Monica was too tired to join him. "No, no," he said when she apologized. "Heidi will stay up with me, and soon my brother and his wife, who are working in the shop below, will join us. We shall tell sad stories, we shall weep together, it will be a beautiful experience. We shall toast your health and beauty as you sleep."

The alcove was completely dark except for a weak bar of moonlight from the room's single window which illuminated on the mirror over the dresser a reflection of twinkling rhombi. Monica slept fitfully, awakening occasionally to the drone of low voices. About one she started, fully alert, suddenly aware of a new sound insinuating itself into her consciousness, a series of arpeggios on a *quena*, the reed flute favored by the

Indians of the North. The sound was clean and young but melancholy, as if full of an infinite but unnameable longing. The preliminary warming-up gave way to a tune which Monica thought she had heard before although she couldn't identify it. An unfamiliar voice called out simply, "A Lament."

Monica propped her head on one elbow and strained to listen. She was tempted to get up and join the people in the living room who had pleasantly interrupted her rest, but there was a curious satisfaction in grasping secretly onto the liveliness of others when she had barely emerged from the death of sleep. "So an old person must feel," she thought, "who as he apparently dozes off while rocking to and fro in the cool of the patio, listens contentedly behind closed eyes to the stir of activity around him."

A strong male voice had begun to sing, a challenge to the honeyed tone of the flute:

In the afternoon of September 11
They killed our president,
They murdered with machine guns
Our chief, elected by the poor and despised.

There were no sobs, nor tears
There were no flowers, nor priests' prayers.
Nobody could protest
It was forbidden to cry.

There were a few harsh, discordant notes on the *quena;* then a woman's voice, sweet like chimes in the wind, joined the other singer:

Let us remember our president
He who gave his life in
His search for justice
He who poured forth for us his consecrated blood
In a searing confrontation
Between reason and force.
He gained for Chile in his thousand days of government
Copper, land, the productive forces

But he left in liberty his profaners
With their infamous newspapers and their trucks.

The mournful mode modulated to a major key, and the
rhythm of the lament became jerky and syncopated:

Now it's late, now more than ever
Lift up your voice, though heavy laden
Proclaim to the world
From the tomb of hope
What we have lost in this unforgettable afternoon.
Say that in the afternoon of September 11
They killed our president.
How hard is a bullet, how fragile a word
It is prohibited to cry.

6

Monica had been seated alone in the faculty lounge for over
an hour, hoping to grade a set of papers before she had to
attend a four o'clock meeting. She couldn't concentrate. Some
problem seemed to be teasing her, but when she paused, intent
to capture the prize, it hid itself among the crowd of tiresome
errands and duties which cluttered her mind as well as her
engagement book. She closed her eyes, determined to give
herself a respite from her cares. "I'll think of Felipe," she said
to herself. Yet to her astonishment it was Carlos' image, not
Felipe's which suddenly appeared to her, somewhat blurred
but lifelike, as in a faded photograph. She attempted to ac-
commodate herself to it, but the likeness disappeared, and
although she frowned in concentration, she could not conjure
it up again.

She returned to her papers, eyeing the clock impatiently as
she marked three or four, when abruptly she was struck with
insight. She put her pen down and rose from her chair, pacing

up and down in the smoky lounge with her hands under her armpits.

"Carlos has won," she whispered to herself. "I waited for years for him to join me; then unwittingly, unconsciously, I joined him." She wanted to protest against the revelation, poke it with the pricks of subtle qualifications. Yet in her amazement she could only wonder at her discovery and admire in stunned surprise this unexpected turn in her life.

She sat down again and began to doodle with her pen. A host of smart arguments began to elbow their way across the avenue of her mind, each clamoring for attention. She was already quarreling with Carlos, denying him his victory. "My illegal and clandestine activity under a ruthless totalitarian regime is much different from your trying to undermine a benign leftist government," she began. "Look, you helped to bring this country to such a pass; a lot of people who before wouldn't have considered running a red light now must lie and cheat, hide and rob."

"It's what I always said," replied the faded simulacrum: "the struggle will intensify before the people triumph, and all of us will be called upon to show which side we're on. As for the present situation, it is only a stage in an inexorable historical process."

She listened to the charges and responses which buzzed remorselessly about her mind. She had heard them all before; it was a dialogue which was written in her own blood. She couldn't remember a time when her relationship with Carlos hadn't resembled a courtroom scene, both of them endlessly justifying themselves before an invisible jury, appealing to sound principles. She found herself waving her hand before her eyes as if to clear the chamber. Suddenly she felt the futility of having opinions. She had spent her life in framing elaborate alibis for herself, justifying her every arrangement, insuring herself against costly moral mistakes. Yet in a few September days the world in which she had so admirably situated herself had disappeared, leaving her with the necessity of beginning over again.

She would have liked to cry, but tears no longer came easily to her. Then she thought of the telegram from Felipe: Carlos had asked for money and crossed the border to Argentina. She wondered if he was bothered by the same doubts which persecuted her.

7

Monica supposed that don Julio César Verdugo's garrulousness was an occupational disease. He had lectured to so many generations of captive audiences in his career as university professor that he assumed he deserved everyone's undivided attention. His dinner party was turning out to be a stifling affair. Conversation was impossible, thought Monica, in that steam bath of hot air.

His soup spoon arrested in its passage from plate to palate, don Julio César droned on and on, occasionally interrupting himself to ask if everyone understood. To Monica it was amazing how his guests put up with his unqualified arrogance. "They are old *momios*, one and all," she thought. "They tolerate him because they recognize their own opinions in his crabbed, perverse pronouncements."

"Our efforts to restore private ownership of property," he was saying, "would have failed if we had yielded to that nervous pusillanimity, typical of certain Christian Democrats, in regard to the use of force as the faithful handmaid of justice."

He paused to acknowledge a hum of approval. "Our instincts and the procession of history tell us that private property is a prerequisite to freedom and to the normal satisfaction of human needs. I don't mean to imply that there is any advantage in a universal distribution of property. It will suffice if enough families have sufficient property to set the tone for the entire society. And to those who object, saying that this or that value, which is incompatible with freedom and private property, is to be preferred, or that the military forces are not the proper guardians of our values, let us assert, ladies and gentlemen, that there is no room in the present Government for so un-Chilean, not to say unmanly, a viewpoint."

The dinner guests seated at the long table burst into a spontaneous round of applause. Monica felt obliged to join them. Ben leaned towards her and murmured, "You're a good, sensible girl, Monica." She replied ironically, "Isn't Julio César a wonder!" Then she smiled brilliantly at all those guests who were eyeing her curiously.

She was slightly drunk, but much to her surprise she was no longer afraid. When she and Benjamin had arrived, late, she had observed an ominous silence descend upon the guests, but Hector had immediately taken her under his protection, fussing over Monica as if she were a prized possession. He had put on weight since she had last seen him, and as he waddled about in his distinctive manner, she was amused by his phocine proportions. He kept winking at her conspiratorially as if to say, "It's you and I against all the old biddies." It was exhilarating, this playful and foolish camaraderie, but it was as dangerous for Hector, who stood to lose his good standing with the momios, as it was for her. Even as the pisco dulled her wits, she wondered why Hector should choose to parade his affection for the sister of Señora Allende's assistant; it was even possible that someone there remembered that she was married to a Mirista.

Monica glanced around the table at the guests who were trying to have a good time. It was an unusual and not altogether successful effort to welcome home a son who had three years previously declared his unwillingness to submit to Marxist totalitarianism. These social events had gone better, Monica thought, in the old days, when Señora Verdugo had been there to soothe the wounded feelings of don Julio César's victims. With her death, the old man had grown more irascible than ever. This evening he had managed to insult the wife of the Minister of the Economy, who was there with her stepson, and the new Director of Primary Education. Even when his guests tried to agree with him, he found fault. "No one," he seemed to claim, "can possibly capture the subtlety and brilliance of my opinions: kindly keep your mouths shut."

His most sensational outburst came with the fish course. As two flustered maids smelling vaguely of perspiration and garlic cleared the soup bowls, Señora Encina, wife of the well-known surgeon, Dr. Rodolfo Lobos, made a wry comment on the photos of Allende and his mistress which had recently appeared in the *Mercurio.* The slight gasps of surprise and expectancy which came from the diners suggested a lascivious relief in the turn the conversation was taking, but don Julio César cast a cold eye upon the author of the flippant remark. Monica thought for a moment that he was going to play the outraged keeper of the public morals—a role that would ill become him—but the old man had more wicked resources at his command than she had given him credit for. Little dots of light flashed from his ginger-colored eyes which were set deeply into incarnadine hollows. He allowed a hint of a smile to pull at the corners of his lips, as if in anticipation of his own drollery.

"Would someone kindly tell me," the old man demanded, "why—when the mass media have at their disposal such an instructive and edifying example of a man who by selling his soul gained mastery over the minds and hearts of millions— why, I say, they parade before us continual examples of his only admirable sentiment: that is, a profound sense of appreciation for the feminine gender? I see that some of you suspect that I am jesting; not so. Anyone who knew him can tell you that Allende was worshiped by his wife and three daughters, by his sisters, by a faithful mistress, and by a lifetime of sweethearts. They adored him because he adored them, adored all women, in fact. During his first year of office an old toothless grandmother from our former *fundo* was among a delegation of peasants invited to the Moneda for one of the Government's extravaganzas. I heard about it. Allende treated her like the Queen of Spain—holding her by her elbow, making her sit in the chair of honor. You may laugh, ladies and gentlemen, you may suspect his chivalry to be feigned, but if you do you are unschooled in the crooked paths of the forceful human personality; sometimes as it advances, mowing down people and institutions, a bit slops over into an emotional landscape altogether alien to the owner's normal habitat: that is why conquerors and dictators are frequently famous lovers."

Monica could see a gleam of humor in don Julio César's eyes, but as the group began to titter somewhat uncertainly, in their confusion uttering such neutral banalities as, "What a golden tongue he has!" or "How well he puts things!" the old man reassumed a grim aspect. "Such truths as I have uttered tonight will not be common currency, I can tell you." He sighed. "Everyone in this country has been corrupted by foreign standards, by middle-class values. Read the *Mercurio*: you would think that they were aiming their pitch at a nation of English parsons. There is no room anymore for the man of destiny, the one who—rather than bowing to the spirit of the age—creates it. I am not referring to vulgar opportunists, like Allende, who play to the masses; men with cloven hooves can only destroy. But what would our nation have to say to Pedro de Valdivia if he were to appear today: instead of...."

His voice trailed off as he turned his gaze to the door by which his son had recently left to answer the phone. Hector stood there now, gesturing discreetly to his father, who in a sudden, odd gesture covered his heart with both hands and wheezed, "Ladies and gentlemen, you must excuse me."

The guests, suddenly deprived of both garrulous host and puckish son, glanced at one another in silence for a few seconds and then began to giggle self-consciously. The man on Monica's left took out his handkerchief and wiped his brow. In the schoolroom recess atmosphere, both Monica and Ben began to relax somewhat. It was as if, having suffered uncomfortably together under a torrent of words, the guests were willing temporarily to forget their differences. Yet the respite from don Julio César soon proved to be more trying than his presence, for the sudden quiet seemed like a void crying out to be filled. The guests continued to eat quietly, their forks ringing against their plates, wishing that the Verdugos would return. The conversation alternately sank under the weight of indifference and bobbed up unexpectedly in simultaneous splashes of exclamations ("Delicious!" "Exquisite!") which left behind them an embarrassing silence.

But the reappearance of Hector and his father failed to relieve the tense atmosphere. Don Julio César, instead of finishing his story, set himself to examining his guests' plates, demanding to know why they hadn't eaten this or that, and forcing more food upon unwilling recipients. Hector began an interminable explanation of the American Watergate conspiracy about which no one seemingly knew or cared. They retired to the living room for coffee and brandy, and although the Verdugos urged all to relax and enjoy themselves, Monica suspected that they were as relieved as their guests when the clock chimed at nine. "You wouldn't want us to be shot for staying out after curfew, would you now?" asked Dr. Lobos with a stentorian heartiness.

Monica and Ben were the last to go. Hector accompanied them. They detoured first to stroll towards a domed gazebo, where Señora Verdugo had long ago established headquarters for her little rock garden. They sat down on a stone bench. There was a sweet odor of jasmine and a full yellow moon; Monica felt relieved to be finally alone with her two friends. She took Hector's hand. "Hector, I had a feeling that you and your father were disturbed this evening by your phone call. But perhaps I'm being intrusive."

"Not at all. I'm glad you brought it up. There are some things I need to talk to you about, Monica. And I feel bad after the way my father carried on. I hope you weren't insulted. I warned him before the dinner to avoid offending you."

Monica suddenly felt a flutter of anticipation. "No, never mind, go on."

"It's my uncle. He's killing himself with worry about his son, my cousin Orlando Verdugo. You don't know him? He's a young fool, about eighteen or nineteen, and he got mixed up in things. . . . He disappeared on September 12 and hasn't been seen since. We can't track him. We thought that you. . . . My uncle was calling to see. . . . "

Monica studied Hector's face for a few seconds and then burst into edgy laughter. Confused, Hector began to stammer, but Monica reassured him. "Dear friend," she began, "I have been speculating for days as to why you invited me to your party; but my mind has been corroded with worries, you see, and in my anxiety about my own problems it never occurred to me that you might think I could do you a favor! No, it's all right"; she covered her face and attempted to control her nerves. "What are friends for? It's just the irony of it, your thinking I could do something for you. . . . "

"We've heard that the MIR is still in operation," Hector continued. "There are reports that some *Miristas* will attend an international meeting of guerrillas in Argentina; they're going to divvy up five million dollars' worth of arms. I thought perhaps you knew if Carlos will attend. Orlando was a protégé of Carlos'."

Suddenly Ben squeezed Monica's arm, as if in warning. She felt annoyed at having to suspect Hector's motives, and her words, now slow and deliberate, almost betrayed her depression as she answered. "Hector, you seem to know more about Carlos than I do. I haven't heard from him since July. Nor do I know anything about your cousin." His face drooped. "I'm sorry. You see, I'm as barren of favors as I had first thought; you mustn't count on me."

Later when Monica let Ben off at the Plaza Italia bus stop she said, "Well, Benjamin, I wonder if you are going to fail me as I just failed Hector. Maybe I'm asking the impossible."

"About Eve, you mean? I'm pretty optimistic, Monica. I'm working hard on it. So is Anna."

She reached out and patted his cheek. "I know you are. I'll never forget this no matter what happens. I hope you know that."

8

For the past three Sundays Monica had eaten with her family and then spent the afternoon in bed at her mother's house. It was ridiculous, she knew, to take to bed like an old woman who couldn't keep warm. But she felt comforted by her girl-hood room with its floor-to-ceiling shelves, still housing her collections of shells and fossils picked up at the beach during her childhood summer vacations. And, although she protested vigorously when her mother babied her, bringing her a tray with tea and pastries about five and keeping her company for a while, Monica was grateful for these sabbath indulgences.

This afternoon she glanced at the stack of books she had left on the bedside table the week before, choosing the one on top to browse through. It was Felipe's *Past and Present in Rural Chile*, well worn and dog-eared. She had read it, she supposed, a hundred times; there was no need to turn to it again. But a long-distance love affair needed some tangible signs besides the telephone, she thought. Seeing the words upon the page, smelling the dusty odor of cheap paper, she somehow felt closer to Felipe.

"Sixth edition, 1965, first edition, 1960," she read on the title page. That was long before she had met him; indeed, she had been a girl of fifteen when he had broken into print. He had started his book when he was a graduate student in agronomy at the University of California at Davis, making of it an extraordinary jumble of his memories, term papers, letters from home, and family history; there had been no thought of publishing it then. But over the years, as he had moved from one post to another as a consultant or student, touring agri-businesses in California, vineyards in France, and communes in Israel, he had become ever more absorbed in the writing project which at first had been a casual pastime. In 1957, depressed by his recent divorce from a North American and grieving for his absent son and daughter, he had taken a year off to perfect the work, retiring to his family's country house near Talca.

The work had aroused no interest when it had first appeared. The big growers, as Felipe was fond of pointing out, inattentively cultivating only two-fifths of their property, never dreamed that a book on agriculture could be interesting; and other readers, with the self-deprecating attitude of the provincial, preferred more cosmopolitan settings than rural Chile. It was not until the book had been translated into French and favorably reviewed in *Le Figaro* that Felipe began to receive attention in Santiago as a man of letters. He was thirty years old when the second edition appeared, suddenly elevating him to modest fame. Respected by the aristocrats for his impeccable lineage and his literary gifts and by the technocrats for his careful analysis of Chile's complex agricultural ills, he soon became a frequently quoted author. Within a few years a scattering of eager epigones, paying him the ultimate compliment, had named a school of writing after him and claimed to be inventing under his inspiration a new *genre*, one that would ultimately replace the novel, that of the "concretive essay" suffused with "spirit of place."

Felipe protested against manipulation of his work into the procrustean bed of literary genres; objected, further, that he disapproved of "layered" essays and of "local color." He considered himself a Chilean author, without doubt, but even more he saw himself as a modern Pascal, with a sense of humor, and as a technocrat; he continued working for the Food and Agricultural Organization, treating writing as an avocation. Yet Monica was certain that his unexpected prominence as a widely discussed literary person was immensely satisfying to him. ("Of course," he had once said. "Why else does a man write but to be loved and to avenge himself on those who didn't believe in him?") But he wore his distinction casually and playfully, adopting a faintly ironic tone, as if dubious about staking too much on such a slender volume. His fame seemed less like something earned than like a delightful prize carelessly dropped in his way. He could not be solemn: recently, when a well-known critic had declared to him at a cocktail party that with Chile's two Nobel Prize winners—Gabriel Mistral and Pablo Neruda—Felipe had put Chile on the world's literary map, Felipe had replied, barely smiling, "But why do you include Mistral and Neruda?"

If he knew a disappointment in his achievement, it was in its tepid reception by a large number of moderate Christian Democrats with whom he felt fairly sympathetic. It was not so much his conclusions which they objected to—for although he refrained from drawing up a detailed program he insisted on the necessity of agrarian reform—as a certain nostalgic tone the book conveyed, like the swan song of a member of a dying class. The criticism rankled because Felipe had recognized that quality himself when he was writing his book. More, he had been astonished how the most unadorned description of his early years on his family's *fundo*, or of the antiquated practices of his ancestors, suggested a hint of regret for the way of life which, Felipe argued, must disappear. It would be different, he supposed, if one of the peasants, a descendant of the long line of workers who had coinhabited the land with the Medina family, were to author the book: but however hard he might try, Felipe could not write from a point of view other than his own. And although he was critical of the claim that art is in any case worthwhile without reference to its social impact, it did seem to him that the ordering of his own impressions and the recreating of the lives of others was in a mysterious way praiseworthy.

Monica thumbed through the back pages, pausing now and then to read a favorite phrase, slowly progressing towards the opening chapter, which described in detail the types of *fundos* which had existed in various parts of Chile during the thirties and forties, when Felipe was a boy. It was the part she liked the best, perhaps because she had visited Felipe's ancestral home, amply described in those pages, and had even met his grandmother, though she was no longer the magnificent lady who, having married a shiftless man, had governed vast acreages as well as commercial interests with considerable skill. "I remember her best presiding over the tea table," Felipe had said on Monica's first visit to Fundo El Consuelo. "The big chapel bell which governed the hours of work and rest would ring about five in the afternoon calling the peasants to their ration of toasted wheat mixed with warm water and a biscuit. In those days I usually went riding with a peasant's son about my own age nicknamed 'The Rabbit.' He would wait for me beneath the chestnut tree in the patio, where our horses were tied, while I joined the family in the dining room. The table would be crowded with homemade bread, avocados, fowl, ham, a roast of beef, fruit desserts, and all manner of pastries. My grandmother would pour the tea; usually six or seven of her children would be there, for of her offspring only my father and his sister Magdalena were grown. It was a noisy gathering carried on in three languages since the governess spoke French with the children, my aunts and uncles and the servants spoke Spanish, and my grandmother carried on in German with the overseer. The big house wasn't lived in except in the summers and during the harvest, when the proprietors suddenly felt called upon to assume their roles. Even as a child I could see something ludicrous about this arrangement, for none of my relatives had ever pushed a plow or weeded a field, or sharpened an ax; their skills ran towards hunting down an occasional puma, and even then a peon dutifully rode along behind the hunter carrying the weapon. But my elders would issue orders about bringing half-wild horses down from the pastures in the mountains, say, or about which peasants' children were to take part in this year's harvest. I absorbed it all, enthralled with life in the country. My uncles could say, 'Remember, Felipe, you were born to command.'"

Monica had seen photographs of the uncles in a gallery at the great house; there were portraits of other ancestors, too, dating back several hundred years. There was even a facsimile of an original grant of *encomienda* which Valdivia had bestowed upon a certain Juan de la Cruz Medina in recognition of his services during the conquest. "To you is given the chief named Pillán, with all his sub-chiefs and Indians and subjects who have their seat in this valley," the charter had read. ("About the grant of *encomienda*, don't be too impressed; it is a forgery," Felipe had told her later. "There is hardly a family in Chile that can date its origin before the eighteenth century. Juan de la Cruz Medina: he is a myth.")

Yet, thought Monica, in spite of the family's stature, there was a fatal flaw in the Medina strain. They had joined with the other creoles under O'Higgins and San Martín, expelling the Spaniards and setting up a "republic" ruled by the old families; they had held prominent places in the succeeding administrations up to the time of Manuel Montt; but a curious lethargy had infected them during the latter half of the nineteenth century, rendering most of the men indifferent to anything save alcohol and *rodeos* and European jaunts. There were a few vigorous individuals, but their accomplishments were often too eccentric to be appreciated by their peers, a landed gentry swelling in wealth: one great-great-uncle, for instance—besides astutely abandoning his own kind to marry the daughter of a fabulously wealthy English merchant—had earned a footnote in the history of astronomy by setting up the first telescope south of the Maule River and making careful maps of his observations. Another had devoted his life to writing a three-volume work on St. Isadore of Seville, with whom he purported to commune in seances. But a fair number, thought Monica, resembled Felipe's father, who had drunk his way through a short and tawdry life, finally creating a spectacular scandal when he was involved in a shooting at the house of his mistress. Only his powerful connections kept him from being tried for murder.

About the other side of Felipe's ancestry Monica knew surprisingly little, for although the Larraín family was the most famous in Chile, it was immense, and Felipe's mother came from an obscure branch. She had been a brilliant pupil of the Sacred Heart sisters and the first woman to study veterinary medicine at the University of Chile, but she had abandoned her career plans to wed Felipe's father, who, after a year or two of marriage, had preferred to seek feminine company in other places. She had attempted to build a satisfying life without him, devoting herself—much to her relatives' perplexity and dismay—to breeding the best herd of dairy cattle in Chile. But the periods of depression she had suffered occasionally in her adolescence had become a regular affliction, keeping pace with her husband's moral deterioration.

Sometimes, Monica had learned, when doña Isabel was not quite in her right mind, she would retreat into her past, recalling scenes from her childhood which she would relate with an eerie eloquence. When Felipe was a boy he had been spellbound by her stories about the Larraíns' *fundo*, Las Tres Campanas, so different from the fabulous El Consuelo of the Medina family which reigned imperiously over thousands of hectares of extraordinarily rich soil. Las Tres Campanas was a mountain property, with only a narrow band of fertile land at the foot of the Andes, where wheat, onions, alfalfa, and beans were cultivated. Unprofitable for agriculture, the *fundo* served as a summer retreat for the family and their friends, who settled in every year about the time the snow line began to retire, leaving the earth dry.

During early summer, according to doña Isabel, many cows, horses, and sheep would forage on paths almost overgrown, making their way towards the half-wild Andean pastures. The shepherds and cowboys selected to accompany the animals would prepare for a nomadic existence, packing cheese, dried meat, and biscuits to last for three or four months. It was an exciting season: Felipe's mother remembered how each year she would vainly beg to accompany the men who lived on their horses, sleeping in the shelters hastily assembled in former years. Nothing seemed more wonderful to her than exploring the top of the world, where enormous condors, strong enough to carry off a sheep, were said to attack a person when they were hungry enough; no scene, she thought, could be as magnificent as the shores of Lake Maule, at 10,000 feet, where in the distance one could see the plains of Argentina. But this was a region she was destined never to visit; by the time she was old enough to insist on having her way, her tastes had changed although occasionally the vision of the shepherds, with their feral smell, tugged at her nostalgically. Even Felipe, who as a child had vowed that he would someday make that trip, knew of Las Tres Campanas and its summer pastures only from his mother's stories; before he had grown up, the *fundo* had disappeared, along with most of the other landmarks of his youth.

Monica put the book aside. A heavy rain had suddenly begun to fall outside, freshening the air and darkening the sky. She reached for a pen and a scrap of paper, acting on an impulse to write a few lines to Felipe. "For a while this afternoon," she began, "I lost myself utterly among the plants and people, textures and odors of your past, and now I feel as if my heart has had a splendid vacation. May you, too, beloved, be as free from care as a summer wind on a mountain meadow at Tres Campanas."

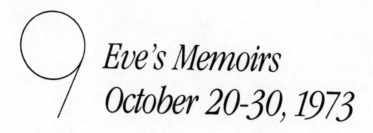

Eve's Memoirs
October 20-30, 1973

While they are partying—
  they are offering toasts—
We are crying in the night
  in the ransacked house.
We are in mourning at the dining
  room table with its empty seat,
Pale and quiet,
Fearful that they might knock on
  the door.
                    ——ERNESTO CARDENAL

Memoirs
Writing: reconstructing the past; groping for an abundance formerly shared with loved ones; reliving a national drama; inhabiting old dreams and visions; diagnosing former illness, having died; deciphering joy.

Helmut
He called on September 12, but I had already been arrested. Wild with sympathy and fright, he told my mother that he

would marry me by proxy. Then I could leave Chile easily as the wife of a German citizen.

"But Helmut," Mother said, "Sergio has never agreed to an annulment; legally Eva is still his wife."

"But Germany is like Chile," he replied. "It does not recognize civil marriage performed in other countries. If Eva could just get into the Embassy we could claim that she wasn't married by German law, and the First Consul, who is a friend of mine, could stand in for me in a hasty wedding."

Mother was unconvinced but spent several days investigating the possibility. Since all foreign embassies were surrounded by heavily armed soldiers who stopped Chileans whom they suspected of seeking refuge, she had to rely on phone calls. It was to no avail.

For several weeks after the coup there was no mail service. When Helmut's letters finally began to arrive, they had the cryptic, sometimes baffling quality of coded messages designed to pass the censorship. The first said simply, "Hold on, somebody out here loves you." The second was in modern Greek, a language I don't know. As I wracked my brain trying to find a way to translate the mysterious looking script, I wondered which had prevailed in Helmut's decision to send it, his caution or his sense of playfulness. It took an afternoon for me to track down the following translation of a poem by George Seferis:

Whatever I loved vanished with the houses
that were new last summer
and collapsed in the autumn wind.

For doña Tencha (a wish):
May you grow old among friends.

Santiago After Curfew (October 1973)
Occasionally sniper shots, a round of fire. Helicopters circle overhead, droning in great spirals. In the distance a siren and

the muffled cry of a man. The tinkling of shattered glass.
Then stillness again: the fear and silence can be heard.

Chile

We like to think of ourselves as a nice, reasonable little country
where nothing exceptional ever happens. Sometimes people call
us "the English of South America," and we swell with pride
thinking about our regular habits, our sobriety and sense of
measure, our customs of taking tea every afternoon and going
to the seaside for the summer.

But there's no hiding the fact that we hold the world's
record in disasters: the biggest and most frequent earthquakes,
the most spectacular volcanic eruptions, enormous tidal waves,
alternating droughts and floods.

There's a limit as to how much this poor land can put up
with: someday, geologists tell us, the country will detach itself
from the rest of the continent and tumble into the sea.

Per omnia saecula saeculorum. Amen.

Then we have the more homely tragedies: Newcastle disease
withers our chickens, and hoof-and-mouth disease decimates
the cattle. Our children suffer from parasites and decalcification
of the bones. In the South there's tuberculosis; everywhere
cirrhosis of the liver and gallbladder trouble.

Does that cover it? Not at all. We're second only to France
in number of alcoholics and to Israel in national indebtedness
(and they've the excuse of a war to pay for); only a few nations
can claim more illegitimate births, higher infant mortality
rates, and in number of abortions we hold the world's record
along with Argentina and Uruguay. We are right up there,
too, in number of pedestrian deaths (it's the way we drive) and
child desertion. As to inflation, nobody can match us; it's a
way of life.

And now, a military government.

Deo gratias.

The Momios

Now we're back to the only kind of rationing the comfortable people can live with: the rationing imposed by level of income.

Uncle Max

He has moved back home; he and Aunt Sara are going to give it a try again.

When he saw me at the dinner table last night, he looked angry. I felt uncomfortable. It seemed likely he didn't like harboring a politically undesirable person. I decided to move on.

Aunt Sara came to talk to me about it. I misunderstood the situation, she said. Uncle Max is sorry about my arrest and torture, but at the same time he supports the general policies of the present government. So he can't think of anything to say. My presence embarrasses him. Yet he doesn't want me to leave. According to Aunt Sara, he's really worried about me.

I thought it over for a while and decided to find another place. Uncle Max makes my head ache.

The Devil

He wears a policeman's uniform. His name is Juan Andini.

Carlos

When he and Monica were going together, I was too young to have any reasoned convictions, and Mother and Dad were too old to change. Simple truths of this sort he failed to appreciate.

On Sundays he would come to dinner and annoy us with his pronouncements. In my anger and ignorance, I hardly listened to him. But over the years, he influenced me. Yes, and Monica too.

It was shortly before the birth of Maria Paz. Carlos, Monica, and I had risen early to do some photographing on Cerro San

Cristobal. As we were walking home, Carlos began another of his little lectures, and suddenly I understood. I felt almost stunned by the force of his argument and disoriented, too, as if I had been living all wrong.

Just what was it he said? Something like this:

"You are not excused from responsibility because you have chosen to do nothing. Your nonaction is just as real as my action. We both face a difficulty in trying to figure out whether our conduct is making us a part of the problem or a part of the solution.

"My opinion is at least an opinion about something, namely about whether I am succeeding in bringing an end to class exploitation, whether I am helping to make the revolution. You, on the other hand, live in order to get what you want out of life, but you don't know what you want. You are always trying to decide. You are asking a question that has no answer because you make up the answer as you go along."

Hard words. Bitter medicine.

Where are you now, Carlos? See? I have not forgotten.

Felipe

He is only of average height, perhaps 5' 8". He has splendid dark eyes, framed by perfect black arcs. Standing close enough to touch him, one can see that his skin, rather than lying smooth, has settled into the hills and rills that acne sometimes leaves behind, the permanent reminder of a difficult adolescence. At first I did not regard him as handsome, but over the years I have come to appreciate his looks.

He was forty when Monica met him, but his crown of thick, glossy black hair, just touched with gray at the temples, as well as his slender build, gave him a youthful air. He had a way of putting people at their ease, always saying the right thing, always being amusing. Although Monica was a strong, self-reliant person, quietly pleased with the way she was managing without a husband, Felipe indulged her like a child.

I remember the first afternoon I spent with Monica and him.

We were standing at a pastry shop in Viña del Mar, where as children on vacation marveling at the rows—identical year after year—of flaky French confectionery, Monica and I confirmed our faith in the permanence of order and beneficence.

On this day Monica glanced cursorily at the chocolate cake, sugar roses, and towers of whipped cream arranged on window trays; she was intent upon the marzipan with almonds, and the brown-sugar paste pressed into familiar shapes of hens and turkeys and rabbits. Her eyes had finally found the object of their search: "Look, Eve: the two-kilo brown sugar hen! You remember how we always begged Father to buy it, but we had to settle for a little chick."

Felipe responded to the cue. When he presented her with the brown and lumpish freak, she smiled and kissed him. We left the shop and flagged a rickety horse-drawn victoria tottering slightly to one side. This was before the drivers took to painting their carriages with floral designs.

We set ourselves to devouring our enormous marvel, quickly dismembering the legs and wings and head until, dismissing the driver and his mangy horse at the beach, we were left with a sticky, formless mass.

"One more bite and we're sick," Felipe said, and, walking towards a shoeshiner stationed near a group of tourists at the clock of flowers, he had called out, "Would you like a hen?"

Seeing the strange gift thrust into his hands, the shoeshiner screwed up his one good eye suspiciously; but later, turning back towards him from the sea's edge, we could see him intently licking his fingers.

Hiding out

The day before yesterday I left Aunt Sara's and Uncle Max's. Yesterday morning my *carabinero* called there asking for me. No one can figure out how he got the number; my location was a secret shared only by Monica, Mother, Aunt Sara, and me. Mother became hysterical when she heard about it, and I was so distraught that I called Dr. Carvajal.

I don't know what I expected from him. I guess I like his fatherly way of handing out advice and consolation. He gave me another bottle of pills and G.'s phone number. G., his niece and daughter of the former vice-rector of the University of Chile at Concepción, said that she would be glad to keep me for a few days.

Talking with Dr. Carvajal, I came to a new resolution: *I want out. I want out of Chile fast.*

The Universities

Last night G. and I stayed up late talking. She used to teach at the University of Chile in Concepción. She reports that of 16,000 students, 6,000 have already been suspended, along with hundreds of professors.

The military encourages the professors and students to denounce leftists. Almost every department in the University of Chile has been assigned a "prosecutor" to receive written or oral denunciations. The accused are not allowed to face their accusers; they are not informed of the charges against them in advance of their trials.

Dr. B. was fired for having applied for a grant to study the Cuban preventive health system and for having worked during the medical strike in August. Now he faces the possibility of criminal prosecution.

Soldiers with machine guns patrol the campuses. The libraries are closed while the books are "reviewed" and many are burned.

Death

When I was being tortured, I sometimes said to myself, "As soon as I have a chance I must make a list of the reasons for staying alive." How ridiculous.

Chile: Excerpt From a Letter to Helmut, October 15, 1973

When Monica's friend Pablo was arrested, he met a Protestant minister, a fellow prisoner—or perhaps he was a deacon or an elder in a church that has no minister. He was a poor and simple man who cried every time the prisoners were fed their bowlful of beans. "It's my family—I have food, and they have none!" he would explain, and he couldn't eat.

One day he offered a little impromptu service for the prisoners in which he claimed that Christ had come again. He had been born in Cautín Province, and now he was in a prison camp, but no one knew which one. Perhaps the minister was speaking metaphorically; perhaps not. "What we must do," the preacher said, "is witness to the newly come Christ just as the apostles witnessed to the Jesus of old. We must brand upon our hearts the scenes of his deeds and of his sufferings." And then he began an extraordinary litany in which he intoned the names of all the places he knew of where prisoners were being tortured. Soon his listeners took it up, repeating after him, until the guards quieted them with blows, the infamous names I am ashamed to say are not yet stamped upon my soul but which I record here for you and for posterity:

Military Academy
Buin Regiment
Tacna Regiment
Telecommunications Regiment
Tank Regiment No. 2
El Bosque Air Force Base
Air Force Polytechnic Academy
Air Force Academy of War
Ministry of Defense (underground rooms)
Central Police Barracks
National Police Barracks of Quinta Buin
National Police Barracks of Renca
National Police Barracks of Puente Alto
Tejas Verdes Regiment

Bucalemu Regiment
Railway Regiment of Puente Alto
San Bernardo Infantry School
Military Quarters at Cerro Chena
Colina Air Base
Colina Parachute School
Chile Stadium
Calle Londres No. 38 (private house used for interrogation)
Agustinas No. 632 (private house used especially for the interrogation of medical doctors)
Police Units of Melipilla and Talagante
Polytechnic for Minors of San Bernardo
Air Force Specialist School

This listing is just for Santiago Province, and it is not all—ah no, it is not all.

The Momios

During the early days of September there were many tables stationed in the downtown areas bearing the legend "Allende Must Go!" There one could add one's name to long scrolls of signatures calling for the president's resignation.

Once, at the corner of Bandera and Agustinas, I saw Julia Stratagopoulos de Benson manning such a table. Of Greek extraction, she was a teacher at the Harriet B. School where, among a faculty remarkable for its height (several women measured six feet), she was the tallest at 6' 1½". She had once invited my class to her house where she had served us stuffed grape leaves, aubergines, and the various sticky sweets of honey and sesame seeds beloved in Mediterranean countries; and when I played the role of Tiresias in the school production of *Antigone*, she presented me with a copy of the play in Greek, from which her father had studied, declaring as she did so that no male actor could have rendered a better performance.

"Julia," I said, "whatever are you doing here? I didn't know you were interested in politics."

"Nowadays everyone is interested in politics," she said. "Be a good girl and sign with the rest of us."

"Julia," I replied, "I don't share your political views. I thought you knew that I'm working in the Moneda now as a special assistant to Mrs. Allende."

She stared at me uncomprehendingly for a second or two and then gave a little gasp, covering her mouth with her hand. Perhaps she had never seen a leftist close up before.

"But why," I continued, "are you in favor of such a drastic step as Allende's resignation? What has he done?"

"There's no freedom left in Chile." She stared stonily ahead. "He's destroying our liberties."

"But here you sit in a public place calling for the downfall of the government; the newspapers are full of it. What do you mean, there's no freedom in Chile?"

She continued to stare, her lips tightly pursed. Finally she said, "I don't talk to communists."

The Harriet B. School

To school every day from eight to three, dressed in navy-blue uniform, carrying a bag of books and notebooks identical with those of my friends, the same since first grade. Networks of secrets, every flutter of an eyelash of deep significance. The positive experience of meeting and overcoming intellectual puzzles. Loving some kind teachers, diplomatically working my way around the neurotics. I never stopped to ask myself if I were happy.

Bitterness

I love my bitterness because it's mine.

Allende

One day after Helmut had been in Chile just a short time, he asked me, "What is it like to work for Mrs. Allende? You've never told me much about it."

"We took a liking to each other immediately. She mothers me and confides in me; and I am worthy of her confidence."

"Would you describe her as a happy woman?"

"I would, although she's had her share of poor health. I think she is like her husband in that she never really expected to make it to the top. It's a tremendous, exciting surprise to her. There were depressing days, especially at the first, but on the whole it's been enjoyable."

"Tell me about Allende. Do you see him often? Do you know him well?"

"Not well, but I see him every day for a few minutes. He always comes to visit doña Tencha sometime during the afternoon. Occasionally I join them for lunch when there is a guest they think I'd enjoy, or someone who doesn't speak Spanish and needs an interpreter. I hesitate to tell you what he is like: how can I presume to know? You've seen pictures of him: he's an attractive, well-preserved man of sixty-three, of average height for a Chilean and just a little stout. With his large, black-framed glasses he looks like a typical bourgeois."

"I've seen him on TV. He seems a man of tremendous energy and self-confidence. But in some ways he's a puzzle to me. He's a Mason, for instance. How can a Socialist also be a Mason?"

"Only a foreigner would ask such a question! It's a family tradition with him: his grandfather was a Most Serene Grand Master of the Masonic Order. Perhaps you know that in the nineteenth century being a Mason was a way of having advanced opinions. I think above all he is a family man. In this respect he is 'Mr. Chilean,' at least 'Mr. Upper-Middle-Class Chilean.' For he considers himself as carrying on a tradition, as being part of a line. His father, for instance, was a political radical; at his funeral Allende promised that he would carry on the social struggle. He is distantly related to Marmaduke Grove, who became Chile's first Socialist president for a few days in '29 or '30. You see how it is: Masonry, Socialism, family ties. His grandfather founded the first lay school in Chile; people called him 'Red Allende.'"

"I wouldn't have thought of him as being family oriented. I understand he's quite a lady's man."

"Women adore him, including his wife and his daughters. He's very much devoted to them and gallant to all women. As to the others—well, he isn't the first Chilean president to have a roving eye. You think perhaps that he is self-indulgent, but it occurs to me that self-indulgent people are frequently good-natured. He is in truth too comfortable, too happy with his life to become annoyed at people's shortcomings. He is even tolerant of people with different political views—rather a rare virtue in a Chilean. I remember in particular how he took me into his office one day and showed me something of which he is very proud, one of the first copies of Ché's *The Guerrilla War* which bore a dedication, 'To Salvador Allende, who is trying to obtain the same result by other means. Affectionately, Ché.' And I noticed, too, on Allende's desk a portrait of Ché with an inscription to the Allende girls. If people seem to have good intentions, he is quick to compliment them even if he himself looks at things another way. I once heard him praise in a half hour over tea a whole cross section of the modern world: Fidel and Ché and Betancourt and Graham Greene and Cardinal Silva and the Beatles and more whose names escape me now."

"Maybe it's because he's been a politician all of his life. He's apt to be charming. But what I wonder is how far such qualities go now that he is president."

"Well, I have confined myself to his personal traits. If you want a political portrait, we'll have to begin all over again."

"No, no; I can read about his politics in the papers." He paused, and then, as if thinking aloud, he said, "Somehow I don't think he's the man that Fidel Castro is."

I felt stung by Helmut's remark, but I replied evenly, "It's probably not an easy thing for a foreigner to appreciate our preferences. Fidel is magnificent for Cuba, but he wouldn't do at all for us; he is an immense hurricane whereas Allende is like the tides, dependable and regular."

Helmut looked at me closely. "Forgive me; I've hurt you."

"Not at all," I replied.

"You must forgive me," he persisted.

"Done," I said. But it was one of those times that I was less than truthful. Even today, when the memory of this little talk lies warped and curled up in my memory, I feel childishly resentful. He shouldn't have said it.

Allende

As don Nestor once observed: a lot of have-nots in this country will identify with a man who's a winner with the ladies.

The Junta's Minister of the Economy

He was on TV tonight. There were no surprises. He intends to use the capitalistic approach to "rebuilding" the ruined economy; instead of deciding what our human needs are and planning how to fulfill them, he will concentrate his efforts on producing a dynamic "healthy" economy, which all of us must nurse along. Soon we shall be at the mercy of this inhuman patient which requires ever more sacrifices from a crushed and sulky labor force.

Ah, *compañeros*, did you hear? Will we endure?

The Minister spoke of the "restoration of free enterprise" and "competition." Is he a liar or a fool? How can there be competition in a nation where a handful of families own all the industries and control all the sources of credit?

Helmut

In Helmut's presence I became a person of consequence. There seemed to be no aspect of my life or thought that didn't arouse his interest and curiosity. Although I recognized that his obsession was born of a fever from which, in the natural course of things, he would recover, I couldn't help enjoying the myths and dramas which he created about my every movement and sentiment.

I remember that once, for instance, when I had recounted to him an amusing story, he chuckled, then remarked thoughtfully, "What is striking about you—I'm sure you know—is your wit, for wit in women is as rare as generosity in men; and wit joined by a taste for making sharp distinctions of a philosophical sort: such abundance is rare in both sexes and rightly feared."

But he wasn't unmindful of my faults, some of which I hadn't thought of before: my indolence, for instance, my lack of interest in people outside the range of family and close friends. Others I prefer not to talk about.

About my looks he once said, "You remind me of the late Byzantine madonnas, those young girls with almond-shaped eyes, hair parted severely in the middle and waving to each side of their faces, with round cheeks and sober little mouths. How undisturbed they appear to be by the commotion they are creating!"

On another occasion: "When I was a boy I was vastly impressed by the liturgy of the Lutheran Church. In my mind's eye I could see God the Father, Jesus, and the Holy Ghost, who looked like our bishop. But other abstractions were more difficult to grasp: free will, for instance; consubstantiality. But once in a while, as in a vision, I am slapped, so to speak, with an intuition as to what those great words mean. Seeing you sleep this morning, your lids slightly fluttering when I disturbed you: suddenly I seemed to know what Sanctifying Grace is."

The Mercurio

Ten days after the coup some of their editors interviewed General Pinochet and congratulated him on taking power. He assured them that the coup couldn't have succeeded without the help of the *Mercurio.*

The MIR used to write articles for the leftist press in which they claimed that the *Mercurio* was subsidized by the CIA and that some of its articles designed to create fear and havoc were actually composed at CIA headquarters in Virginia. Felipe, who knows the people at the *Mercurio*, dismissed the charges as propaganda. (Incorrectly? Correctly? Who knows?) "Surely," he used to say, "our own *momios* are clever enough to fill the pages of the *Mercurio* with their calculated hysteria without any help from the *gringos*."

Irony (Benjamin Willing) :
Monica has found a Guardian Angel to rescue me from these burning fires. He turns out to be a *gringo*.

The Doe
Sometimes I used to see her at official receptions, this splendid looking person of forty-five, her magnificent, velvety eyes surveying everything, her thick cascades of black hair, just touched with gray, setting off the ivory whiteness of her face and neck. No ordinary secretary, this tall, leggy woman so impeccably dressed, but mistress to a president and a political power in her own right.

She would arrive early at a government function, taking everything in, laughing and chatting indolently, apparently prepared for a long stay; but without fail, five minutes before doña Tencha's entrance, she would discreetly disappear. Wife and mistress must never meet: that was one of Allende's unwritten laws. His chivalrous, thoughtful attention to such sentimental details he took great pride in. Humiliating a woman—any woman—was for him worse than rude; it was barbarous.

Twelve years; for twelve years these two women shared his life. More years than I have been grown up.

The doe must have been to him like a summer cabin on the shore; doña Tencha, his legal wife—she would have been a solid country place with sounds of dogs and children and roundups.

And the others? Some other sort of haven altogether, no doubt.

Torture

Among the women who were arrested with me was a dentist, an Oriental political refugee from Brazil, named Akiko Hombo. Though I knew her for just five days I shall never forget her: we were bound in that quick and absolute intimacy that links the victims of total disaster.

When I first saw her, she was in the posture all prisoners were to assume before their interrogation: knees on the floor, back straight, arms stretched straight ahead with hands flat on the wall. It was the simplest of the tortures I was subjected to, yet in some respects the most intolerable since it lasted for several days and aggravated my bad back.

"Let me pass on a useful warning," she whispered to me as the guard paced towards the other end of the room. "When you are called for interrogation, they will first ask you which of your kin should be contacted in case of your sudden death. Don't be frightened; it's a gimmick to loosen your tongue."

Later that afternoon we were separated, and when I met her again after several days, I could hardly look at her for her nose was bleeding profusely, and her stained clothes gave off a stench. "It is something the Chileans have learned from the Brazilians," she said without emotion. "Tubes are inserted in the nose, through which water and tobacco powder are poured to produce a shot of euphoria in the victim and drive him mad.

"No, don't weep over it," she added. Then she said, "My hand, my right hand: they have killed the feeling in three fingers. What is a dentist with anesthetized hands?"

When we were released together on September 17 she embraced me. I looked at her hands; some of her fingernails had been ripped out. I wanted to comfort her, but she was the one who found healing words: "Never forget your failures, never forget your shame. They are the sadly beautiful part of life."

Discovery

Felipe, with his passion for biology, has explained to Monica and me how human evolution has worked, how the evolution of the brain conformed itself to the exigencies of the hand. First we "do"; the nervous system responds; then we "think."

We give too much credit to the eye, as if it were by seeing that we learn.

Many languages reflect this confusion; in Spanish, "I see" frequently means "I understand." But at least for those of us who have grown up outside the contemplative Eastern religions, it would be more precise to say "I do" when we mean "I understand." How peculiar, then, that we should seek to discover truth by "gazing inwards."

The Devil

Juan Andini stopped by Monica's apartment last night. He was surprisingly polite and friendly. He's so unpredictable. Monica promised that I would be there soon. He said he'd drop by next week.

How long can this go on?

Torture

For a week or two the horror stories have been circulating systematically among the clandestine groups. Ten thousand dead the first week; twenty thousand imprisoned, of whom an estimated 75 percent have been tortured. It is just as I overheard General Prats predict several months ago to some Christian Democrats waiting outside Allende's office: "A coup in Chile will not be like Brazil or Peru; it will be another Haiti."

I am haunted by the story of the Socialist deputy Perez who was detained in the little port of Los Angeles. One of the officers there, reminded of the song about the mouse named Perez who fell in a pot and squeaked, forced the deputy to crawl on the floor on his hands and knees and imitate the mouse, Perez. While being beaten, he had to turn in circles and squeak as his fellow prisoners looked on.

It was not unlike the worst inflicted on me. Some things I try not to think about.

Diary

At first my writing was taut, unsupple, but over the weeks I have grown more relaxed and expansive. I am reminded of learning to knit as a child. At first I clutched the needles and pulled the yarn too tightly, producing a matlike effect. In time I learned to relax, developing a natural rhythm, no longer throttling every stitch.

History

Bolívar said that making a revolution in Latin America is like plowing the sea.

Anna
October 1973

In this time of the swollen grape,
the wine begins to come to life
between the sea and the mountain ranges.

In Chile now, cherries are dancing,
The dark mysterious girls are singing,
and in guitars, water is shining.

The sun is touching every door
and making wonder of the wheat.

. . .

I have no wish to change my planet.
————PABLO NERUDA

Lunch would be late today. Anna and Carmen had lingered
with Damaris at the river's edge to watch a truckload of
Gypsies who had come for a feast.

They had been singing and shouting as their truck inched its way to a parking place along the sandy bank. In an attempt to escape the fierce heat of the noonday sun, the women had scrambled fully clothed into the gelid, swift-moving water. Children and babies had joined them, and as they splashed about, their mothers had washed their youngsters' hair with detergent. Soon grandmothers were scrubbing clothes, leaving them to dry on rocks, or expertly dicing onions and garlic, evidently to be used in a blood pudding, for a number of the younger men, knives in hand, were conversing earnestly over a noisy young pig.

Some of the adolescent girls insisted on telling Anna's fortune. She successfully resisted at first, repulsed by their grimy reptilian hands and by their quaint way of cleaning their noses by leaning over, blowing, and pinching their nostrils. At last she yielded to a pretty, green-eyed child dressed, like her elders, in three or four layers of bedraggled chiffonlike skirts. From her pocket the little girl extracted several walnut shells, dyed red, which she offered to Anna as love charms. The fortune was very simple: "You will always be in love," the child said.

"You can at least give us some cigarettes," one of the older girls added.

"I don't have any." Anna heard the nervousness in her own voice; she wondered how she would extricate herself from the center of the Gypsies' attention.

Carmen came to the rescue. "We don't have any cigarettes, but we can give you some advice about butchering your pig. I have been listening to the men over there." Carmen gestured with her head. "They're not getting off to a good start." Then she walked towards the men, followed closely by the Gypsy girls, Anna, and Damaris.

It seemed odd to Anna that the Gypsies were innocent of the art of butchering a pig, but it was possible, she supposed, that they survived on plain, almost vegetarian fare. At first they listened noncommittally to Carmen's advice, but soon they obeyed her instructions as if accustomed to her rule. "That's the way it always is with Carmen," Anna thought. "She ends up bossing you. And even though you may resent it, you realize you have no alternative; like a petulant child, you give in. Because she's right. She knows. She knows how, no matter what it is."

Anna moved closer to the squealing pig. Carmen was offering it something to eat. Kneeling down by the pig's snout, Carmen looked up at the men and motioned: "Now," she said. They hit him twice on the soft part of his skull where the bones, as in an infant's crown, had not quite grown together. The pig was dazed. Anna felt stricken by the violence which was about to be committed. Damaris moved closer to her and clutched her hand, yet neither made an attempt to leave the scene of slaughter.

Damaris tugged at her mother's hand: "Look." The men were carrying the pig to a tub, where they laid him with his head slanting forwards. Suddenly a hunchbacked crone crept forwards and stabbed a kitchen knife into the pig's heart, causing a heavy spurting of dark blood. The child covered her face for a few seconds, then sought Anna's hand again. "Oh, mama, mama," she whispered.

"The skin must be removed while he's still warm," Carmen was shouting to the men. "You've got to keep him warm." They responded by covering the animal with burlap sacks over which they poured boiling water from a cauldron on an open fire. Then the skinning commenced.

Carmen walked back to stand by the group of women who were surveying the scene. The corners of her mouth turned up almost imperceptibly; her eyes seemed to register a sense of professional approval. "In our family we keep a special large ladle with sharp edges to scrape the hide with," she explained to Anna matter-of-factly. "In the North people finish the job with a razor; I've never tried that."

When the butchering began, the Gypsy women gathered around closer as if waiting for the succulent organs and the blood to make pudding. Anna felt a horrified fascination with the proceedings and still she didn't move. Damaris stood transfixed, her gray eyes pellucid behind owllike glasses. One of the men slit the pig down the middle, carefully removing his digestive system. Then the bony carapace over the heart was cut away. Finally the animal was quartered; the women rubbed the pieces with salt and garlic and oil and hot peppers before hanging them on a line.

"Tomorrow we'll bring you some," one of the Gypsies called after Anna, Carmen, and Damaris.

Anna felt slightly ill; the noonday sun as well as the bloody scene had made her head ache. "I hope they don't," she said. "I don't want any. Why did I stay?" She squeezed Damaris' hand. "Let's go home."

2
_____

Anna had arisen at six to light the oven to warm the house, for the mornings were still chilly; in the frigid dawn air she could see her breath. With Carmen she went out to feed the animals, returning in time to awaken Damaris for school. Normally Anna would ride Damaris to school on the bicycle, but last week she had punctured the tire, and it was still not repaired. Now they had to walk to the bus stop at the end of Amunátegui Street and wait about twenty minutes, since the service was poor. Anna rode with Damaris as far as the city square, depositing the child in her classroom and going about her errands.

She stopped for bread at the baker's and for vegetables at the community market. After the warm, homey smell at the baker's she pitied the greengrocers who stamped their feet on the dank earth in an effort to keep warm. They wore dirty white garden gloves while they sawed chunks from enormous squashes and dipped their hands into long burlap bags of onions and potatoes. With two housewives whom she knew slightly Anna stood and talked while they waited their turns. Señora Flora began to mutter about prices which skyrocketed from day to day. The women talked softly, almost in a whisper, for every type of complaint was taken as a criticism of the Government, and criticism of the Government was illegal. Anna felt a little uneasy. She nodded politely in agreement as Señora Flora and Señora Juana talked, but she had little to add. Only yesterday, when Anna had gasped at her bill for oil and sugar at the drygoods store, the woman next to her, the wife of a trucker, had said edgily, "Yes, but we're better off than before; now we have our freedom back; or don't you think so?" Anna was forced to agree; and she tried to sound enthusiastic. She said to herself, "I keep swallowing my choler, I and everyone else; all this emotional flatulence can't be good for people."

On the way home Anna stopped at the Ortegas' house to use the telephone. The maid answered the door. "The Señora is in bed," she said.

"What, is she ill?" Anna asked.

"Oh no, she's just knitting and keeping warm."

"It's turning out to be quite a nice day though, don't you think?"

"Yes. But the Señora doesn't warm up before noon."

After her phone call Anna stopped by Señora Ortega's room to say hello. It was a large, comfortable room, she noted, with expensive furniture, for the Ortegas had grown rich raising tomatoes, and their lifetime savings had gone into their house. "And yet they don't have decent heating," Anna thought. "It seems so strange. The richest people in town have to huddle over their kerosene stoves or take to bed to keep warm."

Anna sat on an overstuffed chair by the TV. The women chatted awhile. "I love to watch you knit," Anna said. "The needle moves so fast, like hummingbirds' wings. I couldn't begin to do it, yet for every Chilean female over seven or eight, it seems to be second nature."

Señora Ortega, whose brilliant black eyes set off an otherwise nondescript grayish face, darted a meaningful glance at Anna. "We knit our way through our lives," she said. "In

Chile there is an eternal clacking of needles and of tongues. Both are expressive, but it is with our needles that we women let out the anger and resentment and sorrow that we'd best keep quiet about."

Anna was surprised. Señora Ortega, although obliging about the use of the phone, was normally distant with her neighbors. Anna waited, hoping the woman would explain herself, but she quickly staged a retreat to her wool, merely nodding as Anna made conversation. "Well, thank you," Anna finally said. "I'll be going now."

At home Anna found Carmen heading towards the garden with baskets to pick vegetables for lunch. "Don't forget I won't be here," Anna called. "It's just you and Damaris today. I'm going to Valparaíso."

3

The motion of the train made Anna drowsy though she raised her eyes to register the passing of the stations which still separated her from Valparaíso. There was a basic sameness among most of the well-vined, pumpkin-colored villages along the coastal range, but some of them had impressed themselves on her by virtue of their peculiar histories. She remembered that the devil had been seen on Urmeneta Street in Limache as recently as 1969, and about the same time a mysterious stranger, an *anciano*, had appeared in Olmué, to chastise the town's richest man, who owned most of the land the buildings stood on as well as fertile farmland. Anna had been assured that his arms had been permanently crossed behind him, prisoner-style, by the awful visitor, as penance for binding in chains a peasant who had stolen a cow for his starving family. Closer to the coast, in Villa Alemana, say, or in Quilpué, one couldn't expect such miraculous events, since the inhabitants—

many of them working in the port—had grown too sophisticated for such homely displays of divine interest in human
affairs.

The conductor paused to collect her ticket. Fares had
doubled since last week; Anna could no longer afford the rather
luxurious trips to Valparaíso· which she was accustomed to
taking three or four times a month. Had it not been for her
knowledge that she and Ben and Damaris would soon be leaving Chile, she would have despaired at the relentless and predictable drop in their standard of living. It was a serious moral
failing, she supposed—her inability to embrace the fate of
Chile as her own. But it was not her country, she thought
furiously, clenching her toes tightly together as if in defense
against an invisible attack; and although the pain and suffering
of Chileans was as significant as those of other peoples, it
wasn't more so. "If I am to burden myself with a comfortless
history, a future without hope, let it be in a more congenial
environment," she had written to her sister, Ingrid. But loath
to register any specific complaints against a people who were
down and out, she hadn't sent the letter.

The train rounded the bend which revealed a sweeping view
of Viña del Mar, vineyard by the sea, Pacific pearl, opulent
precinct of the well-to-do. Anna loved to walk through its
ample, flower-filled plazas in the winters, when the coastal
breezes preserved the city from the Andean cold found further
inland, but in the spring and summer, when thousands of
tourists descended on the limited number of sandy beaches, she
preferred Valparaíso which, while grimier and more tempera-
mental, had elements of greatness about it. The train was
closely paralleling the ocean now, and soon, at some imper-
ceptible point, it would leave the stylish city for its once
splendid but now fairly dowdy twin, with its wooden clapboard
construction, bedraggled and decaying. Most of the passengers
would descend at the central station at the port, but Anna
intended to ride to the end of the line. She watched the people,
preoccupied with their bags and children and newspapers,
wondering if they were as indifferent as they seemed to their

city's extraordinary geography. Valparaíso had to be the hilliest city in the world, and from the rows of houses, propped up precariously on mounds of earth and stone, like inverted cups of various sizes, one could view the magnificent bay, once the major Pacific port and still an active one, with its fringe of solid and aggressive buildings, suggestive of a former British influence, of wide commerce, of imposing wealth.

At Caleta Membrillo she descended from the train and began a short walk to her destination, a seafood restaurant which—up two flights of stairs—allowed one to commune at eye level with the gulls which dived for fish in the ocean far below. It was in truth a shabby café, badly in need of paint, and the interior—if it could be called that, for the dining area consisted of a windowless porch—was furnished with insipid, formica-topped tables. In the corner was a jukebox which always had the same records, including "Anna's Song," which someone inevitably played every time she was there:

> Anna's leaving on the night train
> Don't wait up, don't wait up
> Sweet Anna's leaving, leaving with me.
> Bought her ticket at the station
> Made her midnight reservation
> Sweet Anna's sure this time,
> She's leaving, leaving with me.

Yet, in spite of its almost formidable humility, there was no restaurant in Chile which Anna liked as well, and she was convinced that the *pièce de résistance*, a fish soup, would steal the honors from the most widely acclaimed Mediterranean bouillabaisse. And even if the fare had been less than sublime— even if the spectacle of the gulls turning gracefully in their wide arcs over the milky froth of waves breaking on promethean boulders and, farther out, of the dolphins leaping and flying in a sea of deepest lapis lazuli, had not filled her heart to brimming—she would have come to listen to the moan of foreign passenger ships drawing near to port, to the whisper of gentle favonian breezes drifting in from Robinson Crusoe's island and Tahiti, to the monotonous slapping of waves on the shore: all of these beloved sounds reminded her that Chile, though situated at the world's end, was bathed by the same tides and currents that visited the rest of the globe. It soothed her spirits to catch the rhythm of these eternal movements which challenged her own insularity and Chile's, and sang of the North, of home.

She ordered quickly without consulting the menu, always the same, and turned her attention to the discourse of the wind and the sea. She had made this journey—she knew it well—not as she had once been used, to pass a few pleasant hours. She was here to commune with her memories and to immerse her senses in the scents of other days. She had come to induce in herself a mood of nostalgia which would become a source of exquisite melancholy pleasure. It seemed foolish, even morbid: it was the sort of womanish behavior, she thought ruefully, that lends itself to persiflage. Yet life being what it is, rich in impertinences, prodigal in stinging cruelties, why should she reject a bracing tonic of beautiful moments, however self-conscious and contrived? Besides, now that she knew she was leaving Chile, now she needed to read its character, not in the endless streams of words which she and her loved ones had said and thought about the place in the past six years, but in the wordless language of the elements which had shaped the contours of the country, those primeval forces which did their work undisturbed by the human dramas which ended by defeating their actors.

"No," she thought to herself, "that's not quite it. It's not Chile that I'm seeking to come to terms with: it's myself."

She lingered over her fruit and coffee. She watched the vault and plunge of whewing birds and the journey of a solitary cloud across a blue landscape. Everything seemed easy at the sea's edge—the gliding of wings, the ebullient play of foam, the dystole and systole of the waves' coursing. "Perhaps it's the example of nature's refusal to ponder or regret that purges us," Anna thought, for although she meditated on her situation, she no longer brooded. Indeed, it came to her that for an hour or more she had felt nothing at all except the clean physical sensations of sunlight and a full stomach. But she was happy—she sought no further benediction—and as she stretched, as if to take deeper into herself the peace she felt everywhere, she suddenly saw without emotion the cause of the maelstrom which had been threatening her inner harmony. "I've outgrown my own wishes," she said to herself. "I persist in mouthing sentiments which I no longer feel." And she recalled her first conversation with Ben after the coup, when she had extracted from him a promise to leave Chile. It was a triumph over him so long delayed in coming that, when she failed to rejoice, it was easy to attribute her lassitude to an exhaustion of will. Or to pity and remorse: for in spite of the series of hurts he had dealt her, he was still her most trusted friend; when his hopes were crushed, he always seemed so vulnerable, so innocent of saving self-deception and cynical connivance that she was tempted to yield to his maiming goodness, his foolish—she searched fruitlessly for the right word—sanctity. "It is difficult to exult," she thought, biting her lip to keep from smiling at her own conceit, "when one has downed an adversary who is as placid and artless as a plant."

But the consideration which had struck her only a minute ago, that in truth she was beginning to truly like Chile, was so at variance with her habitual way of looking at things that she could only nudge at it playfully. It seemed to her that, ever since Ben had conceived of the quixotic idea of becoming a Chilean, her longings had been in permanent anabasis: not because she especially loved the land she was born in, not because she identified herself with Anglo-Saxon values, but because she needed to belong somewhere, and this was not the place. Chile, this physiological abortion, this grim chronicle of historical mishaps, bereft of form, of muses and majesty—she could compose an endless litany of its detestable characteristics. She had a score of well-turned stories about the native temperament and its essential attributes: vainglory, saturninity, venality, mendacity, sensuality. She thought of the typical Chilean, whether aristocrat or *roto*, as a consummate con man; insincere, rapacious, clever, indolent.

And yet, as she sat studying the geometry of her feelings, she began to recognize a certain shoddiness in what had seemed like elegant demonstrations. She remembered her dismay the year that she and Ben had returned to San Francisco: far from falling into a familiar posture among the cultural landmarks of her youth, among a people with whom she shared an emotional alphabet, she had vacillated at the periphery, unable either to take a place in the conversational field or to formulate precisely the reasons for her unease. It was less that the country had changed—in any case the continuous flashy racing of modish concerns across the national consciousness was something she was used to—than that she no longer felt the significance of either the terms or the syntax of the ongoing dialogue. Even her sister Ingrid and her new husband, Miles, a philosopher who intimidated Anna with his moody brilliance, had been hard to talk to. The couple, deeply committed to the humane and generous causes available to them, nevertheless struck both Anna and Ben as captives of arguments which could never be carried to their farthest conclusions without floundering in contradictions. They were for patching up this, doing away with that, unaware that the reforms they advocated would end up destroying the very economic and social system they proposed to save. When Anna tried to talk to her about it, Ingrid would become defensive: "You've become too ideological, Anna. Maybe you can get away with such talk in Chile, but here you'll just get yourself branded as a bellyaching agitator."

So Anna had been forced to recognize the fact that her long residence in Chile had undermined her life's integrity. It seemed to her that formerly she had been, like Ingrid, a creature whose responses, however varied, at least swirled around durable and significant points in a comprehensible emotional plane. But now a whole new set of references had formed a layer of meaning which, while it never totally obliterated what lay beneath, subtly transfigured it and competed with it. She didn't feel at home anywhere. "Some people, like Ben," she reasoned, "choose a physical landscape which corresponds to their inner geography: a true marriage results; then there are those of us, philanderers of the soul, who are only wounded by the spirits with whom we coinhabit a place."

Anna glanced at her watch and knew that she should go; but at the horizon the sea had turned the color of ripe plums, and the sunlight which fell upon the granite boulders where the gulls nested was benign and golden. She lay her head on her arms and viewed the scene through lowered lids. "I'm happy"; she whispered the words to herself, half-afraid of this novel proposition. And this "puny-souled country?" This "pointless exercise in joyless and rancorous subsistence?" Suddenly she remembered the story about the political prisoners in the Valparaíso jail who had sung their party songs defiantly even though they were tortured for it, and she thought of the long lines of wives standing patiently outside countless prison walls every visiting day, heavy laden with buckets of food and bundles of soap and blankets and photos. She winced at her own glib sarcasm; it was as if the swarm of outrages that the *milicos* had visited upon the country had picked her clean of bitter invective.

She paid the bill and made her way down the steps, where two brindled cats were lazily stretched. The path to the bus stop was littered, and as she passed a circle of fishmongers, they began to ogle her although, as she observed sardonically, she towered a head over the tallest of them. The sense of serenity so lately achieved began to desert her: she had known it would. Somehow the emotional guidelines for living in Chile which she was forever formulating for herself were strained beyond limit by the exigencies of day-to-day affairs. "Happy or not, resigned or not: whatever I am to be, let me at least be it wholly, without this eternal meandering!" she exclaimed to herself. Then she searched her purse for a wad of bills with which to pay the fare and composed her list of errands as she waited absentmindedly for the next bus.

4
_____

Her old parents would appreciate this place, thought Anna, as
she walked into the vastness of the city market of Valparaíso,
for they felt a loving reverence for food, its aesthetic and useful
properties. She could hardly remember her early years on the
farm in Idaho, before her family had moved into Caldwell,
but her mother had often described the manmade cave near
the kitchen where she put up food for the winter: row upon
row of jars of yellow corn and tomatoes and stringbeans and
pickles and peaches and apricots and pears; there they were,
colorful soldiers lined up on the shelves, ready to defeat the
long winter. There were potatoes too, and onions and squashes,
and the pig her father had butchered, big chunks of it dried
and hanging from a line.

The cave had been low and cozy, barely large enough for
its stores; the effect must have been just the opposite of what
Anna always felt in the market, for it was huge—vaguely suggestive of a cathedral with its high ceilings; and the hurried
bustle of people constantly coming and going, of boxes and
bins always filled and then emptied and quickly filled again,
made her think of the vast labor of thousands, their eagerness
to sell immediately, while everything was fresh, and the practiced customers' insistence on pinching and poking and testing
for the best.

She followed along behind a couple of chattering women,
eyeing the enormous yellow squashes, with diameters of tree
trunks, and purple aubergines, and shiny green avocados piled
negligently in great heaps, and the knobby *chirimoyas* and
lucumas which, in their plain dress, concealed their sweetness
and delicacy. Then she walked to the fish counters. Only another who had grown up a thousand miles inland, she liked to
claim, could understand how she felt there in the presence of
such fantastic living forms. For they were still squirming, most

of them, the barnacles and sea urchins, the scallops and mussels, the clams and crabs and oysters and lobsters and shrimp. She gasped in astonishment at their endless variety and their salty sea smell. Then she turned her eyes towards the enormous and shapely fish hanging from hooks above the vendors' heads: they were always there, the princely *congrio* and *corvina*, shimmering in their unique iridescent tones of gray and violet and flamingo pink: the most beautiful colors in the world.

5
_____

"Suddenly, just as I was about to leave, a dozen customers descended on me," Paulina whispered to Anna. "I can't go until Roberto is here to relieve me."

"That's all right—I don't mind waiting," replied Anna. She took the only chair in the delicatessen and arranged her shopping bags at her feet. She had had a long walk in the inspiriting, hot afternoon air, and her legs were tired. It would be pleasant to sit for a while and watch the most beautiful woman in Chile reigning over a cash register. She suppressed a smile at her own tendency towards idolatry. "One of the strange things about you," Ben had once observed, "is your determined search for exemplary persons and your willingness to prostrate yourself before them. You must have some sort of recessive, geniculated gene, the kind which inspires people to fall to their knees."

He was exaggerating, of course, but it was true that with Anna praise was not merely an expression of approval but also a reverent testimonial to human excellence. It seemed to her that, in a world where grace and wisdom were occasional visitors, their manifestations should be causes for public rejoicing. She considered handsome people to be human benefactors, not only because of their intrinsic worth but also because of her superstitious conviction that there is a necessary correspondence between inner and outer beauty: a hard doctrine, she thought wryly, for a homely woman.

As for Paulina, she was the proprietor of the Copihue delicatessen which Anna had stumbled on quite by accident about a year before; she had been excited to see rich Greek pastries attractively displayed in the window, and a notice that feta cheese was available on Fridays. She rather expected to find a Greek family running the establishment, but Paulina was a "Turk," as the Chileans commonly termed members of the large group of immigrants from Middle Eastern countries and their descendants. Many of them were very wealthy, and along with the Jews, the English, the Germans, the Italians, and the Slavs, they exacted from the old, traditional Chilean stock the tribute which, in the modern world, landowners owe to industrialists and bankers. At least this was commonly said: it seemed to Anna, however, that through a system of judicious marriages of sons and daughters and capital, each of the powerful groups had allied itself with the other, and all had allied themselves with the multinational corporations so that such distinctions were meaningless except to the shoppers who resented the prices charged by the "foreign" merchants. In any case, Paulina's father, a fervent Muslim who had bequeathed to his daughter a meager collection of rugs from his shop, had never known the measure of worldly success widely considered to be appropriate to one of his origins, and although Paulina did somewhat better—supporting a crippled husband, Roberto (injured in an accident which Anna had only heard mention of), and their son, Gonzalo, of high school age, she was a poor cousin to the Hamidi family, the Yayurs, the Hosnanis, and the Haddads.

"I have found the woman referred to in the Song of Solomon," Anna said to Ben after her first visit to Paulina's shop. "She has cheeks of pomegranates, teeth like ewes, and her breasts are twin does." She paused, "At least they were in her youth; in her maturity she's more filled out." When Ben had finally met Paulina, he too had been struck by the thrilling freshness of her skin and hair, her eyes like heavy topazes, the mysterious penumbra which seemed to define the space she inhabited. "It's your secret little desires which determine what you are," she had once said to Anna; and then, as an addenda, "It's not what you are but what you wish to be that counts." Behind the cash register she had posted a sign inscribed with an equation which Ben had copied and sent to his brother; it said simply: "A great civilization=good dreams."

It had been easy for Anna to strike up an acquaintance with the shopkeeper, for Paulina was curious about the *gringa* who lived in such an obscure place as Villa Inez. Soon a day in Valparaíso seemed incomplete without a visit to the Copihue. Whenever she could, Paulina left the delicatessen to Roberto and went with Anna for a break at a nearby bakery, but often she heated a kettle on a hotplate in the bathroom, and the two of them took tea over the counter as they watched the shop.

Anna heard the familiar squeak of Roberto's wheelchair; Paulina would be free to go. Anna rose and gathered her packages, impatient for her friend to join her, but suddenly she observed that Paulina stood perfectly still, her eyes glistening slightly, listening to a customer, a big man of fifty years, who gesticulated widely as he talked. "My son Raul is a pilot with Lufthansa now; it was his bad luck to have to fly the Chilean leftists out who had taken refuge in the German Embassy. He said it made him sick to look at them; he hadn't realized that Chile could produce such trash. We're better off without the vermin, yes, but it's revolting to see them getting off so lightly after committing so many crimes."

Another woman seemed eager to join in the discussion, but Paulina, in a voice that suggested the rustle of satin, said simply, "Raul: it's been so long since we have seen him. You must send him to visit us when he's in the city again." Her vibrant smile spread its arc across the room, and, as she backed out of the shop, almost whispering farewells to her regular customers, it seemed to Anna that the very atmosphere was suffused with her resonant presence.

Outside, however, Paulina allowed herself a few tears. "Anna, my dear, where have you been the last few weeks? It's been bad, very bad. Did you get the message that I phoned to the Ortegas? It was important that I talk to you. But wait a minute; I've got to pull myself together," she said, dabbing at her eyes with a handkerchief. "Maybe a cup of tea will cheer me up."

"Now you must tell me everything," Anna began as they settled down at their regular spot, an upstairs table in the Cologne Bakery. "Are you in trouble?"

Paulina frowned. "Not exactly—not yet. For the moment it's a matter of coping with provocation. That man who was speaking about the Chilean refugees, for instance: he has been a customer for years; he knows I'm a revolutionary. He was baiting me. Frequently people stand around watching, amused at my helplessness. If I were to fall into the trap, I'd of course be denounced as a dissident. Listening without comment, having to take it all, I'm a hypocrite; I feel everyone despising me for it."

"It's because of the JAP," said Anna. "When you agreed to use the Copihue as an outlet for the JAPs, you revealed your political colors. I started to worry about you the day of the coup, Paulina. I imagined that the *milicos* had computerized lists of everyone who had cooperated with the Government food program."

"It seems like a pitiful offense, doesn't it, Anna? I was so careful in other ways. Every time the merchants called a strike, I shut my doors like a true *momia*. I was afraid. You remember what happened to the owner of the ice-cream parlor when he refused to strike: the Patria y Libertad thugs broke his windows and machines, and ice cream flowed into the street."

"So it's the JAPs. That's all they can blame you for."

Paulina sighed deeply and seemed to unwind. "Do you recall how it was back in the days when we set up the JAPs? It was bad, yes—we were fighting for survival—yet we knew we were winning, we knew we were developing the organs of mass power which were essential for the creation of a true socialist society. Every day was an adventure; how alive, how dynamic we were! My role was small, for I'm cowardly—I admit it. But I did use the Copihue as a JAP center; it was a little something. Were you ever here when we were distributing food? I'd put up a notice a day in advance, and at the proper hour the women would come, grateful to get whatever there was. Roberto would be at the scales. 'Containers,' he would say, and everyone would hold out wicker baskets, burlap bags, pillow-cases—whatever they could find—for even if we managed to keep ourselves in food right up to the end, we never had containers. I would fill up empty bottles with oil and cross names off my list."

"I've always meant to ask you: did you ever have occasion to distribute food to members of the opposition, too? I'm curious because of my own experience: since Ben and I are *gringos*, we are frequently taken as *momios*. We half-expected to be rejected by the neighborhood JAP, but whatever their mental reservations, they let us in."

"What questions you come up with! Actually I wouldn't have turned a *momio* away, but by the time the JAPs were set up, the country was completely polarized. Everyone had taken a stand, and no one crossed the line."

"Well, and will there be reprisals?"

"Exactly. I'm to be driven from business, Anna. Merchants who cooperated with the left are to receive stiff fines. You know how the Chilean economy is run: the guilds fiercely protect their own interests; if you're blackballed, you're ruined."

"I'd like to help you. Maybe if you sold out fast, you could salvage something. I'm working with some other Americans and a Canadian couple; we're trying to set up new businesses and cooperatives for people who have lost their jobs; and we collect information to send out of the country."

"Setting up businesses—that's expensive. Where do you get the money?"

"Here and there. Lots of church groups abroad are helping."

"All of this talk is so depressing, Anna; I don't know why we go on and on about things. That's how we spend our evenings:

friends drop by, and we feed on death and torture and unemployment and starvation. I suppose it's inevitable, isn't it? Yet I wouldn't have guessed that a group of *gringos* were mixing themselves up with us. You shouldn't follow our example, Anna; this isn't your country, we're just a dot on the earth's surface."

Anna suddenly felt a surge of sorrow which pulled at her mouth and constricted her throat. She attempted to make a joke. "Why should I bother myself about you? Chileans are like non-Chileans, really, seeking happiness and truth—"

"But more quarrelsome. . . ."

"Braver in adversity. They've known so much of it."

Paulina's eyes lit up in pleasure at the turn of phrase which presented itself to her. "Chileans are like non-Chileans in that they use their knowledge and power not as a lamp with which to illumine the way for their fellow men, but as a club with which to beat them into submission."

Anna was shocked at Paulina's mockery. "I don't think that was true of the left—honestly I don't."

To Anna's surprise, Paulina covered her mouth and laughed deeply. "Ah, what babes you and Ben are," she finally said. "You are with us, yet you're not. How extraordinary it must be to be so innocent!"

Anna fought a twinge of irritation. "You put me in a difficult position: surely you don't want me to agree with you."

Paulina reached out and squeezed Anna's arm. "I'm being dreadful—forgive me. In truth I envy the way you have managed to stay clear of our sectarian quarrels although it puts you at a disadvantage in analyzing our debacle."

Anna glanced around the bakery as Paulina continued to talk. In the upstairs portion they continued to be the only customers, but looking down from the balcony Anna could see a roomful of tables crowded with sandwiches, pastries, and brass and copper pots. It was pleasant sitting at a ringside seat watching the patrons—mostly women—chatting animatedly. Even as she followed Paulina's remarks, Anna found herself reading the lips of a woman below whom she thought she recognized—a salesclerk at a nearby bookstore. There was an agreeable odor of coffee and chocolate and warm bread.

"I don't have the advantage of university training," Paulina was saying as she emptied the teapot, "but I was still at home when my brothers were studying, and I've listened to thoughtful talk all my life." She paused as she stirred a spoonful of sugar into her cup, and then she smiled bashfully. "You will think I'm boasting, but I must tell you that sometimes I suspect that I have the best of all possible perspectives: I'm familiar with all the theoretical positions, but I'm also by necessity a sensible, down-to-earth person."

"About the theoretical positions, I don't follow you."

"I'm not surprised. Listen, Anna, you have been isolated out in Villa Inez, and Ben, for all his fine qualities, allows himself to be led around by the nose by his priest friends. I don't think you've had a chance to arrive at a correct understanding of the situation we're living through."

Anna suspected what was coming. "The Communists are to blame," she offered.

Again a fleeting smile lit up Paulina's face, and her eyes, still glistening from her recent tears, seemed to take in her friend with pleasure. "Well, yes, in so many words. It was the Communists who put most faith in the whole notion of a peaceful road to socialism, a revolution by stages, and they were Allende's most loyal supporters in attempting to limit the process to the immediate needs of overthrowing imperialist and oligarchic structures."

"I've never quite understood what you have against that position," replied Anna, and as she spoke, she lowered her voice, for a couple with two children had climbed the stairs and taken a table by the windows at the opposite side of the room.

Paulina also lowered her voice. "It's simple, Anna. The Communists are fifty years behind the times, and they still take their orders from Moscow. What does Moscow know of socialism? The Russian type, of course, the top-heavy bureaucratic state socialism with no workers' power at the base. That's not what we Chileans want; we don't want to trade domination by a small bourgeoisie for domination by an all-powerful government run by technocrats."

Another table in the balcony had been filled by teenagers, and Anna felt obliged to lower her voice. "Well, that seems reasonable, but I don't think anyone in the UP, including the Communists, wanted to copy Russia's errors. As I understand it, the Communists were for proceeding one step at a time, moving with great caution. I suppose it's true that nationalizing the basic industries isn't everything, but it's something."

Paulina replied in an earnest whisper, "Anna, you can't freeze the revolutionary process that way. You can't force a preplanned, parliamentary mold on to the dynamics of history without destroying the whole movement. That's what the UP did; that fact has to be faced. I supported them, yes, but only insofar as they were permitting and implementing the organization of new structures appropriate for self-rule by the masses."

"I hear your words, but I honestly don't understand you."

Paulina hesitated for a few seconds and then whispered rapidly. "Let me give you an example: the strike of October 1972."

"The strike of the rich and their lackeys."

"Exactly. The first massive mobilization of the opposition to bring down the Government by economic pressure."

"But they didn't succeed. Or rather, they didn't succeed in October of 1972."

"No, they didn't. And why not? Because the workers and the masses kept the productive forces in operation. They were forced by circumstances to mobilize spontaneously on a greater scale than ever before and to solve such problems as finding supplies for the factories, transport, and so on. They requisitioned trucks and drove them themselves; when shops closed down, workers organized protection for those who would stay open; they set up committees for vigilance and self-defense. They walked to work, since there were no buses, and they distributed food. If the owners tried to join the strike, closing down their factories, the workers would occupy them and run them; they took over more than a hundred that way. The workers with medical students and a few doctors kept the health facilities in operation. The Socialist Party newspaper put it in a nutshell: 'Chile is now functioning without employers.' "

"Then there were the *cordones industriales* set up in the industrial zones as paramilitary organizations."

"Well, that was in 1973, actually, when everyone could see that a coup was coming. But the idea was the same; it was to strengthen the network of organizations which the people created and ran."

Anna glanced nervously about to see if she and Paulina were attracting attention, but the patrons, occupying nearly every table now, scarcely seemed to lift their eyes from their well-filled plates.

"Well, you don't think the UP was against you, do you? It was they, after all, who called upon the people to mobilize."

Paulina's eyes flashed contemptuously. "They were scared to death of us at the same time they needed us. 'Setting up dual power': that was the name of our error. Once we had saved them, they wanted us to hand back to their owners the factories we had taken; they wanted to reserve the defense of the country to the Armed Forces and the Police." She suddenly burst into tears. "You see where that got us."

"Paulina. . . . "

"They gave the army the right to search the factories for arms held by the workers. Such insanity! It wasn't until the Armed Forces had thoroughly scoured the *cordones industriales* that they dared to rise against the Government!"

Anna was smitten with sadness. A confused cluster of replies crowded her mind, but she resisted the urge to verbalize them. "What's the use?" she thought. "Everybody predicted this disaster, but from a different point of view, and once the coup was effected, they said 'I told you so.'" Maybe Paulina was right; maybe Ben was. She wanted desperately to know, but at the same time she felt the hopelessness of ever being certain.

Paulina was discreetly drying her eyes and blowing her nose

in a lavender-scented handkerchief. "Do me a favor, dear friend. Don't give me any of Ben's standard answers. Don't talk to me about the necessity of staying on good terms with the middle classes as represented by the Christian Democrats. I'm going to tell you a bitter truth which the so-called moderate leftists would never accept: it's a disastrous illusion to think that you can win over the middle classes. Why? Because the initiation of socialism in a formerly capitalist economy is bound to cause an imbalance in the functioning of the system for a while. You have to expect a certain period of economic difficulty with inflation, shortages, and so on. The poor can put up with it, but the middle classes—who, in comparison with the proletariat, are materially and socially privileged—are bound to resist it." She returned her handkerchief to her handbag and snapped it shut energetically. "The UP couldn't bring themselves to choose: would it be the poor or the middle classes? Allende tried to straddle the fence, tried to woo the opposition with his personal charm: that was his tragedy."

They left the bakery and strolled at a leisurely pace back to the Copihue, where Roberto, about to close shop, was carefully wrapping in cellophane some wheels of cheese and a rasher of bacon. Paulina took Anna's hands in hers. "I don't know why you put up with me," she began.

"Don't be silly; don't apologize."

"I'm always preaching at you in an unconscionable way."

"Nonsense."

"You're a North American; I shouldn't expect you to understand. In any case I think you've been splendid." She reached suddenly towards the counter where from under one of the tiles she extracted a postcard on which were typed several addresses. "I want to ask a favor of you: keep this for me."

"Whatever—"

"Don't ask why. These are addresses of some relatives in Europe. If anything happens to Roberto or to me, please contact them immediately."

Anna felt a shiver of fear. "Paulina, you're holding out on me. You're in some kind of trouble."

"No, but anything is possible." She suddenly smiled radiantly. "Sometimes it's better not to know things; I'm not going to burden you."

Anna gave her a quick embrace. "You know where to reach me," she said.

6

When Anna reached her house a bit past nine, she was surprised to see Dorothy Hemming's van parked in the drive. From Damaris' room she could hear the murmur of children's voices.

Dorothy was already dressed for bed and, half-in and half-out of a sleeping bag which she had arranged on the sofa, she was reading about the Watergate case in an old issue of *Newsweek*. "I just hate it when people drop in on *me* unexpectedly," she began apologetically.

"Well, I love it," interrupted Anna.

"Zachary is with me. We were in Viña today. When we were driving through Villa Inez on the way home, Zachary twisted my arm about visiting Damaris. I was so embarrassed about arriving unannounced that I decided to stop at a public phone and call you at the Ortegas', pretending to be still in Viña and asking if you could put us up. Poor Mrs. Ortega's maid had to run all the way here to fetch you, but you weren't home. We came anyway. Carmen let us in."

"For a minister's wife, you're pretty crafty."

"Yes, I am. I'm also intrusive. Ben told Alan and me that you've decided to leave Chile. I wanted to ask about it."

Anna, who had been filling the cupboards with her parcels, frowned suddenly and came to sit on the floor. Then she smiled crookedly. "Yes, you're right," she replied, "and I need to talk about it."

"Well, it's what you always wanted, isn't it? I guess I should congratulate you."

"It's what I always wanted. Yet when Ben finally agreed to it, I didn't react as you might expect. I felt confused for several weeks. Then today when I was having lunch at Caletta Membrillo, the truth suddenly sprang at me: leaving Chile wasn't what I wanted after all; it was something else. . . ."

"What?"

"I wanted to punish Ben."

"Well, that's easy enough. Why upset all of your arrangements for it? Why don't you just shout and pout like most people?"

"That's not my style, Dorothy. I'm much more inclined to punish people with kindness and pity and mercy."

Dorothy leaned her head back and laughed a light gossamer laughter. "I can see what your problem is: you've rebelled against the natural dialectics of marriage: charge, rebuttal, reconciliation: thesis, antithesis, synthesis."

Anna got up to talk to Damaris, who had been calling from her room. She tucked both Damaris and Zachary into bed, and when she returned Dorothy was doodling on the back cover of *Newsweek*. "It's Pinochet," she explained, "but you can see that I've dressed him up like Diego Portales, Chile's founding father, Chile's Alexander Hamilton, the super *momio* whose successor Pinochet fancies himself to be."

Anna admired the cartoon. "It's very good. But if I could draw, I'd dress Pinochet in kingly robes and scepter and crown and set him in a draughty castle in Scotland where he'd mumble in true Shakespearian style, 'To be thus is nothing. . . .' "

Dorothy giggled and quickly sketched a king, but to Anna's surprise the features weren't those of Pinochet. "You've drawn Allende's predecessor," she said.

"Well, if you're going to talk about the crimes of vaunting ambition, I think he wins hands down. What can you say of a man who—not content with having been president once—does everything in his power to bring down a legitimate government under the false impression that the *milicos* will put him in office again? What can you say about a presidential aspirant who accepts money from the CIA?"

"You really hate him, don't you?"

"Let's just say I'd like to see him tried for treason someday."

"I don't think you will."

"Neither do I." She threw down the magazine and the pen. "So much for *l'art engagé*; let's get back to homelier themes. Tell me now: what are you punishing Ben for?"

"For being unfaithful to me."

"Be serious."

"I am serious."

"I don't believe it. How do you know? Did he tell you?"

"He has tried to tell me several times, but I wouldn't let him. I figured that confession would make him feel better, and I wanted him to suffer. I put on an innocent act; I seemed so fresh and warm and trusting that ultimately he had to back down; he decided to live with the hair shirt of his own guilt."

Dorothy looked at her closely. "Then how do you know?"

"Some things about your husband you just know, that's all. I can tell you something about it; it was the wife of a professor of chemistry at the Catholic University whom we met in San Francisco in 1971. You could feel the magnetic forces pulling them together even then though it wasn't until we had returned to Chile that Ben started up with her—it was an intense affair that lasted about two weeks."

"This is fantastic, Anna. I don't believe it." She scratched at her temples several times. "But let's for the sake of argument grant your point: let's say that Mrs. Chemistry really did get through to Ben; maybe she kept him aflutter for a few weeks. You say he was sorry, he wanted to apologize; maybe you've built it up into something more important than it is."

"Of course I have, Dorothy! You can't imagine how foolish I feel! How can I explain it? It's partly because of Ben's character, of course. He's so guileless, so well meaning, and so free of that nearly universal urge to sacrifice others to one's own pleasure that I really gave myself to him utterly over the years: I held nothing back. So when he succumbed to his passions like a typical philandering husband, I felt betrayed."

"Well, that's understandable, but at the same time—if you don't mind my saying so—it's a hard judgment. You've been married how long—twelve years? If Ben has behaved himself in a saintly way for eleven years and eleven months, I think you might find it in your heart to forgive him for the momentary lapse."

"You think I'm neurotic, don't you?"

"We're all a bit neurotic; let's not go that route."

"Look, when a husband is unfaithful, a wife has two options: she can leave him or she can forgive him. The first option is ridiculous, as you've suggested, unless, of course, the husband prefers his lover to you. As to the second, it's what wives have been doing for thousands of years; they grant their husbands absolution, and the men cheerfully assume there's no harm done."

"There's another option; you might neither leave him nor forgive him; you might merely make his life miserable."

"The flaw in that plan is that you make yourself miserable too. To some extent that's what I've done the past few years; in avenging myself on Ben—criticizing our way of life, Chile, his opinions—I seem to have become desperate myself without affecting him much."

"Why don't you come clean with him? I should think you could clear up the matter in fifteen minutes."

"It's too late for that, Dorothy. If he knew I'd been silently bitter against him for several years, he'd be appalled. It would have a terrible effect on our marriage—worse than his adultery."

"Well, I have a suggestion."

"Good. What is it?"

"Treat Ben the way he treated you. Have a two-week affair with somebody. The balance he upset by his original transgression will be restored; you'll feel better, and you won't be obliged to talk the whole painful mess over with him."

"Believe it or not, I've actually thought of that," replied Anna. She walked to the window where she pulled the curtains shut and then she sat down out on the Indian rug in the middle of the room. "But restoring the balance is harder than you think. My adultery would have to be equivalent to his; I'd have to feel the same degree of attraction for somebody as he felt for his lady. And I never do, Dorothy. Maybe I could in the U.S., but in a culture where I tower over most of the men, and where all that the men want in a woman is good looks, I don't rate."

"Ridiculous; you aren't trying."

Anna laughed. "You have certainly upset all the ideas I ever had about ministers' wives." She paused. "By the way, would you act on the advice you just gave me? Have you . . . ?"

Dorothy grinned and stretched herself languidly, pushing her toes against the surface of the sleeping bag about midway down. She seemed even smaller than she was, about 5' 2", and in the dim light Anna could barely make out the faint signs of age which had just started to appear on her friend's face, the deepened lines running from nose to mouth and the web of wrinkles under the eyes.

"Just once."

"And?"

"I think that for some women adultery can be interpreted as vengeance. I was furious with Alan; we had had a quarrel the day before I was to fly from La Paz to New York, and he wouldn't make it up before I had to leave. I kept begging, but he gave me the silent treatment. On the plane I had fantasies that there would be a crash and he'd mourn me forever; that would show him! When I arrived in New York, where I was to attend an international two-week session on the Church in the Third World, a handsome fellow immediately attached himself to me. His name was Wafik Badawi. . . ."

"Wafik Badawi? It doesn't sound like a Methodist name to me."

"He was a Catholic from Lebanon, to be precise. He kept propositioning me, and in my pique at Alan, I finally agreed that if I didn't receive a letter from home within ten days, I'd yield to Wafik."

Anna laughed astonished. "And what did Wafik think of it?"

"Whatever his private opinions, he went with me twice a day to check the mail, and when there was nothing from Alan, he would cross himself in gratitude. On the tenth day I felt obliged to live up to my promise. That's not putting it quite honestly: he was an attractive man with a fund of beautiful things to whisper in my ear; he had been singing his own praises as a lover since the first day I saw him. Perhaps I was in some respects glad Alan hadn't written—I'm really not sure."

There was a pause. "Well, you're not going to stop there, are you? What happened? How was it?"

"It was fine although I can't resist observing that the delights of new flesh are easily exaggerated. After forty minutes we finished, and the inevitable regrets set in; I was afraid I wouldn't forgive myself. Grumpy Alan seemed infinitely preferable to the most charming of Arabs. I pushed Wafik out of my room and made a reservation to fly back to Bolivia the next day."

"Did you ever tell Alan about it?"

"Oh, right away. Perhaps it was to make myself feel better or more likely it was to make him feel awful. I confessed it all."

"How did he take it?"

"He was immensely relieved, as it turned out, having himself been seduced by a graduate student in anthropology who had arrived about the time I'd left. She wanted him, and he's always trying to please people. He felt—and quite rightly I should say—that I could hardly hold it against him under the circumstances."

Anna stared at Dorothy in wonder. "You mean it turned out OK? Neither of you felt bitter afterwards?"

"I'd almost forgotten it until you asked. I'm sure Alan never thinks of it either."

Anna shook her head. "Why is it some people seem to glide through their days as if life were a sleigh ride while the rest of us flounder around in agony and self-doubt?"

The bright look on Dorothy's face suddenly dimmed, and she seemed pensive. "I must seem foolish to you; forget what I said, Anna."

"You take back your advice?"

She smiled enigmatically. "Who am I to give advice? To each rabbit his own carrot."

7

Since the early morning train connections to Santiago were bad, Anna had been forced to take the bus, leaving Villa Inez at 7:15 and changing at Quillota an hour later. She walked around the city square several times, watching the children on their way to school and trying not to stare at the legless beggar on his little wheeled platform. He was always there, near the newspaper stand by the bus stop. With little stumps for legs, clothed in knitted stockings, he looked as if he had been sawed off at the thighs. Expertly he propelled his platform along the road with his gloved hands. Anna was ashamed of her morbid interest in him; she brooded on his condition, imagining to herself his wife who cooked for him and clothed him and sent him to the plaza every day for work or recreation; at night she knitted stockings for his stumps. The astounding thing was that at the other end of the line in Santiago, she had seen another sawed-off man on a nearly identical platform though he had appeared grimmer, more sinister, like the city he lived in.

After a twenty minute wait the Santiago bus came. The driver, as he collected the tickets, munched grapes which he kept in a water-filled can near his seat. Anna made her way to the center, choosing a place on the aisle. To her right a plump old lady sat dozing, her bundles neatly stacked on her lap. On her left a young man who stood grasping the handrail was deeply absorbed in *The Day of the Jackal*. He didn't look down at her, and she was glad; she disliked making small talk with strangers on buses, especially Chilean buses, for she had to concentrate on the driving. No, that wasn't quite it, she thought to herself; she had to focus on divesting herself of her will to control her own fate. For once on the bus, there was no chance of her proceeding at her own rate—prudently, deferentially. It was as if she had boarded a bomber, diving now this way, now that, braking with an abrupt lurch, or starting forwards suddenly, causing her to brace herself, steady herself. Even the humblest old vehicle became transformed under the guidance of a Chilean driver into something ruthless and proud; a great potentate, a viceroy or bishop.

She took the *Mercurio* out of her shopping bag and began to read from the back, starting with the ads. American movies were making an appearance again, and there were numerous reviews of *Klute* and *Cabaret* and *The Godfather*. For filler there were the various familiar patriotic slogans and a few she hadn't noticed before. On the business page she spotted one in large print, arranged on the page like a poem:

> More than a hundred
> fatal victims
> was only the preamble
> to the massacre
> prepared by "Plan Zeta,"
> the conspiracy among Chileans
> and sinister foreign adherents
> of Marxism
> to destroy Chile
> and the Chileans,
> This is Marxism!

She turned the page. There, next to a transcription of a speech by the president of the Chamber of Commerce, her eye caught a small article entitled, "The youngest child of Alberto Aragon revealed his hiding place." Skimming the description of Aragon's arrest, made the day before, she found the part about the little boy:

> It turned out that Aragon was found because of an involuntary indiscretion by his small son. When asked by an officer as to how long it had been since he had seen his father, the child replied,

"I see him every day." The officer ordered his men to repeat their search of the house, which had formerly revealed nothing. This time they discovered their man hiding in the attic.

Reading on a moving bus always made Anna nauseous; she put the paper down for a few minutes to compose herself. She drifted off into a disturbed sleep in which she dreamed about a man digging himself out of a dirt cell with a tin scoop similar to Damaris' sand shovel. She knew that she was dozing, but she wanted to continue the dream. Finally the cell and the man disappeared, and she saw instead the poster which Ben had described to her, the one he had seen at the Air Force Headquarters near UCADULTOS. Mounted at the front door, where guards were always stationed, it stated, "If keeping watch tires you, remember that in September you were to die!"

Suddenly the bus came to a complete halt, throwing all the passengers forwards in their seats. Anna was fully awake, attempting to breathe calmly. "Patrol": the word was whispered through the bus. A soldier appeared at the front, instructing everyone to line up on the outside, men in front and women behind. Anna followed the others, who looked cautiously sullen. "Identity card, please," the soldier said to the crowd. He barely looked at the documents; the search was evidently perfunctory. With the men, however, Anna could see that it was different: they were standing, arms over their heads, while the soldiers frisked them.

The passengers boarded the bus and started off again. There was an oppressive silence everywhere. Suddenly the young man standing in the aisle next to Anna looked down at her and said, "Why do the *milicos* always travel in threes?"

"Tell me," she replied.

"There's one who knows how to read, another can write, and the third is there to make sure the two intellectuals don't go over to the left."

Anna chuckled. She immediately liked the stranger, yet she knew she should be cautious; he could be an informer. "Are you in the military?" she asked.

"What do you think?" he replied.

"Do you have a brother in the Armed Forces?"

"No!"

"A cousin? A brother-in-law?"

"No!"

"No relatives in the Armed Forces?"

"Of course not!"

She smiled. "In that case would you please stop standing on my foot?"

8

Anna arrived at the "Andes Mar" bus terminal at 9 A.M. Since her friends weren't expecting her for another hour, she decided to walk rather than to wait for one of the city buses, which were always crowded. These weekly activities were becoming a pleasant routine, she reflected. For the past three Wednesdays she had left the terminal shortly after nine, strolling along the Parque Forestal, under the well-barbered trees, blue-gray in the morning mist. There was a hint of the sea in the dense air when the day was cloudy, and a rustle of excitement among the few beings she encountered: stray dogs mostly, with tails wagging furiously; fat birds vaulting from complaisant branches to manured flower beds; and an occasional human too, usually a sleeping drunk but once in a while a checkered-aproned maid swinging a child who screamed in delight as she sliced like a scythe through the air while his sister, thumb in mouth, tugging at the maid's skirt, begged a turn.

Still, it would be more pleasant if it weren't so warm, Anna reflected. A month ago she might have known the joy of walking in the rain under an umbrella, peeking out at the other pedestrians who, half-hidden under identical black umbrellas, looked like sea lilies on slender double stalks. It was the only time she felt an affection for Santiago, when the rain, submerging the city and vivifying everything, rendered ordinary sights and odors exhilarating—the color of brick buildings, for instance, the smell of wet sidewalks, the chrome of passing automobiles glittering like Christmas tinsel. She would gaze into the shops where customers in damp hats and raincoats conversed with salesclerks by means of signs and gestures. Turning down Agustinas Street, dominated by gift shops which catered to the tastes of tourists, she would admire the native wares made from abundant Chilean raw materials. They dominated the window: shiny copper plates, brass teapots, jewelry of lapis lazuli, chessmen carved from onyx. They were pretty but they were depressing, the window dressings of underdevelopment.

But on this December morning there would be no rain, and the heat threatened to be more intense than Anna had anticipated when she had left Villa Inez early in the morning, with the chill of night still hanging about everything. She had dressed in a woolen skirt and cotton blouse with a heavy cardigan, and now she was sorry. Her nose was shiny with sweat, and her hair damp and limp. She stuffed her cardigan into a shopping bag and unbuttoned the top button of her blouse as she mentally reviewed her itinerary: she would cross from the Parque Forestal to Bellas Artes and then proceed along Agustinas Street to the Marie Antoinette tearoom, where Paul Pouillon would be waiting.

She looked forward to seeing Paul and Evelyn Pouillon, the newest members in her circle of friends. Ben, she remembered, had first introduced the couple to Dorothy Hemming who in turn had presented them to some of the other Protestant ministers' wives, like Elise Cooper and Kay Duncan, who would be there today. Anna had known Dorothy and Kay and Elise for years, yet she had lost contact with them after moving to Villa Inez. Ironically it was the tragedy of the coup and Dorothy's suggestion that Anna help in gathering information for the foreign press that had agreeably enlarged her horizons. All of these people, who a few months ago had hardly penetrated Anna's consciousness, had come to share her life so intimately that they seemed like essential elements in her own identity.

She was nearing the fine arts museum where, succumbing to the heat, she decided to stop for a few minutes. She found the ladies' room, dingy and smelly like most public lavatories, and searched for the cleanest sink. After splashing water on her face and the back of her neck, she pinned her hair up in a bun. She paused for a moment to look at her reflection: eyes good, though rather small; nose bony and narrow; mouth a thin line; teeth passable; skin olive colored; hair thick and brown, with a few strands of gray. "Nothing is terribly wrong, and nothing is quite right either. Maybe I'll improve with age." Yet she resented her own longings, felt offended with that part of herself which so mercilessly judged the facts of her physical makeup. "It's dreary, being a woman," she thought. "Is it any wonder that some females prefer to do away with their bodies, hiding them behind nuns' habits?" She pictured to herself her tall frame clothed in Franciscan brown; a decided improvement, especially if the habit would cover her long neck.

Out in the street again her thoughts turned to Paul and Evelyn Pouillon, who, although newcomers, had somehow assumed the leadership of the group. They didn't have jobs— that was one reason, of course—but they were also devoted to the project and they seemed to have access to whatever was needed: Xerox machines run by people sympathetic to the left; free paper; foreign newspapers; contacts in other cities; money. Most of all they exerted a strong moral influence over some of the Protestant women like Elise and Kay, who unaccountably enjoyed being bossed by a couple a dozen years their junior.

The first time Anna had met them was at the Marie Antoinette. Over avocado and chicken sandwiches the couple had described to the American women their experiences since the coup and the week that they had spent in the Canadian Embassy. "We were not welcome," Evelyn had said. "The Ambassador and his wife thought we were making a big fuss about nothing."

"Welcome or not, at least you got in," interrupted Kay.

"The American Embassy took no one. A woman we know who was frantic with worry about her personal safety was told, 'Why don't you go to the Chilean police?' That's how the Embassy helps its citizens!"

"Yes, well, there are worse bags than being Canadian." Paul smirked at his own assertion, and behind his thick lenses one could see the golden flecks in his eyes. "But in fact it was a pretty bad scene in the Embassy. There were six or eight Canadians and a dozen Chileans to one bathroom, and sleeping accommodations were crowded. It was no one's fault; we could hardly complain. The worst part anyway was the disunity among the Chilean refugees—all the quarreling over whose fault it was that the UP fell."

"One guy, a Communist newspaper editor, kept ridiculing the MIR," Evelyn continued. "He described with great sarcasm the way the MIR would agitate the *Lumpen* over issues that were peripheral to the program of the UP. In San Bernardo, for instance, the citizens took possession of the city hall under the motto 'Pavement or Death!' He made it sound ridiculous, the way he would roar 'Pavement or Death!' in his heavy tone. And then he would add, 'Imagine going to your death because your streets aren't paved when the control of the means of production is hanging in the balance!' "

"Then it was the *Mirista's* turn to come on with the sarcasm," interrupted Paul. He lit a cigarette and inhaled deeply. "His name was Lucho. 'What you fatuous reformers lack is a sense of history,' Lucho would begin. 'The question isn't what program to adopt and how to implement it; the question is one of *power*. Take the case of San Bernardo: the point about "Pavement or Death" isn't pavement; it's rather the mobilization of the people around an issue that is real to them. You can't turn people into revolutionaries by preaching at them or by nationalizing a few industries for the technocrats to run. People become revolutionaries by acting. What is essential is that they become agents in the making of their history instead of victims of it. The incident in San Bernardo is a good example. All those people who occupied the municipal building are now men and women. No amount of repression is going to make them retreat from the state of revolutionary consciousness that they reached through their own efforts. Multiply that example by thousands and you've got a revolution. We'll have our ups and downs, yes, but eventually we'll get there. But you people: you limit your objectives to creating a welfare state, and you fail even at that. Look where Chile is now. It's just as we predicted when Allende assumed office.' "

Anna admired the ease with which Evelyn and Paul could work the doughty world of Chilean sectarian disputes. "You've learned in two months what I can barely grasp after six or seven years," she had once observed to Paul.

"It's because we never had a chance to be mere spectators," he answered. "We've been faced with one dilemna after another ever since we stepped off the plane."

Anna was nearing the Marie Antoinette. She stopped for a minute or two at a kiosk to read the headlines of the various morning papers and to change her shopping bag from her right hand to her left. The heat was causing her feet to swell in her shoes, and she felt dusty and tired. Suddenly she thought she saw Paul Pouillon walking just ahead, but when she hurried to meet him, she realized her mistake: it was another young man with a similar bald patch creeping inexorably from his crown, and similar thick glasses. "It's strange how close I feel to Paul considering how little I know about him," she reflected. She remembered the hours they had spent together clipping articles from newspapers, filing accounts of tortures and deaths, and typing up newsletters. In some ways it was a horrible time they were living through, an inauspicious hour for forming friendships. Yet they felt drawn to one another— Paul and Evelyn and Kay and Elise and Anna and a few others —by the danger of their enterprise and by their commitments. In some obscure way Anna felt confident that these were, in spite of everything, moments she would remember with pleasure.

She had just entered the Marie Antoinette and ordered a café au lait when Paul approached. He was dressed, as usual, in a yellow hooded windbreaker, blue jeans, and Indian moccasins. It could not be said, Anna thought with one corner of her mind, that he was a handsome man; if he was attractive to her, it was due to his peculiar blend of energy, intelligence, and diffidence. As he kissed her cheek and pulled up a chair, she was struck with the poignance of something he had said to her the week before: "My father has always been younger than I am."

She quickly finished her coffee and allowed him to pay the bill. Then they walked to the Pouillons' apartment on Eugenia Street where the others had gathered. When they entered, Anna was vaguely aware of a mild disorder, as if someone were packing up, but there was plenty of space for them to spread out their files and papers. It was a pleasant apartment on the ninth floor. Anna liked the easy comfort of it, the "sofa" constructed of a mattress and footlockers, covered with a Mapuche blanket, and the various wicker chairs and tables. There were vases of enormous paper flowers, and on the wall were prints of Indian women and children. A set of French windows opened off the living room onto a small balcony. They were open today, admitting a pleasant breeze.

"Anna, you're here; good!" called out Evelyn. "You can contribute something to our discussion. Are Chilean women less intelligent than the men?" Her thick red hair was gathered in a ponytail, giving her rounded, freckled face a youthful appearance.

"To be more specific," corrected Elise Cooper, her folds of fat settling comfortably around her middle, her several chins sinking into her neck, "did the women oppose the UP because they didn't understand what was going on?"

"Some understood it very well," replied Paul. "They opposed the UP for the obvious reason: it was in their class interest to do so."

Evelyn rubbed her bottom lip with her finger and fixed her vision on the ceiling. "We weren't thinking of the *momias* so much as the wives of some of the workers. A number of them can always be depended upon to vote conservative. Elise suspects that they're weak in the brain department, but there must be a better explanation."

"Maybe you think they're born conservative?" asked Elise. "That's a common Chilean point of view; the official view of the present government. Women by nature of their physical makeup and their maternal instinct are more conservative than men and, consequently, more mature and responsible. What about it, Anna? You've been here longer than the rest of us." She crossed her legs, solid like great tree trunks. Her plump bare toes seemed to nestle comfortably in her sandals like the piglets in the children's rhyme. In spite of her size and her years, she exuded volcanic vitality.

Anna gestured helplessly, turning her palms upwards. "In truth most of the women I know voted the way their husbands did, but I have heard of poor women going along with the *momios*. I'll tell you my theory: the women aren't as well educated as the men, and once married the wives cease to be intellectually stimulated because they're always at home. What a contrast to the men! Have you ever met a worker who didn't know the Chilean situation backwards and forwards? They're politicized at work by the unions and the political parties."

"Brainwashed, some would say," interrupted Evelyn.

"One man's brainwashing is another man's education," continued Anna. "In any case they learn to consider problems and how to solve them. Those social facts which formerly seemed 'natural' and uncontrollable suddenly show themselves as human arrangements which can be altered. The wives seldom experience that. They can't escape from a primitive fatalism typical of barely literate menial servants."

Paul lay lengthwise on the sofa, supporting his head on a pile of sofa pillows. "Even without the 'consciousness-raising' sessions at the factories, I think the men would have a better awareness than the women of what's going on. The women are merely consumers. All they know is that goods are scarce or abundant, expensive or cheap. The men on the other hand take part in production; they understand the relations of the social forces to the productive process."

Kay Duncan, who had been in the kitchen making sandwiches, suddenly entered, tray in hand. With her prominent
bust and skinny legs, she reminded Anna of a pigeon. "I think
you're all wrong," she said. "The women vote conservative to
oppose their husbands, whom they hate. And why shouldn't
they? The men drink all the money away, don't they? They
hit their wives and kids. So the women sneak an act of defiance
in the secret, dark polling booth. You can't blame them."

The sandwiches were passed around, and Paul produced a
bottle of red wine. "I like Kay's theory the best," he smiled.
"It's the sexiest hypothesis."

"Look, I feel sorry for the working-class women," said Elise.
"They seem to be the losers no matter what happens. How are
they going to get along now that their husbands are imprisoned
or dead? In spite of Kay's hypothesis, I think it's better to have
a morose, alcoholic husband, if he's a breadwinner, than to have
no man at all." She started to play unconsciously with the
wedding ring imbedded in her fleshy finger. Anna wondered
what was on her mind.

"Are we ready for horror stories?" demanded Paul. "I know
that Anna has a number to report this week."

"What I dislike about the Pouillons' place is the dinner conversation," Kay said, pursing her lips. "It's always so ghoulish.
But go ahead—now we're dying of curiosity." She curled her
long legs under her body and smiled at Anna. She always sat
with her back straight and her hands folded under her ample
bosom, as if about to sing in a church recital.

"I'll begin with an old doctor I interviewed in Zapallar,"
Anna began. "He was arrested the day of the coup. First of all,
it's amazing a UP doctor ended up living in such a snobbish
town. Don't ask me how it happened. He had a spectacular
house overlooking the beach and a large, well-tended orchard,
but after the *milicos* broke into the place the first time, it was
repeatedly ransacked by marauders. Everything of value was
carried off. The doctor's wife told me how the *milicos*, on the
day they came to arrest her husband, kept searching every
square inch over and over again. They even dug around in the

orchard. 'What are you looking for?' she asked. 'For arms.' 'Arms," she replied. 'They are there,' she pointed to her books. 'You are nothing without your weapons,' she hissed, 'but we carry our weapons in our heads, and we will defend them with our hearts!'

"As for the doctor, he was taken to a prison ship where he was held for a week. He's dying from a rare disease, and his diet is restricted. After he finished the saltless bread which his wife had stuffed into his pockets, he had nothing to eat. His torture was mild compared to some although it could have caused a heart attack: he was made to stand under a current of ice water. Do you know, when the *milicos* released him, he was dressed in his bathrobe and slippers and he hadn't a cent. He had to beg some money from a stranger. He's so old, so frail: it's a wonder he made it home."

"What was his crime?" asked Evelyn. "What did they punish him for?"

"For working during the August strike and for helping to design the UP's health program. Now the old man and the other UP doctors are being retired without pension."

"They seem to have it in for the doctors, don't they?" asked Paul. He took off his glasses, rubbed his eyes for a second or two, and looked about in the vague way that sightless people have. "Let me tell you about Dr. Pedro Astaburuaga; he was head of one of the biggest hospitals in Santiago and an administrator in the public health program. The *milicos* arrested him and took him to a discotheque. You've heard the expression—a torture chamber where they play music really loud so that the neighbors won't hear the screams and blows. Anyway, they tortured Dr. Astaburuaga for an hour or so and then they took a coffee break. One of the torturers, a cat with a high-class accent, approached the Doctor and said, 'You know, Dr. Astaburuaga, I have a little problem that no one has been able to help me with; maybe you could give me a good diagnosis. It's my breathing. I have difficulty inhaling deeply; something seems to catch. I end up gasping a lot of the time. It's very uncomfortable.' The Doctor didn't know what to say. 'How can

you do this to me?' he asked. 'How can you torture me foi
an hour and then ask my advice?' You know what the *milico*
said? He said, 'Don't misunderstand me, Doctor. I don't have
anything against you. My job is to interrogate people, and I'm
a professional. But once it's done, it's done. I never take these
things personally.' "

"Well, that must be a new high in lows," said Kay. Her
lips assumed their natural pouty position.

"I can give you another example of torture, this one on a
prison ship," continued Anna. "I heard it from a woman who
lives in Copiapó. When she was released, she came to Villa
Inez to visit her daughter for a few days. Since she has to sign
in every Friday at the Copiapó police station, she wasn't in
Villa Inez very long. This is the story: she was arrested two
days after the coup and taken to the Naval School in Valparaíso. All the prisoners there were stripped naked; the
milicos searched the women's vaginas for explosives, can you
imagine? Then the women were blindfolded for three days.
Outside the school they executed people; she had to listen to
it. Before she was released, she was raped repeatedly; she's
fifty years old. Do you know, a priest came to talk to her; he
was for the Fascists, but before he left, she made him cry. She
said, 'You are supposed to be the Christian, and I'm a Communist—an atheist. But I have devoted my life to creating a
wholesome world for everyone, and you are with *them*. Priest,
I have a seventeen-year-old daughter; I would rather see her
killed than let her be submitted to what's gone on here!' "

Kay Duncan, who had been rummaging in her purse, produced a small scrap of paper folded many times. "I interviewed
a girl of twenty who had been on the Maipú," she said; "I
suppose conditions are the same on the other prison ships." She
began to read from the paper. "They had no water for several
days, and no food, until the Red Cross provided toasted wheat
with sugar. Every night the officers selected young girls to
sleep with. One was only fourteen. Now she's under psy-
chiatric care."

"Savages, that's what they are!" exclaimed Elise. "Perverts!

See how quickly a man's good manners rub off when he's sanctioned to rule with a gun!" Her chin quivered in indignation, and she raised herself slightly from the depth of her chair as if about to make an announcement. "Did you hear about the owner of the leftist radio station in Pillán?" she asked. Her eyes flashed as she turned her attention on each of her friends. "His station was dynamited early in the morning of the eleventh. He and his eighteen-year-old son were taken to the Belloto Naval Station. The man I interviewed saw them there; they were forced to do oral sex with each other while the other prisoners watched."

Everyone in the room made small, restless noises, and Paul whistled in low sounds between his teeth. "That story makes the others seem pretty insipid in comparison," he said. "But once soldiers have been ordered to act like beasts, how do you choose the worst examples of torture? How do you choose?"

9

When the meeting was over, Paul walked Anna to the nearest bus stop. "I have something to tell you," he said as they turned off Eugenia Street onto a broad avenue. "Evelyn is about to leave Chile."

Anna's heart give a loud thump, as if anticipating danger. "That must be the explanation for the boxes and books strewn all over your apartment. I should have guessed."

"You know she's pregnant. It's important that there be no slipups this time. We decided it would be better for her to return home. Maybe she told you that she has to spend months in bed. Otherwise she'll miscarry."

"No, I didn't know."

"Anyway, I'm sticking around here for a few months, and I'm apt to be lonely. I hope you'll come and see me."

Although he was speaking civilly, even formally, Anna felt as if he were trying to peer behind the shutters of her mind. She drew them tighter. "Well, you live in the same apartment house as Jaime, and Ben is usually there during the week; it should be easy to get together."

He put his arm around her casually. "Evelyn and I talk about you sometimes; we both admire you very much. When you're around—it's hard to explain—you're unpredictable. You're full of life and fun and wisdom." He laughed awkwardly. "What I mean is that I thought I'd just about memorized all the possible human types, but you're always new—you're exciting." Then, in a half-whisper: "Don't take that from me."

"Ah, I am becoming afraid of him," Anna thought, with dismay. She avoided his gaze, looking down at her feet. "Sometimes you really throw me into a muddle," she said. "Once in a while I can't think what to say."

He laughed again, a little too heartily, and removed his arm from her shoulder. Suddenly he looked sad and distant, as if he were viewing the scene from faraway. She tried to follow the sweep of his eyes around the busy, dusty street, languid now in the hot afternoon air; she wondered which secret velleities, which consuming passions were waiting to be discovered in him —discovered by her, if she would say the word.

"Here's your bus." He gave her a quick smile. "Remember what I said."

"Yes."

"It's important to me."

"I know."

"It could be important for you too."

She didn't answer.

"See you next week." He turned, hands in his pockets, and retraced his steps.

10

Anna ran up the steps to Ben's office in the UCADULTOS building. She detested being late for appointments, but whenever she felt anxious about something, she fell behind schedule. Her conversation with Paul had disturbed her: she resolved to shelve it for a while. "Later, in Villa Inez, I'll be able to cope with it," she said to herself.

She tried to concentrate on Monica Araya, whom she was about to meet, but thinking about her also made Anna uneasy. "Why is it I find it impossible to be natural around her?" Anna wondered. She remembered the social events from the days when she and Ben had lived in Santiago. Often Monica had been there, beautiful and smart in her stylish clothes. She would speak rapidly in her throaty way, gesturing widely and making people laugh at her string of amusing observations. She could be serious, too. She would sit on the floor, kicking off her shoes, and run her long, ringed fingers through her abundant golden hair as she consulted her personal taxonomy of responses to every type of problem. "She's the kind of woman I admire," Anna thought; "I wanted us to become friends." Yet every time Anna tried to strike up a conversation with her, Monica seemed to look right past Anna's face. Anna couldn't overcome the feeling that directly behind her own head there was a mirror in which Monica was admiring herself. Once she had even turned to see, surprised by the bare expanse of wall which faced her. "It's because you suspect Monica of using knowledge as an ornament," Ben said; "you think she's vain."

"And am I unfair?" Anna asked. "Am I making it up?"

Ben looked at her affectionately. "I'm not sure the word applies. Anyway, she's one of those rare and fortunate people who has never questioned that she deserves a personal symphony orchestra to accompany her through all the moods and movements of her life."

Anna reached the top of the stairs and glanced at her watch: 4:15 P.M. Her meeting had been scheduled for 4:00. Hurrying down the hall and past the foyer where several secretaries sat typing, she looked in the direction of the glass window of Ben's office. She saw opposite his door the wall which was papered everywhere with photos of children and food and people working in the country. At first she didn't spot Ben, who was leaning back in his chair, his feet crossed on his desk, talking to a young woman. Anna turned her attention to his guest, surprised to see that it was a stranger. Having prepared herself to confront Monica, Anna felt alarmed and betrayed, as if the line of defense she could use against Monica might be all wrong in the case of this other woman. "But how absurd!" she exclaimed to herself; "what's wrong with me!" She forced herself to breathe deeply and assume a pleasant expression before tapping on the door.

As Anna entered the office, she took in the young woman's appearance. Seated in the depths of an easy chair, her feet barely touching the floor, she seemed small and vulnerable. Her dark brown hair, parted in the middle, was hidden behind a scarf which was tied at the back of her neck; she was dressed in a brightly colored dress, vaguely Mexican, with enormous sleeves. Anna wasn't at first sure if the young woman was pretty; her small round face, with its sober mouth, was dominated by her dark, narrow eyes and heavy brows. She wore no makeup—unusual for a Chilean woman—and no jewelry except for the heavy golden hoops which hung from her ears.

"Anna, this is Eva Maria Araya," Ben was saying. Anna extended her hand and the young woman rose, smiling shyly. "I feel as though I already know you," said Anna.

There was a pause. Ben—overcome, as he sometimes was, by a fit of embarrassment—evidently hoped that Eva and Anna would begin the conversation. They did. Each decided to plunge into speech at the same second, interrupting the other. Giggling nervously, they turned to Ben, appealing to him to get things right. "Well, at least we can all sit down," he said, clearing his throat. He brought forwards a folding chair for

Anna and returned to his own seat. "Maybe we should begin by filling her in on your situation, Eve," he began. "As you can see, Anna, our plans have changed."

"Then I'm not going to visit embassies tomorrow to find a place for you?" Anna asked Eve.

"I think not," she replied. "It seems that Father Jaime has already arranged things in a satisfactory way."

"That's splendid," replied Anna, but in truth she felt disappointed. She had had two or three occasions to call upon some of the ambassadors who were most cooperative about taking refugees. It was exciting to hear their evaluation of the current Chilean situation and to take an active part in helping someone escape into extraterritorial safety.

"You remember that we were counting on the *sueco chueco*." Ben referred irreverently to the Swedish Ambassador, Mr. Lindquist, using the title "crooked Swede," which the Junta's press had bestowed on him. "It happens that Jaime is a friend of his. Since Jaime wanted to intervene with Mr. Lindquist on Eve's behalf, we of course encouraged him to do so."

"Then it's settled? Eve is to enter the Swedish Embassy?"

"No, it's a bit more complicated than that." He threw a glance at Eve, who was absentmindedly playing with the wooden buttons of her dress. "It turns out that the Junta is angry with the *sueco chueco* for taking refugees. The Latin-American countries, you see, long ago signed a covenant to accept one another's refugees in case of political upheaval, but no such agreement exists with regard to other countries."

"But most of the European embassies have accepted some refugees," said Anna. "Is the Junta angry with all of them?"

"Perhaps. But it is vocal only about the case of Sweden. Ambassador Lindquist, in addition to accepting the refugees, also took over the settlement of Cuban affairs once the Junta broke diplomatic relations with Cuba. That was one unpopular move. Then in general the Swedish Government is obnoxiously persistent about the right, the good, and the true."

"Well? And will they take Eve?"

Ben pushed both his palms hard against his forehead and

closed his eyes. "Mr. Lindquist agreed, but there would be a little problem. She might have to stay there forever." He avoided Eve's eyes, which, as far as Anna could tell, expressed nothing. "You see, the usual procedure is for an Ambassador to accept a refugee and then to ask the Military Government for a 'safe-conduct certificate' so that the refugee can travel safely from the embassy to the airport. Normally the certificate is granted if there are no criminal charges outstanding against the individual. However, Lindquist says that the Junta is so hostile to him that they refuse to grant him any certificates. His refugees will be his guests—who knows?—perhaps until the end of time."

Eve suddenly looked intently at Anna as if to see if she understood the situation. Anna felt confused and frightened. "Ah, yes, well, so that's it."

"Both Jaime and I wanted Eve to accept the Ambassador's offer, but she declined. It's a tough choice. Fortunately another alternative unexpectedly presented itslf. There is an opening at the Italian embassy. Or, rather, there will be."

"The Italian Embassy? I understood they were overflowing with people."

"They are, for the present. But eventually a planeload will be leaving with sixty refugees on board. Then there will be room for Eve at the Embassy. The Ambassador made a promise to Jaime."

"Ah, Jaime. What would we do without him? I suppose he knows the Italian Ambassador too?"

"They're old friends."

"So my services aren't needed?"

"Yes, they are, Anna, though not in the way we had expected. Since Eve can't enter the Embassy for three or four weeks, we need a place to hide her. It occurred to us that Villa Inez would be suitable."

"I'd love to have you," Anna said to Eve, and she smiled to put the young woman at ease.

"I'm very grateful to you," Eve said. She tried to mouth the courteous formulas that are appropriate for such occasions, but

Anna felt Eve's misery and uncertainty. It touched her heart.

"I'm ashamed of all the trouble you and Ben have gone to for me," Eve concluded. "I don't want to make demands upon your hospitality too."

"No, no, not at all, it's no trouble," returned Anna; and they continued to try to reassure each other. "*She would like to cry,*" Anna thought. "*Her eyes and skin and the timbre of her voice are suffused with the tones of unshed tears. She must constantly be on guard against the temptation to give up. To give up: she would like to, but her sense of dignity will not permit it. It's all she has now, her longing to do the right thing, to rise to the terrible demands of this extraordinary occasion. There she sits, speaking in the courtly tongue of a civilization that is in her blood. Everything about her is refined and beautiful. But she has no home, no country, no income, no sure future, and she must throw herself upon the mercy of strangers whom she has no reason to trust with her life. She's truly a sojourner in her own land, a reluctant pilgrim. And she is perhaps a little quaint and old-fashioned, with her cultivated ways, her unquestioned adherence to the traditional humane standards. How passionate she is, under her ladylike talk! Do I approve of such passion? I do. Then don't let her break down. God, no, no, no. Don't let her break down, no.*"

Eve's Memoirs
November 1973

Why the devil do I write?
So that they might respect me and
   love me
To do my duty by God and the devil
In order to keep a record of
   everything.

To cry and to laugh at the same
   time
In truth, in truth
I don't know why the devil I write:
Let us suppose that I write out of
   resentment.
                    ——NICANOR PARRA

Hiding Out

Another move, this time to the apartment of Monica's friend, Pablo. The quarters are cramped, and when his friends are here in the evening, I find myself joining in as they talk and drink and sing. It makes me tired and nervous, but nevertheless I'm comfortable—I feel almost safe. But somebody else needs the space more than I; soon I'll have to be on my way.

Abortion

A few days ago Mercedes, the maid my mother employed until recently, returned for a little visit. She is retired and living with her son who has seven children. She told Mother that her pension isn't nearly enough and her son can't keep her, so she is starving herself to death. She would eat nothing Mother offered her. She didn't seem to think her behavior remarkable in any way; perhaps it's the old Indian habit at work.

It was probably Mercedes' visit that prompted my dream about Rosario, our maid when Monica and I were young. We were very fond of her. I remember vividly that when I was eleven or twelve, she disappeared for a week or two; and when my mother discovered where she was, there was a lot of whispering and tiptoeing about. Monica and I weren't slow to find out what happened: Rosario had had an abortion; it had been performed by an amateur midwife in her neighborhood.

Monica induced Rosario to tell us about it, although Rosario had been forbidden to do so. First, she said, the midwife had dissolved some pills in lukewarm water in a lavatory and then she had poured the water through a rubber tube with a bulb at one end into Rosario's womb. This was supposed to dissolve the fetus, but Rosario felt as if she were going to explode. It was obvious that something was wrong—she became quite purple and began hemorrhaging—so a friend took her to a hospital. The dead fetus was inside her, and the doctors had to operate. She nearly died.

Monica, who at sixteen felt very grown up and read books on the social sciences, gradually dropped her air of disinterested inquiry and displayed a horror as great as mine. "How could you do such a thing?" we asked. She replied, "So many kids and so many problems: I'd rather die than have a child." Then she added, "Some people get away with abortions. My sister, she has had seven, but her husband is a trucker: he earns good money; she went to a private clinic where everything is nice and clean."

Excerpt from a Letter to Helmut, November 10, 1973

Last Saturday I sneaked over to Mother's house for a few hours in the morning. I devoted myself to the most forlorn of household tasks: sorting through old things—discarding most—in preparation for a new life. Discerning the treasures among the detritus of the past requires a more discriminating taste than I have; I finally blinded my heart and consigned a trunkful of memorabilia to the flames. Mother helped me, and it was she who came upon an issue of *Le Monde* which I had long ago saved for its excerpt from Régis Debray's interview with Allende. You will perhaps want to laugh when I tell you that the discovery was providential; it wasn't so much that we found the paper as it was that the paper imposed itself upon our attention. Alone among its peers it refused to burn, and its letters seemed blackened and enlarged among the smoke and ashes.

"What was the message?" you will ask. I shall tell you. Allende was speaking to us, and I felt his energetic presence as palpably as if he were visible before us. His words, it is true, dated from 1971, but they were a legacy which we had to wait until now to take possession of. They were good words; I'm glad he spoke them. I have felt better ever since this strange experience:

> They can lay no accusations at my door—all the civil liberties have been maintained: freedom to hold meetings, freedom of opinion, freedom of the press, etc. . . . The social process is not going to disappear because one of its leaders disappears. It may be delayed or prolonged, but in the long run, it can't be stopped. In the case of Chile, if they assassinate me, the people will carry on, they will follow their course, with the difference that things will be very much harder, much more violent, because it would be a very clear and objective lesson for the masses showing them that these people stop at nothing.

Felipe

Felipe flew in last week. I stayed with Maria Paz at G.'s house one evening while Felipe and Monica went out. I amused myself by going through his journals, more fun to read than his book though, oddly enough, less personal and autobiographical. But I can see that the coup has changed him. He's become more bitter, more sardonic, and—in spite of himself—more involved. One of his entries, on imperialism, I copied.

THE LOGIC OF POWER (1)

THE RICH COUNTRY: If you people want to develop rapidly, it will be necessary to attract capital, and since we are the ones with the capital, you will have to please us by offering guarantees to investors.

THE POOR COUNTRY: But it isn't just that foreigners profit from our earth and our sweat.

RULERS OF THE RICH COUNTRY (in a low voice among themselves): It seems that the country in question is led by ideologues and theoreticians; it needs to be straightened out by a strong man, a no-nonsense military leader.

THE LOGIC OF POWER (2)

THE THIEF (knife in hand): Give me your money or I'll kill you.

THE VICTIM: Jesus! Mary! Joseph! Think of my wife and children! How will you live with yourself?

THE THIEF: Enough of your metaphysical twaddle!

Sergio

As Monica has put it: if you ask Sergio what he thinks of something you've done, he regards it as a long-awaited opportunity to remake your whole personality. He is a master of gratuitous insult. Even in his music criticism, admirable as it is, he sometimes comes on as a cheeky boy challenging the grown-ups.

Sergio

If his obsession with his health seemed morbid, his attention to his own funeral struck me as downright macabre. He had purchased the burial site and the coffin and selected the church. About the flowers and music he tended to change his mind periodically, but when we separated, he had settled on poinsettia, some preludes and fugues from *The Well-Tempered Clavier*, and the "gloria" from an old Mapuche Mass.

"You misunderstand," he used to say. "You think I contemplate my death with fear and regret. Well, perhaps I do, to some extent. But my aim is to look at these things as the ancients did, for whom happiness and dying a peaceful, honorable death went hand in hand. It is only in modern times that we have come to hate death so intensely. We should regard our good-bye to the world as an important statement, worthy of a great deal of careful planning. We owe it to life, to our loved ones. A little reflection will show you that my way is better."

In the last few weeks it has occurred to me now and again that Sergio wasn't always wrong.

The Devil

Juan Andini was supposed to drop by Monica's early this week to find out when I was arriving, but he didn't show up. I feel encouraged; maybe he's forgetting about me.

Allende

His immense patience.

Everyone wanted a private audience with the President, perhaps a dinner invitation. Not just Chileans: from all over the world they came—the adulatory, the critical, the merely curious. He was at home to the great majority of them, and he flattered them with his respectful attention.

The one I remember best was Cunningham P. Edwards.

One morning Allende's secretary informed him that he would be entertaining Cunningham P. Edwards at dinner that evening. No one could think who he was. Since Allende's staff was involved in preparing a big rally, I was asked to check up on Mr. Edwards and to accompany him to Allende's house on Tomas Moro.

I called the American Embassy. Mr. Edwards, I learned, was an agronomist and chief editor of *New World Agriculture*; he had written widely on potatoes. He was staying at the Hotel Mapocho. No one could quite recall how he had swung an invitation to dine with the President.

I called him at the Mapocho to welcome him and to inquire if there were anything special he would like for dinner. (I expected him to ask for *empanadas*; foreign guests almost always did.) "Of course not," he responded, surprised. "I'm bringing the dinner."

I thought I hadn't heard right. He said it again: "Didn't anybody tell you? I'm bringing the dinner."

At seven I met him in the lobby of the Mapocho. Surely enough, he had in one hand an enormous thermal pot. In the other he carried a short, bushy plant.

Plump, of medium stature, with a long black beard and thick glasses, he beamed at me as if happy to be doing me an enormous favor. He made me think of Father Christmas.

We climbed into the back of the presidential limousine. I carried the plant. On the drive, as I remember, we discussed potatoes.

Allende and doña Tencha had been warned. They made room on the dining table in the small salon for the plant and pot. A maid brought dishes and silver. We stood around admiring the plant while Mr. Edwards described its virtues.

Quinoa, he said it was; a hardy Andean summer crop tolerant of the poor stony soil on which it is often cultivated. Its main use is as a flour-yielding grain. The protein content is higher than in most cereal grain, and it is of excellent quality.

Conclusion: quinoa could save Chile. If only the people could be persuaded to grow and eat it, we would have a cheap and excellent source of protein.

Allende said he was very eager to try it. He opened the pot and dished a portion of quinoa porridge for each of us into the soup plates stacked before him. "I hope it's not too bitter," said Mr. Edwards anxiously; "it has to be washed very carefully to remove the bitter taste."

I thought it was OK for porridge. Allende professed himself

to be delighted with it. Mr. Edwards blushed with pleasure. "You can make spinach from the foliage too," he said.

The Laying on of Hands

All the photographs I took, all the archives I kept, all the papers I filed were destroyed when the Moneda was bombed. So much for history and art.

But maybe something remains.

Yesterday at the outdoor market I ran into Gloria Alicia Flores. I recognized her immediately although I had seen her only briefly two or three times, in December of 1970, in doña Tencha's office.

Marisol had shown her in. "This woman has been waiting all day to see you," she said to doña Tencha.

Gloria Alicia Flores had the eyes of a trapped animal, and her voice was like a whimper. "It's about my child," she said. She motioned to a little girl, about two years old, whose expression was pure suffering. We waited for the woman to continue, but she stopped suddenly, removing the child's panties and lifting her dress.

She turned the child around; I saw deep, ugly burns engraved in the child's behind and upper legs. Her gashed skin was raw and purple, glistening with the oil her mother had rubbed into it.

"I had to leave Rosita with the neighbor lady when I went to work," the woman said. "My husband has left me—there is no one to help me." She put her hand to her mouth; a long shudder escaped her. "Two weeks ago the neighbor became enraged at the child for wetting herself; she punished my baby by setting her on a kerosene stove. Rosita almost died."

Doña Tencha, Marisol, and I stood staring incredulously at the hideous sight. The child began to whimper. "Señora, I have never heard of such an outrage," said doña Tencha. Her voice was shaky. "Please, tell us how we can help you."

Within a few weeks we had found another job for the mother and a doctor and nursery for the child. It was at this time that we rearranged doña Tencha's schedule, limiting her contact with these pitiful petitioners. She herself was ill and high-strung, barely taking care of her health under the weight of her new duties.

Yesterday Gloria Alicia Flores tapped me shyly on the shoulder as I waited at a fruit stand. "I just wanted you to know that things are better," she said. "I've married again: he's a good man. We have a TV. The little girl enjoys watching the shows. I'm very grateful to you; I'll never forget you."

History

Today the newspapers tell us that the U.S. is about to award to Chile's new Junta a wealth of grain credits. I remember that the week before the coup the Americans turned down Allende's request to buy a few tons of wheat.

Was there ever any hope for the UP Government? Were we doomed from the start? I recall Felipe's prediction the day after Allende's election. "You may remember my brother-in-law," he said, "the one who works as a district manager for ITT. He was notified this morning by his boss that, as of this date, no telephones are to be repaired in Santiago. A small matter, but only one of the innumerable details that the U.S. State Department, the CIA, and the multinational corporations— aided and encouraged by the *momios*—will see to. You wait: they will ruin us."

Today Monica met H. who, as a *Mirista*, takes grim pleasure in seeing his prophecies fulfilled. He quoted Saint-Just: "He who carries out a revolution halfway is only digging his own tomb."

But perhaps we theorize too much. Now that the social sciences hold dominion in the universities, we see patterns everywhere, overlooking the element of luck: bad harvests, the low price of our only dollar-earning export (copper fell from 70¢ to 49¢ a pound), Russia's unwillingness to keep us afloat when the Americans cut us off. Had even one of these factors been different, we might have made it.

Hypocrisy

After a hundred and fifty years of the social sciences there are still those people who assert that they are apolitical and without ideology. "I am against taking sides in a political drama," they say. "Politics is self-interested, corrupt, incapable of improving people. I am in favor of individual charity. Doing the best we can each day, building a satisfactory private world: that is my advice."

These people refuse to recognize that their "anti-ideology" is another ideology: that of individualism, with layers of assumptions about presumed laws of social life which work independently of human will.

They are rewarded for their views, which maintain the status quo, with respectability and good jobs.

In August, during the strikes, when food lines were ever longer, Señora Sara Silva, well-known chef and cookbook writer, gave a demonstration on TV of how to prepare lobster thermidor. Someone asked her, "What do you say to those who claim that in a poor country recipes for luxury foods like lobster are somewhat inappropriate? On Radio Portales, for instance, they've gone in for recipes which combine grains to yield high-protein dishes."

Señora Sara, as if in imitation of the crustacean in her hands, seemed to set about herself a stiff protective shell. "I don't believe in dictating to people what they should cook. I'm here to show people how to prepare gourmet dishes; whether they do or not is up to them."

The Doe

They say she stayed with him till the last, but Allende would not permit the self-sacrifice of those dearest to him. Mistress, daughters, *compañeros*: they left the Moneda shortly before it was bombed, hands over their heads in sign of surrender.

She was ill, they say, and she was driven to a hospital in an ambulance. That was all: then she simply disappeared. Days later the Swedish Ambassador informed the Junta that she was in his embassy; he asked for a safe-conduct pass for her so that she might leave the country.

Where is she now, the mysterious woman of a thousand secrets, whose flame and shadow dazzled us so?

Chile: Copper

When Helmut and I left Peru for Chile, we stopped at the port of Antofagasta. There were some Americans there who wanted to see Chuquicamata, and we agreed to share a taxi with them. It was a dreary ride through the Atacama Desert. The monotony of the scene was oppressive to me although I have known people who, having grown up on the desert, see endless variety in the sands, which turn different colors every hour of the day.

When we arrived at the mine, it looked like a colossal inverted step-pyramid sparkling gray-green in the bright sunlight. But the busy activity on the various terraced steps as well as on the bottom of the pit testified that this monument of faith and human ingenuity was not completed. Indeed— and this thought struck me as profound though I couldn't say why—once the last blast of dynamite had deepened the cavern, once the final ton of material had been removed, this prodigious artifact would lose its power to awe and subdue us. Unlike the ancient stone ruins we had just seen in Cuzco, this human enterprise signified nothing beyond the activity which deepens the mine's dimensions day by day, decade by decade.

There we stood looking at the mine. Everyone felt obliged to express some sort of reaction, and we simultaneously oohed and aahed at the edge of the enormous manmade hole—two miles long and one mile wide—in which superhuman labors were being performed by massive machines. That fact, it seemed, had to be taken account of; one couldn't simply shrug and turn away.

We walked along the mine for ten or fifteen minutes, unwilling to admit that we were bored. "Those posters we see everywhere; what do they say?" asked the American lady.

"They say, 'Copper is ours,' " I replied.

"But what does it mean?"

"It refers to the nationalization of the mines. Now the mines are owned by the Chilean people. Formerly the Americans owned them."

"Oh," she replied, already uninterested.

Chile

Government of *milicos*: organized spite.

Allende

This morning the newspapers informed us that the Convent of St. Michael the Archangel has been closed by the military authorities. The local bishop has protested, but to no avail. The problem, it is said, is the mother superior: she has been accused of having danced with President Allende.

A blurred photograph was attached to the news story. It showed Allende facing the camera, embracing or dancing with an unidentifiable bundle with a covered head.

The mother superior was emphatic: "I don't dance with anyone," she said. "I don't dance."

People are likely to believe Sister Teresa, but this is one time I'll have to side with the newspapers: I know it's Sister Teresa because I took the photo. I wonder where they got it.

It was on September 18, 1971. Allende had made half a dozen appearances in honor of our national holiday, and by 4 P.M. he was tired. He returned for a nap to his house on Tomas Moro where I was helping doña Tencha with arrangements for the dance that would be held that night in the large patio off the main reception room. "You must stay for tea, Eva," she said. "We are having a special guest: Sister Maria Teresa Valdez."

I was surprised. The Allende family, as far as I knew, did not socialize with the Catholic clergy. "I don't think I know her," I replied.

"She is now an important person, a mother superior," doña Tencha said. "But to us she will always be Salvador's old friend. Her parents had a summer place next to Salvador's in Valparaíso when he was growing up. The families were close. Sister Teresa was quite a tomboy; she and Salvador were full of adventures. They continued their acquaintance even after she entered the convent. She's coming to tea, you see, because it's her birthday. Salvador has always remembered her on her birthday. They get together; sometimes they attend one of the patriotic festivities. It's a little custom."

Sister Teresa turned out to be round and jolly with three chins. She was dressed in street clothes except for the veil on her head. When she laughed her little eyes disappeared into folds of fat. We drank our tea at a small table in the patio, since it was a lovely day, and while the family reminisced about other September eighteenths, the orchestra which was to play in the evening warmed up for a practice. I sat by doña Tencha most of the time, but I also roamed around the patio taking pictures since the light was just right, and I was preparing an article with photos about the president's house.

Finally it was time to go. We had all stood to say good-bye when suddenly the orchestra struck up "The Merry Widow Waltz." Allende, who was standing next to Sister Teresa, turned to her and beamed. "Teresa, do you remember? We danced to this back in—" And he took her in his arms and swung her around.

She was flustered. "Salvador, I can't...how...for Heaven's sake....I haven't danced in forty years!" She stepped on his feet a few times, apologizing as she struggled to get away. He blithely ignored her protests, and finally she gave in, seduced by the charm of the song and Allende's sure steps.

There were lots of people in the house that day. They came to the French windows to watch this strange sight. The band-leader seemed delighted. The odd couple improved as they danced, cutting wide arcs across the patio. Round and round they swang, Sister Teresa leaning back and half-closing her eyes, her lips slightly parted in a smile. In spite of her portly shape and lack of practice, she was lithe and graceful. Finally the music stopped. The couple was breathless and giggly. Sister Teresa leaned slightly on Allende's arm for a few seconds, flushed with pleasure as the onlookers burst into applause.

I had taken a photo, of course. In truth it didn't come out well, but I gave a copy to Allende and sent one along to Sister Teresa too. She responded with a note. "Thank you for the picture," she wrote. "It reminds me of a happy occasion. All my days with the Allende family: they have been happy days."

The Elevator

Finally it seemed as if I had to return to Monica's apartment to pick up some clothes and money I had left there. I figured that if I went at seven-thirty or eight in the morning, when the streets were crowded with people going to work, I would be inconspicuous. Besides, sometimes I suspected that my fears of running into Juan Andini again were becoming paranoid. Presumably he had to work; presumably he had other things to do besides walk the streets looking for me. He hadn't called for me in a week. It seemed safe enough.

The bus connections were bad. By the time I reached Monica's apartment building, it was 8:40. I stood alone waiting for an elevator. It was only as I stepped in that I saw his reflection in the mirrored paneling.

I darted back towards the closing door, but he grabbed me. I started to scream, but he looped an arm under my chin and pushed me to the wall. The elevator began to rise. With his free hand he felt for the control buttons. He pushed "emergency stop": we were between floors.

Drawing on the surprising reserves of brute strength that I seem to possess in emergencies, I struggled free from his clutch and pushed him backwards. He staggered, amazed. I screamed, alarming both him and myself with the horrible, echoing sound. He came at me again, this time covering my mouth with his hand. He was breathing hard; I could feel his heart pounding fast.

He forced me to look up at his face. His eyes were scared

and anxious. "Why do you make me act this way, Evie?" he said. "I don't want to be bad to you, baby. You've been hiding from me; don't lie, I know you have."

He took his hand from my mouth. I was crying hard. "Let me go!" I screamed. "What more do you want from me, you animal!"

He shook me. "What are you talking about?" he said roughly. "If you stop to consider that I've got the goods on you, you have to admit I've been nice—pretty damned decent, I'd say!"

Suddenly the elevator began to move. Startled, he looked around and pushed the "emergency stop" button again. We continued to move. He started to bang angrily on all the buttons. At the next floor the elevator halted. As the door opened he hastily let go of me and moved a step or two away.

Señor Gomez, the building superintendent, was standing there with a janitor whom I'd never met and two women with shopping bags. When I saw them, I started to cry frantically.

"Señora, good Lord, what a terrible fright; I'm so sorry," Señor Gomez began. "Please, step out." He took my arm and gave me a pat. "Nothing like this has ever happened before—we've never had trouble with our elevators. I'm going to call the company and have them send a man right over. But why don't you come down for a little brandy—you need to calm down."

Juan had stood by me uncomfortably all this time. Señor Gomez finally seemed to notice him. "And you too, señor. Please accept my apologies. My, how frightened the little lady is. Won't you—"

"The brandy," I interrupted. "I'd be very grateful, Señor Gomez." I clutched his arm.

Juan gave me a hard look. "I'll see you here tonight at nine," he said. Then he nodded towards Señor Gomez and turned on his heel without a word. I watched him descend the stairs. When he had disappeared, I fainted.

Juan Again

By nine I was ready for him. It was much like the last time, except that I hadn't prepared myself like a sacrificial victim: I was beyond melodrama. I lay on the bed waiting without looking at him. He piled his clothes on the dresser and set his shoes together neatly under a chair. He let himself down on the bed heavily, sighing as if tired from a long day's work. He took me in his arms, burying his face in my neck, and then, without further ceremony, he mounted me.

I didn't cry; I merely waited for him to be finished. It occurred to me: this is what it's like between many married couples. He didn't seem angry at my indifference. It's possible, I thought, that this is what he's used to.

Only when he was half-dressed did he strike up a conversation. "Bet you were surprised to see me this morning, weren't you?"

"Well, kind of."

"Intuition, pure and simple. Something told me to come by your place just then." A shadow crossed his brow; he sat on the edge of the bed again, his hand on my arm. "But you acted bad, Evie. I didn't know you hated me so much."

I remembered the power he had over me and felt afraid. "It isn't that, Juan. But it isn't nice to threaten people. How can I relax with you when I'm worried that you may turn me in? If only you'd promise never to mention to the authorities about those arms you found in Allende's basement, I'm sure we could be better friends."

He sniggered contemptuously. "How can I make a promise like that? A policeman's got his duty." He gave my shoulder a squeeze. "But there's no hurry, is there, as long as you're here when I come calling...."

He left shortly before ten, just as Monica was returning. Monica and I stayed up late talking things over.

"It wasn't so bad this time, was it, Eve?" she asked softly. "Not like the first time?"

"No."

"I don't mean to sound crass, but maybe you could put

up with him for a few weeks more. You'd be safer, you know. If we could just keep him quiet long enough to get you into an embassy.... Do you follow me?"

"Yes."

"Your life comes first; you've got to think about how to stay out of trouble."

I mulled it over for a while. "It's impossible, Monica," I finally said. "I've got the smell of him all over me; it won't wash off. I know it must sound stupid. I really can't bear him, can't abide him...." I started to cry. "Waiting around for him, listening for his steps.... How could I.... Life's not that important to me anymore; there are some compromises I'm not ready for."

Monica reached over and brushed my cheek. "You don't have to explain anything, Eve," she said. "Do what feels right to you. We'll get you out of Chile one way or another. Tomorrow you can go back into hiding. When Juan comes around, I'll butter him up. I don't want to make any high-sounding promises, but maybe I can put him off for a while. I'm good for a few more lies."

Leaving

This afternoon I am going to see Benjamin Willing in his office. I think his wife is coming too. Benjamin and Father Jaime Venegas are lining things up for me to leave. Soon. Soon, soon, soon, soon, soon, soon....

Advice to the Supreme Being

This world is very difficult for creatures like us. It would be better to create another, easier world.

The earth ought to be populated by people with harder hearts.

Mother

Unable to close the hasps of my burgeoning suitcase which she has filled so lovingly.... She is in the unhappy position of longing for a fate for me which she herself cannot live with. But there will be a stopover before my final departure, a stay of several weeks in Villa Inez de Suarez, where Mother can visit occasionally, postponing the final wrenching. . . .

Memoirs

I have been writing continually for several months now. When Dr. Carvajal suggested that I verbalize my problems even if I had no audience to listen, I started producing my memoirs religiously, as if the written word would, like a forthright friend, buttress me against danger by revealing me to myself.

But to seek solace solely in oneself is impossible; I rapidly abandoned the enterprise. I don't want to be relieved of a profound heartsickness which I came by honestly. I'd rather take vengeance on all those who have wrecked us, on those fattened cows of our country who not only strip the lean of the modest measure of power won over so many generations at such cost but who also, as they inundate the cemeteries with our poor relics, sanctimoniously insist on believing in their own virtue.

What can I confront them with? Words, ridicule, contempt: the weapons of the humiliated.

Chile

Why do I sabotage the voyage I must make?

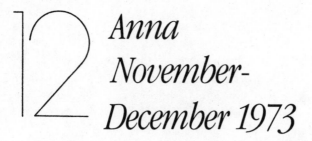

Anna
November–
December 1973

It is well to note two things: The first is that love
should be more in deeds than in words.
Second, love consists in giving between the two parties.
That is to say, in the lover giving to the beloved what he has,
or what he can do; and, similarly, the beloved to the lover.
So that if one has knowledge, honor, or riches, he gives to the
one who has it not.

——ST. IGNATIUS LOYOLA,
Spiritual Exercises,
4TH WEEK, 2ND CONTEMPLATION, NOTE.

1

For a half hour or more Anna had been lying beside him listening to the rustling of the curtains and to his soft breathing. She started to arise. Without opening his eyes, he had touched her gently on her arm: "Let me lie with you for just this little while."

She lay down again, turning her head towards this strange man. His lonely-sounding words had touched her. In the late afternoon sunlight the abundant hair on his body glowed auburn against his bluish skin. She wasn't used to hairy men; it took an effort not to feel repulsed by the heavy shadow on his chin and neck, the disordered curly growth that covered him like a frayed rug. "Why Paul?" she found herself wondering. "Why did I let him work himself into my life—or was it the other way round?"

He turned towards her, throwing his arm across her breasts and smiling slightly without opening his eyes. "It's been a good day," he whispered. "I can feel that you're about to leave; psychologically you've already gone. But I want you to know that, for me, it's been very good."

She wanted to reply truthfully, but she was out of touch with her own feelings. Although she had, in the beginning at least, appreciated being enjoyed by an enthusiastic lover, and although the novelty of the situation had been exciting, she was not at all certain now that she had had a "good day." Indeed, as the hours wore on, she had found herself responding less to the eager touch of his hands and lips than to a certain physical and verbal ineptness which aroused her pity. His eagerness to please was so apparent that it embarrassed her. In order to avoid disappointing him, she found herself faking her sexual pleasure, a deception she was totally unacquainted with. She did not resent the ruse he had inadvertently forced her to; but at the same time, she no longer understood what she had expected from this adulterous liaison. In any case, rather than setting her straight with Ben—which, she was certain, at one time had been her primary interest—her intimacy with Paul had left her more isolated than ever. For now (and this reflection made her smile sardonically) she was trying to befriend not one man but two, and in each case her efforts had led to lies and deception.

She gently moved his arm and rose. This time Paul did not resist. He watched her as she dressed, smiling with his eyes. At length he sat on the edge of the bed and lit a cigarette. "Are you going to tell Ben about this?" he asked.

Anna was shocked. The question seemed crude. Her relation

with Ben was the one subject she did not want to discuss with Paul.

"No," she said. "No."

He inhaled deeply, looking at her hard. "Why not?"

"Don't ask me," she said. She stooped for her handbag and stood halfway between the bed and the door as if eager to get away. "I know you and Evelyn have another way of handling these things, but I—"

"Don't underestimate him. Ben could take it."

Anna was so taken aback by Paul's assertion that she dropped her purse and slowly slid to the floor. She closed her eyes and swallowed hard. "I hope you're not going to lecture me on my husband's virtues," she whispered. "It's a subject I know by heart."

She felt him rise from the bed. He quickly dressed and crossed the room, kneeling down and taking her face in his hands. Her tears were flowing in rapid spurts. "That was dumb," he said. "Forget I said that. It's just that I'm kind of worried about you. Sometimes you look so goddamned vulnerable. And you've never said it, but I can't help suspecting you've got some queer old-fashioned ideas. Maybe you've set yourself up for a guilt trip or something. I don't want to see that."

She struggled to her feet. "Maybe we can talk about it another time; I've got to go."

"The next time?"

She faltered. "Well, sometime. I'm really moved that you care, but it's too soon for me." She walked to the door and turned the handle. She wished she didn't feel apologetic, as if she owed him an explanation. "It will take me a long time to figure out what I really feel about all this."

2

When Anna learned of Eve's imminent arrival, she threw herself into a systematic spring housecleaning as if in preparation for a visit from a proverbial mother-in-law. But with relief and disappointment she acknowledged the futility of her efforts: the shining floors and polished doorknobs remained unremarked by the young woman who, retiring and preoccupied, seemed more oblivious than most people to the ordinary domestic comforts. With total indifference she slept on the sofa, with Damaris, in Carmen's bed, or in a sleeping bag on the floor; and unless reminded she was apt to forget mealtimes. At least it was so in the beginning.

Looking after Eve's needs and facing the challenge of getting to know her provided a distraction that Anna grasped at. Only by submitting to an exhausting regimen of frenzied activity could she still the prickling sense of unease, of danger even, that spread over her spirits like an emotional rash whenever she had a moment or two to herself. It was an old malady, she reminded herself; she had suffered from it now and then for years. Since the coup it had seemed especially stinging and cruel, and after her last trip to Santiago and her day with Paul Pouillon, it had threatened to turn into a more serious disorder altogether.

Once in a while she felt tempted to confide in Eve about Paul. It might be helpful to hear the reactions of a disinterested observer, and, yes, it might be a delicious pleasure to explore a world of feelings so new she barely recognized them. But she was uncertain of her abilities to do justice to the complexities of the situation, and, even more, she feared that no matter how carefully she proceeded, she would do an injustice to Ben who, if responsible in a major way for her present anguish, was also at the same time wholly innocent of it. Besides, she told herself, it wouldn't do to pick at a sore so recently erupted.

Some conditions, however dolorous, may well take care of themselves if one can bear to wait on them.

3
_____

Eve spent most of her time with Damaris. Anna was amazed to see how quickly the young woman's shyness disappeared when she was with the child. They cooked, they sewed, they took long walks in the late afternoon, and they whispered together in the dark once bedtime came. By the end of a week Damaris had decided that she was her best friend.

Shortly after Eve's arrival, since the weather was fine, Anna decided to fill the swimming pool. She and Eve and Damaris spent a day cleaning out the winter residue and another day and night supervising the slow but steady flow of water from the irrigation ditch into the long, concrete oblong with an inclined floor. The conversion of what had been a reservoir into a pool had been one of Ben's pastimes for several years, and he was proud of his newest invention, a series of cement chambers filled with sand which served as a filter system. Eve said she thought it very clever. Damaris watched its successful operation with a self-satisfied interest, as if for reasons of propinquity she deserved to be congratulated for her father's handy tinkering.

When Ben returned to Villa Inez on the weekend of November 25 the usual round of work and rest was pleasantly interrupted. From morning until night someone was sure to be splashing about in the chilly blue water, or sunbathing, or taking a meal in the shade of the orange trees that bordered the west side of the bathing area.

It was a happy time for Anna. For hours on end she forgot the problems she had been living with, the itch that both tormented her and excited her. Only occasionally, and with a start, did she recall the weight of worry that had been burdening her. With the memory came a sense of guilt, as if she had allowed herself to be distracted from her primary duty: to fret, to anticipate disaster. She would set to it again, gnawing on her knuckles or chewing on a blade of grass. But under a cloudless sky, swimming langorously or drying off on sun-warmed tiles, she would soon forget again, at peace with herself and the world.

4
_____

On Tuesday morning when Anna was walking to the bus stop with Damaris, she heard someone calling her name. It was Rosita, the Ortegas' maid. "You're wanted on the phone," she said.

It was an odd hour to be receiving a call. She ran to the phone, her heart thumping due to the exertion and to her unease. "Anna, this is Hector Verdugo," she heard a voice say.

"Hector? Oh, hello," she responded. She was astonished that he should be calling her, for it was several years since she had seen him, and they had never got on well. He was more Ben's friend than hers. ("What I can't stand about him is the way he throws roses in front of himself as he struts about," she had said to Ben, "the way he bestows his smiles like autographs." Ben had understood her point of view but he preferred to overlook his friend's faults. "I seem to have a fair number of conceited friends," he once observed. "Personal vanity is a failing I frequently find amusing but almost never annoying— I don't know why.")

"You must excuse me for bothering you at this hour," Hector was saying. "It is very important. Have you seen this morning's papers?"

"No, no, I—"

"Thank God. I wanted to catch you before you showed them to you-know-who." (Anna supposed he was referring to Eve; she felt anxious because the conversation seemed about to take a political turn.) "There's a front page item about Monica's husband and my cousin. . . ."

Anna began to tremble. "Monica's husband: ah, that's Comandante Carlos," she said to herself, surprised that she remembered. "Hector is trying to give me a message about Comandante Carlos." It had been years since she had given Monica's marriage a thought. Anna had never met Carlos, and he seemed like a mythical person to her. She was aware that Monica was involved with someone named Felipe Medina. It was a bewildering situation to Anna; she was afraid that in her ignorance she wouldn't catch Hector's message.

"I don't want to go into it by phone," Hector continued, "but it occurred to me that someone should break the news to you-know-who. That's why I'm calling. I didn't want her to read about it in the papers."

"Dead: Carlos must be dead," Anna thought. Aloud she said, "How is Monica taking it?"

"I called her as soon as I learned of it, about 2 A.M.," responded Hector. "The Minister of the Interior had phoned me. He's a personal friend," he added importantly. "When I first talked to Monica she seemed calm enough, but when I dropped by her place this morning about seven, she was pretty wrought up. She's bound to be."

Hector's tone was doleful. Anna suddenly remembered his cousin. "About your cousin: I'm very sorry," she said. She felt inept when talking to bereaved people she didn't know well. How inadequate the old formulas always sounded.

"He was only twenty years old," Hector said. "I was very fond of him."

After Anna left Damaris off at school, she bought the newspapers at the stand on the plaza and devoured them on the way home. There were three morning papers; all three showed pictures of Comandante Carlos, of Orlando Verdugo, and of two or three others Anna hadn't heard of. "Extremists make suicidal attack on an armory," the headlines proclaimed. It had been in the South, near the Argentine border. According to the news, they were part of an international group of extremists who were accumulating arms and supplies for a coordinated effort which would begin the following year. Apparently the "Comandante" had counted on the cooperation of some soldiers on guard who at the last minute had got cold feet. Carlos and his men had been executed on the spot by a firing squad.

Anna dreaded facing Eve with this dreary news. She still did not know her well and did not converse easily or naturally in her guest's native tongue; nor did she know how Eve felt about her late brother-in-law. She didn't even know for certain what her political views were. She took the bus down Amunátegui Street, getting off where it ended, and walked hurriedly down the road to her house. Trying out phrases, she attempted to fit words together to present to Eve. At the same time she felt like whimpering over the unfair burdens which befell her: "Why me, O Lord—why me?" She wondered if she should be ashamed of her selfish reaction. Even as she put on a brave front for her guest, she tried to console herself.

The two women spread the newspapers on the floor and examined every article about Carlos' death. At first Eve seemed subdued, stunned. She read silently for a while, then asserted hopefully, "This could be a tissue of lies; maybe he's alive." But overwhelmed by the evidence and by her own feelings, she finally turned aside from the papers and from Anna and, clutching her temples, began to moan monotonously as she rocked from side to side. It sounded less like a dirge than like a chant sung absentmindedly by a monk. Anna had never observed anything like it. She picked up the papers and proceeded with the housework. After ten or fifteen minutes Eve stopped moaning as suddenly as she had begun. She turned to Anna and said, "I must call Monica. She will be needing me. She's probably at my mother's."

Anna and Eve walked to the local telephone company where there were three or four phone booths. Anna waited outside.

"I hope you won't mind that I invited Monica and my

mother out for a day," Eve said when she returned. "I thought they could use a change of scene." She spoke dryly, almost coldly.

"Of course I don't mind—that will be fine," Anna replied. And although she meant it, she also felt as if she were being swept ever deeper into a world of uncompromising emotional turns and violent upheavals that she wasn't prepared for. "But then who is?" she thought. "How do you prepare yourself for misery and calamity?"

5

When Ben returned to Villa Inez the following Friday evening, he seemed moody and solemn. "I had tea and a sandwich on the train," he said. "Don't bother about me." And while Carmen and Anna and Eve ate a warmed-over lunch, he and Damaris went swimming. From the house the women could hear the two of them laughing and splashing, and the sound of the water's still surface being torn apart by steady kicking. Then the swimmers lay on the tiles by the pool, drying off slowly under a setting sun.

When they returned to the house, Ben seemed more relaxed, but it was obvious something was on his mind. Eve, apparently unaware of the whisper of anxiety in his movements, had retired to the sofa where she seemed to be filling the pages of a notebook with a tall, feminine script. Anna, who feared a new assault upon her scanty stores of self-control, attempted to compose herself. "Speak sweetly, love," she begged Ben with her eyes, but he seemed unable to heed her plea. "Anna, something has come up that you should know about," he began. "Paul Pouillon has skipped out: he's left the country."

She felt an earthquake in her middle; she began to tremble. "Ah, Paul . . ." she whispered.

"Don't be alarmed for his safety—it's not that. He left a

note, you see, saying that he must fly immediately to Canada. Thursday night he showed up at Dorothy's house with all the files your little group has put together, and the other supplies too. He mumbled something about an emergency, urged Dorothy to read the note, and hastily drove away, explaining his need to rush because of the approaching curfew."

"So this is it," thought Anna. "This is how the affair ends." She groped behind her for a straight-backed chair and sat down near the table. "Paul," she whispered aloud. "I don't understand. What are you trying to tell me about him?" She entwined her fingers into a ball which she clasped between her knees.

"It's his honesty we wonder about, Anna. Dorothy found out that he lied about his destination. He flew to Argentina instead of Canada."

"What do you mean?" Anna was staring at Ben's face as he spoke. His mouth had an odd, pinched quality, as if it hurt to release his words.

"Well, now there's some suspicion in the group that maybe things aren't quite right—maybe he wasn't on the level. What did we know about Evelyn and him, after all? Why did he lie about his plans?"

"You mean you think he's a spy? You think maybe Paul Pouillon was spying on us!" Anna began to laugh shakily, and then she buried her face in her palms and heaved a great sob. Eve looked up from her writing. Ben put his hands on Anna's shoulders.

"I didn't say that. What I said is that maybe he wasn't on the level. He could be an agent, but then again, who knows? Maybe he's just what he appeared to be. In any case your little group is dissolving. Dorothy has already hidden your papers, and she's doing what she can to protect everyone who has been involved. She and Elise and Kay have been very upset."

Ben was waiting for a reply from Anna, but when she attempted to speak, she choked on the words. There was an uncomfortable silence punctuated only by the hoarse sound of her weeping. Carmen, who had been drying dishes, hung up her towel and tiptoed out the door. It was Eve who finally spoke. She folded her notebook and capped her pen with an emphatic little pop. Her tone was tranquil and thoughtful. "I have a suggestion," she said timidly. "There's no point in living under this cloud of uncertainty when you could perhaps find out the truth about your friend's activities."

"You're right," said Ben, "but it's hard to know whom to ask. You can hardly call the U.S. or the Canadian Embassy. You can't possibly go to the police." He shrugged apologetically at his own little joke, hastily replacing his hands on Anna's shoulders.

"It's too bad Felipe Medina is in Concepción," said Eve. "This is the sort of problem he's good at solving. He knows everybody, and even better, everybody seems to owe him a favor. If you want, we can try to contact him."

"But there should be somebody in Santiago," persisted Ben, "somebody who has his finger on everybody's comings and goings."

It seemed to Anna that Ben and Eve were making a commendable attempt to keep up a conversation in the face of her own uncivil conduct. She resolved to pull herself together. She uncovered her face and dabbed at her tears with a swimming towel that Damaris had draped over a chair. The child, alarmed by the unaccustomed sight of her mother's crying, had ceased playing with her dolls and now ran to bury her head in Anna's lap. It was the knowledge of her unquiet presence that restored Anna to the edge of control.

"I have one friend who might be able to help," Eve said. "He's a fashionable tailor who is always in the thick of things."

"You don't mean don Nestor!" Ben seemed genuinely surprised and pleased.

"You know him too?" Eve smiled. "But of course you would. He specializes in foreigners. I'm sure he can tell you about the Pouillons if anyone can."

Ben looked at Anna, whose sobs had changed to hiccoughs. "I'll go see don Nestor," he said. "Dorothy is following some other leads." He patted Anna affectionately. "So there's no need for lamenting—at least not yet. Maybe you'd better save your tears until you're sure you really need them." He was peering at her anxiously, affecting a playful, reassuring tone that somehow irked her.

"Of course, of course," she blurted out, and she attempted to smile. Instead her words caught in her throat. She buried her head in her arms and gave herself up to her sorrow.

6

The next morning Anna could not get up. Ben pretended to agree that she was coming down with a summer cold and treated her to breakfast in bed and frequent glasses of lemonade which she obediently sipped. At noon he served her some red wine and meat pies that Eve had bought at the bakery. After a quiet dip in the pool Ben returned to the house to keep Anna company. He moved the single comfortable chair into the bedroom and sat near the lamp reading *A Passage to India*. He had been reading it for over a year, Anna remembered. He was the sort of person who read fiction only in his leisure time, and he was almost always busy.

She turned towards the wall and allowed her face to fall into a mournful expression. "Maybe I'll never get up," she thought. "Maybe this is it; perhaps my will to live has permanently snapped. 'Flash! December 14, 1973: Anna Willing's residue of resilience was gobbled up by evil news at 7:57 P.M.; she realized that she had had an affair with an unkempt little James Bond from Quebec; she will never recover!'"

She felt rather than heard Ben's reply to her secret thoughts, for the room was utterly quiet except for the buzz of a fly at the window and the occasional turning of a page. *Well now,* he said, *let's not jump to conclusions. This isn't the first time that Anna has wanted to crumble up like a piece of parchment and wither away, but she never does; her will to survive is actually rather tough and sinewy.*

Yes, Anna replied. But who could deny she has a morbid side?

Shouldn't she? At this time and place in history?

You are too kind. The littlest things can set her off, you know. Remember the other occasions. . . .

I always thought she came through admirably in an emergency.

You're thinking of the time her college roommate died of an overdose of sleeping pills.

Yes; some other misfortunes too.

But she can also feel suicidal just from reading about this heartless world. She took to bed after finishing Notes from a Warsaw Ghetto, *you remember.*

It's the way she sometimes has of regarding life as a series of outrages perpetrated against defenseless people.

Nobody asked to be born.

One doesn't need to look at things that way; that's what I always tell her.

It's the way that comes naturally to her.

Not always.

Listen, do you remember the book of modern German poems that Ingrid sent her? You finally destroyed it because it brought black moods crashing down on her. But by then she'd already learned it—that one poem. And some things, once learned, can't be erased from the memory no matter how hard you rub away at them.

I remember.

Then let me repeat it, just the end.

No.

I wish that we were our first ancestors
A lump of slime in a warm swamp
With life and death, conception and birth
Sliding out of our mute juices.

A leaf of seaweed, or a sand dune

Formed by the wind and heavy-bottomed.
Even a dragonfly, a gull's wing
Would be too highly evolved and would suffer too intensely.

In truth she hated that poem; that's why I threw the book out for her. She rejected the poet's point of view.

Protesting too much, as usual. Listen, about Paul Pouillon: she doesn't know how much you've guessed.

Some things it's better not to pry into. It will blow over; Anna is probably exaggerating its importance.

She's not even certain now why she went to bed with him. It seemed important to do it. It looked like a selfish act, but she did it for you, for the marriage.

Yes.

Well, there's no reason to jump to any conclusions, is there? About her feelings for you, I mean.

No.

You know she loves you.

Yes, that's the one thing I know.

It's all you really need to know, isn't it?

Yes.

You think she'll forgive herself? Forgive whatever it is. . . . Life?

I'm sure she will. She always does.

She always does.

About that other unpleasant thing—the thing she's been punishing you for. . . . Your infatuation with the gorgeous woman. . . .

I've tried to tell her in every way I know. There's nothing to it: she invented the problem.

You've never said it in words.

She's never accused me in words. Why does she torment herself with painful fantasies when the world is filled to brimming with real calamities?

Why indeed? You think she's a little bit crazy?

About the same as the rest of us.

You really mean it? There was nothing to it—the famous affair?

You know there wasn't.
Then what should she do?
Well, what about getting up and taking a swim?
Really, you're too much.
A little exercise is good for the nerves.
You're making light of Anna's troubles.
No: I love her, I need her.
Really?
You know I do.

Anna stayed in bed on Sunday and on Monday until teatime, when Eve got a bad burn from the oven. Having been forced up by one necessity, Anna soon felt besieged by others: the laundry that Carmen had brought in that afternoon remained unfolded, and Damaris' school uniform, along with Ben's shirts, needed to be ironed. At eleven-thirty she listened to the last news broadcast and drank a glass of cider with Eve. Her spirits seemed mysteriously calmed. While her sense of impending disaster remained, she no longer feared being buffeted like a frail vessel in treacherous currents. It was less that she had summoned from her depths a salvific force than that she had inexplicably arrived at a numbing indifference as to her fate. It was the first time in weeks that she had been relaxed, yet she could not say that she was free from care or that she was happy. It was as if her real self had departed from the scene, leaving behind a fossilized shape about whose performance she could be—if not amused, comforted, or entertained— at least objective and detached. She did not, however, put much store in her present mood; she had reason, she thought, to distrust her own wily disposition. But there was no longer any call for either lying in bed or running about frantically: she might as well behave sensibly, as her friends expected her to, methodically setting about effecting her own improbable deliverance. First one move and then another: it might even prove a healthful distraction to weave a set of plans—however flimsy—with which to confront her trouble-infested existence.

With Eve, Anna did not share these thoughts. It seemed to her that the young woman understood her very well. Verbalizing what was already perfectly clear would be useless and tiresome. Finally Eve rose and washed the glasses; it was time for bed. "You're going to Santiago tomorrow?" she asked.

"Yes. Dorothy and the others are expecting me; Ben too."

"It's probably a good idea. I'm glad. I'll take care of things while you're gone. Don't worry."

"We're a strange and sorry pair," thought Anna as she turned out the lights. "It's not clear who is, or should be, comforting whom."

8

When Anna arrived at Dorothy Hemming's house early the following morning, Elise and Kay were already there. The three women had evidently breakfasted together. On the coffee table in front of the sofa Anna noted absently some crusts of toast and half-empty cups. Elise filled a small glass with orange juice and passed it to Anna, who had taken a seat on the floor. "You're too late, love," she said amiably. "The excitement is over. We've already decided what to do."

"You're very cheerful," observed Anna. In truth, however, she thought that both Elise and Kay seemed nervous.

Dorothy, who had been talking on the phone, suddenly hung up the receiver and turned to Anna. "We're cheerful on principle. What do you expect us to do—whimper and take to our beds and cover our heads with our blankets?"

Anna felt herself reddening; she was speechless. She wondered how her friends had learned so quickly about her collapse.

Dorothy sat down near Anna and threw her arm around her. "Ben called last night. He told me you felt down. Do you think we haven't had our moments of depression too?" Her voice was gruff and gravelly.

They spent a half hour reviewing what they knew of Paul and Evelyn Pouillon, searching fruitlessly for clues to explain their puzzling conduct. Then it was time for work. "The question is," said Kay, "where do we go from here? Let's assume the worst: Paul informed the *milicos* of our fact-finding activities. How do we stay out of trouble?" She drew deeply on a cigarette as she talked. Anna as usual was amazed at the childish impression Kay made when she smoked, pursing her lips into an exaggerated pout as she inhaled.

"Hide the evidence," replied Dorothy promptly. She ran her pencil through her blond hair as she talked. "It isn't as if there's very much. In fact"—she turned towards Anna—"Elise and Kay and I have taken care of almost everything except the file on torture victims. We thought maybe you could handle that, Anna."

"OK. What do I do with it?"

Dorothy wrapped her arms around her knees. To Anna, gazing at her figure, folded up like a jackknife, she seemed extraordinarily small. Small but capable: in her presence Anna's self-confidence, as if in imitation, began to expand.

"The best thing to do is to send it abroad," replied Dorothy. "We certainly would rather not destroy it. But the only safe way to mail something out of the country is to use the diplomatic pouch. Then the Chilean authorities can't touch it."

"You mean the U.S. Embassy's diplomatic pouch."

"Yes. Of course, we'll have to cut all the proper names out of our files to protect our informants from the CIA agents who read the mails."

"Do you think we should risk that?"

"Once they've read our stuff, they'll have to mail it since it will be in the diplomatic pouch. It's guaranteed to reach its destination. If proper names are missing, it shouldn't hurt anybody."

Elise, who had been occupied sorting through a stack of papers in front of her, suddenly looked up and removed her glasses. Her green eyes looked thoughtful behind the puckers of fat. "I'm afraid it won't be easy to get permission to use the diplomatic pouch," she said. She fingered her broad chin with her hand. "It's meant exclusively for diplomatic correspondence. Our best bet is to try to exert some influence—if we have any."

"I can think of someone who might be willing to help," said Anna. "The head of the North American Cultural Institute: Seymour Johnson. I used to know him when I lived in Santiago. I was on the library committee with him at the Institute. He's the sort of fellow who will bend the rules when there's a reason. If he could exert some influence for us at the Embassy, I think he would."

"Seymour, I know him too," said Dorothy. "Fine; let's start there."

Anna stood up and gathered her things. "If I hurry maybe I can catch him today," she said.

"That's true," replied Kay. "But don't you feel as if we've lots of unfinished business to talk over?" She ran the back of her hand across her forehead and looked around timidly.

"If you mean to ask even one more time how we're supposed to cope with our fears, I'm leaving," interrupted Elise. She seemed to quiver in indignation. "For five days now we've been terrifying ourselves with speculations about what the *milicos* might do to us. I'm sick of it." She crossed her arms emphatically and settled her face down into her neck.

Dorothy leaned over and patted Kay's hand, and then she turned to Anna with a little half-smile. "You weren't here with us this weekend," she said, "but maybe you can imagine how we carried on. We half expected the entire Chilean army to descend on us." She continued to hold Kay's hand. "All the same, I think Kay has a point. We shouldn't just sit around waiting for trouble. We should put our heads together and plan our stories."

"You mean fabricate alibis," said Anna. Her phrase made her want to laugh. A tittering arose among the group.

"OK, maybe we have illusions of grandeur, but it's possible that Paul Pouillon has denounced us and we'll be interrogated. Stranger things go on every day. It wouldn't hurt to get our stories straight, would it? And maybe in the process we can calm ourselves. What do you think, Anna?"

For a second or two the room was silent. It seemed to Anna that she could feel wordless currents of anxiety and sympathy pulling at herself and her friends. "Agreed. But not now, I've got to run."

"What about tonight?"

"Yes. If you want to put me up, I'll sleep here. We can think of answers to every possible question."

Elise rolled her eyes and slapped her temple dramatically with the palm of her hand. "All right, all right. But I still think all these group fingernail-biting sessions will end up driving us crazy."

Dorothy walked Anna to the door. "Will everything in Villa Inez be OK if you spend the night?" she asked.

"Yes."

"Eva Maria Araya is still there?"

"Yes. And strangely enough, instead of being troubled by her presence, I'm comforted."

"Great. See you later. Good luck with Seymour." Dorothy opened the door for Anna and gave her a quick hug.

9

The North American Cultural Institute was not in a fashionable part of town, nor was it housed in an attractive building. Although it was not as charming as, say, the British Institute, Anna was fond of the nondescript, four-story structure where lectures and concerts started on time and one could find a library-full of last month's American newspapers. She was sorry to see that great progress had been made on the new building located next door, scheduled for opening next year.

She eyed it as she passed: all glass and steel and artificial glass. Its opening was sure to cause a great fanfare.

She walked directly to Seymour's office where his secretary informed her that an appointment was impossible: Mr. Johnson was out of town. "His assistant, Mr. McNair, however, is in. Would you like to see him instead?" she asked.

"That would be fine," Anna replied, and she followed the secretary into Mr. McNair's office. A ruddy-faced man of medium height, he had a slightly gnomish appearance, due in part to the shape of his head, which was bald and shiny. At the base of his neck he displayed a ruff of unruly, platinum blond hair, and his great shaggy eyebrows, which grew over his bright blue eyes, displayed the same disorderly characteristics.

"Mr. McNair?" Anna began.

"Call me Frank, Anna," he replied heartily with a slight Western drawl. He stood and leaned across his desk and pumped her hand a few times. "It's a pleasure to meet you. Where are you from?"

"My husband and daughter and I have a place in Villa Inez de Suarez." Anna lowered herself into the leather chair directly fronting Mr. McNair's desk. It felt very warm, as if it had recently been occupied.

"No, I mean in the States; which state are you from?"

Anna hesitated, then smiled. "Like most Americans I've lived lots of places. I grew up in Idaho—Caldwell."

"No kidding. Carson City, Nevada, here. We're almost neighbors." He stood and reached for her hand again, giving it a good shake. "We're almost neighbors," he repeated.

He walked across the room to a table where an automatic coffeemaker was plugged in. He poured himself a cup and turned towards Anna. "Could I offer you a cup of coffee? No? Well, please don't mind me while I finish mine. I'm bushed. I just spent two hours with Major Clemens and Colonel Ross. They're representing the U.S. Army in their negotiations with us. And they're wicked at the bargaining table, I can tell you." He looked at Anna out of the corner of his eye and smirked, as if sharing a joke with her.

Anna felt bewildered. "Negotiations?" she said. "You have some differences with the U.S. Army?"

Mr. McNair guffawed loudly as he took his seat. "It's about the special training in English we give to the Chilean Armed Forces. Who's going to pay—that's the question. It used to be taken for granted that we gave one or two scholarships and the Army paid for the rest. Now they're economizing; they want scholarships for everybody!" He laughed heartily again, and Anna felt obliged to join him.

"I didn't know you had special courses for members of the Chilean Armed Forces," she replied. She tried to sound relaxed and friendly, but in truth there was something about Mr. McNair's conversation that made her uncomfortable.

"Just for those who are working in *English-language-sensitive areas*." He emphasized the words as if to suggest that they were an important phrase in some sort of technical vocabulary.

Anna again felt at a loss. "English-language-sensitive areas?"

"Well, you can't have these people running around translating word by word from their U.S. Army instruction manuals, can you? It makes a bad impression, very bad."

"Yes, I suppose so," Anna replied feebly.

"But why am I boring you with all this shoptalk? What can I do for you, Anna?" He had folded his hands loosely on his desk and assumed a confidential tone.

"My problem is that I want to send some papers out of the country, but I'm afraid of losing them. You know how unreliable the Chilean mails are."

"Yes indeed."

"I was hoping that I might be permitted to put my papers in the diplomatic pouch."

A curtain of distance slowly descended Mr. McNair's eyes. He began to tap his fingers together as he talked. "I'm afraid you came to the wrong place, Anna. That's Embassy business. But let me warn you, you're not likely to get anywhere with those people. There's a rule: the diplomatic pouch is for diplomatic mail."

Anna forced herself to smile cheerfully; she hoped her voice wasn't shaky. "So I understand, Frank; yet I've heard of some exceptions. Occasionally they'll accept a doctoral dissertation for safekeeping, or perhaps a will."

"May I ask what the papers are that you're so anxious about?"

Anna had prepared her answer. "I've been taking some notes on life in rural Chile. Nothing technical, you understand. I'm collecting folk stories and legends and practical lore."

Mr. McNair stared out the window for a minute or two as if lost in thought and then he looked at her again out of the corner of his eye; this time he winked. "What would you say if I put in a little phone call for you?"

"I'd be very grateful."

"I can't make any promises, you understand, but I like to lend a helping hand when I can."

"Thank you very much." Anna rose and extended her hand, assuming that the interview was over.

"Just a minute," said Mr. McNair. "It occurs to me: maybe you can do me a good turn." He began to leaf through the papers on his desk. "You've been in Chile a long time—you've probably read some Chilean authors: you're just the person I need."

Anna sat down again, but on the edge of her chair. She was eager to go. "Actually, Frank, Chilean literature isn't a strong interest of mine. What do you have in mind?"

"Ah, here we are!" he exclaimed, smiling broadly. "You see, the folks here at the Institute are planning a surprise for the officials of the Chilean Government. We're giving them a little party in six weeks; they think it's just a reception to welcome our new director—I guess you know that Seymour is leaving us—but in truth it's a bigger affair."

"How very nice."

"Yes. The four members of the Junta are invited, plus fifteen or twenty others. And this is the surprise: we're having facsimiles made of the four treaties that Chile and the United States have signed. They will be excellent reproductions—very costly, I might add, but very good. We're going to present them to the Junta."

"I suppose the originals are in a state of disrepair?"

"Ah, of course, I forgot to tell you: they were housed in that part of the Moneda that was bombed to smithereens the day of the military pronouncement. All kinds of historical records were destroyed including, unfortunately, the treaties I've mentioned. We're having copies made from the American versions in the Library of Congress in Washington. Each one is costing us over a hundred dollars. So you can see that we're eager to make it a nice little affair. Our program adviser suggested that we set up a display of historical memorabilia including books written by Chileans about the United States."

"I'm sure you'll do a wonderful job. You have a splendid program committee."

"Well, thank you. But I must say we're not having an easy time of it. The problem is finding suitable material. You can't think of anything you've read that we could use? Poems, stories, anything?"

Anna felt obliged to come up with a name or two. Her effort was almost like a payment for the favor Mr. McNair had agreed to do her. But she was nevertheless annoyed; even the idea of sponsoring a party for the murderous Junta and their lackeys made her wince. "There's always Benjamin Vicuña MacKenna," she said. "I understand he had something to say about Lincoln, Seward, Grant, and the other leading Americans of his day."

"We've already got him." Mr. McNair sorted through some papers as if in confirmation of his assertion.

"Well, there's Pablo Neruda." It was a bad little joke, Anna realized, but it made her feel better to fling it out.

Mr. McNair looked Anna straight in the eye for a second or two as if she were an unruly child. "It's a question of tact, you understand, common courtesy. The present Government has no use for Communist poets. Besides"—he coughed into his fist—"it's not as if Neruda ever said anything about the U.S. worth listening to."

"I'm very sorry I can't come up with some ideas, Frank, but as I said, I don't really know much about Chilean literature." She rose from her seat. Her skirt, limp and sweaty from the warm leather, stuck to the back of her legs.

Mr. McNair also rose and extended his hand. "Well, we really appreciate your interest, Anna. Give us a call if anything comes to mind." He walked around the desk to where Anna was standing. "In a day or two my secretary will notify you to tell you what the Embassy says about your request. If they allow you to use the diplomatic pouch, you must consider yourself lucky indeed."

"Oh, I will; I will."

They walked to the door. Mr. McNair held it open for her, peered out at her from beneath his shaggy brows, and began to pump her hand again. "It's been nice talking to you, Anna," he said. "Drop by sometime when you're in town. I'll tell you what: if you can see your way clear to helping me out with our little party, I'm sure I could swing an invitation for you and your husband."

"Thanks, Frank. How nice. I'll keep in touch," she said.

The community Christmas party was scheduled for December 13. Anna had first read about it in the papers in early November: "This year every child in Chile will receive a Christmas present," the headlines had proclaimed. "In every town there will be a party where Santa Claus will distribute gifts." Anna had given no thought to this exceedingly improbable proposal of the Government's supporters to make Christmas a happy occasion for everybody. But towards the end of November a bright-faced, plump woman whom Anna knew vaguely had appeared at the door, clipboard and pen in hand. "We're doing a survey of the town to ascertain how many children we have," she had said brightly. "Let me see—you have a six-year-old daughter, don't you?"

Anna would have preferred to be overlooked by the *momias* who were preparing the gifts and the party. She tried to avoid giving a direct answer, but the woman, Señora Lyon, had called to Damaris, who was playing by the house, "Little girl, did you know that Santa Claus is coming to town?" Damaris' enthusiastic response had made Anna back down; reluctantly, she saw her name and address added to the roster.

"And do you really expect to have a gift for every single child in this town?" Anna had asked.

"We do," Señora Lyon had replied. "We have women making dolls full time. Some of the men are helping with wooden toys. We're buying things too, I'll have to admit: time is running short, and there's so much to do! Many women are baking cakes, and others are arranging for a Santa Claus and a band. Oh, there's lots of energy in the air!" she had said, and she had rocked back and forth slightly on the balls of her feet as if to illustrate vitality and health. "Now that Chile is free again, we women want to do something for the country. Women who were formerly on the brink of despair are now as happy as can be with the Christmas party. And you know what we're planning for next year? A coat for every child in Chile! Yes! As soon as the Christmas party is over, we're going to get busy!"

On the morning of the party a youngster of six or eight appeared at the gate to beg for a pair of Damaris' old shoes. "I want to go to the Christmas Party," she explained, "but I can't go barefoot." Anna lent her Damaris' rubber sandals and found a dress for her too. "What time are you going to the party?" Anna asked.

"When Santa Claus toots his horn," the child replied.

"But will he toot it this far out in the country?"

The child smiled. "You'll be able to hear him when he's at the end of Amunátegui Street," she explained.

By two o'clock Damaris was delirious with excitement. Anna decided it was time to start walking to the bus stop. On the way the child with Damaris' sandals joined them, but they seemed to be the only people walking down the road. Anna had the unpleasant sensation of being watched. At the gates of houses on the left and the right, unsmiling children stood staring at the pedestrians. Finally she saw Leonardo Olivares approaching. "You're not sending your family to the Christmas party?" she asked.

With his eyes he expressed a great symphony of complicated feelings, but he uttered only a solitary "No."

"And these others?" she motioned with her head towards the clutter of houses at the roadside. "No one is going?"

"No one," he replied.

At that moment they heard the din and clatter of noise-makers and barrels being beaten with pans. Anna raised her eyes to see the green pickup truck ahead which, with a sound system, urged everyone to hasten to the plaza for the celebration. Damaris and the beggar child started to run, and Anna caught up with them just as a bus approached the stop. It was crowded with shoppers and teenagers, but no young children.

The town plaza had been festooned with strings of Chinese lanterns and a large crèche flanked by decorated bushes. At the center of the grassy area a dais had been set where a well-dressed lady, Señora Bastiás, the mistress of ceremonies, spoke into a microphone which wasn't working properly. She kept glancing anxiously behind her, where a lanky, bedraggled Santa Claus, struck by stage fright, nipped surreptitiously at a bottle hidden in his bag. Señora Lyon was attempting to keep the band together. Evidently discouraged by the delay, its members kept wandering off. "We really must begin," she said imperiously to Señora Bastiás. Noting her look of bewilderment and disappointment—for there were no more than twenty children, mostly middle-class, gathered about the dais—Señora Lyon straightened her back bravely, squared her chin, and smiled encouragement.

The mistress of ceremonies looked as if her eyes might overflow, but she gave the signal, the band struck up the Chilean national anthem, and everyone began to sing a thin, wobbly melody. The children were perhaps not quite sure of the words. As the band proceeded to a number of Christmas hymns, Anna glanced at the crowd—two curious bystanders, mostly *rotos* and shoppers, for every child. To each side of the dais there were tables heaped with gifts and with elaborately decorated cakes. Several women were already busy slicing generous pieces and placing them on slips of newspaper.

The Santa, who was curtly commanded by the mistress of ceremonies to cut short his winy welcome and get on with his work, dutifully distributed gifts to every child present. To Damaris' doll a paper had been pinned which read, "Damaris Willing, age six."

As Anna ate her cake she kept glancing at the women who were busy with the arrangements. Watching them was painful, but she wouldn't resist the temptation. "What will they do with all the leftover gifts?" she finally asked the Irish priest who had come to stand by her. "How much work they represent!"

"Oh, I imagine they will be delivered to the children one way or another," he replied.

It was time to leave. Anna went to thank Señora Bastiás, a buxom matron of fifty who wore her glasses around her neck on a silver chain, and Señora Lyon, who had finally allowed herself to sit a minute on the dais. Anna attempted to say the appropriate thing and she was surprised by the emotion in the women's response. "How kind of you," they each replied, taking her hands, and as they said their graceful little speeches Anna felt touched by the brave show they were making in the face of their disappointment. "It is easier to despise these *momias* in the abstract," Anna thought ruefully. "In the flesh they seem like the people I grew up with: the qualities of mind and heart they admire and cultivate I know and understand."

"I felt sorry for them," Anna explained to Eve when she reached home. "I couldn't help it. It was the way they had of trying to shine like cheerful suns in spite of their miserable flop of a party. I caught myself thinking, 'Is that the way life is? We spend half of our time urging ourselves on to perform noble deeds which other people will only hold in contempt.'"

"Yes, but you are too generous. Noble deeds went out of style in Chile when capital and interest came in."

"You don't think you could feel sympathy for a *momia*?"

The corners of Eve's mouth turned down in an ugly, sardonic way. "No. No I don't. How can you ask?"

The next day, as the Irish priest had suggested, the green pickup truck, loaded with gifts, could be seen inching its way along from door to door. Señora Lyon, crisp and efficient as always, ticked away the names on her clipboard as the deliveries were made. Damaris and Eve, who couldn't resist eyeing such a spectacle, walked over to the row of shanties down the road and stood around.

"The mothers accepted the gifts; they had to," Eve explained afterwards to Anna. "But there was no gratitude on their faces or on their children's."

"The parents I can understand, but the children: it doesn't make sense to me," Anna replied. "This is Christmas; won't they break down even for a little holiday cheer?"

"Accept charity from those people?" Eve asked. "No!" She paused and then suddenly began laughing. "The lady with the clipboard exchanged a few words with me between houses. She mistook me for the wife of one of the Ortega brothers. You know what she said? She said, 'The people who need help the most are the ones it's hardest to do anything for. Sometimes it seems hopeless. We've been doling things out to them for years, and they continue to live in their miserable way. We're just going to have to try harder, I guess. But one lesson I've learned: you can't expect any gratitude—absolutely none. The Chilean *roto* is by nature an ungrateful creature!'

"And then she assumed her military posture and proceeded on her way."

11

Eve's departure from Villa Inez was scheduled for Saturday, December 15. Anna had been present at the meeting in Jaime's office on December 11 when the final arrangements had been confirmed with St. Joseph's Convent in Santiago. Eve was to enter the convent on Monday, December 17 and remain until Wednesday when Ben and Jaime would assist her in scaling the wall of the Italian Embassy. "Sorry she can't get in through the front door, but the Chilean guards on duty would stop her," the assistant to the Ambassador had explained. "But at least I can assure you that she'll be flown out of Chile with a group of refugees within a few weeks."

It was happy news for Eve, and Anna shared in her sense of liberation. Indeed, Anna had felt no cause for worry ever since she and Dorothy had safely deposited their file on torture victims in the U.S. diplomatic pouch. With the disappearance of tangible evidence against her, she was presumably beyond suspicion. Besides, it had been over a week since Paul Pouillon's hasty departure from Chile. Since the *milicos* hadn't yet bothered them, Anna and Dorothy and the others allowed themselves to hope that their fears had been groundless.

Late Friday afternoon Anna decided to join Eve, who was sunbathing by the pool. Now that Eve's departure was imminent, Anna realized how much she would miss her. At the same time she felt a certain guilty gladness to see her new friend go. It was no doubt a coincidence that Eve had arrived in Villa Inez at the very time that Anna had been beset by terrors, real and imaginary. Yet in her irrational depths she could not help associating the young woman's presence with pain and suffering. It was most unfortunate: she admired Eve, she enjoyed her company, she was grateful for the emotional support Eve had provided. But at the same time she could not be at peace as long as Eve remained in Villa Inez.

"It seems that everything is ready," said Anna as she took a seat by Eve under the tangerine tree. "There isn't even any last minute packing up to do. I want to tell you how happy I am for you."

Eve, who was bent over a pile of notebooks, looked up and smiled. "Thank you. But am I myself happy? I'm afraid that you and Ben and Damaris have spoiled me. I can't think of another place I'd rather be." She motioned vaguely towards the intense blue sky which found its reflection in the limpid water, and at the scene below them. The waxy leaves of the avocado trees were shimmering in the heat of the day, and along a section of the adobe fence an abundance of bougainvillea seemed to grow ever brighter. "That's what I've been writing about," she said, indicating her notebooks. "About how confused I feel about myself and everything that has happened to me the past few years."

"You seem to have written a great deal," observed Anna. "I had never noticed before what a load of notebooks you carry around with you. But tell me what you say. I'm fascinated by people who love to put words together. What do you write about?"

Eve shook her head. "No, I am not a writer by nature, I assure you: a doctor friend recommended it. And I soon became addicted to my medicine. There is a great satisfaction in taking vengeance against everyone who has hurt me. But most of all, I love setting down my memories. Those of us who endure are saved by our store of memories—don't you think?"

Anna wasn't sure she caught Eve's meaning. "I'd never thought of it quite that way."

Eve smiled. She scooted to the edge of the pool where she dangled her legs in the chilly water. "That's why it's important to have them—memories, I mean. Yet you can hardly set about stockpiling them systematically in case of emergency."

"I love to hear you talk," murmured Anna. "You seem so wise for your age. I've been slow to grow up—too slow, I'm afraid."

"I don't think there's such a thing as 'growing up,' Anna. You change all your life—don't you agree? It seems to me that I've changed even in the few months that I've been writing these memoirs. In the beginning I think I was still pretty much wrapped up in my love affair with Helmut. I wanted to relieve it by writing about it—by writing about him."

"And now?"

Eve turned her eyes on Anna: they were large and sad. "Somewhere along the way I'm afraid I've lost him. Most of the time he doesn't seem real to me. He's like a wonderful dream I once had. Writing about him is like writing about a character in a book I read a long time ago. But I keep trying; I know he's out there somewhere."

"That's understandable. You've been separated too long. You'll probably feel differently when you see him in a few weeks."

"Probably."

They were silent for a while. Finally Anna began to gather her things together to return to the house. She glanced at her friend. Eve had grown very tan since she had come to Villa Inez three weeks previously. Taking in her olive skin, her extraordinary black brows like circumflexes over narrow and lambent brown eyes, her childlike proportions, Anna was once again struck with the astonishing contrast the Araya sisters presented, the strophe and antistrophe of a familial genetic dance. Monica, she supposed, was the more beautiful: golden to the tops of her eyelashes and to the fine down on her arms and legs, ripe and fulsome like summer, she was as breathtaking as a cloudless, indigo sky, as impossible to ignore or forget as the relentless February heat. But it was Eve whom Anna loved.

12

On Saturday morning Anna, Ben, and Damaris accompanied Eve to the train station. Arriving half an hour early, they had plenty of time for last minute good-byes, but Anna, at least, felt shy about expressing her feelings in so public a place. Eve, apparently as cool and serene as the morning glories which climbed along the station wall, sat on a bench beside the tracks and read the morning papers.

Yet Ben surprised Anna by his air of nervous distraction. He paced up and down the sidewalk outside the station, pausing now and then with a word for Eve and Anna and to play with Damaris, who was lost in a game with her favorite rag doll. Occasionally he would sit down, pushing his palms hard against his forehead as if trying to recall something, but soon he was on his feet again, retracing his steps.

It was only when the train approached that everyone seemed ready to acknowledge the fact that this leave-taking was final. Damaris went to Eve's side and hid her face in Eve's full skirt. As she caressed the child, Eve whispered to Ben. Anna could not hear their conversation nor did she wish to. Yet the picture of them standing there together, talking earnestly, smiling and touching and embracing in a troubled way, brought a lump to her throat.

Then Eve turned to Anna. They threw their arms around each other and stood silently for a minute or two. Anna was afraid that she would cry. Finally Eve raised her dark eyes and said in a husky voice, "You won't forget me, will you, Anna?"

The question was spoken with such a fervent simplicity that Anna knew it was neither polite nor rhetorical: it was a cry from the heart. "Never, never," she whispered, and she drew Eve towards her again. It seemed to her, in those brief seconds before Eve boarded the train, that this leave-taking would always be as moving and vivid to her as it was then, and as fraught with deep and unnameable feelings.

Then it was all over, an event of the past. Eve boarded a coach along with a dozen other passengers from Villa Inez. She found a window seat and waved idly at Ben and Anna and Damaris as the train slowly pulled out of the station. The three of them stood at the edge of the tracks until even the echo of the wheels' turning had died away. Then they walked wordlessly to the bus stop, feeling as if a part of themselves had just died in the balmy summer morning.

13 *Eve's Memoirs November and December 1973*

When men carry the same ideals in
their hearts, nothing can keep them
isolated, neither the walls of
prisons nor the sod of cemeteries,
for a single memory, a single spirit,
a single consciousness, a single
dignity, will sustain them all.

———FIDEL CASTRO

Fate

Here I sit, a supposed outcast and refugee, in the most beautiful
spot in the most beautiful valley of central Chile (according
to some, the loveliest of all countries). I walk and swim and
talk and eat and write letters and think of the others now in
prisons and concentration camps and cemeteries. There is no
justice and no equity. There is no explaining anything.

Memoirs

When I reread what I have written, I am amazed at the
sketchiness of it, the way it settles here and there over my life

like a butterfly in an orchard which it takes for the world, flitting randomly from flower to flower, without regret for those not visited.

Reconstructing my life from these memoirs would be like discovering the design of an ancient textile, having only bits and pieces to go by—a fragment of sky, a spear, a foot.

Lesson: the uncertain correlative between what is written and what is lived.

Carlos

He was the only person I ever knew who hungered and thirsted for righteousness' sake. His life was evidence for a proposition I would otherwise have doubted: that justice can be the object of a passion.

Anna and Ben

They treat each other with exaggerated respect and concern like strangers trying to make a good impression on one another: great seas of feeling acting like little shadow rills.

Anna

Her Spanish is stiff and unsupple. It is only in English that she reveals her stunning verbal powers. I have come to regard a talk with her as an unforgettable entertainment. She begins her paragraphs by breathing a little gasp and wrinkling her forehead. Her eyes, her eyebrows, her facial muscles: they are all alert and quick, the diacritical marks of a mobile intelligence. She sends forth a phalanx of clauses and conjunctions, of sturdy nouns and verbs, all marching to a cadence so brisk and tricky that one marvels to see them reach their destination. She speaks as if she had memorized everything in advance. The steady roll of her phrasing can lull one into a false sense of security, as if her conclusions were inevitable and predictable; in fact her conversation is a series of tiny surprises.

Monica and Carlos

The day she learned of his execution she spent at Mother's.
In the morning she wrote letters to his brothers, Alejandro and
Jorge, who are in Argentina. She did not allow herself to think.

It seemed improbable that there would be callers, for people
are afraid of being associated with the wife of so notorious
an extremist. Yet at two the bell rang. It was Sergio, whom
she had not seen since he and I separated a year and a half ago.

"But why do you look so astonished?" he said. "Carlos and
I were family, after all. It's true we seldom saw each other in
recent years, but quite by chance I happened to run into him
on the streets of Valdivia shortly before the coup. He must
have had a premonition of what was coming, for he asked me
to perform a favor for him in case of his sudden death. I was to
deliver this to you."

He withdrew from his pocket a heavy envelope. Inside
Monica found Carlos' wedding band and curls of Maria Paz'
baby hair tied with ribbon. She sat on the sofa and cried while
Sergio comforted her.

Ben

How his moods affect his walk. When all is well he sets his
heels down an instant before the rest of his feet, so that a
happy slapping sound results. When he is depressed, he tends
to limp, favoring his left leg. Once or twice I have seen him
groping, stooped and somehow sightless, like an old man.

Monica

She sits at home nights chewing her nails and wondering what
she will do when she is fired from her job. Once you've been
fired for political reasons, you're done for.

The Devil

Monica promised Juan the last time she saw him that I would
be home last night. We were both beside ourselves worrying

that he would show up. "Let's face it, Eve," she said. "He's not going to take any excuses. If he comes for you, I'm going to have to call you in Villa Inez, and you'll have to speak to him. I'm afraid you'll have to see him one more time. Just once: it wouldn't be so bad; just once, probably, to keep him from denouncing you."

But he didn't stop by. Monica called me at the Ortegas' this morning, and we talked our worries away. We think everything is going to turn out all right: the Devil is forgetting about me.

Allende

I dreamed of him last night. He was speaking to Ben by the swimming pool. He said, "Balmaceda was the only Chilean president to commit suicide. That was in 1891 or '92, when he was up against the British imperialists and the Chilean bourgeoisie. You see how it is with us Chileans: for all of our indolence and our egotism we have dignity. Sometimes we have majesty, and we know how to die. In other countries there is a coup or a civil war, the president flees, living comfortably in exile, perhaps he returns, perhaps he doesn't. Balmaceda is our conscience. He was drawn into a great civil war, he fought for noble principles, and he was defeated. He took his own life. Now every little town has a street or park named for him."

Imperialism

First it was the English and then the Americans. But why deny it? There were always those Chileans who couldn't wait to sell our national wealth to the imperialists. They were glad to be rid of the mines: industry and trade were ungentlemanly activities. They looked down their noses at the vulgar foreigners who so quickly reduced us to a state of economic dependency from which we have never recovered.

Before the advent of imperialism—before our civil war in

the nineties which the British instigated to protect their interests—we were notable for our stable institutions, our stable currency, our prosperity. Extraordinary. How will we ever undo the follies of our ancestors?

Childhood
Hard kernels of experience which only later burst their coats, scattering their riches in sweet memories.

Ben
Pride in reverse: to avoid giving offense, perhaps, he acts like an unprepossessing little barge though he knows beyond doubt that he is in fact a great vessel.

Chile
BEN: Let's for the sake of argument grant that a majority in Chile favored a coup (although I'm certain they didn't). We are still left with a dilemma: can majority rule be legitimate when it imposes by force, on a sizeable minority, a system which brings about economic growth—if there is any—through further impoverishment of the poorest classes?

This is the kind of question Ben loves to throw out, and I always fail to make an adequate reply, for no Chilean would ask it. Ben must be measuring us against the norm of majority rule to which we were accustomed but never wholly reconciled. A *momio*, for instance, is indifferent to the opinion of his inferiors (the majority), whom he sees as ignorant and impressionable if not morally undeveloped, and a leftist to that of his opponents (the majority), whom he would claim are spokesmen for a false and self-serving ideology. For Chileans the ballot is only an indirect—and not always efficacious—means to determine who is going to command.

Memoirs
What have we here? My own cellar of memories with its stores going to root or ruin—musty-smelling, domestic.

Excerpt from a Letter to Helmut, December 8, 1973
I am sitting at the edge of the Willings' pool. I see this blank white paper, so expectant, and my new green fountain pen, a gift from Damaris, and I am happy. The immense pacific quality of this place casts a spell over all living things; it quiets my troublesome dreams and reconciles me to my fate.

Above my head three clouds pass in formation like Spanish galleons, the *Niña*, the *Pinta*, and the *Santa Maria*. In the West, La Reina attempts to impress with her majesty, but she is old and benign. When Darwin was in Chile, he climbed to the top and sat upon the same fossil-encrusted rock that I sat on last Sunday. The universe and eternity, how vast; I feel a smile of gratitude radiating from my being, as if this splendid cosmic drama were just for me. With the trees I nod a thanks in every direction and sigh with pleasure.

How *right* everything seems! My words will give utterance to my feelings, and I shall write beautifully. You will be amazed and delighted by my letter. Or will you frown and scold me for my metaphysical fancies? Will you say, perhaps, that I do not appreciate the seriousness of my situation?

Carmen
"Carmen," I asked her this morning, "don't you ever get homesick? This must be very different from the South. It must be hard to stay here when your parents are so far away."

She was adamant. "No, I'd never go back. It's a horrible life. In the South the *campesinos* live like animals, without the sacraments."

Ben
Anna assumes that, since he bends with the breeze in a seemingly effortless way, he is an utterly natural creature (though

very clever)—without memory, and without hope. "He simpli-
fies everything, even suffering," she says.

I presume to think she doesn't understand him. Without
a great passion, he cannot live. He has a sense for all of the
mysteries of the world, all of the tragedy of life. He traces
imaginatively with his fingers the curve of the letters of an old
illuminated manuscript. He is the only person I have ever met
who might want to emulate those monks of medieval times
who slept in their shrouds to remind themselves of death and
eternity.

Chile

No longer a home or an identity, but a critical condition, a
situation.

Anna

Her anguish: we have no polestar here. For us ambiguity is a
natural zone; for her it is one step away from loss and destruction.

Helmut

Last night I dreamed of him. We were walking hand in hand
along a sidewalk covered with autumn leaves. Sometimes he
would stop and kiss me. Occasionally the dream changed and we
were in bed together in the room in Valparaíso that we used
to know.

When I awoke, I realized with a shock that it was not
Helmut's face but Ben's that I had seen in my dream. For a few
hours I felt sheepish around Anna, as if she could read my
thoughts; and I was afraid that my subconscious was trying
to deliver a message to me that I most definitely did not want
to hear.

Now that it's evening, my anxiety about my dream has faded,
and I no longer expect that seeing Ben will throw me into a
muddle. At the same time, I'm sad to realize that I can't

recall Helmut's face very vividly. I keep wondering if he is in truth the man I remember or a phantom lover I invented after his departure—just to keep myself going.

Fate

S., who took refuge in the Mexican Embassy the day of the coup, is now in Sweden. She wrote Monica that the only job she could find was washing corpses at a hospital.

When Allende back in the thirties started to work as a pathology student, that was his job—carrying out autopsies, washing corpses.

Chile: Departure

Did you hear that, heart? It's been arranged. Next Wednesday we're to shed our old self and on Thursday grow a new one.

Do you think we can do it?

Memoirs

These puerile writings reveal nothing, signify nothing. But I'd be wild without them, lost without my memories.

The Devil

He dropped by Monica's last night. He apologized for not showing up a week ago (he was on duty, he said). Monica replied that I had been waiting for him all that evening. She went on to explain that I was again with the sick aunt in Osorno but that I could see him next Thursday. That's the day after I'm to enter the Italian Embassy.

He was polite, he voiced no objections, but Monica had an uncanny feeling that he didn't believe her. Why didn't he say so?

Both Monica and I are nervous, but we remind ourselves

that once I'm in that Embassy, he can't hurt me. It's less than a week now....

Chile: A Farewell
The newspaper owners with their lying articles; the bought labor leaders; the industrialists with their foreign bank deposits; the military officers trained in the United States, bereft of natural human sympathies; secret agents; torturers and interrogators; infiltrators; the middle classes, their consciences stultified by coarse rhetoric; servile party leaders; fawning professors; grasping landlords; smart economists who offer the country's resources for sale and lend the public pension funds to the capitalists; grasping, venal, lascivious souls: this is their Chile, they earned it, they're welcome to it, I leave it to them!

Ben's Theology
Ben quoted his friend, Jaime Venegas: "Only those of us who have traveled much and have witnessed with our own eyes the depths of human cruelty and self-deception are capable of appreciating the staggering miracle of charity and loving kindness. And perhaps for this reason we are most in danger of losing perspective, of prostrating ourselves before a generous sentiment or an upright act, as if such isolated and fleeting instances of goodness were capable of rejuvenating the world."

Chile
It isn't one country but many worlds. Its geography unrolls in my mind like a crumpled ribbon—deserts; worn, tired hills; volcanic rock; stony quays; *pueblos* of mud and sticks; paths overgrown with blackberries; sea; secret coves of coast; sweet acres of grain; *rodeo* rings; forests of mahogany; gelid peaks, cavities of open mines, red earth, swift rivers with Indian names (Mapocho, Bio-Bio), played-out silver mines, intact mummies

with burial offerings, onyx and lapis lazuli, copper tools, olives and grapes, avocados and lemons.

Let me leave it, let me stay, don't let me yield to the temptation to make it more beautiful than it is!

Chile

So many have died, and you leave.

14 *Ben*
December 1973

I have always known
That at last I would
Take this road, but yesterday
I did not think that it would be today.
——NINTH-CENTURY VIETNAMESE POET

When things happen suddenly,
and against all calculation,
it takes the heart out of a man.
——THUCYDIDES

Ben had spent a long weekend in Villa Inez, and it was almost sunset on Sunday evening when he boarded a train for the three-hour trip back to Santiago. A Sunday night train ride was an experience he normally avoided, for the seats and aisles were filled to brimming with passengers who, like him, had to report for work on Monday morning. He had found a place opposite the latrine where the odor was stifling in the summer heat, and even by the time he had reached Quillota, he was exhausted from the effort of standing up, threatened on all sides by careless elbows, heavy feet, and greasy heads reeking of onions and wine and hair lacquer. No one ever seemed to get off, but at each small town another couple or family would stoically push their way into the car, bracing their suitcases or baskets before them like armor. At Llay-Llay Ben had finally maneuvered himself into a corner where he could sit astraddle his bag and rest his back against the sack of homemade bread that Carmen had prepared for him that afternoon. Some of the passengers nearby eyed him glumly as if envious of his commodious arrangements. Only at Patuco did he finally get a seat, but by then he felt feverish and shaky, barely able to keep his head erect. When the train finally arrived at the Mapocho Station in Santiago, he was so weak that he took the unprecedented step of hiring a taxi for the ride to Jaime's apartment.

"You should have waited till morning," said Jaime as Ben collapsed lengthwise on the sofa. "Nobody would mind if you showed up a few hours late on Monday." He poured some whiskey into a coffee mug which he urged on Ben. "This should kill all but the most diabolical germs."

"I'm getting a cold," Ben rasped. "I get one every summer, but I always forget until it attacks me. Why does it have to be this week? This is an important week. For Eve, and all of us."

"Did she leave Villa Inez yesterday?" asked Jaime.

"Yes. By now she should be at the convent. The sisters were expecting her this morning. I believe she spent last night at an aunt's house."

"About your cold, don't worry," said Jaime. "I'll nurse you back to health in no time if the whiskey doesn't cure you. You'll love being a patient here; it's a delightful experience."

In the morning Ben arose to prepare breakfast, but he still felt feverish, and his throat was sore. He scrawled a note and left it on the table for Jaime: "There's a bread wrapped in newspaper on the table. If you want some tea, just boil some water and pour it over the bag I left in the cup." He returned to bed and fell into a light sleep, soon to be disturbed by the creaking of the floorboards as Jaime tiptoed to his side.

"You're awake, I see," Jaime observed cheerfully. "I'll prepare a splendid breakfast for you. What would you like?" He rubbed his hands together briskly.

Ben pointed to his throat to indicate his malady. "You think you could make a little lemonade?" he whispered.

"Willing, considering the patronizing way you treat me, going so far as to leave written instructions on how to boil a cup of tea, you don't deserve to taste my lemonade; it's a secret family recipe. If it weren't for the examples of the saints which come to mind when you provoke me, I'd push you down the stairs. But no matter, no matter," he concluded, holding out his hands as if in protest. "You'll have your lemonade as soon as I can find a lemon."

Ben continued to doze, half alert to the sounds in the kitchen: the squeaking of cupboard doors, the shattering of a glass on tile, water running. Then there was a long silence followed by the slamming of the front door. Ben dropped off. When he awakened, he saw on the floor beside his cot a pitcher of lemonade and a note folded neatly in a glass. "Sorry to take so long," he read. "I had to borrow the lemons and the sugar."

Jaime returned home briefly at one to warm some soup which he had brought from the lunch bar near his office. Although he was certain that his illness was causing Jaime some inconvenience, Ben felt too apathetic to object or to propose other arrangements. Besides, his throat hurt; he could speak only in whispers.

"Eva Maria's at the convent. So far so good," said Jaime just as he was about to leave again. He was whispering as if in imitation of Ben.

"Great. And the Italians are expecting her on Wednesday night?"

"Right. I'm just now confirming everything."

Ben dozed lightly all afternoon and could barely rouse himself for dinner. By the following morning his throat felt worse. "I'm getting a doctor for you," said Jaime.

"Don't be ridiculous, I'm a doctor," whispered Ben.

"So you are. It's easy to forget. You're a poor ad for your profession, friend."

At noon Jaime had returned with Dr. Wong Lee. Dr. Lee poked at Ben with his pink hands which smelled pleasantly of disinfectant and sandalwood.

"Strep throat," Dr. Lee pronounced solemnly, and he eyed Ben accusingly, as if he were to blame for something. "I hardly ever have strep patients in summer."

By four o'clock the antibiotics which Dr. Lee had prescribed had begun to work, and Ben felt simultaneously healthier and more miserable. There was no lamp for reading, and the maid's room in which he was resting, dimly lit by one small window set high in the north wall, was dreary and depressing. He couldn't sit up comfortably on his cot, nor could he stretch out languidly. He watched the shadows on the walls which grew larger and more mysterious as the hours passed. Twice he drank some cold mint tea which Jaime had left on a tray beside his cot. He began to feel anxious, even frightened, just as he had when, as a child bedridden with polio, his mother had left him alone while she ran some essential errands. Yes, that was it, he told himself; in a helpless state you frequently revert to childlike reactions. He used to observe such behavior among his patients. So he reasoned, but his explanations could not still the queer terror which had taken possession of him. It was as if the world outside had ceased to exist while he lay in bed, or had altered beyond recognition. He strained himself to listen to the movement of traffic on the busy avenues which intercepted Eugenia Street, and he was smitten with melancholy by the distant honking of horns. He waited impatiently for Jaime who had promised to return at five.

At six-thirty Ben was still alone. He roused himself to the task he had set himself earlier in the afternoon. At first it had been a fantasy, his changing location from the cot to the sofa. He craved the comforts of light and books and fresh air from the large windows in the living room. Some of Jaime's notebooks lay on the desk, he remembered; it would be pleasant to read at them in a desultory way. At midafternoon, however, he had lacked the animus required for a major move; it would take two trips, he reasoned, before he could comfortably settle in with sheets and pillow and medicine. Finally he had risen for a trip to the bathroom, and petulantly, like a distraught child, he had grabbed for the bedding and stumbled to the sofa. With furious exertion he had devoted himself to tucking in the sheets and setting up everything he needed: water, aspirin, pills, Jaime's notebooks, a lighted lamp. Then he had lain quietly, inducing in himself a fitful sleep.

At eight Jaime, heavy laden with bundles, finally made a noisy entrance. "Ah, there's a feast for you tonight, Willing," he said as he dropped the parcels on the desk and nearby chairs. "If your throat is too sore, we'll mix a little milk with everything, and you can drink your dinner." He paused to mop his brow and catch his breath. To Ben, Jaime appeared abnormally excited and a bit vague, as if his mind were elsewhere; but slightly feverish and out of sorts, Ben declined to trust in his own perceptions.

"You must have thought I'd forgotten you," continued Jaime. He blinked nervously behind his spectacles.

"Not at all."

"I'm really sorry, Willing. I was going to close up shop at four, but, with the relentless regularity to which we're becoming accustomed, a crisis arose at 3:55. I got here as fast as I could."

"Anything I could help with?"

"Not until you recover."

With a domestic efficiency unusual in him, Jaime arranged the dinner on plates and set the kettle on to boil for coffee. The sun was low in the sky, and rather than turn on the overhead light, to which he claimed a peculiar aversion, Jaime lit a kerosene lamp and set it on a straight-backed chair near the sofa.

They ate silently, commenting favorably from time to time on the rice and chicken and the cool, tart wine Jaime had chosen as accompaniment. Ben forgot his former misery; indeed, he felt almost well except for the swelling in his throat. The sun disappeared in a cloudless sky. The world outside the windows was alive with the sound of crickets and the occasional murmur of voices in the patio below. The kerosene lamp cast a warm bar of light across the sofa and the bookshelves above, leaving the rest of the room in a friendly half-shadow.

Jaime cleared away the plates and brought Ben a fresh pitcher of water. "Shall I read to you for awhile? That might be a pleasant way to pass the time."

"Fine," Ben said. "Why don't you start with something from your notebooks?"

Normally Jaime loved to read and discuss his writings, but tonight he seemed moody and diffident. He moved his chair and the kerosene lamp to the windowsill. Ben propped his head on the arm of the sofa so that he could see his friend better. "The lantern is casting a halo about you, Jaime; you look beatific."

"It goes to show you can't trust in appearances. The devil is full of tricks." Jaime bent his head over his notebook and, squinting slightly, began to read in a soft, expressionless voice. As so often happened with him, Ben was struck with the difference between the writings and the man. It was as if the writings were an image of Jaime's secret life, not urbane and unruffled, like his public image, but convoluted, sometimes quarrelsome, frequently nervous and paradoxical. He borrowed liberally from other works, especially the writings of the saints, which he inserted among his own entries in an apparently random order; and he switched from mood to mood, subject to subject without explanation and without apology.

The Lord bless you and keep you, may He show His face to you and have mercy. May He turn His countenance to you and give you peace.

For a moment Ben wasn't certain whether Jaime was reading or quoting from memory. Evidently it was the latter. Jaime looked into the lamp for a second or two, apparently on the brink of speech, for his Adam's apple began to work, then promptly returned to stillness. Again Jaime looked down and turned the page.

There was never a struggle or battle which required greater valor than that in which a man forgets himself.

Meister Eckhart? Ben thought that he had heard the quotation before, but he wasn't certain. Jaime sighed deeply, as if he were disappointed with himself; Ben was tempted to laugh.

Jaime's communication with his conscience [in his notebooks he always referred to himself in the third person] was clouded by mutual suspicion. He had severe doubts as to whether his inner self was sincere when it applauded features of his conduct which were from some conceivable viewpoints open to charges of self-serving hypocrisy. As a consequence he sometimes hurt his own feelings, to the point where he would sulk until he had satisfactorily apologized to himself.

Clever and well put, thought Ben, and he was about to express his admiration when suddenly he was startled by the anguished look on Jaime's face. Jaime closed his notebook and set it on the floor. He rose and paced a few times across the small empty space near the sofa. Finally he sat down in the rocker and turned his troubled eyes on Ben.

"Willing, something terrible has happened. Something involving you. I had wanted to spare you until you were better, but it struck me just now that I haven't the right."

Ben felt a sense of alarm racing through his veins in a futile search for safe exit. He craved a minute alone in which to pull himself together. He fought an urge to snap at Jaime waspishly: no big build-ups, please. Let's get it over with. "Ah, Lord, Lord," he heard himself whisper hoarsely. He sank his head back into the pillow and fixed his eyes on the ceiling as if succour were to be found there. "It's something about Anna." The realization struck him suddenly and conclusively. *Lord, don't let it be Anna.* He lay still and silent, but inside he heard a shrill, despairing cry which wrenched his heart.

"Anna was picked up by the police today." Jaime's tone was thin and taut. "She's in jail, Benjamin. She's in the Valaparaíso Municipal Jail."

Ben blinked and closed his eyes. He could feel the beads of sweat forming at his hairline and above his lip. The soreness in his throat seemed to expand to fill the cavities in his face. He should respond. He looked at Jaime whose eyes were smarting with tears.

Jaime suddenly leaned forwards in the rocking chair and grasped Ben's wrist. He lowered his forehead to the back of Ben's hand. "Oh, Benjamin, that I could take this trouble from you...."

There was a moment of silence, then Ben forced himself to a more upright position. Images of Anna played across his mind—her long, pointed fingers dicing onions, her garden boots, shaped like her feet, waiting crisscrossed at the shed where she usually left them; her reading glasses resting on a book. Jaime was speaking. He was saying a string of touching things, and Ben half-listened and responded. Yet, incredibly, he felt himself reaching through the heavy drapery of his memory for a scene which had lain dormant since its occurrence when he was fifteen. His mother had called him at his after-school job to tell him of his father's end. "Your father has had a stroke," she had announced in a stringy, wavering voice. "You must run home and take care of your brother." She had spoken without expression. It was the same tone with which she said, "Stop by the market for a dozen eggs." Steely self-control, no childish displays; he had taken in the message.

"What have they done to her? Have you talked to her?" Even whispering hurt Ben's throat.

"She hasn't been tortured."

"How do you know?"

"Let's take it in order. The police came for her today in Villa Inez about three. Carmen was there. Like most of us, Anna had foreseen such a possibility, and she had left instructions."

"We had talked about it. Carmen was to call me at work."

"Yes. But you weren't there. I took the call. It was about 4:00. I immediately phoned everyone I could think of—the American Ambassador, who is out of town, the First Secretary at the Embassy, some contacts I have in the Chilean Armed Forces. Finally I had a bit of luck; I called the American Ambassador's deputy for Valparaíso Province, a Mr. Eric Anderson. He's head of the North American Cultural Institute there. Fortunately he knows Anna and took an immediate interest in her case. In an hour or so he was able to determine where she is being detained."

Now that Jaime was recounting the circumstances, his spirits seemed to revive. He reached for the water pitcher and half-filled Ben's glass, which hadn't been touched, and sipped at the liquid. Like Ben, he had been sweating profusely. Ben watched absentmindedly while rivulets made their slow progress down Jaime's cheeks. Unconsciously Ben wiped his own face on the sheet, already damp from the heat of the day and his fevers.

"But did he talk to her? Did she tell him she's all right?"

"Don't strain your voice, Willing. I'll cover everything if you will give me a minute." He filled the glass with water a second time and ran his index finger around the rim. "Mr. Anderson talked to the Chief of Police and insisted on seeing Anna immediately. The Chief was polite but firm: he no doubt has his reasons for ignoring Anderson's veiled threats. Who's Anderson, anyway? The chances are the U.S. Ambassador, once he's returned, will approve whatever the Chilean Armed Forces choose to do with Anna; he's on the best of terms with them, to all appearances. Excuse me for speaking brutally. However—and this is after all what matters—the Chief seems to have his own reasons for going easy with Anna. Maybe she's not the one he's really after. Anderson got the impression that she's being questioned about someone else's activities rather than her own."

"Whose?"

"I don't know."

"It seems odd they took her all the way to Valparaíso. Why didn't they question her in Villa Inez or some closer city?"

Jaime did not respond immediately. His eyes, which had

been staring absently at the shadows on the wall, suddenly darkened as if to match the grayish pallor of his skin. "Whatever the reasons, let's be glad it's the police rather than the DINA."

Ben heaved a great sigh and groped for a neutral tone in which to continue the conversation, but at each turn of his mind he caught a glimmering of dark possibilities which threw him into a panic. "But why Anna?" He heard his voice crack even as he whispered. "I can't make sense of it. She didn't do anything the rest of that little American group didn't do."

Jaime shot him a meaningful look. "I've already checked it out, Benjamin. Dorothy Hemming was taken into custody late this afternoon. The other members, however, haven't been touched."

Ben rubbed the back of his hand across his lips. They were chapped and cracked. "Paul Pouillon?" he whispered.

"Maybe. I don't deny I've thought of it. But it's a sheer guess, Benjamin. We still know nothing about the mysterious movements of Pouillon. No matter what people say, I still can't see him in the role of spy or informer."

It was a topic which evidently agitated Jaime. He began to pace around the room again, reviewing his acquaintance with the Pouillons in detail. It was like a recital of arguments long ago worked out and committed to memory. "Don't worry about it," Ben wanted to say, "no one is blaming you." But Jaime, absorbed in his monologue, appeared to be unaware of Ben's presence. Ben found himself unable to pay attention, uninterested in what Jaime had to say. Towards Paul Pouillon he felt neither hatred nor resentment although, when he speculated on how betrayed Anna must feel, he had to fight back tears. "Paul Pouillon may have his own reasons, his own secret explanations," he said to himself. And then he recalled something that his catechist had once said to him—one of the scraps of religious instruction that had left an impression. "Sanctity is transparent and open, unlike sin. A man reborn in the spirit has no more secrets than a babe."

Jaime continued to talk. Ben could think only of Anna and

Damaris. He closed his eyes and searched for Anna's presence.
He tried to see her sitting straight-backed on a narrow bunk,
hands folded in her lap, nunlike, staring uncomprehendingly
at the bars of her cell or at the cinder-block wall. She would be
thinking of him, waiting for a message. He tried to reach her:
Anna, where you are, there's life; we are one. It was futile: he
could not penetrate the mysterious world of prison walls and
bars, as strange to him as an unvisited planet. Old conversations,
then: he sought to catch the tone of her voice, the turn of her
lips as the two of them sat lazily over breakfast reading the
morning papers. Mechanically he reviewed the corners of the
house and land which were most of all hers—the screened
shed where she shelled peas, the spot under the tangerine trees
where she rested after a swim. And finally he was with her
again. She was sitting on a narrow bed in an apartment in San
Francisco. Naked, sitting cross-legged, she was lifting a broad-
toothed comb to her wet hair, working through it in long,
even strokes. As she raised her arms Ben could see the small
swellings of her breasts, her ribs standing out defenselessly
against her whitened winter skin. From behind her crossed
ankles only a suggestion of pubic hair was visible. She spoke
softly, self-consciously, as if afraid of articulating her confes-
sions. "I am not a connoisseur of life," she said, then bit her
lip. And again, fighting back tears, "I never seem to get the
hang of it, this so-called art of living that some people master
so effortlessly and lovingly. The universe and I: we're hardly on
civil terms, do you know what I mean?" Ben opened his mouth
and struggled for a reply, but he could only fumble for the right
words, conquered in advance by his fear of failing her. She
swung her legs to the edge of the bed and leaned over and
kissed him. *Thank you,* she whispered. *Thank you for rescuing
me from myself.*

Suddenly Ben felt smitten with anguish. "Jaime, stop it, we
must go to bed," he said irritably.

Jaime turned to him, embarrassed. "Of course. You need
rest—lots of it. You must excuse me for forgetting." He put
his fingers to his mouth and coughed self-consciously. He

reached for the kerosene lamp and prepared to leave. "Is there anything you want?"

"I'm worried about Damaris. She must be terrified. She's just a baby."

"I'll call the Irish priest in Villa Inez first thing in the morning and have him go over there. Anyway, Carmen will know what to do."

"Well, I'll be OK now. I just need some sleep."

"Don't lie awake worrying. I'll take care of everything tomorrow." He paused. "By tomorrow night it will be over."

"Yes."

"You're not to get up tomorrow. I can manage."

"Yes."

"Good night. No worrying, now." He disappeared with the lamp, leaving the room in a shadowy darkness. Ben folded his hands on his chest and waited impatiently for relief from consciousness and pain. *Anna*, he whispered, *Anna*.

2

The day was golden and cloudless. Even in the early morning hours Ben could feel the slow swelling of heat which would weigh heavily upon the city by noon. He had slept badly until six or seven, apparently dropping off about the time Jaime arose. At 8:10 the telephone rang. Ben stumbled from the sofa to answer it, surprised, when he spoke into the receiver, to hear himself utter an audible sound instead of a whisper.

"I called the Irish priest. He promised to help out with Damaris." On the phone Jaime always sounded cool and professional, as if he had no time or feeling to spare. "Dorothy Hemming is out. I thought you'd like to know."

"Great. What does she say?"

"I haven't talked to her. The U.S. Embassy informed me. They say she was interrogated last night from six to eight, then released; plenty of time to make it home before curfew."

"And Anna?" Ben affected Jaime's dry tone.

"Nothing to report yet, Benjamin. The Embassy has no word. But I'm working on it."

Jaime urged Ben to rest, and he agreed to, but even before hanging up the phone he had made his morning's plans. He dressed casually and took his medicine and some aspirin for his low-grade fever. Rather than cope with Jaime's bare kitchen, Ben decided to eat a continental breakfast at the Cafe Monjitas.

Orange juice, croissants, café au lait: Ben tried to linger over his meal, skimming the paper as he ate, for it was still too early to make his calls. A lady burdened with parcels eyed him accusingly as he took his time. Finally he surrendered his seat and paid the bill. He walked to his bank, where he cashed a check. At the cavernous post office, which was still cool and damp from the night air, he stood at a counter and wondered what to write. "Here's two for the censors," he thought. To Anna's parents he wrote a brief note: "The weather is fine, but as in years past we miss the prospect of a White Christmas. We may be home sooner than you think." He still had a half hour to spare. He took another aerogram and after a few false starts scrawled a note to his brother Hugh: "Life imposes upon us the obligation to master certain skills which, once learned, are no longer of any use, as language students must memorize their conjugations and declensions until, having learned to speak fluently, they may forget them." He paused. He would have liked to have added, "I feel desolate, bereft." But instead he merely signed his name.

At 10:10 he stood in front of the building that had once housed the French Embassy. He walked past the main entrance to a door on the right. "Nestor Salas, tailor," announced a discreet bronze plaque just under a doorbell. He opened the door and entered, impressed by the bustle of movement inside, for he had never called on don Nestor in the morning and half-expected the establishment to be slumbering.

The interior dazzled with the radiant sunlight which the abundant windows admitted. Later, Ben supposed, they would have to be covered, or the place would be an oven. There was more greenery than Ben had remembered—one wall seemed to be covered with climbing plants—but otherwise it was painfully familiar, reminiscent of other visits he had made—when?—eight or ten months ago, maybe, in another life, when there had been time and inclination for a little laughter and carefree talk. Ben was suddenly tired, and in his left leg he felt a shooting cramp. He looked around for a chair to sit on.

Don Nestor was evidently in the fitting room. Ben could hear the occasional rise and fall of his voice. Several assistants nodded politely at Ben as they hurried across the salon, cuts of material draped gracefully on their arms. Ben slowly became aware of his tacky appearance. Clothes which had seemed perfectly satisfactory when he had put them on were now, he observed, all tatters and puckers and loose threads. He gave himself a quick once-over to see if he had, perhaps, put his shirt on inside out or neglected to zip his fly. He crossed his ankles to hide his unpolished shoes.

Apparently don Nestor had been informed of Ben's presence, for he suddenly appeared, arms outstretched, full of affection and reproach for his old friend who had so shamefully neglected him. He was a bit grayer at the temples, and the circles under his eyes looked dark, almost bruised. Yet his bearing and presence were always an event. He was dressed in a brilliantly colored knit shirt, a silk scarf at the collar, and yellow linen pants with flared bottoms. Everything about him was an argument against thoughtless insouciance.

"And now I suppose you are expecting your suit by next week, maybe? ¡Ay, los gringos! ¡Por Dios! But why you are sitting there when you have such a rush? Come, come, amigo. In the storeroom I find your suit."

"Suit?" Ben faltered. Then it dawned on him, as he followed don Nestor through the salon to a large closet-lined room on the right, that he was expected to participate in a ruse for the benefit of the other customers and the employees.

Don Nestor closed the door and fumbled in a closet for some garments loosely basted together. "Ay, how overgrown you are, *amigo*. But this should do. Here, step into these pants," he whispered, "in case anybody should walk in and see us talking together."

Obediently Ben stepped out of his own pants and into the strange pair offered him. They were too large around the middle and too short. Don Nestor took a measuring tape from around his neck and a pincushion from a nearby table.

"And what you will tell the owner of these pants when he comes for his order?" whispered Ben.

"*No importa*, don't trouble yourself," replied don Nestor. "We pin up one side, then we sit down and talk. Afterwards I unpin it. *Ay*, times have changed as you can see. How careful I must be—every day it is harder. There now, that should do."

Don Nestor chose a straight-backed chair with a soft leather seat, leaving Ben with a dainty, silk covered overstuffed rocker of petite dimensions. Ben balanced on his left hip and crossed his knees as he attempted to pull his thoughts together. Don Nestor spoke first. "If it's about Anna, I can tell you now. She's OK. She will be released at noon." He glanced at his watch.

"I knew you were a man of many resources, but I must admit that today I'm astounded. How did you know?"

Don Nestor took a cigarette from a silver box lying on the table and inserted it in his holder. "It is my—how you say?— my melancholy duty to know *todo*." He lit up and inhaled deeply, squinting as if the smoke hurt his eyes. "In truth I expect you yesterday. I wait here until nine in case you come."

"I was sick."

"For Anna I am happy. I congratulate you, but for Paulina I grieve deeply, and for her husband Roberto. Yesterday he closed their shop, boarded it up. Above the door he put a sign, '*Cerrado por duelo.*' How you say? 'Closed for grief.' That is what we are, a whole people shut up in our mourning."

Ben stared at him, dumbfounded. "But what are you talking about? I don't follow a word you're saying."

Don Nestor tapped his cigarette against a copper ashtray and smiled grimly out of the corner of his mouth. "*Por Dios*, poor fool, you really don't know nothing?"

"Evidently not. My friend Jaime Venegas was informed that Anna was arrested yesterday at three or four, and her friend Dorothy Hemming about six. We thought there was a connection." Ben felt alarmed by his own ignorance. Beads of sweat appeared on his face and back.

"Dorothy Hemming? That was a mere nothing. The police weren't really interested in her."

"Anna and Dorothy were involved in a fact-finding operation. They interviewed people who had been tortured and so on. They had a little group."

Don Nestor squinted and the corners of his mouth turned up slightly. "Of course. That harmless little group."

It wasn't the response Ben expected. He fought a childish urge to exaggerate the scope of Anna's activities, to paint her in heroic colors. "You may be right, but we've thought for a week or two that their group was infiltrated by an informer. One of their members suddenly and mysteriously disappeared. You ever hear of a Canadian named Paul Pouillon?"

Don Nestor threw back his head and closed his eyes as if about to laugh, but instead he sighed deeply. "Ay, there he is again, Mr. Pouillon. One thing I can promise you: he has nothing to do with the arrest of Anna. Beyond that? Where is your intuition, friend? Have you no imagination? He is part of a new, international liberation group that spans the Americas from Quebec to Chile. It's so secret that even the MIR isn't in on it."

Ben was stunned. "I'll be damned." He was curious to know where don Nestor got his information, but it seemed pointless to ask.

"Pouillon was sent down here to represent the Québecois in some big confederation the extremists are planning. Things became too hot for him, though. He was afraid of being arrested, so he moved on. That's all I know for sure, *amigo*. In a week or two I could tell you more, but by then, of course, you'll be gone. Deported. Well now, don't look surprised. You didn't think the *milicos* would let Anna return to her bothersome little activities, did you?"

"Somehow I thought we'd have more time." Ben shifted his weight to the other hip and extended his left leg which ached dully. "It's not as if I'm ready to go, Nestor. Abrupt changes have never agreed with me. Both Anna and I are in the middle of things."

"Saturday. It's already decided. The authorities are even now processing your papers."

"What's the charge against us? Against Anna?"

"Concealing information about illegal and clandestine groups. Cooperating with Marxists."

"Want to spell it out?"

"First you must get it out of your mind that Anna is the Big Fish they wanted. It was Paulina."

"Paulina. I hardly know her. I've seen her just a few times."

"Her brothers were way up in the left wing of the Socialist Party. One of them was a speech writer for Pedro Montero, so it is said. Well, after the eleventh, here is a thing for Paulina. Her brothers ask her to shelter some of the big names the *milicos* are after." He paused to extinguish the cigarette and immediately lit another. "Paulina, she doesn't think twice. Her house becomes a hideout. Roberto, he is plenty scared, but Paulina tells him to mind the cash register and keep quiet." A fleeting smile played across his face. "An excellent woman, Paulina."

He turned suddenly towards the door, evidently hearing footsteps that had escaped Ben's notice. An assistant knocked and mumbled something about the *señor* who was still waiting. "I'll be just a minute," responded don Nestor, and he rose and walked to the large closet where he removed a garment from a hanger. "Here, try the jacket on while I'm gone," he said to Ben. "We keep up the appearances."

When he returned, don Nestor led Ben to a long mirror and again began altering another man's clothes to fit Ben's build. He worked fast and efficiently, taking the pins he needed one by one from one of the enormous silk-covered pincushions found on almost every table in the shop.

"Do you really think this is necessary?" asked Ben. The day

was growing warmer and in the jacket he felt hot and uncomfortable.

"Don't tell me my business, *gringo*," murmured don Nestor. "Compared to me, what do you know about living on pins and needles?" He chuckled at his own pun. "Hold out your arm, there—just so. Now, where was I? Oh, yes: Paulina's distinguished houseguests. Some say Pedro Montero himself hid out there, the old devil; then there was Miguel Enriquez, the MIR's number one boy. Who else? Roberto Montt before he moved on and got captured. It sounds like a *Who's Who* of the left, no?"

"I'm amazed. Paulina's house isn't especially isolated. You'd think somebody would have noticed."

"Arms down, please. I think I sit now. You stand there, please, before the mirror, in case somebody looks in. Keep the jacket on." He pulled a wooden chair from under a long work table and perched on the edge of it, crossing his right knee with his left ankle. Ben turned his back towards the mirror. "She was denounced several times," Nestor continued "and the *milicos* went to search. Luck was with her: her guests were transients, so to speak, and it happened that whenever the *milicos* showed up, the house was empty. But she was being watched, and she wasn't cautious enough." He frowned. "A little example, *amigo*: one day last month your lovely wife she goes to tea with Paulina at a bakery in Valparaíso. The ladies think they are alone. Paulina is upset: she cries and carries on. She is indiscreet; so is Anna. Spies are listening."

"You don't mean that Paulina confessed to Anna that she was hiding fugitives!"

"This I don't know. In any case the spies are now on to Anna as well as Paulina." He paused.

"Go on."

"Last Thursday the *milicos* pick up a *Mirista* named Guillermo Bustos who had before been at the house of Paulina. He is tortured, he talks. Paulina is implicated, some others too. The DINA do a roundup. They take Paulina on Friday and torture her. On Sunday night right before curfew she is released; she refuses to go out at that hour. They shove her out the door and shoot her in the back. The time is 10:05. The official reason for her death: violating the curfew."

In his anxiety Ben could feel neither pity nor anger, but his hands began to tremble, so he clasped them behind his back. A pin in the jacket kept pricking him as he moved. In the warm clothes he was sweating. It occurred to him that he was probably still feverish.

"As for Anna, she is almost—how you say?—a last minute detail? An afterthought?" Don Nestor took his cigarette holder from his pocket and began to play with it. "The *milicos* know who are the friends of Paulina. Somebody at DINA gets the bright idea that maybe Anna hides extremists too, you see? They tell the police to investigate it. A *milico* talked to your neighbors in Villa Inez: yes, indeed, somebody from Santiago is there at your home almost three weeks, maybe more...."

Ben's trembling spread from his hands to his back and knees. "Ah, no, Eve, they mean Eva Maria Araya...."

Don Nestor raised his eyebrows. "So that's it? But it seems she is gone from your house by yesterday when Anna is arrested."

"Yes. She left Villa Inez on Saturday. Now she's at the convent of the Sisters of St. Joseph."

"A convent. Any special reason?"

"The convent faces San Martín Street. If you walk out the back door and climb the wall, you're in the Italian Embassy. And that's just what she is going to do tonight at nine-thirty. We arranged it, Jaime Venegas and I. She's taking refuge; in a few weeks she'll be in Europe."

"Well, that explains something, maybe; it tells why Anna implicated Mrs. Hemming. Yes, that must be it. She reported that Mrs. Hemming is often at your house, that the neighbors must be referring to her. The police therefore check out her story with Mrs. Hemming who knows how to talk her way around things."

"Nestor, you were always a mine of information, but I must confess I always thought of you as a raconteur and a harmless gossip. Today I stand corrected. You seem to have joined the ranks of the professional spies. Tell me—your secret is safe with me: how do you keep track of what's going on at, say, the Valparaíso Municipal Jail and everywhere else too? Somebody must feed you information the day it happens."

A shadow crossed don Nestor's eyes. He inserted a cigarette in his holder and lit up. "You have heard no doubt about how the left was completely infiltrated by the time of the coup?"

"Of course."

"It is only a slight exaggeration. Now we infiltrate the right. Slowly. But in a year or two we will have informers in all the key places." He fixed his eyes on a coffee stain on the carpet. For a moment he seemed to forget Ben's presence. Suddenly he stood and arched his back and stretched. "The fitting is over, *amigo*. You behave yourself well. Change back into your own clothes please. You can hang up the suit you've got on over there in the closet. Then come and see me in my office. We must discuss the bill, no?"

Ben followed don Nestor's instructions. The office, which had been remodeled since Ben's last visit, proved to be in stark contrast to the rest of the shop, for although large, it was bare of furniture except for a long, heavy table with a bench to each side, a shelf lined with catalogs, several sets of files, and a copper fireplace. Two small windows admitted a modest suggestion of light. The floors were tiled and bare except for a few Peruvian throw rugs.

"I want to thank you," Ben began. "You have proved more helpful than I even dared hope."

"You don't seem an especially hopeful type," replied don Nestor. He was sitting at the table, one of his knees drawn up to his chest. "Anyway, there's a bench, sit down. I have something to say to you, something *muy interesante*."

Ben sat down opposite don Nestor. "What could be more interesting than the news you've already given me?"

"This." Don Nestor tapped a manila folder lying in front of him. "Compared to this, your little drama is a piece of lint. You excuse my frankness." He pushed the folder across the table.

"What is it?"

"A set of documents showing step-by-step the U.S. involvement in the overthrow of the Allende government."

Ben pushed the folder back towards don Nestor. "Well, it doesn't surprise me. Nothing you've got there is likely to surprise me."

"Step by step. Display number one: a letter from the U.S. Ambassador written to Allende's predecessor, who didn't want to make way for Allende. 'Don't worry, we'll wreck the economy for you,' says the Ambassador. 'Not a nut or bolt will be allowed to reach Chile under Allende.'"

"What else?"

"Next: a letter from the White House to the head of the CIA telling him to make our economy scream. Next: positive proof that the CIA was behind the murder of our Commander-in-Chief back in 1970." He pushed the folder towards Ben again. "Here, see for yourself."

Ben pushed it back.

"What's the matter? You're not interested?"

"I feel as if you're pushing me somewhere I don't want to go. Why are you showing me these things? How do you know I'm reliable?"

"We have checked you out, believe me. I confide in you because I need you—we need you."

"You forget I'm being booted out of Chile in a few days."

Don Nestor seemed to look Ben over thoughtfully, as if perhaps measuring him for something. "It's true you aren't perfect for the work I have in mind, but you are the best candidate we can come up with." He shrugged almost apologetically. "We want you to publicize U.S. involvement in the overthrow of the Allende government once you get home."

Ben was taken back. "There are a good number of Americans already devoting themselves to that task."

"Yes, *amigo*, but they are there, and you are here."

"Meaning . . . ?"

"The Americans busy themselves with policies in Washington and tricks on Wall Street. That is all very fine, but one thing they neglect: the U.S. Embassy here in Santiago. What

I mean is the complicity between the Embassy and the Junta."
Don Nestor was fumbling in his shirt pocket again for cigarettes
and lighter. "You know that two Americans were killed by
the *milicos* after the coup?"

"I heard only that they were missing."

"Mr. Frank Teruggi. He died from multiple gunshot wounds,
at least two in the head. Mr. Charles Horman: for a long time
Horman is listed as missing. Then his body is discovered. The
deaths remain uninvestigated. The U.S. Government does not
complain. Does that not seem a strange way to react when
American citizens are murdered?"

"Not if Horman and Teruggi were UP sympathizers."

"Exactly. At the U.S. Embassy they keep files on Chileans
and Americans alike. I think they denounce Teruggi and
Horman and a few others to the Chilean *milicos*. Your boys
prefer supporting the Chilean Junta to protecting their own
citizens. So what is an American passport worth these days,
amigo, I ask you? Whose side are your officials on—whose
side?" He inhaled and for a moment sat lost in thought. Then
he rose and walked to a file cabinet. He opened a middle
drawer and extracted a bottle of *pisco* which he banged on the
table dramatically as if to emphasize a point. From the top of
the files he took two glasses and filled them, passing one to
Ben.

"You knew the CIA financed the famous middle-class general
strike of August, for millions of dollars?" Nestor asked suddenly.

"Of course. Everybody knew."

"The Americans always have plenty of money. I have a U.S.
Foreign Service acquaintance. Back in 1972 he asked me if I
had access to information about the MIR that I would be
willing to put at the service of the U.S. Government." Suddenly Nestor laughed deeply, closing his eyes. "The Embassy,
he said, had managed to infiltrate all the major UP parties,
but they hadn't cracked the MIR. He wanted me to help them
crack the MIR!"

"Bastards, all of them." Ben felt tired and morose. He wanted
to go home and rest.

"So will you?" asked don Nestor suddenly as he returned the *pisco* to the files.

"Will I what?"

"Publicize all the evidence we have here?" He tapped the manila folder lying before him. "About the U.S. Embassy, I mean, and the CIA agents around and about. We've got names—there's solid stuff there. You do not have quite the talents for the job, it is true, but you're the best we can hope for."

Ben felt mildly amused by Nestor's severe opinion. "You mind my asking what you see as my major shortcoming?"

Nestor in his habitual way squinted at Ben through a haze of cigarette smoke. "*Amigo,* one human dimension you never reveal (I wonder if you have it): a capacity for *righteous indignation.* A splendid English expression: in Spanish we have nothing so good. *Righteous indignation,* yes. You are *responsable,* you are *inteligente* (that we have reason to know), but you are cold. You will perhaps fail to arouse others to a—shall we say—heated concern when you yourself are like ice. But wait, now it occurs to me that you have an admirable *compañera:* Anna will help you. She knows how to *exclaim.*"

"Anna?" Ben chuckled.

"What's the matter? You underestimate your wife. Like all husbands you fail to appreciate your woman's talents."

"You are a great one to be lecturing me on the state of matrimony."

Don Nestor's eyes lit up, but he didn't smile. "*Bueno.* But about women I am still the super number-one expert; even if"— he sighed deeply—"under the present circumstances I must neglect my *tesoro,* a dream of a girl you must someday meet. But about Anna, you will see, I am right. She will want to help."

"She's the wrong person, Nestor. She's so self-conscious about writing that she can't sign her letters 'Love, Anna' without fear of being misunderstood."

Don Nestor seemed to consider for a moment, and then he rose. He took the manila folder to its hiding place among the catalogs on the shelf. Ben felt as if he were being dismissed.

"Well, *amigo*," said Nestor, "*es obvio*. The two of you must put your stunted personalities together and do the best you can. Rome was not built in a day and so on. We must work with what we have. None of us is perfect."

Ben felt moved to laughter. He chuckled silently at first, and as Nestor watched, he seemed to be affected. Soon both of them were laughing aloud. "So that's how you expect to build up an organization?" asked Ben. "By insulting the people whom you must rely on?"

"Not everybody," Nestor replied. "Just you." He narrowed his eyes thoughtfully. "You do not appreciate the fact that I understand people. I understand you. And I have succeeded in persuading you. You will see."

3

It was an evening Ben was to remember all his life. It was as if his sickness and his anxiety about Anna had separated him from the city and its inhabitants, intensifying his perception of his own feelings, the voices and gestures of his friends, the tone and texture of what was to be the last gathering of those who had come to mean most to him, a handful of refugees and dropouts from a country which was no longer theirs.

He had taken the bus as far as the corner of Las Violetas and Pedro de Valdivia. It was still early, about 7:45, and he decided to walk to the Italian Embassy where he was expected at 8:15. Slanting rays of warm sunlight threw their bluish shadows across the sidewalk, and a breeze rustled the leaves of the cherry trees which bordered the street. He noted that there was no moon. It was an evening like hundreds he had known in Chile, with the odor of jasmine and wisteria and a hint of sea-freshness. Hearing his footsteps slap against the sidewalk, he found his thoughts keeping rhythm. "When calamities strike, killing even the smallest chance of enjoying innocent satisfactions, it's hard not to give up," he said to himself. As if in response to his brown mood, his feet slowed their movement. "I said, I will go softly all my days in the bitterness of my soul": the rolling wave of psalm came to him unexpectedly, as if it had been waiting within him for years, just for this occasion, to comfort him and sadden him in his moment of need.

He lifted his shoulders and quickened his pace as he crossed the street, suddenly aware of the peacefulness of the scene and its contrast with his own sense of want. It was the kind of summer evening in which children revel until after dark. He noticed them now, riding bicycles in the street and running about on the tailored lawns, well-fed and comely, the happy children of the *barrio alto*. He thought of Damaris who all day yesterday and the day before must have grasped wildly and unbelievingly at Carmen's promise that her parents would return, her mother would return. A pain rushed through his side; for a second or two he couldn't breathe.

He approached the Italian Embassy, noticing—as he never had before—the height of the walls that surrounded the building, the sweep of lawn which stretched langorously from the front gate to the main entrance. The tallest man, he figured, would have trouble jumping the fence even if the two *milicos* stationed at the premises were suddenly to disappear. He noticed a parked car with three men in it a quarter of a block away. This Embassy was no doubt carefully patrolled. He remembered that in spite of the Junta's displeasure and the *milicos'* watch, a hundred and more suppliants had found sanctuary within the walls.

"Passport, please," said one of the soldiers when Ben arrived at the entrance. For the first time Ben felt a surge of anxiety, as if he might have overlooked something. He handed the document to the beardless youth who skimmed through the pages two or three times. Ben wondered absently if the soldier could read. "Your passport is not in order," the *milico* snapped, and he eyed Ben accusingly.

Ben breathed deeply and resolved to keep calm. "Excuse me," he replied. "I think you'll find on the second page that the passport is valid until 1976. It was issued in San Francisco. On the last page my date of entry into Chile is recorded." He made a motioning gesture with his index finger, as if to encourage the soldier to turn through the pages again.

"All foreigners are supposed to register with the authorities; you have not registered."

Ben took from his pocket a piece of blue paper which the American Embassy had issued him the week before. "This must be what you want," he said. The blue paper merely affirmed what the passport said, but, as Ben expected, the signature of the Ambassador and the official seal had an impressive effect.

"What are you here for?" demanded the soldier. His presumptuousness would have been amusing if Ben had not felt nervous.

"To see the first secretary, Señor Covelli."

"What for?"

"It's a tax matter. It concerns some property of mine in Italy."

"You're lying. You're seeking refuge in the Embassy." The soldier bared his teeth belligerently and raised his automatic rifle slightly.

Ben had trouble concealing his temper. "Not at all. What would be the point? As you can see, my papers are in order."

The other *milico* on duty decided to join in. He was older than the youth who had been addressing Ben, and in his corpulence he seemed almost square. "Let the man by," he said out of the corner of his mouth. As he spoke, he turned the key in the gate.

His companion made no objection, but Ben could feel their mutual hostility as he passed between them. He could imagine the dreary, sun-drenched hours they had shared, displaying threatening attitudes towards anyone who approached, in their boredom finding fault with each other. It was a variation of human wretchedness he hadn't thought of.

In the Embassy waiting room sat several men bent over Italian newspapers. Ben approached a counter where a stocky, gray-haired woman stood sorting through a card file. "I'm to see Señor Covelli at 8:15," he explained. "My name is Benjamin Willing."

"I'm sorry, Señor Covelli was called out suddenly. He won't be able to see you." The woman carefully kept her finger in place in the box of cards as she talked. Ben felt a twinge of irritation. Señor Covelli was perhaps a less reliable accomplice than he had been led to expect. "Did he leave a message for me?"

Reluctantly the woman withdrew her finger from the file box, leaving a pencil in its stead. She walked to a desk where an appointment book lay open. "No message," she said. "But it says here, 'Señor Willing and Father Venegas at nine-thirty.' Señor Willing: would that be you?"

Ben relaxed a little. "Yes. I just wanted to confirm the hour. Thank you."

He left the same way he had come, through the enormous hand-carved doors which stood open to admit the evening air. He strode rapidly down the walk to where the *milicos* stood at the gate, now studiously ignoring him, and turned to his right. He felt mildly excited, as if the evening's adventure had really begun.

He walked quickly around the block to the convent the grounds of which stood back-to-back against the Italian Embassy. Eve was waiting for him, he knew, and perhaps Jaime too. He glanced at his watch: eight-thirty.

He was about to ring at the gate when he was surprised by a man coming out the front door. Taller than average, with a thick shock of gray hair and an ascetic-looking face, he looked rather familiar. "No need to ring; I'll open the gate for you," the man said in a cultivated tone, and as he spoke, he smiled at Ben as if he recognized him.

It was only as he slammed the heavy iron gate behind him and crossed the sidewalk to the front door of the convent that Ben could place the man's face. "Sergio Sotomayor," he said to himself, astonished. "Eve's husband, Sergio Sotomayor." Ben had met him once or twice back in the sixties, but that was before Sergio's marriage to Eve, and Ben had never grown accustomed to thinking of them as a pair. For the first time, it occurred to Ben to wonder about them—when they had married and separated, for instance, and about the present status of their relationship. Eve had never mentioned her husband to Ben. Indeed, it struck him that, in spite of the curious quality she had of speaking earnestly and intently as if her listener were a trusted confidante, she revealed very little about the actual circumstances of her past, the fabric of events which most people would point to in identifying themselves, explaining themselves. And though he felt close to her— though he would feel free, for instance, to trouble her to perform any number of favors—there were certain questions he would never presume to ask her: questions which, addressed to another, would seem innocuous or even trite.

Eve met him at the door and greeted him with a kiss and hug. As Ben had anticipated, she made no reference to Sergio's recent visit. She appeared as calm and serene as the nuns he could see in a sitting room to the left. It was yet another facet of her life which would remain forever hidden and mysterious. There was probably no woman, he suddenly realized, to whom he felt more drawn; yet she was inaccessible not only for the obvious reason of her imminent departure but also because of the impenetrable recesses of her private world. He felt suddenly burdened by a new and unwelcome fear that a person's most cherished experiences leave him disappointed if not grief-stricken in the end.

Eve took his arm and led him to a small parlor dominated by a plaster statue of the Virgin and a Victorian overstuffed settee of indeterminate color. Ben felt oppressed by a sense of cleanliness, as if the odor of wax and ammonia had driven out the genial spirits which might have inhabited the knickknack shelf, say, or the old-fashioned, pedal-type sewing machine which supported a thriving collection of African violets. Only a profusion of cakes and sandwiches and a tea service on the low coffee table before the sofa suggested—along with the lively conversation of the room's inhabitants—a touch of human warmth and comfort. Jaime was there, seated in the armchair, talking to Monica and a middle-aged man seated next to her. They rose to greet Ben, evidently interrupting a story Monica had been telling.

"Don't mind me," said Ben. "If you continue your story, Monica, I'll soon catch up."

"But first you must meet Felipe," she replied. The man extended his hand and looked at Ben in a quizzical way, as if he didn't know how to act. Monica gazed at the two men with a fond, proprietary interest, as if their presence there were somehow a credit to her. Ben found himself answering Felipe's expression with an embarrassed smile. "We've heard too much about each other," Ben thought to himself. "Monica has a way of sharing her friends' experiences and feelings as if they were communal property."

They sat down again, and Monica continued with a story which Ben only half-followed. Having expected to find Jaime and Eve waiting alone, nervously eyeing the clock, he was unprepared for the show of festivity which had greeted him. Eve evidently read his thoughts, for she leaned towards him and whispered, "I bet you are amazed. That's the way we Chileans are, I'm afraid. Here I am, about to scramble over the wall to the Italian Embassy, and we're making a party of it, as if it were a splendid occasion." She paused for a minute or two, evidently following the drift of the conversation, and then she whispered again: "At least Mother isn't here. We knew she couldn't take it. I spent the afternoon with her."

Monica finished her story and disappeared for a few minutes, reappearing with a bottle of chilled champagne. Everyone seemed eager to make of this improbable farewell gathering a happy experience, and Ben found his own spirits rising. Monica uncorked the bottle and filled the glasses, talking as she worked, exuberant and witty. "With every look and gesture," Ben reflected, "she has a way of suggesting that her life—and by extension all life—is filled with ecstatic moments: what kind of childhood does it take to produce such a woman?" Jaime was evidently similarly moved; he turned to Ben and murmured, "Whenever Monica is around everything suddenly seems thrilling; have you ever thought about it? You find yourself believing that an important letter will come, or a check in the mail, some wonderful change of fortune...."

They lingered ten or fifteen minutes over the champagne, touching lightly on the weather and the European winter and the Cardinal's recent trip to Rome to see the Pope. About Eve's departure they spoke only obliquely. Everyone in the room, Ben suspected, had his own anxieties to cope with. No one spoke of them, yet the sense of unease, of possible calamity, which permeated the group was like a password granting immediate access to an abject fellowship. They laughed, they chatted, but their sad and secret knowledge seemed to govern the convivial scene like an unobtrusive but persistent countermelody in an otherwise merry little piece. They were extending benevolent feelings towards one another, acknowledging their gratitude at being included in this melancholy fraternity. It was as if each of them were saying: "At last I have found people worth living with, worth dying for, and they are leaving; *we* are leaving—scattering in time and space like flotsam in water."

It was 9:15. They rose and walked out the back door of the convent into a grassy garden that was almost bare except for a grape arbor on the left and two huge avocado trees. Against the tree by the arbor a ladder was leaning, like steps to a house hidden in the leaves. It was this scene that was to be imprinted on Ben's mind with extraordinary vividness. His senses had been sharpened to an edge by his recent illness and by the splash of ebullience he had found in the champagne. Normally somewhat unobservant of his environment, he felt overcome by the mysterious friendliness of a modest garden when the weather is fine, and by the beauty of familiar forms—the tree he stood before, the ladder, the garden wall. Space itself seemed palpable. He could almost feel the distance which separated him from the nearest object, and the immense reaches that stretched between the leaves. He sensed the possibility of happiness and peace. And though he was excited, even tense, as the moment for Eve's escape approached, he also seemed detached, as if he were viewing the scene from a great distance.

Jaime rubbed his hands together and glanced at his watch. It was 9:20. "Since Señor Covelli didn't call, I assume everything is according to plan," he said to Ben.

"Apparently. I stopped by the Embassy on my way over here. He wasn't in. There were no messages for us." He moved to help Jaime, who had begun to carry the ladder from the tree to the wall.

"This is the spot, ten meters from the left boundary post," Jaime said. "There should be a ladder at this very place on the other side."

Ben left the ladder and approached Monica and Felipe and Eve, who were standing under the tree. It was the moment for good-byes. Half-expecting a show of tears and desperate embracing, Ben was surprised at the conversation, for Monica— evidently in response to something Eve had said—sputtered, "Eve, you're overflowing with venom. If you were to bite your tongue, you'd die of poisoning."

Eve laughed a sad little laugh, then turned towards Felipe, resting her hand on his shoulder. "You were right about what you said this afternoon, Felipe. It's time to leave. I'm becoming the person I have written about in my memoirs. I will them to you—all my notebooks. You'll know what to do with them. I'm not planning to take my past with me, you know. I depart with nothing but a change of underwear and a mildewed rag of a heart."

She turned towards Ben. Something about the slenderness of her neck, the smallness of her hands, caught in his throat. She asked to be remembered to Anna and sent love to Damaris. He felt cross with himself for his inept responses. Jaime signaled: it was 9:25. Everyone seemed reluctant to move, as if something important remained to be said. Yet the moment had passed for the baring of intimate secrets. Finally Eve sighed deeply and offered her hands to each of her friends in turn. Then she said (or so Ben was to remember), "Dear friends, those of us who have been seized by the spirit of hope and solidarity know neither victory nor defeat. During Allende's first year we hadn't really won, and even in prison we weren't vanquished. In spite of everything, I am confident that history is on our side. This Chilean tragedy we've lived through is bound to end. At last our dreams will come true, though I don't expect to live to see the day."

She walked to the ladder, pausing to embrace Jaime. It was 9:29. She waited for a minute until Jaime gave the signal. "Now," he said. She started to ascend slowly and deliberately, as if she were navigating through an unfamiliar element. Jaime put his foot on the bottom rung in readiness to reach upwards and help her over the wall. Ben went to stand by Jaime's side.

It should take just a few seconds, Ben assured himself. He glanced at his watch: it was exactly 9:30. He held his breath as he watched Eve sit briefly on the top of the wall and swing her legs to the other side. "It's almost over," he thought. Behind him he could hear Monica: "Hurry, Eve, you've almost made it." He unclenched his fists, aware for the first time that he had dug his nails deeply into his palms.

But then, to his dismay, he heard in the distance a round of fire and closer a sharp crack. Ben cried out involuntarily.

Eve stopped. She sat stiffly on the wall for a few seconds, her back to Ben, and then she suddenly slumped. She fell backwards, hitting her head on the ladder, and collapsing near Monica's feet. Behind her she left a trail of blood.

Monica screamed. As Ben sprang to Eve's side, he heard the staccato of gunfire and the ping of broken glass. In the Embassy, people were shouting and crying. Somewhere by the north wall a deep, male voice roared in agony.

Ben felt himself panic. He was overwhelmed by his fears and by the noise and confusion about him. He knelt down by Monica, who was cradling Eve's head in her lap: looking at the bloody pulp that had been Eve's skull, he was sure there was no hope. Monica was talking on a constant stream as she waved her hands, now bloody, in the air; she was cursing some unidentified malevolent power and commanding Eve to wake up. Monica's skirt and blouse were soaked in blood. Felipe tried to calm her. "Let Ben get a look at Eve—he's a doctor," he said. "Wait, I'll go for some water." He rose just as a nun appeared from the convent door, pitcher and towels in hand.

In the meantime Jaime had ascended the ladder as if it were a battlement, his face diffused with a terrible rage, and he stood at the top, gesturing and exclaiming wildly. "Down, Jaime, get down! This is insane—you might get shot," Ben yelled; and he ran to the ladder and tugged at Jaime's legs. Finally Jaime was silent. He descended the ladder and came to stand over the group that huddled around Eve. Monica gazed at Jaime, a film of hopelessness shadowing her eyes. Ben started to cry in great, heaving gasps. The nun, who was mopping Eve's head, kept rolling her eyes back. Ben thought that she would faint. "Ay, Lord, Lord, Lord," she moaned.

"Covelli was on the other side," Jaime said. He reached for Felipe's arm to steady himself. "I just found out from him. There are two dead people in the Embassy, and somebody was injured on the north side as he was walking down the street."

"But why?" asked Felipe. His eyes were wide and terror-stricken. "Were they after Eve? Somebody else?"

"I don't know. How will we know?" Jaime didn't try to stop the tears which rolled down his face.

From the convent came the shrill sound of alarmed voices. A door slammed. A crowd of nuns was approaching with two men who bore a stretcher. Suddenly the air was heavy with the shriek of sirens.

Slowly Monica lowered Eve's head to the ground. "Help me—we must take her in." She knelt at her sister's side, bowing over her chest. Monica's long hair, now splashed with blood like her face and clothing, hung in disarray over the victim's face and neck. "Oh, Eve, don't die, don't break our hearts," she sobbed.

Afterword

The press gave a prominent place to the events at the Italian Embassy on December 15. According to official sources quoted in the newspapers, dissatisfaction had arisen among the refugees in the Embassy due to crowded conditions and to general anxiety. One of the refugees had secured a gun and resolved to keep watch at a window to prevent others from seeking asylum. After killing Eva Maria Araya and injuring Señor Artemio Lucero as they scaled the Embassy walls, he quarreled with two refugees within the building who attempted to disarm him and killed both of them.

On the morning of December 16 Father Jaime Venegas and Benjamin Willing met with the Ambassador and the First Secretary of the Italian Embassy. According to their testimony no one in the Embassy had any weapons. They claimed that the firing had come from military men stationed on the roof of the house next door. Señor Artemio Lucero, they believed, was a passerby who had been mistaken for a refugee. The Ambassador suspected that the motive was to discourage embassies from accepting refugees and to discourage refugees from seeking asylum.

Monica Araya made many attempts to find and interview Señor Juan Andini about the circumstances leading to Eva Maria Araya's death, but she never saw him again.

On Saturday, December 18 at 10 A.M., Anna and Benjamin Willing were expelled from Chile. They now reside in Oakland, California.

On Saturday, December 18 at 2 P.M., Eva Maria Araya was

buried. Helmut Luhrs of Berlin, Germany, attended the funeral. On that occasion Señor Felipe Medina presented him with the journals of Eva Maria Araya upon which this account of her life is based.

Monica Araya and Felipe Medina were married in the spring of 1974. They currently reside in Rome, Italy.

In 1975 Jaime Venegas received a postdoctoral fellowship to study at the University of Louvain in Belgium, where he now lives.

About the Author
Caroline Richards was born in Atkinson, Nebraska. She presently lives with her husband and two children in Richmond, Indiana, where she teaches history at Earlham College. Richards has been the recipient of an NEA Fellowship and the Great Lakes College Association New Writers' Award for Fiction. From 1966 to 1974 she lived and taught in Santiago, Chile. *Sweet Country* is Caroline Richards' first novel.